PRAISE FOR GAIL LINK'S *NEVER CALL IT LOVING:*

"Never Call It Loving is an enthralling tale of beauty and the beast....It's obvious Gail Link was born to write romance!"
—Jayne Ann Krentz

"A tale that kept this reader eager to turn each successive page until the very end!"
—Joan Hohl

"Never Call It Loving is a gift to the senses....A provocative read!"
—Kasey Michaels

"An exciting blend of revenge, intrigue and sexy romance. Gail Link's best book yet!"
—Barbara Dawson Smith

"A winner! Gail Link's writing has never been better!"
—Susan Wiggs

D1040707

A NIGHT TO REMEMBER

Determined to melt Marisa's icy facade, Cam opened his lips, skillfully coaxing hers to surrender. She stood still, twists of sensation flickering across chilled nerves as her husband's mouth moved from her lips to the sweep of her neck.

"Art a virgin?"

"Of course, my lord," Marisa stated, bending to pick up her discarded robe.

Cam stayed her hand, forcing her to stand upright once again. "'Tis naught of a certainty."

"'Tis so for the women of *my* family. Now, if thou art satisfied, my lord husband, I will don my robe."

"Think you that I shall be *satisfied* with only a look?" he demanded. "Know you what passes between a man and a woman, my lady wife?"

Other *Leisure Books* by Gail Link:
ENCANTADORA
WOLF'S EMBRACE

NEVER CALL IT LOVING

GAIL LINK

LEISURE BOOKS   **NEW YORK CITY**

A LEISURE BOOK®

October 1993

Published by

Dorchester Publishing Co., Inc.
276 Fifth Avenue
New York, NY 10001

The name ''Leisure Books'' and the stylized ''L'' with design are
trademarks of Dorchester Publishing Co., Inc.

Printed in the United States of America.

DEDICATION:

To Patricia Reynolds Smith: a very big thank you for all the support you've given me and my work over the years. For the friendly ear and the nourishment of a writer's dream; and, also, for understanding and promoting the value and importance of women's romantic fiction.

ACKNOWLEDGMENTS:

To Carolyn, Joan and Kathie: *Amigas Para Siempre.*

To Pat Snow: in gratitude for all your enthusiasm and encouragement of this book. It meant a lot.

Once more to the special customers (and coworkers) of WaldenBooks #668 who cared. You know who you are. Thanks all!

To Joan Bradshaw: for your letters—always a joy to read!

To Deborah A.: for the great concert seats in Washington, DC, to see you know who!

To Michael Ball: for the face of a hero.

To Michael Crawford: for the soul of a man. All acting should be this brilliant.

And, as always, to my parents. I love you.

Prologue:
So Dark the Day
London, 1655

"Some wine, my love?" purred the sweet voice.

His arms bound above his head, his legs shackled, his response was to spit in her direction, for which he received another blow from the short, beefy man to his already bruised body.

"Come now," she said, walking closer, "'tis not like you to refuse a glass."

"'Tis the company," he answered, doing his best to ignore the pain his body had already suffered. Sweet Jesu, was it only a few hours ago that he and this woman had enjoyed the softness of the very bed he was now held prisoner in? His flesh still bore the marks of her passionate scratches.

Cameron Buchanan found it hard to believe he'd been duped so easily. The scheming, lying bitch was an actress of rare talent. She'd played the part of the loyal Royalist to the hilt. He'd never suspected she was instead an agent of the hated Commonwealth, intent on destroying the king he served.

It mattered little to him that he wasn't the only man to be taken in by her cleverness. Others had trusted in her—and had paid the price with their lives, she'd gleefully informed him.

Cam's large hands clenched into fists. He'd never struck a woman before; if the opportunity presented itself, this cunning whore would be the first. But he reckoned he wouldn't get the chance. He, too, would soon be a dead man. As a trusted agent of the rightful monarch, Charles Stuart, Cam knew names, codes, ciphers. His value was in the information he possessed. Once it was extracted, he would cease to be of value.

Well, Cam vowed, he'd be damned before he would betray his king.

Faith Bellamy poured herself another flagon of wine. Her shrewd eyes narrowed as she watched the man on the bed, and a small, selfish regret tugged at her. This morn had been her last to enjoy the delights to be found in Cameron Buchanan's strong arms. God's Blood, but he was a lover to savor. With him it had been so easy to forget her task, if only for a while. But she would never consider returning to the meager existence she'd endured before she became a spy. The Commonwealth paid far too well. Her late husband had left her nothing but debts. The fool had been on the wrong side in the struggle between Parliament and the king.

Faith smiled. She hadn't made that mistake. She was making a comfortable living with the winners.

"Has he spoken yet?"

She turned her head toward the doorway. A slender man walked in. His dress was conservative, marking him a Roundhead.

His dark eyes went to the naked man on the bed. He walked over, looking his fill. Then, without warning, he drew back his hand and slapped Cam, hard. "Traitor!" he declared, then turned his back. "I will take the prisoner," he announced.

"No," Faith stated.

"Who are you to deny me?" the man asked.

"He's mine."

"He is an enemy of the Commonwealth, and as such he belongs in gaol, until he can be tried. This is no ordinary man you hold here, Mistress Bellamy."

"Think you that I do not know that?" she countered.

"Then release him to my custody."

"No." Faith laid her hand on Cam's chest, her fingers threading through the soft golden hairs that feathered his skin. "I am sworn to get information from the Buchanan, and get it I will."

"Your duty is ended, Mistress Bellamy," the man insisted.

Her eyes glittered with money lust. "I've been promised a sizable purse if I can persuade him to talk, to tell what he knows."

"You said he told you nothing," the man stated.

Faith wet her lips in a gesture that caused a shiver of revulsion in the man who stood beside her.

"I haven't truly begun. Watch if you've a mind to," she said, her voice once again taking on the sound of a purr.

"Styles," she demanded.

The beefy man who'd been waiting patiently in the shadow of the bed stepped forward. "Aye, mistress?"

"We have been very gentle with our Scottish friend. 'Tis time to amend that." Faith pointed to his right hand.

Styles nodded. He calmly took Cam's bound hand and methodically broke each finger.

Blood dripped from the wound Cam made as he bit his lip to stifle the intense pain.

"Such a pity," Faith mused aloud as she bent to place a kiss on the tightly closed fist of his other hand. "He has such lovely hands, capable of giving a woman a taste of heaven."

The man spoke up, looking deeply into the prisoner's sapphire eyes, which were misted with pain. "We need to know the names of others who share your misguided loyalties. Don't you know how foolish it is to cling to the idea of a monarchy, especially that of Charles Stuart? Admit your error. Tell us what we want and your life may be spared. Others have already died in this foolish attempt to restore Charles Stuart to the throne."

Cam was already aware of the scattered bands that had risen in March of that year. Instead of the promised legions, there had only been a handful of men who tried to lead a rebellion against the government. They had failed miserably, resulting in imprisonment for some and death for others. He'd been charged with finding the leak. It was known that somehow agents of Cromwell had infiltrated the Royalist organization known as the Sealed Knot. Now he'd found out one of the traitors to his cause. A pretty face had hidden a conniving soul.

"Mayhap a stronger lesson for our *guest*." Faith laid her hand once again on Cam's body, skimming across the muscles in his chest, lightly touching his flat belly in a loverlike caress. She continued until she held him in her hand, cupping the very essence of him.

"You can't mean to geld him?" the man beside her asked, incredulous.

"No," she said softly, releasing Cam's manhood. Faith addressed her prisoner. "Do you wish to confess?" she whispered to him in a seductive tone.

Silence greeted her and gave her his answer.

"'Tis a pity that you are so very stubborn, my Scottish fool. Think you that your fine king, that whorespawn, would show you the same consideration should your roles be reversed?" Faith did not let him reply. "'Tis sure he would not. Cam . . . " Her voice took on a coaxing tone. "Do not force me to continue."

Cam stared at her. Faith could read the disgust in those cold blue eyes.

"'Tis on your head then," she stated. "Styles." She pointed to Cam's right leg.

A scream of pain erupted in the small chamber before the man on the bed could stifle it. Tears wet his lids from the impact of the smithy's hammer on his knee. The bones were shattered.

"Enough," the other man said, his voice laced with disdain. "His station demands better treatment."

"Think you that Captain Fairchild would spare him?" she asked. "'Tis he who charged me with procuring the information."

"I should not think that he would want you to damage a man who could be of use to us." He took another look at the prisoner and felt the contents of his stomach rise so that he could taste the bitter flavor of bile. "Cease this until I can talk to Captain Fairchild myself."

Faith smiled once again. "I shall give you one

hour, Mr. Covington. 'Tis enough time to secure
a writ from Captain Fairchild. Only that will persuade me that you have the authority to take the
prisoner from my custody."

"I will return within the hour then," he concluded and left the room.

"That be all you was needing me for, mistress?"
asked Styles.

Faith nodded.

Styles shuffled out of the room, leaving Faith
and Cam alone.

"I never wanted to hurt you," she said, pulling
up a chair beside the bed.

A sardonic smile tugged up the corners of Cam's
wide mouth. He took a deep breath; pain shot
through him. "Pray forgive me if I find that difficult to believe, Mistress Slut." His blue eyes were
cold with contempt. His anger overrode his sense
of caution. "That I ever slept with a creature like
you is beyond my ken."

Faith recoiled as if physically struck by his
words. "You well liked our tumbles, my fancy
lord."

"Like pissing in a pot, my dear." He sneered the
last word. "'Tis all that it meant. A way to relief."
Words were now his only weapons, and use them
he would.

Faith's hands curved into talons. She would
rend his beautiful face, tear the flesh from it with
joy for what he'd said. She'd make him pay. Aye,
that she would.

Then, hot anger was slowly replaced by cold
vengeance.

She stood up, pushing back the chair methodically. It was a chilly day, so a fire blazed in the
hearth. She would be the one woman he would
remember the rest of his miserable life. The last

woman to seek his bed willingly. He would carry her mark to his grave.

She took the poker and plunged it into the flames, watching as the metal grew hot.

Bastard, she thought as she pulled it from the fire. Faith turned, once again facing the man on the bed.

Cam saw her approach, watched with dawning horror the calm look on Faith's face, viewed the white-hot tip of the poker as it came closer.

He heard the sound of a man drowning in pain, little realizing that it was he who uttured the harsh cry as he slipped from consciousness.

Part One:
Hard as Lightning
London, 1662

Chapter One

With my body, I thee worship.

The irony of that phrase twisted Cam's full mouth into a sneer after he'd uttered it. *Worship.* He worshiped nothing, least of all a woman's body. That notion was for fools and poets, of which he was neither. A woman bent on revenge had destroyed part of his soul, the part that could, or would, love a woman. And to be frank, nothing he'd ever seen gave him the slightest reason to believe in that lie called love betwixt men and women. Lust—aye, that he could understand. Greed. He could accept the grasping coldness of that also.

But love—that was a tale for children who knew no better. Not a thing for men, especially not for a man like him. Cam had seen things, done things in the struggle to restore Charles Stuart and the monarchy. He'd achieved his particular goal: his king was once again on the throne of England, where he so rightfully belonged.

Cameron flicked a swift glance towards the dark man dressed in velvets and silks—his sovereign lord. The woman standing next to the king, her hand resting on Charles's arm, he knew to be the king's mistress, the sensual Barbara Palmer, Countess Castlemaine.

It was for his king that he was here now, participating in this farce. Another mark of royal favor was the large sapphire stone set in a thick band of gold that he wore on his left hand. It had been delivered early this morn by a servant while he was breaking his fast.

Cam recalled how he had opened the velvet pouch and removed the gift. He'd examined the workmanship, then noted that there was an inscription inside.

"It reads, *In gratitude: Carolinus Rex*," spoke a deep voice from a connecting doorway.

"Majesty," Cam responded, rising to bow to his king.

"Odd's fish, man, sit down. No need to stand on ceremony with me, Cam."

"As you wish, sire," Cam said, reseating himself.

Charles walked around the room. "You are comfortable?"

"Aye," he answered. "Who wouldn't be in apartments such as these?" Cam glanced around the newly refurbished room he'd been given in Whitehall Palace. It was a significant mark of Charles's regard for him. Cam was well aware the court was full of men—and women—who envied his position with Charles Stuart.

In truth, Cam appreciated the loyalty of the king. As a landless third son of a Scottish earl, he had had to make his own fortune. In service to his king he had found ample rewards.

A bittersweet smile tugged at his lips, interrupting his memories. He'd been an eager youth, who hadn't grasped the fact that life's games were not always played according to plan.

"Art happy?" Charles asked, pouring himself a goblet of wine. He then sank into a chair opposite Cam, his heavy-lidded dark eyes focused on the other man.

"I am grateful to your Majesty for the favors you have bestowed on me."

"'Tis not what I asked," Charles said.

Cam decided that to dissemble to his king would be a waste of his time. Charles Stuart was a very perceptive man; he'd had to be, else he would have lost his life long before.

"I am content."

"God's blood, in this kingdom 'tis a rare state," Charles muttered, standing up. He looked into the fire that burned low in the grate. "At times I feel that I must be a magician, if not the great Solomon himself, to satisfy the requests that daily flood in. This family wants its lands and titles restored, no matter that another family now owns the property. Someone else demands money for his glorious service to the crown." Charles spread his large hands, catching what warmth he could from the flames. "'Tis as if everyone believes England's coffers—and mine—are overflowing. I do what I can."

Cam understood Charles's position. He'd seen first-hand the people who petioned for the restoration of lost property and titles, who besieged the king for money and influence. Cam knew Charles was a man who wanted to help his friends, reward the sacrifices they'd made for him. Yet there was only so much he could do.

Charles turned and sat down once again. When he spoke, his voice was sincere, roughened with emotion. "I owe you a debt I can never fully repay."

"Your Majesty knows full well that you owe me nothing. I did what had to be done."

Charles smiled. "I think you underestimate your service to me, my friend. And," Charles said with a deepening grin, "I think that wedding you to such a bride as Marisa Fitzgerald is the clearest way I can show my appreciation. Besides, I would rather you have her to wife than another. I trust few men with an heiress such as she."

"I am your Majesty's humble servant, in this and all else," Cam replied.

Charles raised a thick black brow. "Indeed?"

Cam laughed at the slightly cynical inflection. "Mayhap not quite so humble."

"'Tis an honest fellow you are, Cameron Buchanan."

"'Twould be foolish to be otherwise with your Majesty."

"Still, I wish you joy of this marriage. I know 'tis perhaps not what you may have wanted. At times every man must bow to the demands of policy, no matter how highly he is placed."

Cam nodded his head in understanding. He knew his king also would be taking a bride soon, the Portuguese princess, Catherine.

"I have sent to your lady a matching necklace, with a note that 'twould please me should she wear it when she weds with you this evening." He stood up, his dark eyes merry. "Now, I needs must return to Barbara. Till later then," Charles said as he left.

* * *

The bishop's voice brought Cam back to the present.

The lights of the fragrant candles flickered within the private chapel at Whitehall Palace, casting a soft glow on the wedding in progress.

The bride was stiff as she, too, listened to the words the bishop intoned. She tried to keep her thoughts focused on the ceremony, but she found them straying back to a conversation she'd had with her grandmother a month previous.

"'Tis lucky you are, dear gel, that His Majesty's seen fit to honor my son Derran's wishes," the old woman said, her face still possessing the remembrance of youthful beauty despite her 80 years. Her thin mouth curved into a bittersweet smile. "He was wise to ensure that you would have the favor of Royal wardship should aught occur to him and to your brothers. Now your claims to the property and title will be acknowledged as true and just.

"Aye," said Barbara Elizabeth Tremaine Fitzgerald, Dowager Countess of Derran. "He had the Stuart's word on it, signed and sealed. Now none dares gainsay your right." Her sparkling green eyes, which she had passed along to her only grandchild, still held the luster of finely polished emeralds. The Countess reached out her hand, taking hold of one of Marisa's. "'Twould seem that there is something that his Majesty requires of you in recognition of your inheritance. 'Tis the king's wish that you be wed to one of his minions."

Marisa wasn't surprised. She was well aware of the size of the estates that she controlled, the wealth of her purse. She was the last of her line in England. She knew enough of politics to realize that a legacy such as hers would have to be given in marriage only at the king's pleasure. 'Twould be by his command that she would find herself wed. But the choice. Who was this man?

She was to ask herself that question again and again in the weeks following her arrival in London. Taking up residence in her magnificent house in the Strand, Marisa was determined to find out what manner of man she was to take to husband.

She found on her entrance to the court that there was a unified reluctance to impart any information concerning her bridegroom. Since gossip was the delight of the court, Marisa expected to find some tidbit, some story. Even the king told her only that her future husband was his Majesty's "most trusted friend."

If so, why was not this *most trusted friend* at court? What was there to hide?

The only information she'd managed to glean was from one of the courtiers. At a small dinner party given in her honor by one of her mother's cousins, Marisa quietly left the drawing room for a breath of air. Upon entering the gardens, she found herself face to face with the man who'd been seated next to her at dinner.

"My Lord Hartwelle," she acknowledged.

"Countess, your servant," he responded with an elegant bow.

Marisa caught the heat in his gaze as it remained fixed on her chest, where the tops of her breasts were revealed by the square cut of her bodice.

"I understand that you seek information about the Buchanan?"

"'Tis only that I am curious about his whereabouts, my lord," Marisa said as she began to move away from him. "I deem it odd that I have not seen this man whom I am to wed."

"Nor are you likely to, my lady."

"Why say you that, my lord?" she queried.

"Call me Thomas, my dear." He moved closer, forcing Marisa to step backwards to avoid him. That move only brought her closer to the cold brick wall that surrounded the garden. "God's blood, to waste you on such a creature as Buchanan." A lascivious grin twisted his small mouth. "Rather, you should have a man in your bed who knows how to pleasure a wench."

"You, sirrah, forget yourself," Marisa stated, her voice cold.

"Come, my sweet, let us be honest. You need not be coy with me. I understand your wish to be discreet."

Marisa had had enough of this ignorant boor. "Discretion has naught to do with it. Stand aside, I said." God's truth, but she was tired of the men she'd met since coming to London. All these gallants seemed to desire was a willing body and a passably pretty face. They cajoled, flattered, and courted; all with the intent of seducing her to their beds. Marisa wasn't angry; who could be angry at boys intent on their games? But she was contemptuous of their silly ploys and pretenses.

The feel of Hartwelle's clammy hand on her arm brought her up short.

"How dare you put hands on me?" she demanded. "Loose me, now!"

Marisa's glance dropped to the offending appendage. His hand was pale, weak, with stubby fingers that resembled thick sausages. A shudder of revulsion skittered along her nerves.

"Think you that you'll like the touch of your braw Scottish fellow?" His laughter rang cruel. "Come the morn after your wedding, you'll be wanting a true man to ride you."

"Should that occur," Marisa retorted, her green eyes as hard as stone as she dropped her gaze to judge his own virility, before returning to look him full in the face, "I shall at least know where *not* to look."

"Haughty bitch," Hartwelle sneered and turned on his elegant heel, coming face to face with a rapier pointed at his heart.

"I would suggest a hasty apology to the countess, my lord, else I shall be forced to teach you a much-needed lesson in manners."

Marisa could see the bulge of Hartwelle's protruding eyes as she stepped around him, her skirts trailing on the flagged stone. Fear was clearly visible on his face as the blade pressed closer.

"Please do forgive me, my lady." Hartwelle swallowed quickly. "I meant no harm," he added hastily.

The man with the rapier bent his head slightly. "An excellent choice, Hartwelle. You are indeed a *wise* man, for not only is the Countess Derran affianced to the Buchanan, she is kin to Killroone of Ireland and Ravensmoor of Wales. 'Twould be foolish to anger them. Or," he added softly, "me, for that matter."

"I understand," Hartwelle said, his voice lowered to a mere croaking whisper. As soon as the blade was lowered, he fled.

"Your servant, my lady," the other man said as he replaced his blade in its scabbard, sketching a bow towards Marisa.

Marisa rewarded him with one of her most charming smiles. "I thank you for the kindness you have shown me, most especially in ridding me of such a nuisance."

"'Twas a pleasure, my lady," he responded. "Hartwelle is a bully and a coward, who deserves a good thrashing. My only regret is that I could not give him the lesson he needs." Once again he bent a leg to her.

"Pray, sir, I would know the name of the gentleman who comes to my aid. Surely you would grant me that, as you seem to know much of me," Marisa insisted, much taken with the genuine honesty of his face. She recalled seeing him enter the drawing room just before she left. His clothes were a sharp contrast to the peacoak hues of the other men. He was garbed in dark colors, and his long chestnut hair was clearly his own, not a periwig, as some men wore.

"Covington, my Lady Derran. Jamie Covington."

Marisa extended her hand, which Covington brought to his lips. "I appreciate your regard, sir."

"'Twas nothing, my lady. I am happy to help." He offered his arm. "Perhaps I should escort you back inside?"

Marisa flashed him a dazzling smile. "I would like that."

He stopped after they had taken a few steps. "I would offer you a word of advice, countess."

"And what, pray tell, would that be?" she asked, unfurling her ivory fan with a snap.

"Ask no more about the man whom you are to wed."

Marisa snapped her fan shut, her gaze seeking that of the man next to her. "Why ever not?"

"Because you must be the judge of the man."

"Do you know him?"

Now it was Jamie Covington's turn to smile. "Aye, my lady, that I do. Reasonably well."

"And you will tell me naught?"

"Only this: Cameron Buchanan is a proud man. Do not allow yourself to forget that, else all will be lost ere it begins," he said.

Covington's enigmatic words came back to haunt Marisa as she raised her eyes to the man standing next to her. Candlelight bathed one side of his face with a warm glow. In profile, his nose, which was neither long nor short, was aquiline. Beneath the wide-brimmed hat with its curling plume, his golden hair hung in thick waves past the white lace of his shirt collar, falling onto the velvet doublet he wore. The color of his hat and doublet matched the deep, rich hue of the ring he wore on his left hand, sapphire blue. She noted with pleasure that that same hand, which gripped a walking stick of oak topped with a figurine of gold, was large, the fingers long and slender. He was taller than she by several inches, though not, she judged, as tall as the king.

A smile of gratitude edged her mouth. The man she was taking to husband was a man in his prime, angelically handsome. His voice, repeating the words of the bishop, was deep and clear, with the tiniest hint of Scotland.

A tremble feathered along her flesh when he spoke the line, "With my body I thee worship." Tonight, after the supper given them by the king and Lady Castlemaine, they would begin their wedded life. Two strangers come to share the same bed, to blend their bodies together. Marisa knew what was expected of her this night. Her mother, now blissfully remarried to a neighbor of her cousin Killroone, had prepared her, as had her cousin Brianna, Killroone's sister, herself a recent widow, who'd accompanied Marisa when she returned to England.

So light was his touch that she hadn't felt the ring that linked their fates slip onto her finger.

"You are now husband and wife. This union, which God has blessed, let no man set asunder."

Her husband, now bearer of the ancient title last held by her father, stepped forward slowly, out of the darkness which partially surrounded him.

Her welcoming smile froze on her face. Marisa stifled the gasp that rose in her throat. Sweet Jesu, what manner of man stood before her? Was *this* the man that she had just promised her life to?

The light revealed what the shadows had hidden. Beauty existed side by side with ugliness. Heaven had been joined by hell. Twisted scars bisected the right side of his face and throat. A black patch covered his eye. Her gaze dropped. His right hand was misshapen as well. It resembled the twisted, gnarled branch of a tree.

He came a step closer and Marisa saw that he limped.

"Faith, Beauty," he said, his voice dripping with frost, "have you no kiss for your Beast?"

Chapter Two

Her lips were cool on his, lightly brushing his mouth like the soft touch of a breeze. Her composure was perfect; in no way did she betray what he was sure she was feeling. No outward signs of abhorrence marred her comely features. Aye, Cameron thought, she was indeed a bonny lass, a fit bride for the Stuart himself.

Charles, with Barbara Palmer on his arm, placed a hand on Cam's shoulder. "Well done, my friend. You have made us proud." He then addressed Marisa. "We are well pleased with you, countess." Charles leaned down and placed a kiss on Marisa's smooth cheek. His smile was warm, his dark eyes alight with laughter as he remarked, "You honor us by wearing our gift to you."

Marisa returned the warmth of the king's smile. "'Tis you who pays me honor, Majesty." She raised her hand to the stone, her fingertips touching beautifully faceted jewel.

"Come, let us to supper," said Charles, leading the way with Barbara, who whispered in his ear some remark that caused hearty laughter to erupt from his throat.

"'Twould appear that Castelmaine still reigns over Charles's affections," spoke a voice behind her husband. It belonged, Marisa found to her surprise, to Jamie Covington. She surmised that he must have been standing next to Cameron Buchanan during the entire ceremony. In normal circumstances, she would have paid closer attention to details, to people. This night, however, was far from the normal.

"Indeed," said Cameron, his head turned slightly towards Jamie, "that has not changed ere I quit the court some months ago. Lady Castlemaine is like an exotic spice, once tasted, not easily forgot."

Her new husband's observations gave Marisa pause. She focused her gaze on him in speculation. Had he sampled freely the charms of the king's mistress? Marisa knew that fidelity was not a watchword at court. Here, amidst the splendor of the restored monarchy, men and women played the game of love as it suited their fancy.

"May I offer my congratulations to you both?" Jamie asked, taking Marisa's hand in his and saluting it with a kiss. "I wish you every happiness."

"I thank you, sir," Marisa responded. "I confess I had not thought to see you again so soon."

One of Cam's blond brows arched in puzzlement. "You two have met before?"

"Aye, Cam," Jamie answered, "'twas at a small supper given for your lady wife some weeks ago."

"'Tis passing strange that you forgot to mention it," Cam noted, his hand tightening on the cane. He was too long standing; pain flared to life, shooting through his leg. "Come, my lady," he said, his voice low, his manner dour, "we must not keep his Majesty waiting for us any longer." He straightened, holding out his left arm for Marisa.

Marisa laid her hand tentatively on her new husband's arm, feeling the strength underlying the soft velvet fabric.

Cam looked up momentarily as a footman refilled his wineglass. He was seated at one end of the cherrywood dining table, at the right hand of Countess Castelmaine. Jamie sat opposite; his bride was at the other end of the table, seated next to the king. As he sipped his wine, Cameron used the opportunity to observe his wife. She appeared to find something that Charles said amusing, because Cam could hear the sound of her laughter. It was bright, sweet, genuine, not false patter designed to mollify or flatter. Her chestnut hair was skillfully arranged about her neck; fat curls hung over her ears, skimming the soft, exposed shoulders. The creamy hue of the pearls that she wore around her neck and in her ears complemented her skin. The rise and fall of her breast drew his eye towards the stone that lay nestled there. How well, he thought, that dress of deep rose suited her. God's truth, but she was flawless. His to have and to hold. His hand tightened on the delicate stem of the glass.

It had been so damnably long since he'd had a woman.

"She is lovely," Jamie said, observing how Cameron watched his bride.

Cam's long fingers relaxed somewhat as Jamie's voice interrupted his painful musings. He drank deeply, feeling the need for temporary solace. "Aye, that she is," he agreed. Cam directed another swift glance in her direction, noting that she ate sparingly of the rich food put before her. The king's cooks had conjured up a marvelous feast, both for the eye and the palate, with fish, fowl, and game, as well as an assortment of sweets to tempt the most abstemious. Mayhap she was delicate, lacking a robust appetite. No, Cam thought, she looked like no fragile child in need of fattening up. More likely she had no taste for food this evening. Could it be that the anticipation of coupling with him had spoiled her appetite? What a pretty thing to contemplate— that his physiognomy could render a woman unable to eat. He flicked his glance toward the king's mistress. Obviously it mattered little to Barbara Palmer, for she consumed her food with gusto.

"You will have to inform me just how you met my wife, Jamie."

"'Twas at an informal supper given by one of her mother's relations. I arrived late, though in time to see her remove herself from the gathering, and to see her followed by someone."

"Who?"

"Hartwelle. 'Twould appear he fancied her for himself. He thought to *take* her favors." Jamie's mouth lifted in a grin. "I merely stepped in and forced him to see the error in his ways."

Damnation! Cam swore silently, an impotent rage welling inside him. Once his skill as a swordsman would have been enough to ensure that no man would risk his anger. Now anyone could bait him. For what manner of retribution did he command? Anger sliced like a razor through his veins. With a wife as comely as Marisa Fitzgerald, Hartwelle would be only the first to offer him insult.

"Hartwelle is a boring ass," Barbara put in, joining the conversation. "No doubt he could not resist the lure of a country virgin," she said mockingly. She fixed her blue eyes on Cameron. "'Tis no pleasure you'll be getting out of her this night. God's blood," Barbara swore as she rolled her eyes heavenward, "she looks the type to fall faint at the sight of a man's naked blade."

The Countess Castlemaine's casual observations forced a smile to Cam's lips. He liked Barbara, for there was no pretense in her; the woman was a sensualist and proud of it. Pleasure was her pastime. She was beautiful and without scruples. She'd already presented the king with one son and carried another child of his in her womb. She loved her status as royal whore, and she was courted by others for her influence over the king. Barbara could be a staunch friend or an implacable foe. She had been the only woman at court who had not turned away from Cam's face in fear and disgust. For that, he was grateful to her. That, and the fact that she did make Charles happy. Having shared the king's exile, Cam knew that happiness was often in short supply; one held fast to it whenever it chanced near.

"God's truth," Barabara said, "virginity can be such a chore. 'Tis glad I was when I rid myself of mine." Her dark blue eyes were slumbrous with memories. "I wish you well," she said, her hand resting on Cam's for a moment. "'Tis a cold bed you've been given, I'll wager. She is much too tame a beauty for a beast," she added with affection.

Cameron didn't take offense at Barbara's words, for he knew she meant none. An ironic sliver of a smile crossed his mouth. What neither Barbara nor his bride could know was that this beast was forever caged by the darkness in his soul. No physical act could shatter the bars he'd carefully erected.

"What think you, my lady?" Charles queried.

"About what, your Majesty?" Marisa countered.

"You know full well to what I refer. The man I gave you as husband."

Marisa wiped her mouth with the fine lace napkin. "Truthfully, Majesty, I was surprised." She toyed with her eating knife, sliding it in and out of a slice of roasted wild boar. "No one would say aught of him, including yourself."

"I told you what was most important," Charles declared.

"And your court thought it good sport to make sure I knew naught of him. Even Jamie Covington did not volunteer any information." She dropped her gaze till it rested on the band of gold that encircled her finger. "'Twas your right to secure for me a match befitting my birth and position. I am a Fitzgerald, your Majesty," Marisa said, raising her green eyes until they met those of the king, "with full knowledge of that responsibility. I lost my father in the battle of Worcester; both my brothers and several male cousins also died for your cause. Loyalty is bred in my bones. If you seek to know whether I accept the Scotsman for my husband—that I did when word came from you of your choice."

Marisa sliced a quick look at her husband. "I did dare to hope that the man you chose for me would be neither diseased nor old."

"In truth," Charles insisted, "he is neither."

"Then your Majesty has been charitable in the fulfillment of his duties."

"Think you that I was merely fulfilling my duties?" He signaled the footman to refill their glasses. "I am well aware of my responsibility to you and your family, countess. 'Tis why I thought long and hard on the choice of a husband for you." Though the Court of Wards had been abolished by Parliament in 1645, and officially abolished on his Restoration, Charles was under moral obligation to the late Earl of Derran, who'd made a proviso in his will that should anything befall him or his male heirs, the wardship of his daughter would fall to the king. "The Buchanan is well matched with you in birth. He is a younger son of the Earl of Tairne and was created Baron Buchanan by my hand. He has shared exile with me, doing many services for me and mine." Charles paused, his dark eyes somber. "You have not yet mentioned the obvious."

"I must admit to curiosity, sire," she acknowledged.

"'Twould be difficult not to have been curious."

"Will you tell me how he came to look as he does?"

"Alas, I may not," he said. "For it is not my tale to tell."

"Then I shall curb my inquisitiveness, Majesty." Her small, full mouth curved slightly. "At least, for the present." Marisa focused her attention on the food, finding that she little cared what was being served. Since it wouldn't do to insult the king and his hospitality, she forced herself to eat more. In truth she was apprehensive about the coming night. Under different circumstances, she knew her wedding would have been one filled with people, a glittering court function with her family journeying from their estates in Ireland and Wales to be with her, to share in her joy. She would have expected her husband's kinsmen to have joined in the celebration of the union. Instead of a private chamber with a few musicians playing softly in the background, there would have been a lavish wedding supper, with dancing and merriment filling one of the huge banqueting rooms in Whitehall Palace. Perhaps even a masque for amusement. Bawdy jokes concerning what transpires between the sheets would have been bandied about, to be followed by a public bedding. Both she and her husband would have been stripped of their clothes and examined so that no flaw could prove a hindrance later to the validity of the marriage. No such spectacle would occur tonight. She had been informed by the king as they sat down to the wedding supper that the Buchanan had chosen to forgo the bedding ceremony. She could well imagine why. He would not want to be further exposed to taunts and jests. She would face him alone.

She stole another glance in his direction, noting that he was quiet. Then, as if feeling her gaze on him, he raised his head and looked her full in the face, a slightly mocking look in that very blue eye. Once, when she was a child, she had visited the Highlands of Scotland with her father and mother; it was there she had seen such a shade of blue in the cold waters of a loch. Blue, bright and deep as the sapphire she wore. She could discern no warmth in that cool orb focused on her. In fact, she felt a trifle perplexed by the intensity of the look he gave her.

Would his possesion of her this night also be cold? True, love had not entered into her marriage bargain, yet she had still hoped for some semblance of caring. On her finger she wore his ring. Her name and destiny were now irrevocably linked to his. In a very few hours her flesh would also be joined to his. Heat flooded her cheeks, and she dropped her gaze.

Cameron saw the stain of color flush her cheeks. The chit was obviously conjuring up images of this evening's sport. Barbara was correct—a country virgin, come fresh to the marriage bed. Still, he caught the hint of defiance in those eyes of deepest green. He'd observed her pride and grace. Any man would be happy to have such as she on his arm, wearing his name, sharing his bed. Once, the man he had been would have felt the same. He would have seen happy anticipation in her eyes then, a certain eagerness to be partnered in the dance of life.

A cold, black anger arose in him; he felt as if he'd been given a seat at a feast, then told it was forbidden him to consume anything. And he *wanted* to consume. Lust coursed achingly in his blood, demanding release.

He could stomach no more of this slow torture. Best to end this comedy promptly ere it became a tragedy.

"I thank your Majesty and Lady Castlemaine for this most gracious of meals. But 'tis time my wife and I took our leave of you." Cameron rose, reaching for his walking stick.

Foolish virgin, Barbara thought, observing the scene as she washed down a succulent piece of squab with a glass of French wine. She'd wager a hundred pieces of silver that the Fitzgerald girl was too frightened to do aught tonight but weep. Her glance followed the Buchanan as he stood. It mattered little to her that the man was lame. Barbara reckoned that what was most important hung between his legs, and if all accounts were true, he was just like her Charles, a veritable stallion. That thought brought a coursing warmth to the spot between her own legs. Christ's blood, but she wanted Charles. Now. She licked her lips in anticipation of the pleasure she would soon have. She was in the mood for a long, hard ride.

Jamie Covington's glance swung from his friend to the young woman who stood next to the king. He searched her face for signs of hesitation or fear. Relieved, he saw only a quiet dignity there. She was no lamb to the slaughter nor cowering child. He drew in a deep breath, silently praying that all would go well for the couple. Cameron possessed a fierce temper and a wicked tongue when he was in one of his black humors; Jamie feared that what was to transpire this night could damage the progress that Cam had made. To think, Jamie had once envied Cam's ease with women; they'd once responded to his charm, eager to bed the handsome man with the face of an angel. Now, because of pain and pride, the angel was tarnished, cast out of the heaven of adoration. Mayhap 'twas better to be a dull fellow. One met the world on more level terms.

Charles addressed the couple, pointing to a door carved into a side panel. "'Tis unlocked. Go down those stairs and through the gate. A carriage awaits your use. The coachman's name is Jack." Charles gave them a benevolent look. "I felt 'twas better to begin your wedded life away from the prying eyes of my courtiers."

Cam guessed this was for his benefit. Another gesture of regard from Charles. Christ's blood! Could he take another kindness? Charles thought to protect him. Or perhaps it was the Fitzgerald heiress Charles sought to protect, should she run screaming from her husband's bed in horror. That would not happen, Cam vowed. He would never allow that.

Cameron paused for just a moment before saying, "Your Majesty's genorosity is most kind. My wife and I accept."

Jamie announced, "I shall go down with you. 'Tis late and I must seek my own bed."

After the trio departed, Barbara turned to the musicians and said, "Be gone. The king and I wish a private audience."

The musicians, understanding the ways of the court and the power of the king's mistress, obeyed without hesitation.

"Odd's fish, Barabara, have I done the right thing?" Charles wondered aloud, tossing his fancy doublet to the floor.

"Of course you have, my love," she answered as she kicked off her shoes and with a sweep of her arm sent the china and glassware flying from the table. They lay smashed on the floor, bringing a contented smile to Barbara's face. She angled herself onto the table, her hands busy opening her bodice, freeing her breasts. She leaned back, wetting her lips. "Now, tarry not a moment longer. Come and claim your dessert."

"I will bid you both a good night," Jamie said when they entered the courtyard where the coach stood, ready for its occupants.

"Please, do feel free to call at Derran House. My . . ." She paused, her glance taking in the man who stood next to her. "*Our* door is always open to you," Marisa stated as she accepted Jamie's hand to enter the carriage.

With a slight bow to Marisa, Jamie turned to Cameron, his eyes reflecting his concern. "Have a care, my friend. Your lady is no ordinary wench."

"Think you that I dinna ken that?" Cam asked, slipping with easy familiarity into his childhood speech pattern. "But," he added with a trace of underlying bitterness, "for all that, she's a woman, and I willna play the fool ever again."

That thought kept nagging at him while they rode in silence from Whitehall Palace the short distance to her London house in the Strand. Through a narrowed lid, he watched her, observing the calmness with which she comported herself. Her hands were folded primly in her lap, looking pale against the darkness of her cloak. Her face was turned toward the window, giving him a chance to see the elegance of her profile. Long-lashed eyes, a pert nose, a stubborn chin. Her skin was fresh, with no paint or powder. A right bonny lass indeed, with the pride and bearing, of a *banrigh*—a queen.

Marisa kept her eyes averted from her husband, choosing instead to gaze out the carriage window. What was he thinking? she wondered. An uncanny sense told her that he watched her. She could almost feel his gaze. Was he measuring her? Deciding just how she would look when divested of her garments? Or was one female body as good as another? Were women like Lady Castlemaine what he was used to? What he wanted?

She dismissed the thought. It mattered little to her, she told herself. She was now his wedded wife. The marriage contract was understood to include the sharing of a bed. Such contracts did not stipulate that one must like or desire the partner one was given. Marisa turned her head back toward the interior of the coach. What did she

really know of desire? Having no experience with
the pleasures of the bedroom was to the good,
she concluded. That way, she would not be too
disappointed should they be lacking.

Yet, her mind mocked, what of the blood she
carried in her veins? That lusty Fitzgerald blood,
which ran hot when love was involved?

But, she rationalized, love was not involved.
The best she could hope for was fondness and
solicitude. She wondered if even that was possible.

Derran House loomed before them. Trees surrounded the property, as did a wide stone wall.
The hooves of the spirited team made a loud
noise on the cobbled entrance as the coachman
pulled the vehicle up to the door. A lad of fourteen
jumped down from his seat atop the coach and
opened the door, flipping out the steps.

Within seconds, the entranceway was ablaze
with light as a footman in Fitzgerald livery held
high a lantern while another assisted their lady
from the coach.

Marisa waited for her husband to emerge.

She heard the hastily suppressed gasp from her
housekeeper, who stood in the doorway, a branch
of candles in her hand, when Cameron alighted
from the coach.

He felt an onslaught of pain. The dampness of
the night had invaded his bones, making him
ache. Disembarking jarred his leg even further,
so that he was forced to lean more heavily on his
walking stick.

Afraid that the Buchanan would fall, Marisa
commanded the footman nearest him, "See to
my husband's aid."

Cameron waved him away with an angry slash
of his hand. "I need no help," he said.

"As you wish, husband," Marisa acknowledged, walking up the steps. She entered her house, leaving him to trail in her wake. Once in the entrance hall, Marisa spoke to her housekeeper. "How did you know we were to come?"

"A servant came from the palace, my lady. He said that the king's coach would be bringing you and your husband back to Derran House after the wedding supper." The portly woman threw a nervous glance in the direction of the man coming slowly into the hall, his cane making a decided click on the polished wood. "I thought that you'd be wanting to have the master's old rooms instead of your own, them being that much bigger and all. They've been readied, my lady. Your maid waits you there."

"And what of my cousin, the Lady Brianna?"

"She is asleep, my lady. Should I have wakened her?"

Marisa shook her head. "No. I shall see her on the morrow."

"A tray of food has been sent up, along with some mulled wine, my lady. Would you be wanting anything else?"

"No, Mistress Chatham. That will do us well."

"Then I bid you good night, my lady," the older woman said with a concerned look in her eyes, "and fare you well." Remembering her manners, Mistress Chatham bobbed a curtsey to the countess's husband, saying, "Welcome, my lord. I wish you much joy."

As the housekeeper departed, Cameron's mouth twisted with wry humor. He could tell that Mistress Chatham wished him anywhere but under this roof. It was evident by the look in her eyes. She believed her mistress wed to a monster. He should have been inured to it ere now. Still, it was another wound, another sliver of his soul scraped away.

Cam let none of his pain show.

Instead, he glanced up the long, wide stairway. Gathering his strength, he said, "Madam, after you."

Marisa entered the room that had been her parents' chamber. Memories flooded back. Her mother's needlework stand was still in the corner. The family portrait, painted when she was an infant, still hung above the fireplace. Further up the wall hung two swords, treasured heirlooms of her family. They had been given by Elizabeth to her ancestor Tristam Fitzgerald on the occasion of his marriage. Marisa smiled, remembering the family story that held that Tristam, Earl of Derran, had earned the swords by showing Elizabeth the power and skill of his own strong blade.

A soft snore brought the realization that she wasn't alone. Her maid, Charity, was fast asleep, curled into a chair. It was after midnight. Time for the girl to be in her own bed. As Marisa wished she was in hers.

She gently shook the girl awake.

Charity sprang from her position, wiping the sleep from her eyes. "I'm ever so sorry, my lady," she said.

"Nonsense, 'tis of little consequense," Marisa said. "Help me from this dress and you may seek your own bed."

Charity complied, unlacing the bodice, gathering up the dress when Marisa stepped out of it. Charity hung it over the back of the wing chair while she proceeded to untie the corset Marisa wore. Next came several petticoats. Finally, Marisa stood naked, chillbumps prickling her bare flesh. Charity held up her night rail, but Marisa shook her head.

"I have no need of that this night," she said. "Fetch me instead my robe with the beaver trim."

Charity bobbed her head and removed the clothes as Marisa pulled the jeweled pins from her hair, sending it tumbling down her back in thick waves. She worked her fingers into her scalp, soothing the aching muscles of her neck. Taking a comb from the dressing table, she pulled it through her hair, ruthlessly destroying the curls Charity had created hours earlier.

That accomplished, Marisa picked up a glass of mulled wine. The brew had cooled somewhat, but she cared not. Drinking it down, she reflected on how very different was this night from the way she'd imagined it. There was no one to demand that she meet her husband as God made her; no need to expose herself. None save for her own determination to do so, to show him she had no fear, and nothing to hide. It mattered not to her if there were no witnesses. *He* would know.

Charity hurried back through the door, a robe of green wool edged in beaver fur in her arms. She held it out and Marisa slipped her arms into it, tying the sash of gold around her waist. The fabric felt soft against her naked skin.

A fanciful thought entered her mind. What would his hands feel like against her flesh? Soft and caressing? Or harsh and cruel?

A flutter of panic rose in Marisa's chest. She forced herself to remain calm. She dismissed Charity. "You may leave me now. I will have no further need of you till the morning."

As the maid went to the door, she turned back to her mistress. "May God grant you a healthy son, my lady."

Aye, Marisa thought. A future Earl of Derran. 'Twould make this all worthwhile.

Walking to the smaller door that connected the bedchamber to the sitting room, she turned the handle, leaving it ajar. She strode to the wide bed, sitting on the edge of it near the foot.

Moments later, she heard the sound of booted footsteps in the room. Bracing herself, she rose to face her legally wedded husband.

Marisa loosed the belt, letting the robe slide from her arms to fall into a heap at her slender feet. Her bare skin gleamed in the light of the candles.

"Come, husband," she said, her voice soft, her left arm extended in a gesture of invitation, "your wife awaits your pleasure."

Chapter Three

Mocking bitch!

Cam's mind silently screamed the words as he entered the room and heard his wife speak. Her words hung in the air for an instant before dropping like grains of salt onto the wounds in his heart. *Await his pleasure.* The phrase conjured up bittersweet memories of countless women who had done just that, once upon a time.

He'd paced round and round in the antechamber he'd been given as he waited for the signal that his wife was ready to receive him. Aye, receive him—in the manner of one who was granting absolution to a penitent. Or an audience to a retainer. It was there in the proud tilt of her head, in the way she stood, her arm outstretched as if dispensing the favors of her rank.

Did she think that he should be grateful for her condescension? He was a Buchanan, by God.

Marisa dropped her arm, feeling the coolness

51

of the glance Cameron Buchanan threw in her direction. He advanced slowly toward her, leaning on his gold-tipped stick, treading slowly and carefully, his limp more pronounced than before. She saw that he was still fully dressed, having removed only his doublet. She fought the urge to shiver, fearing he would interpret that as a sign of weakness. Her bold gesture of welcome seemed lost in the moment. There was a strange look of anger on his face, which in turn gave rise to a sense of annoyance in Marisa. By rights, she was the one who should be angry, being bound to a man like him.

However, anger wasn't foremost in her mind now as he stood before her, capturing her chin in his hand, lifting her mouth to meet his.

Her lips were cool, soft to the touch of his.

Determined to melt her icy facade, Cam opened his lips, skillfully coaxing hers to surrender. His tongue traced the outline of her mouth, slipping inside when she dared to take a breath. He could taste the spices and the wine, sweet and provocative.

Marisa stood still, twists of sensation flickering across chilled nerves as her husband's mouth moved from her lips to the sweep of her neck.

"Art a virgin?"

"Of course, my lord," Marisa stated, bending to pick up her discarded robe, feeling suddenly at a disadvantage standing before him naked.

Cam stayed her hand, forcing her to stand upright once again. "'Tis naught of a certainty," he stated matter-of-factly.

Marisa, her green eyes meeting his, said, "'Tis so for the women of *my* family. Now, if thou art satisfied, my lord husband, I will don my robe."

"Satisfied?" He whispered the word in her ear,

his breath warm on her face. "Think you that I shall be *satisfied* with only a look?" he demanded. "Know you what passes between a man and a woman, my lady wife?" Cam straightened to face her.

Once again, Marisa saw the gleam of anger and something else in his blue eye. Had she imagined that it could be pain? Or perhaps vulnerability? Nay, 'twas only her fancy playing tricks on her. There was nothing in his gaze save pride. "'Tis only that I am chilled and would have once again the warmth of the wool."

"Indeed?"

Her green eyes were lit with anger. "You have doubt of my word?"

"Art not a woman?" he questioned, raising his battered hand to push aside the thick curtain of chestnut hair, sending it rippling along her back. His nostrils quivered at the scent of wildflowers that rose from the strands.

"Aye, I am, as you can plainly see," she answered.

"Then there's your answer, my lady."

"You talk in riddles."

"You haven't answered my question. Know you what passes between a man and his wife in the bridal chamber?"

"I am aware of a wife's obligation to her husband regarding her body, my lord," she stated.

Obligation. The coldness of the word chilled him. A duty to be performed, no doubt, under duress. "And art ready?"

"Have I not indicated as much, my lord?" Marisa wondered what game her husband played. She wanted to get this bedding ceremony over with as soon as possible, lest she falter. She owed it to the memory of the brave Fitzgeralds before her to accomplish this with dignity.

Cam reached out his good hand, trailing his index finger along the soft skin of her shoulder. He could feel the pulse beating in her throat. Her lids were lowered so that he couldn't read the look in her eyes. Her skin, a shade resembling fresh cream, glowed with health. Indeed, he could find no blemishes marring her form. Her perfection served to make Cam even more conscious of his own flaws. His wife was a woman of uncommon beauty and poise.

What would it be like to lie with such cool perfection?

"My lord," she said, her voice low, the accent pleasing to his ears, "I crave your indulgence. I must either put on my robe or seek the warmth of the bed, ere I become more chilled. Mayhap, as you are still clothed," she commented, "you do not feel the damp."

"Allow me," Cam said, bending with his good leg to scoop up the robe. He placed it about her shoulders, his hand lingering, then moving lower until it rested on the fullness of one breast. The nipple, puckered from exposure to the air, beckoned to him. He touched it gently, catching the soft intake of her breath, feeling the slight movement of her flesh.

She trembled.

From what? he wondered. Fear? Revulsion?

Abruptly, he dropped his hand and turned his back to her, walking stiffly toward the chair placed before the fire. Sinking into it, he faced the flames.

She was his to take.

So why did he hesitate?

'Twould ease the considerable ache in his loins if he were to bed her now and have done with it.

He could feel himself harden with the thought of sliding between her thighs, of touching that mound of curls, of feasting on the delights of her full breasts, of once more tasting the wonder of her mouth. Aye, all that and more ran rampant through his brain. Yet he knew 'twould be as if he took charity to lie with her. His wife was proud; even he, with only one eye left to him, could see that. So, too, was he.

Marisa stood quietly, observing the man to whom only hours before she'd joined her life. She'd made it clear that she was willing to seal the bargain as was expected. Why did he hesitate to bed her? Was he playing some game? And, if so, for what purpose?

"Would you like something?" she asked, trying to dispel the silence that threatened to engulf them.

"Some wine, I think."

Marisa proceeded to the small table and picked up the mug of spiced wine. "Tis cold, my lord. I shall warm it for you," she said, hastening to the fireplace, where she picked up the poker and put it into the flames. From the corner of her eye, she saw the movement he made in his chair, as if pulling back deeper into the leather. After warming the drink with the hot metal, Marisa turned to him, catching a look she could not recognize on his face. She held out the brew to him.

"My thanks," he said, taking the steaming wine from her hand.

Marisa replaced the poker, her hand shaking just a little. "Would you like something to eat?"

So very polite, he thought. So very formal. One wouldn't think that mere minutes ago she'd been offering herself to him like some virgin sacrifice on the altar of his lust and her responsibility. He drank the wine, little caring that it burned his tongue. Had he really expected her to welcome him? It said something of her strength that she did not run and cower. Was that what he would have wanted? A wife who quivered with fear?

He drained the contents of the mug, knowing where his brooding thoughts were leading him. He wanted something that he couldn't have. Not her body—that was his should he choose to take what was offered—no, he wanted comfort.

Christ's blood, but the wine must have addled his brain. What he needed was to relieve the deep ache he was feeling. His thoughts drifted to the king and his mistress. Aye, he needed a lusty wench like Barbara, one whom he could ride for pleasure's sake and have no regrets once it was over.

Cam rose, leaning once more on his stick. He needed no one's scraps, least of all his Fitzgerald wife's.

"Art tired, my lord?" Marisa asked. God, but she wearied of this trial. 'Twould be better to end this farce soon lest she scream and bring the household awake. Why did he dawdle?

Strange thoughts took root in her brain. Suppose he could not perform that which was a husband's duty to his wife? Or—she cast a quick glance at his still form—perhaps he had no interest in bedding a woman. She knew such men existed, had heard the whispers regarding certain courtiers and their favorites.

"Get thee to bed, wife," he said, his voice commanding her with its quiet power.

"Will you join me?"

He was tempted. She was like a vision of heaven held out to tantalize him, but he was afraid that should he reach out and grasp this cup of pleasure, it would turn into a bitter brew.

"No."

"No?" she questioned.

"*No,*" he repeated. Cam decided that he must quit this place ere he could change his mind. Already regret formed in his belly.

"I wish you good night," he said as he reentered the connecting room, closing the door softly, leaving Marisa to puzzle as to why he left.

What manner of man was he to abandon his bride on this their wedding night? Marisa thought as she shrugged out of her wool robe and tossed back the blanket on the massive bed. His actions made no sense to her. She was as prepared as she could be in the circumstances to do what was expected of her, to honor the vows she had taken.

Hugging a pillow close to her breast, confused by the events of the day, Marisa burrowed into the warmth of the bed, unsure of what was to follow or how she was supposed to feel.

Cam knew exactly how he felt: frustrated. Obtaining a horse from his wife's stables, he mounted, pushing the animal to maintain a swift pace till he reached his intended destination, Jamie's lodgings outside the city.

It was a modest establishment, a small residence that Covington had inherited from his mother's family, prosperous merchants. Cam was familiar with the house, having been a guest there on numerous occasions. It was there that he fled instead of to his large and comfortable rooms in Whitehall Palace. He couldn't face the looks or answer the questions bound to arise as to why he wasn't in residence with his new wife, the lovely young bride provided for him by a grateful monarch, enjoying the delights of the marriage bed.

The irony in that made Cam give a bark of harsh laughter as he brought the animal to a stop in front of the small stone building. He could hear several cocks crowing and sounds of men stirring within as dawn fast approached, sending streaks of color across the sky. Jamie's stables were small compared to those of Cam's Fitzgerald bride. Nevertheless, Jamie prided himself on the quality of his horses.

A big lad of about sixteen emerged from the stable. When he saw Cam astride the big bright bay, he immediately grabbed the reins, holding the horse still so that Cam could dismount.

Hating the fact that he was awkward and would always be so, Cam maneuvered himself from the saddle with care. A flare of pain shot through his leg as he dismounted and stood once again on solid ground.

Cane in hand, Cam leaned on it, gathering strength. He was bone weary, both from the ride and what had passed during the night. He knew that he had no need to instruct the youth to take good care of his mount. It would be seen to without question.

He walked the short distance to the house, making his way up the short set of steps. He knocked on the door.

After a brief wait, it swung open. A tall, angular older man stood there in his hastily assembled clothes. Recognizing the wayfarer who stood before him, he swung the door wide and beckoned Cam in.

" 'Tis early you be, Lord Buchanan."

"I wish to see Jamie," Cam stated, walking into the small hallway.

"Mr. Covington is still abed, sir. If you will but wait, I shall fetch him for you." He showed Cam into a modest room that served as Jamie's library. Bending, the majordomo replenished the wood in the hearth until he had a fire going.

"That should be more comfortable for you, my lord. Shall I see that some food or drink is sent to you whilst I awaken Mr. Covington? We have some excellent Somerset cider."

Cam eased himself onto the couch, propping his right leg full-length upon the silk material. He pretended not to notice the butler's slight frown when his booted foot made contact with the fabric.

Though he thought that he could use something far stronger than apple cider, Cam said, " 'Tis fine with me, Bridge."

Within minutes, a fresh-faced maid entered the room, bearing a tray that contained a jug of the cold cider, along with a large silver tankard and a plate containing thick slices of cheese and ham.

She bobbed a curtsey to Cam, flashing him a bright smile. "Will you be wantin' anything else, my lord?"

The girl showed no repugnance at his face and form, but then, he was no stranger to this household. He felt safe here, able to relax, if only for a brief time. He fixed her with a deep stare. "Not now. Mayhap . . . later," he answered, taking in her tall, full-bodied figure.

"Well, should you be wantin' me for aught else, my name's Lucy, my lord," she said, licking her lips slowly. "I'd be happy to be of any service to you."

"Get back to the kitchen, girl," Bridge said, entering the room. He waited by the door until she left. "My master will be with you soon, my lord," Bridge announced, closing the door behind him.

Cam reached for the tankard of cider and took a long drink. The brew was good and strong. None of that piss-water variety that passed itself off as cider in most of the taverns.

"Shouldn't you still be abed with your bride, my good friend?" asked the voice from the doorway.

When Cam finally spoke, his voice was barely above a whisper. "I need a whore, Jamie."

"A *whore*?" Jamie asked, incredulous. "You've just been wed," he said, coming into the room, surprise written on his still sleepy face, "so why would you be wanting another woman?"

"Can you arrange it for me?"

"You need a procurer," Jamie responded, a touch of frost in his voice, "not me."

"I have need of a friend," Cam replied. "I dinna come here to insult you," he added, weariness bringing old habits of speech creeping back. "I believed that with your—how shall we say—vast circle of acquaintances, you could perhaps tell me of a discreet establishment, with high standards, not a common stew, though one not favored with the royal trade."

"For what purpose?"

Cameron's full mouth quirked into a taunting grin. "Ah, Jamie," he said, "have you been without a woman for that long that you canna recall what you do with one?"

Jamie's fair skin took on a rosier hue at Cam's mocking comment. "I asked you a fair question, Cam. By all rights, you should be with your wife." Jamie moved so that he was sitting opposite Cam. "What happened?"

"Will you help me?"

"If you will be honest with me," Jamie countered. "Why are you not abed with your wife, the Fitzgerald heiress?"

"I refuse favors tossed to me like scraps to a dog."

Jamie heard the underlying bitterness in his friend's tone. "What do you mean?" he asked, his gaze focused on the side of Cam's face that he could see, the side of beauty. "Have you not consummated your vows?"

"No."

Jamie sighed, deciding how best to pursue his questions. Finally, he spoke. "Did the countess reject your favor?"

"My favor?" Cam questioned, giving a snort of derision. "What a lovely way you have of expressing yourself, Jamie." Cam moved so that he now faced his friend. He lifted his damaged right hand, drawing it across the scars that bisected his face. "Nay, she did not."

"Christ's blood!" Jamie swore. "Did you deny *her*?" Jamie needed no verbal answer from Cameron; it was there in the proud look he wore, in the taut pull of skin over his cheekbones. "Cam, have you considered that your wife will see what you did as an insult?"

"No," he stated. "The haughty Fitzgerald heiress will think herself lucky to have been spared the sacrifice of giving herself to a man like me. Aye, she made the gallant gesture, Jamie. But I've no need of her pity."

"Are you so sure 'twas pity she felt?"

Cam breathed a deep sigh. "What else could it be?"

"Compassion?"

"'Tis all the same."

"No, 'tis not," Jamie said. "You both exchanged vows before God, Cam, with the king as your principal witness. You made promises that must be honored."

With my body, I thee worship.

How he yearned to.

How he feared to.

"You cannot pretend that you have not taken her to wife," Jamie insisted. "Have you given thought to what Charles Stuart will say should your bride sue for an annulment?"

"There will be no annulment."

"You cannot be sure."

"Aye," Cam said, his one good eye gleaming brightly, "of that I can be assured, Jamie. She willna admit to strangers that she couldn't entice the beast. Think what the harpies at court would have to say."

"They could just as well say she was too repulsed to honor her vows."

Cam gave a cynical laugh. "Ah, Jamie. You are well aware of the morals at court. Could you find one there, either male or female, who wouldna bed with the devil should they think 'twould advance their prospects at court? Besides, Marisa Fitzgerald is possessed of too much pride to prattle her private business to courtiers."

Cam took another long swig of the cider. "The Countess of Derran shall not die a virgin, Jamie. Have no fear on that. No, she'll be taken, but in my own time, in my own way."

"Don't underestimate her, Cameron."

His hand fell to his leg, massaging his knee. "I never underestimate a woman, Jamie. I've learned my lesson quite well on that score. Now, will you help me?"

Jamie steepled his hands before his face, considering. "Give me some time to see what I can accomplish," he said. "I know of such an establishment, though it may take a few hours to secure a pass."

"Pass?"

"Aye. 'Tis a strictly run house, with a list of entrance requirements."

"To a brothel?"

"Indeed. One usually needs several sponsors to gain admittance. I think, however, that my word will suffice in your case." Jamie stood up. "Now, whilst I see to the details, perhaps you would like to use the bedroom provided for you to bathe and change."

"Shall I be helping you to wash, my lord?" Lucy offered.

Cam did not turn from the window, merely inclined his head and said, "No, Lucy. You've done enough."

"I'd be willin'. . . ."

"Thank you, but no," he said, his tone dismissive.

"I brung you something for your bath what should help ease your body." She glanced at the tall figure who stood bathed in the early morning sun as it streamed into the mullioned window. The tub could have held two, she thought with a sigh as she dumped the contents of the packet she'd brought with her into the water.

"If that be all then," she said with a touch of regret.

"Aye, young Lucy," Cam said, waiting till he heard her close the bedroom door before he turned around. Satisfied that he was alone, he dropped his clothes onto the floor.

Cam eased his aching body into the huge brass tub filled with steaming water. It soothed his muscles, though it did nothing for the ache in his loins, nor the ache he refused to acknowledge.

As he brought the cloth up, soaping his broad chest, he caught the smell of herbs and wildflowers. For some reason, even though the aroma wasn't the same, he thought of the scent that clung to his bride, and the gnawing hunger in his loins grew stronger.

What would she think when she woke to find him gone?

Chapter Four

Charity peeked into the bedroom after no one responded to her soft knock. She had expected to see her mistress abed with her new husband. Instead, as she crept towards the large bed, where the hangings were pulled aside, she saw a lone occupant. It was evident to Charity's eyes that her mistress had been the only person to sleep in that massive bed. The other side was undisturbed. She decided that it would do no good to speculate as to why the countess was alone.

As she started to back out, Marisa's voice stopped her.

"There is no need to creep, Charity," she admonished as she pushed herself to an upright position among the thick down pillows.

"I was just coming to see if you would like to break your fast," Charity said as she approached the bed. "Cook has some lovely ham from the country that she thought you might like." Charity cast a glance at the door that led to the connecting room. "Shall I bring it up here, my lady?" Her gaze swung back to Marisa. "Should I bring enough for two?"

Carefully skirting the question, Marisa asked one of her own. "Has my cousin arisen yet?"

Charity nodded her head. "Yes, my lady."

"Has she eaten?"

"I think not. She went for a walk in the garden, I believe."

"See if you can locate her and ask her to join me here if she would."

"What about the . . . earl?" That word seemed foreign to Charity's mouth.

The earl indeed, Marisa thought. Where was he? And why had he quit the room so quickly last night? She was willing to fulfill her duty. Her body had been his to take. "Send a manservant to attend to his needs." As much as she wanted to go through that door and confront him, she wouldn't. Her pride forbade her. "Should he wish to break his fast, he can. Alone."

Charity bobbed a curtsey and left the room.

Marisa grabbed one of the pillows and hugged it to her breast. She knew there were dark circles beneath her eyes, evidence of her restless night. The gall of the man, she'd thought as she'd slid into the empty bed, smelling the sweet herbs that had been placed there. She was a bride unclaimed. Her servants would know when the sheets were removed. No bloodstains would mark the fine white Irish linen, a gift from her cousin Killroone.

Another thought struck her. Suppose it was thought that there was no blood because she was unchaste? That she had come to her marriage bed having known a man other than her wedded husband? It would matter little to the wags at court, where virtue was considered a foolish practice. It did, however, matter to Marisa.

But how to remedy the situation?

She understood that there were ways. The sharp blade of a dagger could bring blood. It would, also, leave a telltale wound. And how much blood would be needed? There was another possibility. The thought of sneaking to the kitchen to obtain a freshly killed fowl for the purpose of smearing her sheets repelled her—not so much the act as feeling like a common slut having to cover her past deeds.

Marisa threw back the bedcovers, grabbing her robe from where she had tossed it at the foot of the bed. She belted it just as the door to her room opened.

Marisa spun around, beholding the tall, dark-haired woman who entered.

"Brianna."

The other woman drew nearer to Marisa, a curious look on her face.

Marisa noted that her cousin still retained her mourning clothes. Gone were the vibrant lemon yellows and grass greens, the crimson flames and sky blues for which Brianna's wardrobe had been famous. Brianna, only a year older than herself, was already wedded and widowed. While her face was calm and resolved, her gold-flecked brown eyes reflected an inner core of sadness.

"Charity sought me out with a message that you wished me to join you."

"Aye. I need to talk to you."

Brianna's eyes narrowed as she cast a quick look toward the large bed. "About your wedding night?"

"Or what could better be said to be the lack of one," Marisa stated.

"Lack?" Brianna questioned. "What happened?"

At that instant Charity returned, followed by another female servant, carrying a tray laden with food. She instructed the other girl to pour the cold cider while she prepared the small table. That accomplished, Charity dismissed the younger girl.

Marisa saw that Charity was waiting, her face a study in indecision.

"Have you something else to say?" Marisa asked.

Charity's eyes clouded with apprehension as she spoke up. "I did what you said, my lady. I sent one of the servants to attend the earl."

"And?" Marisa raised her brow as she sipped the refreshing cold cider.

"He wasn't there."

"Where was he?"

"'Twould seem that his lordship left very early this morning, my lady."

"He is gone from here?" Marisa questioned.

"Aye, my lady," Charity replied. "One of the grooms said that the earl ordered one of your best horses saddled for him. When that was done, he rode out with nary a word."

Marisa put down the tankard of cider. "Thank you, Charity. You may go now."

"As you wish, my lady," Charity said as she made her exit.

Brianna could see the fury in her cousin's green eyes. "Will you please be telling me what happened?" she demanded, the soft lilt in her tone distinctly Irish.

Marisa took a deep, steadying breath and recited the tale, leaving out nothing, including a physical description of her husband.

"Sweet Mother of God," Brianna exclaimed. "He touched you not?"

"Save only for the kiss."

" 'Tis an odd way indeed to be beginning a marriage."

"I thought it best to show him that I came with no blemish, that I was willing to accept him as my wedded husband, with all that that entailed." Marisa took a seat, ignoring the food before her. " 'Twould seem he has no taste for the wedded state. Or," she added, "for my company if he fled at the first opportunity."

"Where could he have gone?" Brianna asked.

"Mayhap back to Whitehall," Marisa answered. "I care not, save that he leaves me with a problem."

"What may that be?"

"How to make believe that this marriage was consummated. I am the Countess of Derran. Nothing must interfere with that. I am wedded, though not bedded. I want no gossip to stain my name. Better the stain should have been on the sheets so that there would be no question but that I am a wife."

"Where there is no consummation, there is no real union. You could seek an annulment," Brianna suggested.

"No," Marisa said vehemntly. "I cannot."

"Then what shall you do?"

"I needs must provide the blood myself." The color in Marisa's cheeks flamed, tinting her skin a soft pink. "To do so," she said, "I must know how much would suffice."

Brianna's skin flushed also. Marisa's question brought back ugly memories of her own wedding night, when her husband, the boy she'd been so eager to wed, took her with little skill and much pain. He'd breached her maidenhead clumsily, entering her like a battering ram. When it was

over, Brianna's husband had crowed proudly
about his size, telling her that she would be
the envy of all. As evidence of his manhood, he
smiled at the heavy flow of blood that seeped
from between her legs, little caring that he'd
almost ripped her apart with his efforts. When
he went to touch her again, she screamed and fell
into a faint, waking moments later to her maid's
horrified face, tears of pity steaming down her
cheeks. Brianna recalled asking weakly for help
and the old woman barring the door as she did
what she could to repair the damage.

How could she tell her cousin what she hadn't
revealed to anyone else save her retainer?

"There is another way."

Marisa looked at Brianna, her curiosity rising,
especially at the odd expression in her cousin's
eyes. "How?"

"'Tis my time of the month," Brianna said quietly, explaining her plan.

Marisa nodded. She reached out her hand to
grasp Brianna's. "Thank you."

"What if your husband should discover this
deception? Have you given thought to that?"

"No," Marisa admitted. "And I care not. I must
do what I have to do. The Buchanan has been
well compensated for his role in this farce."

"What are your plans? Do we go to your seat in
Dorset?"

Marisa stood up, crossing to the window. She
stared out for a moment. "I shall stay in London
for another sennight. Tomorrow I have a meeting with a man who has several horses to sell.
His Majesty arranged this for me as he himself
has purchased horseflesh from the gentleman. In
addition, there are things to be purchased in the
London shops. As you well know, business has

kept me from seeing much of the city."

"Does the earl accompany us?"

"That will be his decision," Marisa stated. "For myself, I care not."

"Come. Enough talk," Marisa said, coming back to where her cousin sat primly, her hands in her lap. "Let us prepare for a day away from this place. What say you to a ride on the river?"

Brianna rose. "I should like that very much."

"Good," Marisa said. "Then 'tis settled. I will dress."

Brianna spoke. "Do not allow the chambermaid to straighten your bed till I can return."

Marisa hugged Brianna close. "I am grateful, cousin."

"'Tis little thanks I be needing. You have given me sanctuary and asked no questions, when others would have said nay."

Marisa smiled. "Are we not family, sweet cousin?" she asked, her arm about Brianna's waist. "Your brother Killroone gave me and mine shelter when my world turned upside down and I thought to be one more ruined heiress given to one of the Commonwealth's bullies. Nay, Brianna, we Fitzgeralds stand together."

Brianna couldn't repress a grin. "As do we O'Dalaighs," she added.

But what of the Buchanan? Marisa wondered as she watched Brianna slip out the door. Would he stand with her or against her?

Jamie's coach provided the anonymity that Cameron sought. He was on his way, a silent Jamie accompanying him, to the brothel. This was no ordinary stew, he'd been assured, but at this moment all he wanted was a woman to take away the memory that ate at him continuously—

of his lady wife, naked, ready to bestow her pity-
ing favor on him.

Damnation! He'd rather pay for it and have
done. That at least was an honest transaction.
His dignity was perhaps unimportant to his wife;
it mattered much to him. With a practiced whore it
would be merely a business arrangement. No emotions to be toyed with. No games to be played.

He saw that Jamie kept his eyes focused on the
view from the carriage. Though Cam knew Jamie
disapproved, he also knew that Jamie would do
what he could to aid him. Aye, they had a long
history between them. 'Twas Jamie who'd freed
him from Mistress Bellamy, risking his own life
and hidden identity to secure Cam's safety. He had
thought he was a dead man when she'd come at
him with the poker, Cam recalled. When he awoke
hours later, he was in a cart, hay all around him,
heading out of London. A safe farmhouse had
been found, where the family was secretly loyal
to the Crown.

He'd spent months recuperating from his injuries, learning to adjust. She should have killed
him, he'd thought. The bitch would pay, if ever
he found her. At first he was too weak to get
about. He was tended to by the kindly farmwife,
who gently bathed his wounds and fed him. He
wore a thick cloth bandage about his face, so that
he could not see. Gradually, the bandages were
removed. He remembered staring at his mangled
hand, whose bones had healed crooked. He soon
realized that he had also lost the sight in his right
eye and partial use of his leg. The smashed bones
in his knee were beyond repair. No one thought
he would walk again. Instead of giving up, Cam
withstood the pain and forced himself to use his
injured limb, to strengthen it.

Running one gloved hand along the left side of his face, Cam thought back to the day he'd demanded a razor and mirror. The farmwife seemed reluctant to do his bidding. Still, he insisted. When she brought what he'd asked, she left him alone. Even now, he couldn't forget the first sight of himself in the shabby mirror. Sunlight streamed in the open window, fixing him with light. He shuddered at what he beheld. Calmly, he picked up the sharp razor in his left hand and put it to his throat. One swift cut would end his pain.

"No, Cam," had come Jamie's plea.

Cam turned about with a crooked smile on his face, letting Jamie see the damage done. "I dinna have any intention of quitting this life, dear friend," he explained. "Aye, I'll confess 'twas a passing thought. But to kill myself would be to let that filthy slut win. That, Jamie, I'll never do."

And he hadn't. Cam had conquered his despair, realizing the perfection of his face was a thing of the past. He concentrated instead on learning to use his left hand, to make do with what he had. It was only at night, when nightmares plagued him, that Cameron thought about what might have happened if Jamie not come when he did.

Jamie drummed his restless fingers upon one thigh. This journey was madness. Instead of wasting his seed on a strumpet, his friend should be sowing the proper garden, tending it till it came to bloom. To ignore the Lady Marisa was to heap insult upon injury, Jamie felt. Cameron needed a loving wife, not a whore, to lead him away from the shadows. Someone who could restore the faith he'd lost. The irony of that thought was not lost on Jamie. It had been a woman named Faith who had nearly destroyed his friend.

Every so often, Jamie would remember that night, see again the hot metal, smell the stench of burning flesh, hear Mistress Bellamy's crooning voice as she bent over the body of her victim, lewdly fondling her unconscious victim. He had no doubt that she was prepared to do further damage to his friend, all in the name of the Commonwealth. Through bribery, he'd secured an offical document releasing Cameron Buchanan into his charge, then let it be known that the prisoner had died of his wounds. When he went back days later, he found that Mistress Bellamy had fled her establishment. He'd made repeated inquiries, but to no avail. 'Twas probably for the best, for he knew that if Cam had found her, she would be a dead woman.

"'Tis just over that hill," Jamie said, then added, "You may yet change your mind, Cam."

Cam shrugged. "I've no wish to change my mind."

Mistress Cardwell poured herself a glass of sherry, delighting in the fine vintage. All was in readiness for her guests. The urgent message had arrived; she'd read it and replied immediately. It never hurt to keep in the good graces of important men. Sunlight streamed into the room, illuminating the fine diamonds she wore about her neck and fingers. It was true, she could have made more money had she set up shop in one of London's stews, but her expenses would have been much greater. And the clientele less to her liking. All too often, she'd discovered, the fine *gentlemen* ran up debts they couldn't pay and passed along the pox to whomever they slept with. Besides, what with the ladies of the Court and them that called themselves actressess, all but

giving it away, she would have been sore pressed
to keep the kind of customers she wanted. 'Twas
not as if she wasn't ever so grateful for the restoration of the monarchy. Hell, living under the
tight strictures of the Commonwealth had almost
ruined her financially. Indeed, she thanked God
almost daily for the health of his Majesty. 'Twas
he who had brought her country back to life after
the boring, sanctimonious Puritans, and enabled
her to rebuild her business. Seeing a chance to
establish herself away from the glare of compe-
tition, she took the small country estate a happy
client had left her in lieu of a gaming debt and in
little over a year garnered a reputation for healthy
girls and honest dealings.

Men, and occasionally women, who frequented
her place of business had to meet certain criteria,
as did her whores. She tolerated no drunkenness
on her premises, nor overly boisterous behaviour.
She thought of her house as more of a gentleman's club.

She picked up a dainty silver bell on her desk
and rang it. Moments later a tall, slender woman
entered.

"Has all been readied?"

"Aye, Mistress Cardwell," the other woman replied. "The gold bedroom is prepared. Several
of the girls are in the small salon, awaiting the
arrival of the guests."

"Good," she said, standing. "I think they will
be most pleased with the selection we have provided." She walked to the door. "Come. I want
to have a word with them before the gentlemen
arrive."

They walked down the paneled hall, the gleaming oak showing signs of having recently been
polished as it shone softly in the glow of the wall

sconces. Not knowing the likes and dislikes of the man being sponsored by Mr. Covington, Mistress Cardwell had chosen what she thought was a fair representation of what her house had to offer.

Opening the door to the salon, Mistress Cardwell couldn't hide her smile of pleasure. A fire burned in the stone hearth. Five young women sat or stood there, each wearing a differently colored diaphanous wrap, allowing the customer to see what he was purchasing. Her customer couldn't fail to be delighted with the selection offered him—a tall, willowy ash-blonde; a striking, black-haired temptress from Spain; a short, plump golden blonde; a slim, auburn-haired lass; and a handsome-looking brunette with short curls.

From the open window, Mistress Cardwell heard the sound of a coach approaching.

"Jane, please see to our guests, if you will," Mistress Cardwell said, addressing the tall woman who had accompanied her. "I shall meet them in here."

"As you wish, Mistress Cardwell," Jane said, making her exit.

Cam stepped down from the coach, leaning on his gold-tipped stick. His black boots made a crunching sound on the stone path as he walked slowly towards the door.

Before either he or Jamie could knock, the door swung wide. A woman who looked to be about two-and-twenty greeted them with a gracious smile. Jamie doffed his plumed hat, his only concession to vanity, with a wide sweep, giving a slight bow.

"Please, come this way," she said, stepping back just slightly so that they could pass. Jane shut the door, slicing a sideways glance at the man with the cane. He was dressed simply, no fancy town frills to mark him as a court gallant.

They followed the woman down a corridor until they came to an open door, where the sound of female voices could be heard laughing and talking.

Cam stiffened.

"Gentlemen," Jane said pushing the door ajar. "May I present Mistress Cardwell?"

The woman introduced rose gracefully from her chair, holding out her hand. "Mr. Covington?" she asked, addressing Jamie.

Jamie bowed politely and brought the beringed hand to his lips. "Your servant, Mistress Cardwell. Now, may I have the honor of presenting my friend, who has need of the services of your gracious establishment?"

"No names are neccessary, Mr. Covington, if you are vouching for him," she said, wishing to put the stranger who stood in the doorway at ease. When the man entered the room, she noted that he stood still, not doffing his hat as most gentlemen were wont to do. She knew instinctively that it was not because he felt himself above this gathering; rather, it seemed to be some sort of protection. He kept, she noticed, to the shadows.

She gave Jamie one of her best smiles. "I trust in your character and that of any friend you wish to bring to my house." She turned to Jane, who was pouring glasses of vintage sherry for the men. "Jane, please draw the curtains. 'Tis far too bright in here."

Jane did as she was bidden, then returned to her task. Jamie accepted the glass of sherry while Cam waved a gloved hand to indicate that he did not wish any.

"I have assembled several of our ladies," she began, lining them up side by side, "so that you may make your selection. Pray, do not fear that by choosing one, or perhaps two, you will offend the others. We are here to see to your pleasure."

Jamie shot a quick glance at Cam, who had remained standing, silent, throughout.

"Take your time, *messieurs*," Mistress Cardwell said. "Perhaps you would rather finish your drink beforehand."

Cam couldn't quite believe this woman was a bawd. She was dressed with care, her gown modest, her manners above reproach. Her only vanity seemed to be in her jewels. Jamie had been correct; this was no ordinary stew. Cam focused on the prostitutes. Perhaps he should remove his hat, then watch for the reaction to his face before he chose. He'd as lief let Jamie do the actual picking of his bedmate. They all had a pleasing form, one way or another. But none could match his bride.

The clock ticked on the mantel, reminding him that he wasn't here to dawdle.

Lifting his gold-handled stick, he pointed toward the willowy ash-blonde. "I want you," he pronounced, his voice rough with unfulfilled longing.

Mistress Cardwell smiled. This man had made a wise choice. Patience was a highly skilled courtesan who took the business of pleasure seriously. She stood up, clapping her hands softly. The prostitutes quickly left the salon through another door.

"Jane, please escort our guest to the room that has been reserved for him. See to whatever he wishes." As Mistress Cardwell watched Cam make his way out the door, she couldn't fail to observe the slight inclination of his head. In her business, she'd learned to judge people quickly: friend or foe; gentleman or lout; hedonist or prude. This one had the devil's own pride, she thought, coupled intriguingly with a sensual nature. It showed in the way he held himself, in the movement of his hands in the embroidered deerskin gloves, in the penetrating way he focused on the girl he had selected.

She turned her attention to the man sitting opposite her. "What is your wish, sirrah? What can we do to tempt you whilst your friend enjoys himself?"

Jamie relaxed, giving the proprietress a lazy smile. "I would rather have another glass of wine."

"That can easily be arranged," she said, adding, "You have no other needs we can fulfill?"

Jamie paused as if in consideration. He closed his eyes for an instant, pausing as if to weigh how to make his request. "Have you anyone here who can play chess?"

Mistress Cardwell gave a hearty laugh. She saw the twinkle in his eyes. "I think that I can perhaps provide the partner you are looking for. If you will excuse me for but a few moments, I shall endeavor to see to your wish."

Playing chess in a brothel, Jamie mused. How positively absurd. He pulled off his unadorned kidskin gloves, flexing his fingers. He supposed that he should be availing himself of the charms of one of Mistress Cardwell's ladies. Ah, 'twas so much easier said than accomplished. He'd never been one for casual pleasures. And, if he were so inclined, he could have easily slipped into the bed of one or another of the ladies at the court. He knew how some men curried favor with those close to the king, an exchange of flesh for a good word dropped into the proper ear. One woman had even offered Jamie her daughter, a virgin of fifteen, in order to become one of the king's laundresses. Jamie had refused the offer. He'd found out days later that another man had not been so noble.

A faint smile touched the corners of his mouth. He was what others had dubbed him, "the king's Puritan."

And what of the man upstairs? he wondered. Would this excercise be enough to banish whatever demons nagged at Cameron's soul?

Patience entered the darkened room. It was fast approaching noon, and her belly felt the first stirrings of hunger. Perhaps the man wouldn't tarry overlong after he finished. Most men, she found, didn't. They were eager for their pleasure, and then it was over. 'Twas a rare man indeed who cared whether or not she found her own satisfaction. Still and all, she shrugged, she had little to complain over. Mistress Cardwell's customers were basically good men, searching for something and someone to hold on to, if only for a short while. And they would provide her with enough money to secure a proper dowry. She meant to wed a prosperous farmer and have the children she now took measures to prevent.

That, however, was for another time. Her duty now was to the customer who was paying for her skills.

"How may I please you, my lord?" she said, walking slowly towards the mysterious seated figure.

"Come here," Cam said. As she came to stand before him, Cam moved so that the right side of his face was kept hidden. He would have preferred to do the deed in the dark, without candles or conversation, to satisfy his lust and quit this place.

"Shall I fetch more light?" the woman asked, forcing him to leave his thoughts and shift in his seat so that he was now facing her. As he did so, he heard the gasp that came from her throat.

"Now you know why I prefer the darkness, mistress, though 'tis naught of your concern," he said. He could see the outline of her small breasts pressed against the sheer fabric of her chemise. He raised his gloved hand, caressing the material of her chemise before he eased it aside. She gasped again, though he knew it was not from revulsion this time. The scrape of the soft deerskin along the tender flesh of her puckered nipple forced that sound. He drew her down to his lap, bending his head to savor the taste of her breast.

Patience undid the ribons that held the chemise in place, freeing herself so that he could have greater access to her charms. Her eyes drifted shut as she gave herself up to the ministrations of his wonderful mouth. Each tug and lick sent fire into her belly, replacing her earlier hunger with a more basic need. Her hands gripped his head, threading through the thick, dark-gold wavy curls. It was remarkably clean to her touch, and silky soft. The feel of it against her naked skin was a delight as she pressed his mouth closer.

Patience reached for his left hand, tugging the glove off with her teeth, tossing it to the floor.

As she lay across his lap, Cam slid his ungloved hand beneath the scarlet petticoat she wore, seeking the heat of her flesh. As he made his way past the sleek curls, he felt the warm moisture.

Moving so that she sat astride his strong thighs, Patience reached down, working her hand into the petticoat breeches he wore, past the fine linen drawers until she found her quarry. Her fingers freed the strength of him. Within seconds she was positioning herself, bucking her hips against his.

Even while Cam's body was responding physically to the practiced manipulations of the whore, his mind was racing in another direction. Instead of the tall, boyishly slim figure meeting him thrust for thrust, he imagined another, chestnut hair cascading around her supple body, her full breasts pressed against the fabric of his lawn shirt, her hands moving about his chest as he delighted in her deep, intense moans of pleasure.

Marisa, he thought as he reached for his release.

Marisa.

Chapter Five

"Some 'business' outside the city," Marisa said in response to her cousin's query, her tone conveying her skepticism.

"'Tis his excuse for quitting your house yesterday?" Brianna queried.

"Aye," Marisa answered. "'Tis a lie, of course."

"Why say you that?"

Marisa yanked off her thin deerskin gloves, tossing them onto the small marble table in the hall, upon which the note had been left. "What kind of *business* rouses a man before dawn, when he is supposed to be sharing a honeymoon with his bride, and keeps him away all night?" She held the note aloft in her hand, gripping it tightly. She fixed her eyes on her cousin. "You have no good answer either, have you? Because there is none," Marisa said.

"Perhaps," Brianna ventured, "'tis some business for the king."

"Nay, that I cannot believe," Marisa said. "'Twould not be like his Majesty to arrange a ceremony and then send the groom away on royal business ere his wedded life has begun."

Brianna spoke, her golden brown eyes revealing her concern. "'Twould not be the first time a king has used royal prerogative to put aside the husband of a woman he desires."

Marisa laughed. "You flatter me, cousin. His Majesty has little need of my body when so many others are at his disposal, especially Barbara Palmer's. Though I have no doubt that were I the type of woman to make myself available, his Majesty would indeed sample the fruit offered, for 'tis his Stuart nature; but I did not mistake the regard he has for my husband. Charles would not betray a friend; nor would I betray my vows, unlike others at the court."

"Will your husband then join us for supper this evening?"

"'Twould appear so."

"Mayhap you would prefer privacy?" Brianna suggested.

Marisa unfolded the crumpled note, reading it again. "The Buchanan says that he will bring along his companion, Jamie Covington. So 'twould seem he has no wish to dine alone with me."

Brianna insisted. "I think that I should eat in my room."

"Nonsense," Marisa gently scolded. "You will eat at table with me tonight. Let us have none of your protestations. I have said so and it shall be so." Her autocratic words were belied by the sparkle of humor in her green eyes. She picked up her gloves, pulling them on again. "Come," Marisa said, slipping her arm through Brianna's. "His Majesty expects us at Whitehall."

"I would rather not be going, if you don't mind, cousin," Brianna stated.

"Why?" Marisa challenged her.

Brianna lowered her eyes, her voice when she spoke barely above a whisper. "'Tis not right. I am newly widowed and should not break my period of mourning."

"'Tis only an invitation to see the Royal stables and meet with a horse merchant, Brianna, not a grand affair, I assure you."

"Still, I would rather not attend. Where the king is, so is the court." And, Brianna thought, gossip; perhaps someone who had heard of her husband's death and wondered if it was truly an accident. She couldn't take the chance.

"Even in your black you would outshine all the ladies there," Marisa stated, giving her cousin a fond glance. "That is the real reason you fear to go, eh, cousin? You would not have Barbara Palmer as your nemesis?"

Brianna gave a short laugh. "How well you guess my secret, coz. Though I would hasten to add that Castlemaine has more to fear from you than from me."

"If that be the case, then she is a very secure woman indeed."

"Pray you be careful," Brianna hastened to add.

"Of what?"

"The false flattery of the courtiers. You are a stunning woman, coz, and more than that, an important prize."

Marisa heard the undercurrent of fear in her cousin's voice. "Know you not by now, Brianna, my opinion of most of Charles's men? Their honeyed words will not cajole me." Marisa's green eyes grew serious. "'Twould take more than mere clever repartee and a fine handsome face to get between my legs, were I still available—which I am not.

"What shall you do whilst I am gone?" Marisa asked.

"I thought perhaps to sit in the garden. Your library has yielded several volumes of poetry that I should like to read." Brianna stopped and looked at Marisa. "Have I your permission?"

The eagerness with which her cousin made her request gave Marisa a start. "Of course you may," she responded. "Whatever I have is yours to share. I must confess, I haven't really looked at the library in years. 'Tis years since I was last here with my family." Marisa paused, thinking back to when she was a little girl, remembering fondly the happy father on whose lap she would climb as he sat in his huge chair before the fireplace of his library. *Tell me a story, Papa*, she would say. And he had: endless stories about brave ancestors, dastardly villains, noble deeds, love beyond price, honor without end. More often than not, her mother would sit there quietly, applying her needle to fabric, making exquisite renderings of her father's tales. Her mother, she realized now, was an artist who used needle and thread the way others used paint. Her brothers, along with a menagerie of pets, completed the scene. Aye, they'd been happy here, or at their various country estates, before Cromwell and his kind had led the country to rebellion and disharmony. Now all that had vanished. If not for her cousins, she would have forgotten what laughter sounded like, forgotten what happiness could be found in a family, forgotten so much because of the horrible civil war which had rent her land in two.

Now, Marisa acknowledged, 'twas her duty to see that once again her houses were places of joy, of sweet fresh memories.

But how could she accomplish this task when her newly wedded husband had forsaken her bed, ignoring her decision to yield herself to him for honor's sake?

His indifference had been a cold stab at her pride.

Marisa stroked the gold-and-sapphire necklace she wore. She would not make that same mistake again.

"Thank you, Bridge, that will be all," Jamie said, wiping his mouth with the thick linen napkin. His majordomo nodded and left the room, having just delivered a bottle of hearty Burgundy wine, along with a hot game pie for each of the men. A large loaf of still-warm bread lay sliced on a china platter, a small crock of fresh butter next to it.

Jamie poured wine for Cam, giving his friend a searching glance as he handed him the glass. Cameron had been quiet as they departed the brothel. He wondered if Cam had found the temporary solace that he was looking for, or if the experience had proven a disappointment.

Cam could see the unspoken questions in Jamie's brown eyes. He was aware that Jamie was curious about what had transpired between him and the whore. Cam knew also that Jamie's concern was not for salacious details, but for his own emotional well-being. And what could he tell him? That he'd fornicated successfully with the harlot? He had, if one measured success with the completion of the act. He wasn't such a naive fool as to believe that her cries were genuine.

Once he would have cared, if only to prove
something to himself. Now he no longer cared
enough even to speculate. He couldn't confide in
Jamie the coldness that had crept over him as
the whore attempted to move her mouth closer
to his, how he had pushed her away, wishing to
keep the exchange as perfunctory as possible. He
wanted no false closeness to mar the proceedings,
no shallow gestures of intimacy. He'd used her as
he would have a chamber pot.

It had even been so with the woman who'd
borne his daughter.

A bitter smile twisted Cam's full mouth with
the memory. He'd been drunk, using strong drink
to dull the pain he felt, to somehow blur the
rage at what had happened to him. He had newly
returned to his father's estate, and his family was
giving him a wide berth, not knowing how to cope
with the angry, brooding man who'd come home
to them. Once a man given to hearty laughter, he
had become a miser with sound, speaking only
when necessary. One evening, well into his cups,
he'd spied a comely wench, one of his sister-in-
law's servants, walking across the grounds. He'd
followed her, like a wolf after a stray lamb, hot on
her scent. What occurred was a rough coupling,
without time or tenderness.

He'd forgotten that night until several months
later he found out that she'd been sent back to her
own family. His brother let slip that she was dismissed because she was increasing and had flatly
refused to name the father. Cam took matters
into his own hands, knowing he had to do what
was right by the child he knew was his. He sought
the woman out and brought her back, telling his
family that since she was breeding a Buchanan
babe, it should be born within the confines of his

family's home. A cottage was found for her, and Cam made sure she had whatever she needed till she could bring forth the child. He saw her not, preferring to get news of how she fared from his father's steward.

Complications arose with the birth, and the midwife summoned Cam. His child, a daughter, was healthy—and more than that, she was beautiful, a softer, feminine version of himself. It was in that moment, when the midwife put the babe in his arms, that Cam knew he could not keep his emotional distance from the child. It saddened him that the woman who'd given him this precious bundle lost her fight for life. Guilt rose like bitter bile in his throat as he gazed at the still figure lying in the small bed. He said a silent prayer for her soul, thanking her for her sacrifice.

Lest he frighten the child, he visited her only at evening, when the shadows kept his scarred face from her full sight. 'Twas enough that he knew the wet nurse crossed herself whenever he came to call. Sometimes he would sit by her bed, watching her as she slept, his good hand stroking the blond curls. Once, he recalled, he'd even heard her murmur in her sleep, "Daddy."

Cam could feel the saltiness of the moisture in his eye at that memory of a daughter he could acknowledge but never embrace.

"Do you go back to your lady wife's house today?" Jamie asked.

Cam put down his knife and fork, fixing his dark blue gaze on Jamie. "Aye," he answered. "This morning I sent a message to her to inform her of my plans."

"What are your intentions?"

"About what?" Cam inquired.

Jamie, normally of a phlegmatic temperament, felt his ire rising. "About your wife, your marriage, of course," he said, his voice rising just slightly.

Cam slid his fork into the flaky crust of the game pie. "'Tis my own affair," he said as he brought the fork to his mouth, changing the subject. "You've a tolerably good cook, Jamie."

Jamie decided to ignore the compliment and proceeded to what he felt was the heart of the matter.

"What about the earldom?"

Cam shrugged his broad shoulders. "What about it?" he asked, turning the question back to Jamie.

"Has his Majesty given you the title of Derran?"

Cam took a slow sip of the rich red wine, appreciating the flavor. Having once spent some weeks in the Burgundy region of France, he'd come to relish the wines produced there. "Aye. Upon my marriage 'twas duly noted in the Royal court papers. I am henceforth the Earl of Derran." Cam smiled. "Should I die without issue of this marriage, the title reverts to my good lady, who shall again be countess in her own right."

Jamie allowed a mouthful of food to pass his lips before he posed his next question. "Have you given thought to your new status? You are now amongst the most powerful men in the realm, Cameron. And"—Jamie paused—"you know as well as I what that means to certain people. You will be the target of more gossip for the court. Such wealth and position bring with it great envy, my friend."

"Think you that I know that not, Jamie? I would have been content with a small fief of my own, somewhere on the Border perhaps, near to mine own family. I never craved this *honor,* but since 'tis the king's most excellent wish that I have this Fitzgerald woman to wife and take upon myself her family's earldom, then take it I shall."

"And found yourself a dynasty in the process?"

"I know not about a dynasty, Jamie. I would rather think smaller, ye ken. A son. One of my blood. A *legitimate* heir."

"'Tis his Majesty's own concern as well," Jamie said, "and the reason he seeks a legal union. 'Tis well known that our good King Charles has no difficulty in fathering babes, though they all be from the wrong side of the blanket. England needs a legitimate heir for the throne lest chaos rule once again."

"And what of yourself, Jamie? Do you not wish to pass along the accumulated Covington wealth? Do you not yearn for a son of your own?" Cam asked.

"I have given the matter some careful thought, I must confess," Jamie admitted. "'Tis finding the woman I can love that proves difficult."

"You seek a dream, my friend," Cam said with a tartness to his tone. "I have seen little of this thing called love in my life. Lust, yes. That is easy. Get you a wife for breeding and a mistress for pleasure."

Jamie's hazel eyes were thoughtful. "Is that what you have planned?"

Cam took another slow sip of wine. "No. I am wed and there's an end to all else."

"What of yesterday?" Jamie probed.

"'Tis past now," Cam said with a sigh. "It matters not a whit to me."

He took another forkful of pie and changed the subject. "I mean you to take supper with the countess and me this evening."

"Think you that is wise?"

"Oh, Jamie, have done with your concerns. 'Tis settled, I assure you. Now, let us finish this meal. Then what about a game of chess?"

Studs.

She needed at least several excellent ones to make her plans come to fruition. And she counted on her king to aid her in choosing.

"Countess," spoke the deep bass voice. "Odd's fish, 'tis good to see you. Come, give us your hand."

"With pleasure, your Majesty," Marisa said, giving her arm to the king as they strolled across the grounds of the lovely park of St. James. She knew that the king was fond of walking and could often be found up early strolling through the grounds of one of the Royal parks, with several yapping spaniels at his heels. Today was no exception as three small dogs ran about their legs.

"How fare you?"

"Tolerably well, your Majesty," Marisa replied, glad that she had chosen to wear a dress of deep rose velvet as there was a slight chill in the afternoon air.

"Excellent." Charles gazed down from his great height at his lovely companion. Her fresh looks were breathtaking amongst all the painted jades of his court. In truth, had she been wed to anyone else, a man willing to play the *mari complaisant*, he would have considered the notion of a dalliance with her. The Countess of Derran's mind and wit were quick, two things that Charles liked in women. His dark eyes strayed to the expanse of white bosom exposed by the square cut of her bodice. His wedding gift, the gold-and-sapphire necklace, rested on the lush flesh he would enjoy handling. A hot lick of lust stirred his loins.

Marisa raised her head and caught the deep stare of the king. Color flooded her cheeks as she rightly interpreted that look.

The moment was broken by one of the king's spaniels barking excitedly. He'd cornered a large squirrel and was playing at being fierce, standing by one of the trees, his quarry on an overhead branch.

Charles called the spaniel to heel.

Marisa breathed a deep sigh, glad of the dog's intrusion into what could have proved an awkward moment had it continued. Bending, she ruffled the dog's soft fur. She was rewarded with a lopsided grin from the Royal pet and a wet tongue, which licked her hand.

"Art fond of animals?" the king inquired.

"Indeed, your Majesty," Marisa replied, standing up. "Whilst I was at my cousin Killroone's keep, I had several pets, including a very large wolfhound. He was a great hound, fiercely loyal and protective."

"Was?" Charles hadn't missed the use of the past tense.

Marisa's mouth curved into a sad smile. "He died on a hunt. We were on the trail of a large, rather nasty wild boar and had finally found his tracks. My horse came up lame, so I was forced to wait whilst the rest of the party rode on. The others hadn't been gone more than a couple of minutes when I heard a noise. It seemed the boar had made a change in course and was coming back in my direction. I had only a small dagger for protection, which I knew would be of no real use against this creature."

"You must have been frightened out of your wits," Charles ventured.

"Indeed, I was terrified, your Majesty," Marisa confided. "The odd thought flashed through my head that my father had sent me to Ireland for my protection, and a wild creature would destroy what Cromwell's men could not. But I was a Fitzgerald, so I would have been damned had I gone to my death without a fight." Marisa paused, admiring the sight of a small band of ducks floating happily in the water. "The dog came back just as the boar was ready to charge. He saved my life and lost his own."

They had walked farther down the path when, with a gently teasing tone, Charles asked, "How fared you at Latin, countess?"

"My tutors thought me accomplished, your Majesty."

"Can you translate then: *aut Caesar aut nullus.*"

Marisa stood still and thought for a second before answering, her voice clear and sure. "Either a Caesar or a nobody."

"Indeed." Charles rewarded her with one of his dazzling smiles, revealing white teeth which stood out against his swarthy complexion. "In your case, countess, I would hazard to substitute *Fitzgerald* for Caesar."

Marisa laughed, a rich, clarion sound. She took no offense at Charles's perspicacious remark. "I would have to say that your Majesty is quite right in his assessment. It has ever been so in our family and will continue to be so, I would venture."

"In you, my sweet countess," Charles said, "pride is a virtue."

"Your Majesty is as ever most gracious to one of his *humble* subjects."

At that pronouncement, Charles himself let out a bellow of deep laughter, thinking back to an almost identical comment from the lady's husband.

Marisa threw the king a curious look.

Charles responded, "The jest is private, my dear. What you said reminded me of someone else's words. 'Tis of no import. Now, I would suggest that we return to Whitehall, as the fellow I told you about will be bringing his horseflesh there for our inspection."

Charles turned around. As he did, Marisa observed the crowd he drew. Ordinary people welcomed him, calling out greetings and occasionally ribald comments. He was *their* king, a Londoner born, who could stroll through this park in peace and comfort, without fear. Marisa realized that this was indeed very important to Charles—that he let his people see him among them. In turn, they responded to him. It was the force of his personality, not his fine, tailored French clothes, which won him admirers. Charles was at once approachable and regal.

Marisa also noted the sly looks that were cast at her. Like as not they believed her the king's latest conquest, the newest bit of fragrant petticoat to keep him amused. She heard one man say, "Our king does have a keen eye for the choicest females. She's a right proper beauty, that one is."

The comment reached the ears of the king, who immediately swiveled his head in Marisa's direction. "Art offended, my lady?"

Marisa raised her eyes to his. "Prithee, I can take no real offense, your Majesty. While I do not like being mistaken for a whore, even if 'tis a Royal whore, your reputation as the kingdom's premier rakehell precludes innocence on the part of any woman in your company. 'Tis to be expected,

I fear, even if I were a crone."

Charles took her right hand in his, raising it to his full lips. "Odd's fish, countess. 'Tis a rare woman you be."

Marisa smiled. "Perhaps. I rather choose to think I am an honest one, your Majesty."

"Quite so, my dear, which makes you still more rare," Charles replied as they came to their mounts. Grooms awaited them, each bearing the insignia of the house he served.

As they made their way back to the palace, Charles's keen dark eyes focused on the rider ahead of him. She sat her mount well. He couldn't help but wonder if his Scottish friend could, or would, fully appreciate the valuable gift which his king had bestowed on him.

Chapter Six

The small dining chamber of the Fitzgerald London house was ablaze with light. Branches of candles banished the darkness, releasing a sweet smell of lemon and beeswax. On a table made from sturdy golden oak, polished pewter plates gleamed with a dull shine. They were cherished antiques, each bearing the entwined intials of H & D. In the middle of the table rested a large pewter bowl, overflowing with fruit. Costly fragrant oranges, plump red grapes, fresh figs, pungent lemons, and ripe apples rested in a bed of trailing vines. On either side were two smaller bowls which held various nuts, shelled and unshelled. Elegant silver nutcrackers were placed next to each bowl.

Two female servants entered the room, each carrying a pewter tray containing fresh loaves of warm bread. Another servant came in bearing a wooden tray of rich mahogany that held four crocks of cold butter. She placed them at each setting, smiling at the simple elegance of the table. The snowy white napkins were new. Each carried the skillfully embroidered letter B sewn in rich gold threads amongst a series of curling green vines. The servant recognized the lovely needlework of her mistress, the Countess of Derran.

As Marisa and Brianna entered through the door leading from the hall, all three serving women made their countess a dutiful obeisance.

Marisa smoothed her hands together, steepling her fingers as she glanced at the table. Flutterings of unease filled her, though she was determined not to let anyone else see how she truly felt. She shot a quick look in Brianna's direction, glad that her cousin had decided to join her.

"I see that you wear Duvessa's legacy this evening," Brianna said, her eyes on the jewels that Marisa wore.

Marisa smiled, her left hand going to the beautiful necklace of rubies and gold. A matching bracelet circled her wrist; earrings glowed with a rich, dark fire in her lobes. The O'Neill rubies had been passed down through the generations to the next Fitzgerald heir, from eldest son to eldest son. Now it was hers, to keep secure for her own child, should she have one. "They were one of Mama's favorites," Marisa said, recalling that on the day of her mother's remarriage, she had placed a large ivory casket into Marisa's hands. It contained all the Fitzgerald jewels that her mother had managed to smuggle out of England for safekeeping. " 'Twould be a sacrilege to let Cromwell's men get their greedy hands on the family jewels," her mother had said. Tears had welled in her mother's eyes as she finished with, "You are the last of the name, my dearest daughter. Wear it, and these, with pride."

Marisa noted that her cousin wore stark black. The only color Brianna allowed herself was a creamy collar of pearls that encircled her slender throat.

"How went your visit with the king?" Brianna asked.

"His Majesty was most kind," Marisa replied, recalling the hours spent in Charles's company. She had truly enjoyed herself. "His wit is sharp and his knowledge of horseflesh is superb. Though he did confide that my husband's may well equal or surpass his own." Marisa's eyes glowed with a soft light as she confided, "I managed to obtain some quite lovely stock today, especially a matched pair of stallions. Pure white they are. Beautiful brutes," she said with a sigh. "They'll do well for breeding when I choose to use them."

"Shall you breed them with the Irish stock you brought back?"

Marisa nodded. "I think so," she said, reaching for a grape and popping the sweet fruit into her mouth. " 'Tis my dearest wish to see my estates restored to what they were before that damned Cromwell's war. I will employ whatever means I can to see that what belongs to the Fitzgeralds is kept secure." Marisa thought of the looting that had taken place at several of her estates. People who lived on the estates had been displaced. She meant to rectify the situation as best she could. The seat of the family in Dorset had been spared any major harm, thanks to the efforts of the dowager countess, her grandmother. There were, however, several other holdings that needed her attention. Marisa knew that she could not tarry overlong in London; there was simply too much

work that she had to carry out. Like his Majesty's
Restoration, her own was fraught with problems
and responsibilities.

One of the servant girls, a young lass named
Bess, came into the dining room, bobbing a curtsey. "Begging your pardon, my lady, but one of
the stable boys just came with word that your
husband has arrived, along with another gentleman."

"Thank you, Bess."

"Do you wish me to show him directly here?"

"No," Marisa stated. "Bring him instead to the
library."

"Yes, my lady," Bess answered, hurrying away
to do as she was bidden.

Brianna threw a quizzical look in her cousin's
direction. What was Marisa about?

"My lady awaits you in the library, my Lord,"
Bess informed Cameron.

Cam arched a blond brow, throwing Jamie a
quizzical look. "Lead on, lass," he said, his deep
baritone rumbling with a soft burr. He leaned
on his gold-tipped cane, following Bess down the
long hallway to a smaller set of stairs.

At the top of the stairs, Bess turned to see that
the two men were behind her. Satisfied, she went
to a door and rapped gently on the oak. Opening
it, she went in, announcing to the ladies, "My Lord
Derran and Mr. James Covington."

"That will be all, Bess," Marisa said, indicating
with a wave of her slim hand that the men were
to take their seats.

"A glass of wine before we partake of supper,
gentlemen?" Marisa asked politely.

Cam recognized the not-so-subtle insult. Marisa
had not addressed him by his new title. He also

saw the quick look shot in her direction by the woman sitting beside her. It was obvious that she, too, understood the slight. His mouth curved into a knowing smile. "Thank you, *wife*; I do believe that would be most appreciated after our long ride."

Marisa poured each man a glass of the pale liquid, her eyes never leaving Cameron's face.

Jamie rose to take both goblets, admiring the workmanship that adorned the pieces.

"Oh, pray forgive me," Marisa exclaimed in a light voice. " 'Twould seem I have failed to introduce you both to my cousin. May I present the Lady Brianna O'Dalaigh MacBride. She is newly arrived in England, here to visit me for a while.

"Brianna, may I present Mr. James Covington, a valuable asset, I am told, to His Majesty's court."

Jamie stood and reached for Brianna's hand, saluting it with his mouth. "Your servant, Lady Brianna," he said, fixing her eyes with his.

"Thank you, sir," Brianna replied, her quiet, lilting voice barely above a whisper.

"And, sweet cousin," Marisa continued, "I want you to make the acquaintance of the man to whom the king has given me in marriage. Brianna, I give you Cameron, Baron Buchanan, my husband."

"I welcome you into our family, my lord," Brianna said, giving Cameron a shy smile, accompanied by a slight bow of her head.

" 'Tis I who am honored," Cam spoke, slowly rising from his seat and taking her proffered hand in his good one, "to welcome you into *my* family, good cousin, for any of my lady's clan are as my own."

Brianna sat back down, picking up her glass of wine, her smile widening. "Then you take upon yourself a great responsibility with your bond of marriage, my lord, for we O'Dalaighs are a large company with many branches."

" 'Tis of no consequence how large or small be the family," Cam said, "what matters is only that we share the bond—and honor it."

"My brother Killroone will be most pleased, my lord, to hear of your words, for he is very fond of our cousin Marisa, as am I."

"My lady wife has many champions, 'twould seem." Cam raised his glass in mock salute to Marisa.

"What do you mean, husband?" Marisa shot the question to him.

"Only that you have admirers at the court, sweet wife, who are only to ready to sing your . . . praises. They even include the king himself."

Jamie, sensing the tension between the couple, broke into the conversation. "This wine is a most excellent vintage, my lady. Where did you obtain it?"

Marisa, her green eyes slightly narrowed, turned toward Jamie. " 'Tis part of a selection from our wine merchant. I found upon my return to London that the cellars were in need of restocking, so I relied on his good judgment."

"His taste would seem adequate to the occasion," Cam pronounced. "I am familiar with the family that produces this, having been a guest of their house."

"You have been to Germany, my lord?" Brianna asked.

"Aye, cousin Brianna."

"Cam was in exile with the king," Jamie explained.

"Indeed?" Marisa asked, sipping the chilled wine.

"Aye," Cam answered.

"What did you do for his Majesty?" Brianna asked.

Jamie volunteered, "Cam was an agent for the Crown."

Marisa's eyes widened. "What sort of agent?"

"My duty was to secure information that could be of use to his Majesty's cause," Cam responded.

"You were a spy?" Marisa asked.

Jamie put in, "Rather what we would term a plenipotentiary, countess."

Cam shrugged his shoulders. "Do not put it in such fancy dress, Jamie," he admonished. "I did only what had to be done, nothing more." A ghost of a smile curved his full mouth as Cam recalled how he had obtained one particular piece of valuable information that summer of 1654, when Charles was forced to move his court-in-exile once again. Fluent in German, Cam had posed as a mercenary, eager to sell his services to the highest bidder. He was contacted by a wealthy merchant, invited to his home, and asked about his qualifications and whether he would consider a special task—an assassination. When he discovered the target of the plot, he pretended agreement, eager to discover who would hire him to kill the man who claimed the English throne. Cam found the information he sought in the bed of the merchant's garrulous wife, who unwittingly betrayed all she knew to the handsome young man as she bragged about their influential connections in the new English government. He and Charles had laughed about it later over a bottle and two very lovely local wenches.

"It must have been very difficult, husband," Marisa acknowledged, "for the king had many enemies."

Cam was surprised by the tone of understanding in Marisa's voice. A very slight lapse, he was sure, for he hadn't misunderstood the icy civility in her manner earlier.

"He still does," was Cam's reply.

"And does his Majesty yet require your services?"

"No," Cam said wearily. "I am only his friend, nothing more. All else is at an end."

"And what of you, Mr. Covington? Had you also a place in his Majesty's service?" Marisa questioned.

"Please, I would that you call me Jamie, my lady," he instructed. "Aye, I too had a place in the network, albeit a very minor role."

Marisa took another careful sip of her wine. "Every thread has a place in the tapestry. If the tiniest stitch unravels, then the entire piece is spoiled. I suspect that you are too modest by half, Jamie."

Cam watched as his friend received a dazzling smile from his wife. God's bones, but she looked far superior to the harpies at court. Her hair, which he had last seen hanging loose and free down her back, was now curled and styled in the latest mode. Thick chestnut ringlets brushed the pale flesh of her exposed shoulders, swaying as she moved. Green became her, he thought, admiring the dark moss velvet with its striped underskirt, for it enhanced both the color of her eyes and her skin. Marisa was laced tightly into the gown she wore, and the bodice pushed her full breasts even higher, making them swell over the neckline, even as Cam felt himself swell with the remembrance of her standing naked before him. Cold wine and warm flesh. His body stirred at the pictures his mind formed.

The ugly truth of reality blotted out the erotic images from his brain. He was Vulcan, wed to Venus, doomed to have beauty but not to possess it. Once it all would have been his simply for the taking. But no longer.

Damnation! Must he be haunted the rest of his life with what might have been?

Dinner was a quiet affair.

Following the first dish of smoked Scottish salmon, fresh and tender, a carved suckling pig was brought in, along with trays containing roast hare and chesnut-stuffed capons. Servants hovered with the food, waiting for each of the four diners to make a selection before placing the trays on a sideboard.

Instead of asking the servants to wait, Marisa dismissed them. "If we have need of you, I will ring."

The servants bowed and left the room, plunging the foursome once again into one another's company.

Through lashes barely concealing her gaze, Marisa noted that Cameron ate his meal left-handed. He cut the moist slice of pork with great care before laying down the knife and replacing it with the fork. How easy it was to take for granted the simple act of cutting up one's food, Marisa thought. But the man she called husband didn't possess that luxury. Mealtimes must be damned awkward for a man of his resolute pride. It would have been simpler and faster to instruct one of the servants to perform the task. However, the look of quiet determination on his face precluded that.

A wave of unwelcome empathy stole into her, warming the chill in her heart.

She thinks me some kind of freak, Cam judged. He caught the softening look in those frosty green eyes as he met them with his own. A poor fool to be pitied, he thought, misreading what his wife was feeling. He was well aware of how clumsy he was at mealtimes. The seamless grace of his earlier years was a thing of the past.

He picked up the thick linen napkin to wipe his mouth and saw the intricate design sewn on the fabric. His lean index finger traced the raised letter B.

"Is it not an excellent piece of workmanship, my lord?" Brianna asked.

"It is indeed, dear cousin. Is it yours?" Cam questioned.

Brianna colored softly, shaking her head. "No, 'tis not. My skill is just passable, I'm afraid. The honor belongs to Marisa."

He focused once again on the clever detail of the work. So, his lady wife also possessed talent with a needle.

Jamie picked up his napkin as well, admiring the handiwork, adding his compliment, " 'Tis indeed quite lovely, countess."

"I do thank you for your kind words, sir." Marisa took a sip of her wine, her eyes bright with gratitude. " 'Tis part of my bridal dowry. My own addition, if you will, as a gift to him who married me."

Cam raised his gaze to Marisa's face, searching for the truth behind her words. He saw no mockery there, only what he perceived to be an honest statement. Yet, he was well aware that women could deceive even as they smiled, lie even when they lay with a man. Trust was not a word he placed much faith in.

Cam picked up his goblet, saluting Marisa. "I thank you then, wife," he said, draining the wine.

" 'Tis work of high quality. I am much pleased with your gift."

Marisa listened for the mocking tone she was sure that she would hear. When she didn't, she relaxed slightly, though she was not sure why. By rights she should be consumed with anger at the man sitting opposite her for his unforgivable behavior on their wedding night.

Why couldn't she summon that anger now?

Brianna slanted a glance from her cousin to the Scotsman. She recognized his wary look; she herself had been quite intimate with wariness. In Marisa's green eyes she saw the soft glimmer of compassion. It was such a different regard from the simmering anger she'd witnessed in her cousin's eyes earlier this day. Brianna wasn't surprised at the change. Marisa was a passionate creature whose moods were oft reflected in her eyes.

Brianna heard the snap of the nutcracker as Cameron's slender fingers manipulated the instrument. She was facing his good side, noting that he was indeed a handsome man. A man to bewitch a woman's fancy with the countenance of an angel.

When next she raised her eyes, it was to see the man seated opposite her, his gaze fixed on her. Abruptly, Brianna dropped her eyes, feeling a nervous sensation flicker along her skin. It wasn't that Jamie Covington's glance was lewd or lacivious, merely probing, as if she were an object of rare design. Aye, rare indeed, she thought with a twist of melancholy, a barren woman, unable to participate in the joy which she so desperately craved.

Jamie's sharp hazel eyes missed none of the emotional undercurrents passing through the group: his friend's determination to prevail in this uncomfortable situation; Brianna's rueful look, as if some heavy sorrow sheltered in the golden brown depths of her eyes.

He turned to assess the lady Marisa. Cameron's wife was a woman who possessed a mind of her own, as well as a loveliness that surpassed that of many of the renowned court beauties. She was no coy, grasping shrew, bent on furthering her interests at court. He recalled the look of cool appraisal that had flickered in the countess's green eyes when her husband set foot over the threshold of the library. Yet Marisa hadn't recoiled in horror as had some women, and even some men, when Cameron entered a room. That had been a point in her favor. But though there was no fear in her eyes, there was also no love.

What did that bode for the future?

Friendship had given him the ability to see beyond the scars Cam bore. But what of the Lady Marisa? Would she eventually see? Would she even make the effort? Would Cam allow her beyond the facade he permitted the world to view?

"We have been invited to share the king's box at the theater on the morrow," Marisa announced.

"How fortunate," Cam drawled, cracking another nut. "What answer have you given his Majesty?"

"I told him that I was not aware of *your* plans, my lord husband, but that I would be most happy to attend with him." She speared a thin slice of the succulent salmon and washed it down with the wine before continuing. " 'Tis something I look forward to. While in exile I had no chance to see performances of any kind, save for the occasional traveling bard who stopped at my cousin's castle." She paused, taking another taste of the salmon. "I am curious to see women acting."

"That, my lady, can be seen anyplace, for 'tis not an uncommon occurrence," Cam added.

Marisa ignored his cynical jibe, preferring to turn her attentions to Jamie. "Will you attend?"

"I think not," he said. "My humors do not run to the gaudy, my lady. I am at heart a quiet man, who likes the enjoyment of his own house. To have to submit myself to the mob, the smells, the circus atmosphere; no, I may be better served without it." He threw a glance in Brianna's direction. "Shall you go, Lady Brianna?"

Brianna answered quickly though her words carefully chosen. "No, I regret that I cannot attend. I am in mourning and 'twould not be seemly to appear at such a gathering."

" 'Twould seem that leaves only you and me, husband," Marisa stated.

Cam brought his left hand up to his chin, the square-cut sapphire glowing as dark and deep as his visible eye. "It would seem to be so, wife."

"Then you will accept the king's offer?"

"When have I ever refused that which his Majesty has commanded?"

Marisa recognized the soft-spoken barb for what it was.

She inclined her head just slightly, giving her husband a small, knowing smile. *Arrogant jackanapes!* she thought. Did he truly believe that he could best her? Bah!

"A toast, then," Marisa said sweetly. "A health unto His Majesty." *And a pox unto all Scottish husbands.*

Chapter Seven

Londoners, the monarch himself chief among them, loved their theater. Within months after Charles's restoration, he had issued patents for the formation of two theater companies, one to Thomas Killigrew for the King's Players, the other to Sir William Davenant for the Duke's Players.

All of Cromwell's Puritan restrictions hadn't dimmed the spirit of people who heartily enjoyed this particular form of entertainment. From classics to comedies, from serious to bawdy, the theater was something to savor, to experience fully.

Marisa entered the Royal box, her eyes wide as she took in her surroundings. By her side was the king himself, regal in red velvet. Accompanying Charles was the Countess Castlemaine, bedecked with diamonds and pearls, dazzling in a gown of silver and gold.

A loud cheer sprang from the crowd in the pits

as they spotted the king and his retinue. Boisterous men who had been busy haggling over the
affections of several of the female members of
the theatrical company stopped long enough to
hail their sovereign.

Charles, enjoying the crowd's reaction, answered the raucous greetings with a wave of
his beringed hand. Barbara basked in the obvious admiration of the majority of the men in the
theater, having already decided that the country
countess presented no real threat to her popularity
as the reigning beauty of her day.

Marisa seated herself, looking out at the sea
of countless faces both to the side and below
her. She was aware that she herself was once
again the cynosure of many eyes. Neither she nor
the Countess Castlemaine had bothered to mask
their identities as was the fashion of the ladies
of the court. Several women whispered behind
their fans; men ogled her; some made outright
gestures, bringing a slight blush to her cheeks
even as it brought a smile to her face. Nothing
could dampen the spirits of those attending. To
hell with the consequences, to hell with the cir-
cumscriptions of the past, they seemed to say.
Live for the here and now.

Even sharing the box with the king's sharp-
tongued mistress couldn't bank the fires of
Marisa's pleasure in being here. She was well
aware of the looks Barbara Palmer had cast her
way. Nothing overt, merely the presence of a condescending smile on the other woman's face
as Marisa climbed into the royal carriage, alone.
Marisa could still hear the question Castlemaine
had put to her upon entering the coach. "Where
is thy good husband, Lady Derran? Surely not
too tired to rouse himself from his marriage bed?

Faith, have you ridden the poor beast to the point of exhaustion?" she asked.

The king was amused by his mistress's blunt questions. He gave Barbara a fond glance, even as he mildly rebuked her. "We must not pry into another's bed, my dearest Barb," he stated, "lest we play spies in the house of love."

"God's blood, my love," Barbara pronounced, "all London is asking the same questions. Surely my Lady Derran knows that she is amongst friends who would not spill her bedchamber secrets willy-nilly." Barbara slid her hand along the material of Charles's petticoat breeches, her nails lightly scoring the velvet as she touched his thigh. "'Tis not as if our good Lady Derran would be as indiscreet as Lady MacDonald."

"What has this Lady MacDonald's discretion or lack thereof to do with me?" Marisa asked.

Barbara smiled, much like a cat after licking cream. "Why, when she bedded your husband she couldn't wait to sing fulsome praises of his skill. She nearly fainted recounting the descriptions of the Buchanan's prowess, of his size . . ." Countess Castlemaine hesitated for a moment and wet her lips. " . . . his wide-ranging knowledge of how to pleasure a woman in bed. She bragged about his cleverness, both with his mouth and his hands. According to her, he was without compare."

Barbara sliced a quick glance at her lover. "Of course, she has not known you, my lord, else she would perhaps revise her opinion," she added in a honeyed tone.

Charles laughed. "Only perhaps?" he asked with a lift to one thick black brow.

Barbara laughed. "Forgive me, sire," she begged with a slight pout, "no one could ever doubt that you are without equal in all England."

Marisa's hands had tightened on the fan in her lap, wishing instead that she could rap it across Lady Castlemaine's smug face.

"Of course," Barbara said with a small shrug, "that was before the Buchanan's unfortunate . . . transformation. Such things have been known to, how shall I say, diminish a man's performance."

Marisa opened her fan, managing to look bored with the conversation. She wouldn't give that cat Castlemaine the satisfaction of seeing just how angry she really was. "I dare say the Court will continue to gossip no matter what I have to say about my husband. So be it."

Charles gave a sharp bark of laughter. Much as he adored his stinging Barb, it was always good to know that not everyone quaked in fear of her tongue.

Now Marisa was here, on public view, in the Royal box, awaiting the arrival of her husband, who had politely refused a ride in the king's coach, saying that he had something to attend to and would meet them at the theater.

Marisa wondered as the play began just what his business was about, her thoughts once again straying backward. Upon finishing the sweet fruit pie that she had ordered served after the supper was complete, he and Jamie had excused themselves, leaving her and Brianna alone. The evening had not gone exactly as she had planned, so she decided that she would retire to bed, alone, her doors barred to anyone. She lay in her wide bed, all lights extinguished, expecting she wasn't sure what.

When she woke, she found that once again her husband had quit her house to attend to unknown business. Bathed and dressed, she had attended to business of her own, settling the account of the man from whom she had bought the twin stallions. A man in her livery arrived soon after with letters from her grandmother. One long missive asked her advice about one of the estates in need of repair. Marisa sorted out all the correspondence between her grandmother and the factor of the property. Her head swam at the cost of the needed repairs.

She shared a cold luncheon with Brianna as she took the time to read a private message from her grandmother. The old woman demanded details about the wedding, about her husband. And what could she answer? That she was wed to a disfigured Scotsman who had refused to consummate the wedding vows? That he had rejected her? Her grandmother would be angry at the slight to her family and, most especially, to her beloved granddaughter.

Peals of laughter interrupted the flow of her thoughts, bringing Marisa back to her surroundings. She brought a perfumed square of linen to her nose, trying to alleviate the strong odor wafting upwards from the crowd below. The play was in progress, a broad comedy of mistaken identities, starring one of the king's favorite actors, John Lacy, a man known for his skill with dialects. One actress was dressed in breeches and a man's white shirt, pretending to be in disguise. As the shirt was too small for her rather large bosom, and the breeches clung too tightly to her thighs and well-rounded hips, the disguise was rather comic.

Marisa's attention wandered to some of the other boxes, recognizing certain court gallants, entertaining women she suspected not to be their wedded wives. Her green eyes widened in shock as one courtier openly fondled the naked breasts of his companion even as he watched the action upon the stage.

A noise alerted Marisa to the fact that someone had come into the king's box. It was her husband.

His entrance caused quite a stir among the occupants of the nearby boxes. Gasps and whispers were heard. He was clad all in black, save for his ruffled white shirt, with no fancy ribbons breaking the stark look. Doffing his wide black hat with its extravagant plume, he made a bow to the king, and then to Marisa and Countess Castlemaine. His deep, Scots-accented voice murmured, "Excuse my tardiness, your Majesty."

"Consider it pardoned, Derran," Charles said, waving his friend into the empty seat beside Marisa. "You've missed the delightful sight of Mistress Chambers pretending to be a lad." Charles sliced a glance at both of his female companions. "It would be the same for these two ladies should they try to pretend to be boys. No one would ever believe it."

Cam moved behind the chairs and came to the empty brocaded seat. He shifted his walking stick and sat down, giving his wife a sidelong glance. "Madam," he said with a slight nod of his head. The light from the wall sconce tapers caught the long locks of deepest gold, making them shimmer with color.

Indeed, Cam thought, he could hardly think of two less likely women to be mistaken for lads. Barbara was simply Barbara. His memory restored the picture of his wife, naked and waiting in her bedroom; she had the slim hips of a boy, but her breasts were those of a mature woman, full and high.

At that moment, Marisa slid her glance in his

direction, her eyes meeting his. Cam studied that
face, catching her acceptance of his features.
Unlike others, she did not wear her disgust
visibly.

His full mouth curled into a grim parody of a
smile. There were those present, he was sure,
who believed that his polished black shoes hid
the cloven hooves of a devil incarnate.

He expelled a deep sigh. So be it.

Marisa returned to her house on the Strand
after the play was over, politely refusing the king's
request to join him and Barbara for supper.

As she walked up the stone stairs she turned,
watching her husband stop to take his leave of
the king and the countess. She heard the unmis-
takable deep laughter of the king, followed by
a softer, feminine laugh, and then she heard a
sound not familiar to her—the Scotsman's voice,
joined with theirs, laughing.

His laugh was rich and full; Marisa wondered
what jest the trio shared. At that moment she
felt excluded, and not wanting to be thought
eavesdropping, she entered the house, handing
her cape of thick, soft Irish wool to Charity.

"Would you care to have cook serve supper
now, my lady, or would you like to wait?" Mistress Chatham inquired. "The Lady Brianna begs
that you excuse her from joining you this night
as she has taken to her bed."

"I think that I shall wait," Marisa replied. Then,
as she made for the stairs, she asked, "What ails
my cousin? Is she ill?"

Mistress Chatham gave a knowing look. "Only
her female flux, 'tis all."

Marisa nodded, speaking over her shoulder. "I
shall attend her, then. You have my leave to serve

my husband should he choose to dine here this evening," she said, picking up the hem of her gown and dashing up the stairs.

She rapped softly on Brianna's door before entering. How could she have forgotten that it was her cousin's time? Had that fact not saved her from her own disgrace?

Her slippered feet moved softly on the floor as she approached the bed.

Brianna lay there, a pale figure amidst a thick pile of blankets and pillows. Her eyes fluttered open in the dimly lit room.

"How fare you, coz?" questioned Marisa.

Brianna patted the space beside her on the bed. "Sit, please," she requested. "'Tis only a bad bout of cramps that makes me seek my bed. My flux is almost finished."

"And I feel nary a twinge of pain when mine occurs," Marisa confessed. "Can I get you something to ease your pain?"

"There is no need," Brianna said. "I will soon be well again."

Marisa placed her hand on her cousin's brow, smoothing back the damp tendrils of dark hair. "You are sure? What about some mulled wine?"

"No, truly, I am fine, cousin. The rest has done me good." She eased herself up on the mound of pillows. "Pray, tell me about your trip to the theater with the king and the Countess Castlemaine."

"There is little of import to tell, save that the king's whore has little regard for me, and much for my husband."

"Prithee, why do you think that so?"

Marisa frowned. "'Twas in the manner of her speech, and in those greedy eyes."

"Greedy?" Brianna questioned, a puzzled look on her pale face. "How so?"

"As if she coveted what lay beneath the Buchanan's clothes," Marisa answered. "One would think that with the king's child in her belly, and the king between her thighs, she would confine herself to what she has."

Brianna's golden-brown eyes focused on her cousin's face. "And this truly disturbs you? Mayhap 'twas only an innocent flirtation."

Marisa got up from the bed and moved to the mullioned window. She raised her left hand and traced the pattern of the lead. "'Twas no mere flirtation," Marisa acknowledged, turning back to face the bed. "And my lady Castlemaine is far removed from innocence, coz. No, 'twas deliberate."

"What of your husband?" Brianna asked. "Did he respond to the countess's attention?"

"It bothered him not a whit, 'twould seem."

Brianna gave a deep sigh. "I see," was her only response.

Marisa threw her cousin a dark look. "What do you mean by that remark?"

A faint smile raised the corners of Brianna's mouth. "Only that it would appear to have disturbed you greatly. Why?"

"I would think that obvious," Marisa said, her voice cool as she gave her rationale. "'Tis an insult to his Majesty."

"And that is all?" Brianna queried.

"What else is there?"

Amusement underlined Brianna's tone. "What else indeed, dear Marisa?" Brianna inquired.

"Would you care for something to eat, my lord?" Mistress Chatham asked later that evening, walking into the library of Fitzgerald House. She stood some distance away from the man seated beside the roaring fire, a book on his lap.

Cam raised his head from the pages. "Has my lady taken supper yet?"

"No, my lord."

"Good. Then we shall have it together."

Mistress Chatham worried her bottom lip with her teeth as she made no move to exit.

Cam's blue eye pierced her with its intense gaze. "Is there something else?"

"The countess bade me tell you that you may eat without her if you so choose, my lord," she explained.

Cam closed the book quietly. "Did she now?" he asked, a small smile on his full mouth.

"Aye, my lord, she did," Mistress Chatham confessed.

"Well," he said, his voice low and clear, "I choose to sup with my wife. Do you understand?"

"Aye," she replied, thinking that she understood, though she wasn't so sure the countess would.

"Where is my wife?"

"I believe she is closeted in her study, my lord."

He reached for the elegant cane that lay at his feet, shifting so that he could stand. "Where is that located?" he demanded.

"Down the hall, to the right." She watched him move toward her. As he did, Mistress Chatham backed up against the door.

Cam couldn't help but notice her reaction. He halted about a foot away from her.

"My lord," she queried in a small voice, "shall I inform the countess that you would like to dine with her?"

"No, Mistress Chatham," he said. "I will see to my wife myself. I would like you to see that supper is waiting for us."

She bobbed a curtsey. "As you wish, my lord."

"Wait," he commanded. "Before you leave, have we some ale in this house?"

"Aye, my lord."

"Then serve it with our meal."

Mistress Chatham repeated her earlier words. "As you wish, my lord."

Oh, my good woman, it shall be, he thought. It bloody well shall be, no matter how long it takes.

Cam found his wife ensconced in her study, seated behind a large desk of polished wood. Papers were scattered over the top, tossed every which way. His wife appeared to be deep in study of a large document.

"Madam," he said.

Her head snapped up, a distracted look in her green eyes. "What do you want?"

"The pleasure of your company, wife, at supper."

Marisa brushed away a stray curl of hair. On her cheek she still wore a black, heart-shaped patch. Cam knew such items were worn by women to accentuate their best features. He would have chosen a spot right next to her bottom lip, or perhaps along the swell of her breast.

"I cannot," she said and returned to her paper.

If she expected that he would leave after her curt dismissal, she was proven wrong.

Cam advanced until he was beside her. "You will."

Marisa tilted her head and was confronted by the side of his face that wore the eye patch. She wondered whether any woman had bedded with him whilst he looked like this. And, exactly how long *had* he looked like this? The scars that slashed his cheek and throat were not fresh. How had he come by them?

She dropped her gaze. A jealous husband, she would wager. Aye, more than likely.

"I won't."

"Please."

Marisa tilted her head, giving him a penetrating glance.

"What?"

Cam placed his battered hand on the arm of her chair. "Please," he reiterated, his deep baritone coaxing, "come and sup with me."

His request, so sweetly put, worked as no shout or threat could. This man was, after all, her wedded husband, Marisa admitted, and as such was within his rights.

"Very well, husband," she said, starting to roll the paper in front of her.

"What is that?" he asked.

She rewarded his curiosity with honesty. "An architect's plans for one of the Fitzgerald estates. 'Twas destroyed, along with several other Royalist strongholds in the area. A new house is being built, along with cottages for my tenant farmers."

"May I see?"

Marisa unrolled the paper, spreading it flat.

Cam looked over the sketches, admiring the workmanship, "'Twould appear a costly rebuilding," he judged.

She grasped the architect's plans in her hands. "I can well afford the cost," she stated.

"I meant no censure, wife. 'Twas merely an observation, nothing more." Cam straightened, his arm extended for his wife's.

Mollified, Marisa retied the document with the thick red ribbon that had bound it previously, then tossed it back to the desk. She rose, placing her left arm on his.

Supper consisted of a thick game soup served with bread and cheese. Cam poured another round of ale for their pewter tankards.

He patted his flat stomach. "Your cook does you proud."

Marisa rewarded her husband with a wide smile. "I thank you on her behalf, husband. She has been with my family for many years. I think I shall take her with me when I depart London."

"You are planning a trip?"

Marisa sliced a small piece off the cheddar block. She spread some of the spicy mustard she imported from France on the cheese, handing it to Cameron. "Taste this," she said, cutting another slice for herself. "Aye, I never planned to tarry long in London." She popped the cheddar into her mouth, enjoying the blend of cheese and spices. *"Merveilleux,"* she pronounced, following it with a drink of the ale. "The only reason I came here was to secure my claim to my family legacy and to fulfill my duties."

"One of which was your marriage to me?" Cam asked.

Marisa met his glance squarely. Cam had chosen to sit at her left hand rather than at the other end of the table, as was his privilege. "I will not lie, husband. 'Twas one of the reasons, perhaps the most important reason for my sojourn here. But I never intended my visit to be anything other than of a short duration. I am fond of London," she said, reaching for a shelled walnut, "but 'tis not where I would choose to live. 'Tis too noisy and dirty to suit me for long. I confess that I long for the beauty of the country."

"Your family seat is in Dorset, I believe. Do you journey there?"

"Only for a few days to see my grandmother."
Marisa's eyes shone with love for the old woman.
'Without her strength, her cunning if you will, I
might not have had much of a legacy to return
to." She gave a short laugh. "His Majesty refers
to her as the grand Tartar. Even he has been on
the receiving end of her peppery tongue."

Cam took another slice of the cheese. "And after
your visit there, where do you journey?"

"I am eager to see for myself the progress of
the estate, which is being rebuilt after the wanton destruction by Cromwell's men. 'Tis near the
Wye River not so very far from the Welsh border." Marisa pondered over how best to ask the
next question. She drew in a deep breath and
plunged ahead. "Do you intend to stay in London,
husband?"

Cam paused before answering. Did she think
to be rid of him that easily? Did she suppose
that he would be content with the crumbs of
her life? That he would disappear so that she
could pretend that she was not wed? Oh no, he
thought. That was not part of his schemes.

"I have no wish to tarry overlong in London
either, wife. I shall be pleased to accompany you.
I have not seen much of your England and am
therefore eager to rectify that lack."

"Then 'tis settled," she pronounced, hiding her
surprise at his announcement.

"When do we leave?"

"I had thought in two days' time. Have you any
problem with that, husband?"

"None, my good wife."

Marisa rose. "Now, if you will excuse me, I am
rather tired and would seek my bed."

"I bid you a good night then," Cam said, rising. He captured her right hand in his left. He

dropped his gaze, looking at her smaller hand in his, how his fingers wrapped around her slender wrist. He could feel the rapid jump of her pulse. *You may have started it, my bonny lass,* Cam mused, *but I shall surely finish it.* An enigmatic smile curved his mouth as he brought her hand to his lips, touching the smooth flesh, taking the merest taste of her skin with his tongue.

He released her hand when she gave a slight tug. Without another word, Marisa made her exit.

Cam sank slowly back into his seat. He reached for the tankard of ale, quaffing the remaining liquid. A strong feeling of desire gripped his loins, bringing a deep, intense ache to his body. *I will have her,* he vowed, bringing the pewter tankard down onto the table with a bang. *By God's Blood, I will have her.*

The dockside alehouse was filled with the scent of stale flesh and cheap brew. It was dark; all the better to cheat the unsuspecting customer. Whores plied their trade for eager sailors or ordinary laborers; it mattered little so long as it was a cash transaction.

"You be wantin' somethin' else, *sir?*" asked the surly barmaid, her lank, greasy hair hanging over the pitcher of ale, dipping into the foam as she placed it on the table.

"No," answered the male voice. "That will be all."

"Very well" came the reply as the barmaid moved on, eager to earn some real money this evening.

"Why did you insist on meeting in this hellhole?" queried another voice, this one belonging to a woman.

"I thought it safer. No one will recognize us

here," the man said, pushing aside the beverage that he'd just paid for.

The woman gave a snort of laughter. "Thanks be to God for that favor," she said, though she would take no chances. Her cloak was still in place, along with the fancy mask that she had worn to the theater that afternoon.

"Are you sure 'tis the same man?"

"Of course," she hissed. "Do you think that I would ever forget *him?*"

Her companion gave a nasty laugh. "Or he you, eh?"

She gave a shudder of distaste and reached into her small purse, pulling out a tiny silver bottle of scent. Opening it, she took a deep wiff of the fragrance. "It smells like a cesspool in here."

"You've developed quite a sensitive nose over the years, my dear."

"What I've developed," she insisted, "is a taste for the life that I now lead. I want nothing to come between me and it."

"No one wants that, my dear."

"Than what do you propose to do?"

He shrugged his thin shoulders. "Why should *I* have to do anything?"

"I did what I did for you, remember that," she stated.

His mocking laugh made her angry. "I did, damn you," she asserted.

"You did what you did for money, my sweet, greedy bitch, only that and nothing more. Pray, remember to whom you speak. We should at least have some honesty between us."

She gave a short, sharp laugh. "You have as much to lose as I should our secret be discovered."

"Is that a threat, my dear?"

"Of course not," she hastily assured him. God, how she hated this wealthy pig.

"Good. We have need of each other, never forget that."

As if she could. She heaved a weary sigh. "I never thought to see him again," she said. "Christ's blood," she swore, "but I thought his damnable pride would never allow him to show his face again."

"It would seem that since you saw him this afternoon at a very public function, you were wrong."

"I know, and 'tis what vexes me."

He gave her an odd smile, reaching out his thick hand to caress her face. "Perhaps I can help you."

"You must," she pleaded.

"It will cost you."

"How much?" she asked.

"Let me think on that awhile."

"As long as you rid me of the problem."

"'Twould seem that he has aquired a wife whilst in London."

"Bastard," she spat out. "So you did know that he was alive? That he was once more in London?"

"News of the wedding of one of the richest heiresses in all England could hardly be kept a secret, my sweet. Especially not the marriage of so delightful a trophy as that haughty bitch Marisa Fitzgerald."

"What must she think about being wed to one such as he?"

"Do you really care?"

She shrugged her shoulders. "No," she said, "though it gives me pleasure to think of how she must react when forced to accept his touch, how that must make him feel as she recoils in fear, in loathing at the very sight of him."

"You hate him, do you not?"

"More than you can ever imagine."

"'Tis late and I must be going," he said.

"I want him dead," she stated, her voice devoid of all emotion.

He gave his female companion a twisted smile. "Accidents have been know to befall even the most powerful of men."

She returned his smile with one of her own. "'Twould be a pity if so recent a wife was made a widow, would it not?" she asked, her voice rising in a giggle. "A damnable shame."

He steepled his stubby fingers. "Aye," he agreed, licking his thin lips, "a damnable shame."

Chapter Eight

" 'Tis the king, my lady."

The excited voice of her servant broke into the conversation that Marisa was having with her cousin.

"His Majesty is here?" Marisa asked.

Bess, her chest heaving from the thrill of seeing the king and from having to run up the stairs to fetch her mistress, said in a rush, "Aye, 'tis his Majesty, my lady. You'd best come quickly."

"Calm down, Bess," Marisa said, rising from her chair and setting aside her embroidery. She turned to her cousin. "Come, Brianna, I want to present you to the king."

Brianna stood, smoothing her hands down the sides of her black taffeta. "As you wish, coz."

"Just so," answered Marisa. "Where is he?" she asked Bess.

"He awaits you in the stableyard, my lady."

"Fetch Charity and tell her the Lady Brianna

and I shall need cloaks ere we brave the wind outside. Hurry," she admonished Bess, "else we shall keep his Majesty waiting for us overlong."

Bess dropped a quick curtsey and dashed out the door.

"Faith, 'tis a wonder she could deliver the message at all, she is so excited," Marisa said, her green eyes alight with merriment.

"You must remember, cousin, she is but a simple girl, not used to what you are," Brianna said. "And, if I recall correctly, you were yourself nervous when first you had to meet the king."

Marisa grinned. "'Tis right you are, cousin." As they made their way down the stairs toward the door, Marisa asked, "What about you?"

"I am fine, Marisa."

"Good. I would have you enjoy meeting his Majesty." Marisa took Brianna's hands into hers, looking her straight in the eyes. "I must bid you not to take his manner with women seriously," Marisa prompted. "He is a skilled seducer, with a very charming tongue."

"Have no fear on that head, coz," Brianna stated emphatically. "I am immune to being seduced."

"Then we are a pair," Marisa pronounced, "for I too am immune."

"To what, pray tell?" asked the deep voice of the Earl of Derran.

Marisa and Brianna blushed. "Why, 'tis nothing, my lord husband," Marisa confessed, "merely nothing."

"As you will, wife," Cam said, amusement curving his mouth. He had heard the last statements both his wife and the Lady Brianna made. He chose instead to pretend that he hadn't to see if Marisa would repeat her challenging words. For they were a challenge, dangled before him like precious jewels, the reward for a well-deserved victory.

Charity hurried to the hall, carrying the outergarments requested by her mistress.

Cam took hold of the cream wool, sliding it around Marisa's shoulders, leaning his body close to hers, his breath a warm whisper on her cheek.

Brianna, adjusting the black wool cloak she wore, pulled up the hood. As she did, her gaze caught the hot, hungry look in the Scotsman's eye before he stepped back, releasing Marisa. Brianna turned aside, fussing with the ribbon that held her cloak together before she risked another look at her cousin's husband. The unflawed side of his face was schooled in composure, a study in control. Had she imagined that raw, wanting look?

No, Brianna decided, she had most assuredly not. It had been there. Below the Scotsman's cool mien flickered a hidden flame of passion.

A small shiver of fear shook Brianna's body. Her own husband's lust had brutalized her body, forever chilling her to his touch. Could the same thing befall her proud cousin? And what could Marisa do to prevent it? The Scotsman was Marisa's wedded husband, her legal master under English law.

"Come, let us not keep his Majesty waiting for us any longer," Marisa announced.

The wide doors to the stables were open. Voices could be heard inside as Marisa, Brianna, and Cameron approached.

"Odd's fish, but they are magnificent," Charles announced.

The objects of his admiration were two horses, each over seventeen hands high.

"Majesty," Cam said, bending his knee as Marisa and Brianna sank into low curtsies.

"Well met, Derran," Charles said, feeding an apple to one of the horses. "Countess." He took Marisa's hand in his and brought it to his mouth. "A pleasure, as always." Charles's dark eyes focused on the woman standing next to Marisa. His smile was open and warm. "Who have we here?"

Cam happily made the introduction. "Your Majesty, may I present my wife's cousin, the Lady Brianna O'Dalaigh MacBride?"

Charles gave the Lady Brianna a short bow, doffing his splendid hat with a flourish. "Your servant, madam."

"'Tis perhaps what I should say, your Majesty," Brianna rejoined.

"Nonsense. Even the king of England may be humbled by such loveliness as yours, my lady," Charles said, his mood charming, his smile dangerous. "Ah, so much beauty in one family. Two such fragrant roses: the softly blooming English and the wilder Irish." Charles clapped Cam on the back, his words directed to him while he kept his eyes on the women. "Nothing in Holland, Spain, France, or Germany can compare to the blooms to be found in my kingdoms, eh, Derran?"

"I cannot dispute your Majesty's wisdom," Cam concurred.

"One cannot disavow the truth," Charles stated.

"What brings your Majesty to my house?" Marisa asked.

"The animals you bought were delivered to Whitehall this morn and I thought to accompany them."

"'Tis most kind, your Majesty," Marisa said.

"'Tis merely an excuse to make a visit," Charles admitted.

"You need none, your Majesty," Cam answered.

"No, none," Marisa agreed.

"Well, what you think of your wife's horses, Derran?" Charles stepped to one side so that Cam could get a better look at the pair of snow-white stallions.

Each was held by a groom as they pawed the smooth stone floor, preening, as if they knew they were the object of all eyes in the stables.

"Your Majesty said it well enough—they are magnificent beasts."

Marisa strode up to one, taking the bridle from the boy. She led the horse outside as the others followed.

Stroking the long neck, Marisa spoke low to the horse. The horse whickered a response.

His twin moved restlessly until Cam moved to take the reins from the groom's hands. Tossing his walking stick to the groom, he grabbed a handful of the stallion's silky silver mane and mounted him. Pulling slightly on the bit, Cam brought the animal to his hind legs.

Marisa, her hands still in control of the other animal, observed the power of both man and beast. As if one, they moved around the stable area. She longed to jump upon the other stallion's back and challenge her Scottish husband to a race, to see which of the animals was the fastest.

"They are an excellent choice," Cam announced, bringing the animal to a halt. He signaled the groom to him, dismounting carefully, taking back his gold-tipped stick. "What are they called?" he directed his question to Charles.

Charles shrugged his elegantly dressed shoulders. "'Tis for the countess to decide."

All eyes focused on Marisa.

"Have you thought of names?" Brianna queried.

"I have indeed," Marisa said, laying her head against the horse's neck. "Romulus and Remus."

"An interesting choice, countess," Charles pronounced.

Marisa spoke up. "I promise that I will give your Majesty one of the first offspring of either stallion."

"Odd's fish, but I would be most pleased, my Lady Derran. I want to bring the sport of racing back into fashion. God, if there weren't enough reason to hate the usurper Cromwell, I would hate him for refusing to let my subjects gather together for the enjoyment of the horses." He gave a lazy smile. "My brother York may have his hunts and be welcome to them; for me, I prefer watching and wagering on the speed of fine animals such as these. As their namesakes founded Rome, they will breed you champions, to be sure."

Marisa surrendered the reins she held to the second groom. "See that they are fed and watered well," she instructed the lad. "Will your Majesty take a glass of wine with us?" she asked.

"Perhaps another time, countess," he answered, checking the gold enameled watch he pulled from his doublet pocket. "I must attend a meeting of my ministers in under an hour."

"Then I will bid your Majesty farewell. We shall be departing London tomorrow."

"So soon?" Charles asked.

"Yes, your Majesty," Marisa replied. "I have a great amount of work to do at some of my estates. It has been far too long since they have seen a Fitzgerald."

"You will be much missed, countess. My Court

will lose a singular beauty, and I"—his dark eyes
shifted from Marisa to Cameron and back again—
"great friends."

"Your Majesty knows that should ever he have
need of us, we will of course heed his call without
delay," Cam stated.

"Aye, I know that, Derran," Charles said. "'Tis
good to know that there are some in this kingdom
whom I can trust completely.

"I trust that you will grant your liege lord permission for a kiss from your lovely bride, my good
lord?" Charles directed his question to Cam.

"Of course you have my permission, sire. All
that I have is yours," Cam said.

Charles gave a hearty laugh. "Somehow, my
dear friend," he said with a raised black brow,
"I have a doubt you mean quite *all*?"

Cam returned the king's arch look with a smile.
"Mayhap not *quite* all that I possess, Majesty."

Charles touched his wide mouth to Marisa's.
"I bid you safe journey, countess. You and yours
will never be far from our thoughts."

Both Marisa and Brianna gave the king a low
curtsey. "God grant your Majesty a long and happy reign," Marisa said, rising, "and I wish you joy
in your forthcoming marriage to the Portugese
princess, Catherine. May she prove fruitful and
deliver England a Stuart prince."

Cam stood with Charles, watching as the two
women made their way back to the shelter of the
house.

"She will breed you fine sons, Cameron,"
Charles observed. "Mark my words." He signaled
for his mount to be brought to him. In a softer
voice he said, "Have a care for your lady, as she
is dear to us." Charles mounted, waiting for his
own groom. "I advise you to seal your wedded

union with a babe in her belly before too long has passed."

Charles's words came floating back in the early hours before dawn. Cam was unable to sleep for the ache in both his mind and his loins. What little rest he had was haunted by lusty dreams that tormented him, mocking him with their power and alluring beauty.

Out of habit, he made sure that the door to his chamber was bolted from the inside before he rose from the comfort of his solitary bed. Since Cam eschewed the customary nightshirt, preferring the feel of the sheets against his naked skin, he wore a robe to cover his body when he quit his bed. Stretching his aching muscles, he padded softly across the bare boards of the planked oak flooring toward the fireplace. A fire burned low in the hearth, giving off a soft glow. He held out his hands to warm them, for there was a damp chill in the room, caused by the steady rain that beat at the windows.

He turned his head. Beyond that connecting door slept his wife—she who figured so prominently in the nightime musings of his mind. In those dreams he was as he had appeared before—handsome and strong, able and vigorous; a man used to getting whatever he wanted from women, anytime he wanted it. Unchallenged, he took his pleasures whenever and wherever he would. However, throughout the pleasure-filled dreams, he was troubled by the sense that someone was watching him, just out of sight. He searched and found no one. All he saw was a quick glimpse of skin, a scent of perfume, a strand of chestnut hair. The chimera eluded him, yet still he could feel its presence, softly calling his name, even if 'twas only in his mind.

Then, his last dream found him abandoning the bed of yet another faceless woman to follow the voice that beckoned him. He moved through a series of doors, till finally he stood before one that was almost obscured by a dense, swirling mist.

He tried the ornate brass knob and found it stuck. Applying pressure, Cam forced the door open, sensing that what was inside was somehow very important to him. He walked through the thinning fog and beheld a huge canopied oak bed raised on a dais. Instead of elaborate cloth bedcurtains, this bed was surrounded by a curtain of thorny vines. There, sweetly visible through the entwined brambles was a woman, fast asleep, as God made her, her only covering a thick mass of long chestnut hair. Her scent drew him closer to her. She shifted slightly, affording him a glimpse of one full breast, long legs, and a nest of reddish-brown curls that made both his eyes and his loins ache. This was a woman worth taking, a woman worth possessing, a woman to hold forever.

An intense desire coursed through his blood, desire richer and stronger than any he had ever experienced. His flesh responded, his manhood hard and aching with the need to become lost in the depths of her feminine body.

What to do? he wondered. He had no weapons to hack aside the tangled covering that kept her from him. To reach her, he must breach this bower of thorns with naught but his bare hands. To obtain the treasure that he so desperately wanted he must be willing to take a great risk.

He glanced over his shoulder at the open door, no longer obscured by mist. He had only to walk out, turn his back on the sleeping beauty. The world was full of women, women who posed no problems, no complications. They waited for him outside this room.

He turned back his head, looking once more at the woman on the bed. He heard again that soft, feminine voice that called to him even though she slept. *Cameron. To me.* It echoed in his brain like an oft-spoken battle chant. Her mouth was curved in a half smile, as if her thoughts were pleasant and warm. His were hot and demanding, full of the stoked fire of passion.

Reaching out his hand to grasp the tangle of vines, he felt his skin tear as the thorns penetrated it. Bloody scratches lacerated his flesh, tearing small furrows in it. Pain registered in his mind, waking him up.

Cam examined his hands. Strange, the pain of the thorny vines had been so real, so vivid. He half expected to see the marks on his skin. Nothing. Only the very real scars and misshapen bones of his right hand. He gave a snort of derision. So much for the perfect knight of his wild imaginings, seeking to rescue the fair maiden from her lonely prison. More fool he!

Cam paced the room, his sexual energy running rampant. If he were back home in Scotland, a swim in an ice-cold loch would cool this fever of desire. Here there was only the Thames, and no privacy. Or mayhap he would have taken an early morning ride across the hills, pushing his steed and himself to the point of exhaustion. Or he could have simply bought a woman to slake his hunger.

Moving to the window, he placed a hand upon the misty panes. The cool feel of the glass soothed his skin. It was then that he saw the figure in the garden, heading towards the rivergate. He couldn't make out who it was or why, as the mantel clock chimed four, someone in this household would be walking alone. Perhaps one of the servants was meeting a lover?

Since he could not sleep, he would see his curiosity satisfied.

Unable to sleep, Marisa had thrown a plain, serviceable cloak borrowed from one of her servants over her petticoats and long-sleeved chemise. Her soft kid slippers would be ruined by the wet patches of earth she walked on as she made her way slowly through the garden. Most of the blooms were still to come. Summer would find this ground a riot of colors and scents, yet now it was hushed, as if asleep, waiting for the warmth to awaken its bright promise once more.

Strange, but she felt much like a garden herself, waiting for to bloom. It was as if something deep inside her was clamoring to be set free, though she knew not what it was. She did know that most people decried the night air as unhealthy. She, however, loved the night when it was misty with rain, loved the feel of it on her skin. Believing that no one was around, Marisa shucked off her cape, tossing it carelessly to the stone bench. Her hair, brushed loose from its confining curls, was drenched with moisture, waving riotously down her back. She tunneled her hands through it, pushing it up and off her neck.

The solitary figure watching her from deep within the shadows sucked in his breath as her actions drew his gaze to the rise of her breasts. The rain had caused the cloth to cling to her skin, outlining the hardness of her nipples. Once again he felt the ache deep in his loins, twisting with the coiled power of a snake.

Her eyes spied the huge stone cistern that held the collected rainwater. She would enjoy a cool, comforting bath in this water come morning. Were she at one of her country estates, she would perhaps have gone for a swim if there were a lake or river nearby.

Marisa sighed, dropping the heavy burden of her hair. The caress of the rain was like a hand gliding over her cotton-sheathed skin, molding the texture of the garment to her body. Each breath she took forced the cotton against her stiffened nipples, causing a pleasurable ache deep in her belly. It brought to mind the sensation of her husband's hand on her skin the night of their wedding, his fingers sliding over the nub of her flesh.

She understood the purpose and importance of marriage: to beget heirs and secure property. Yet what of the physical side? Her mother had explained so little of that, saying only that it was a wife's duty to submit her body for her husband's pleasure, for from the act of coupling came children. Her mother had added that it was rare that a man cherished and cared for his wife so that she too experienced that keenness of gratification. Her father had been such a man, her mother said with a deep smile.

Marisa wondered if the Lady Brianna had found joy in her husband's arms. Had she too discovered the pleasure of which her mother spoke? Her cousin's recent loss made Marisa reluctant to probe the secrets of Brianna's marital bed.

Still, Marisa thought, there was her grandmother, the tart-tongued dowager countess, famed for speaking her mind, and if rumor had it true, a woman who had taken lovers to her bed before and after the death of her husband. Aye, her grandmother would be the one to ask about the so-called delights to be found in marriage.

What would her grandmother make of the man she had wed? Marisa shrugged her shoulders, walking toward the stone bench. She sank to the seat, feeling the dampness that had soaked through the cloth of the cloak. 'Twas sheer folly to stay here, else she might take a chill. A glass of warm, spiced cider would be to her liking now, though she was loath to wake her maid Charity to fetch it for her.

Rising, she thought she heard a sound behind her. She froze to the spot, realizing that she had been foolish to venture outside with at least some small weapon upon her person.

A cold piece of metal pricked her throat. "Hold," spoke the masculine voice behind her.

Marisa did as instructed, recognizing the voice.

"'Twas foolish to wander about alone at night, my lady. I could have been someone intent on doing you harm. One little flick of my dirk and I could so easily end your existence."

"And by doing so become a very rich man," Marisa stated. They were alone, with no one to come to her aid. She waited.

The sharp blade disappeared. The wet cloak was placed around her slender shoulders. "Get you back to bed, lady."

Had she heard a trace of hurt in his voice? Without stopping to question further, Marisa bolted.

Cam sheathed the dirk, watching her flee. His left hand raked through the wet strands of his hair, pushing it away from his face. She had courage, no mistake about that; much more than many men he'd known. Courage and a strength of will he admired.

And a damnable bonny comeliness he yearned to possess, in or out of a dream.

Chapter Nine

"They're gone," the woman shrieked. "Gone!"

"My dear, there is no reason to scream like a fishwife. I know." God, but there were times he wished the silly bitch dead, though she was still of use to him. A greedy jade, she provided him with information with her whoring ways; he in turn provided her with money, a pension of sorts, to keep her respectability intact.

She took a calming breath, fanning herself as she strolled down the tree-lined lane. To anyone's eye, they were a couple out for a simple walk in the park. The wig she wore to cover her own her hair itched mightily. Her face, denuded of the paint and powder she normally wore, bore testimony to the excesses of her life. Her gown, stolen from a local merchant's wife, was plain, the cut demure, but it was at least silk. "I thought you were to remove my problem. 'Twould seem he has removed himself," she muttered angrily. "And that I cannot brook."

"Did I not assure you that I would dispose of our mutual problem in my own way, my own time?" He doffed his hat to an acquaintance, smiling perfunctorily.

"But I wanted to bear witness, to see him suffer."

"Keep yourself calm. He will soon be no threat to you."

"Or," she added, "to you."

He gave her a syrupy sweet smile. "Of course, to me also," he stated. He understood her veiled reference to the evidence she held against him. Her solicitor, that randy old goat she serviced in lieu of payment, held copies of a letter which implicated him. Should those papers fall into the wrong hands, his position at court would be in jeopardy. His lands and wealth would be forfeit, along with his life. He couldn't count on Charles's well-known charity towards people who worked with Cromwell's government. Even if he should be spared his life, what would he have? No position, no title, no money. And he was a man who depended on that to feed his love of the finer things in life.

They were at a stalemate; both knew it. She wouldn't betray him because her lust for money was consuming; he couldn't kill her because she possessed information that could destroy the foundation of his comfortable world.

"His eyes haunt me," she said, her voice barely above a whisper. "At night, in dreams I can sometimes imagine that he is there, with me, staring at me with those blue, blue eyes filled with hate. I can see his big hands reaching for my throat, eager to still my life." She shivered despite the warmth of the sun.

"Can you blame him, my dear? You cost him an eye and destroyed his angelic face. Though I must add that to have left one side as perfect as it was was a touch of brilliance, sweetling. A continual reminder of what he lost." He chuckled with glee. "A stud that no mare would accept willingly anymore, forced to service Derran's cold filly."

"A creature you wouldn't mind covering yourself, especially with her fortune at your disposal?" she proposed, her voice coated with honey.

Just the thought of having the Fitzgerald heiress as his own, her vast fortune at his disposal, her lush body at his mercy, excited him, but only mentally. He waited for his sex to respond; as usual, it failed. "I won't deny the prospect of rogering the wench a delicious idea," he stated.

And that's all it is, lovey, she thought, an amusing idea. She was aware of his problem. It brought a touch of amusement to her face. She had little doubt that even lame and scarred, the Buchanan could still stand to stud, whilst this pathetic thing that considered himself a man would fail.

"Where have they gone?" she asked, getting back to what was really important.

"To Dorset, I heard. They left early this morn." He smoothed the periwig he wore, beneath which his thinning hair was filmed with sweat. "Tut, tut, my dear. 'Twould seem his Majesty's roads are not always safe. Travel is such a hazard in these times.

"Now, shall we finish our walk? I find this talk of revenge has given me a monstrous thirst."

"What say you to stopping for a meal at the Red Feather? It has been a while since we ate our breakfast." Marisa proposed.

Brianna, conscious of the extended silence in the coach, agreed. "'Twould be nice to at least have a few moments seated on something that is not constantly in motion," she said, her eyes dancing with merriment.

"I'd rather be riding one of my new stallions," Marisa sighed, her tone wistful.

"Then please, sweet coz, do not think that you have to keep me company inside. Feel free to join your husband," Brianna urged.

"Why ever you'd be wanting to ride one of them big things is puzzling to me, my lady," Charity exclaimed. "I'd be so afraid that they would hurt me. They're ever so huge."

"I think perhaps I shall ride after we partake of a meal," Marisa said, tilting her head so that she could see outside the window of their carriage. Just a little ahead of the coach rode her husband. She could see the straight line of his back, the flow of his velvet cape as it covered the fancy saddle. He handled the spirited horse well, his gloved hands secure on the reins of the big animal. Its silvery white tail flowed to just short of the ground.

Brianna, watching the look of pleasure on her cousin's face, glanced out the window, pushing aside the curtain. 'Twould seem the Buchanan could handle a horse well, a point in his favor with her cousin. While Brianna herself was content with a gentle, placid mount, she knew her cousin's horemanship was superb. Hadn't Marisa kept pace with her own brothers, who were judged some of the best riders in all Ireland? She'd even raced against them, and won, the only woman to do so.

"Husband," Marisa called out.

Cam pulled back on the reins, feeling the power

of the horse under him. He longed to see just
what this animal could do on an open field. He'd
wager that no mount could compare, unless 'twas
the twin.

"Aye, my lady wife?" he asked.

"I would have us stop for a meal at the inn
called Red Feather. Please inform the coachman.
It should be just another few miles or so along the
road."

Cam nodded his head. "I shall, wife. If 'tis but
a short distance, I will ride ahead and see to a
private room for you ladies."

"Wait," Marisa commanded suddenly. "Halt the
coach," she instructed Cameron.

Puzzled, he nonetheless did as she requested,
also relaying her wish to stop at the inn as the
coachman drew the team to a halt.

A groom jumped down from his perch and stood
by the door, swinging it open so that Marisa could
alight.

"I shall accompany you," she said. "Fetch me
the other horse," she said to the groom.

He doffed his cap and hurried to do her bidding, returning a moment later with the other
stallion, a saddle already upon its back.

Marisa turned to her cousin. "You do not
mind?"

Brianna smiled. "No. I would not hamper your
desires, cousin. All I ask is that you take care on
that great beast."

The glow on Marisa's face was enough to bring
a smile to Brianna's countenance. "We shall
meet you both at the inn," she said, watching
as the groom assisted Marisa to mount the
horse. She saw her cousin position her leg
about the sidesaddle, then nod that she was
ready.

"Till then," Marisa called, kicking her horse into a gallop.

The animal needed no further excuse to let loose his tremendous power, taking off like a Cavalier with the Roundheads in close pursuit.

Cam gave a surprised laugh, pulling on the reins of his mount so that the great beast pawed the air, then followed its twin.

The sound of racing hooves pounded the earth as both horses ate up the distance between the coach and the inn. Through the woods they ran, the combined laughter of the man and the woman floating on the air as they urged their animals onward.

Not since she'd last been in Ireland, racing free along her cousin Killroone's lands, had Marisa felt so unencumbered. The wind whipped at her, but she cared not. She felt the fetters of duty slipping from her, if only for the time it would take to traverse the road. She could forget her responsibilities and enjoy the sweet honest satisfaction of a challenge to her skill with a horse.

Turning her head, she saw that her husband kept pace with her. Bending low over her mount's neck, she whispered softly to him, urging him to go faster.

Cam, seeing his wife's actions, did the same, speaking to his horse in his native tongue. He was determined to win; not to best her, for he admired her way with the animal, her determination; nay, it was rather to show her his skills, his abilities. That even as he was, he could still command respect. Just why it was so important to him he did not question too deeply; he accepted and acted on it.

His horse pulled slightly ahead of hers, passing her just as the inn came into view. He veered off the road, making for the stables.

Marisa followed mere seconds later, a wide
smile on her flushed face as she pulled hard on
the reins, her horse dancing to a halt next to his.
"Well done, my lord husband," she said, taking a
deep breath as she waited for the inn's groom to
help her from the horse.

Cam, having already dismounted and tossed
his reins to the groom, reached her before the
young lad could. He held up his arms, his gaze
meeting hers before traveling downward to her
bosom. Her pale breasts were rising and falling
quickly from her excitement. He ached to put his
lips to them, to trace with his tongue the deep
cleft, to rend the material of her gown and free
them to his hands so that he could shape and
caress, to suckle the nipples so that she moaned
with a need to rival his own.

She stood close to him, secure in the circle of
his arms, which held tight to her waist. Marisa
raised her head, her green eyes lifting to meet his.
Her heart was beating quickly, much too quickly.
The cause must surely be the race, she told herself
as she lowered her eyes. "Thank you, my lord,"
was all she said as his hands released her.

"Let us see what accommodations can be had
here ere the coach arrives," he said, lifting his left
arm so that she could rest hers on it.

Waiting to greet them at the door was a rail-
thin woman. "Be you welcome to my establishment," she said, her sharp eyes narrowing at the
couple as they approached.

Marisa recognized the hastily hidden look of
surprise on the other woman's face as she beheld
Cameron. 'Twas odd indeed, Marisa thought, that
this face that still bore the ability to shock others held no terror for her. She had realized that

when she had looked up into his face, there in the courtyard. It was simply the face of the man she had promised before God and the king to honor as husband. No more. No less.

Cam's deep voice was authoritative, breaking through the temporary silence. "My wife and I seek shelter for ourselves and our party. We have need of a room were we can dine privately."

"There be more?" the innkeeper inquired.

"My coach is only a mile or so behind," Marisa said, "with my cousin and my maid." She cast a glance over her shoulder. "I would have feed for our animals too, and something for the servants."

"That can be arranged, my lady," the woman hastened to assure her, recognizing them for quality by the cut of their cloth and the splendid horseflesh they rode. "Do come inside." She stepped back to allow them to pass.

A plump, apple-cheeked farmgirl answered the woman's summons. "Jean, see to escorting our guests to the back parlor, then inform Toby to be expecting their coach and servants ere long." The woman introduced herself, a warm smile on her thin face. "I am Mistress Bennett. 'Tis glad I am that you chose my inn to rest."

Marisa smiled in return. "My father once sought shelter here, Mistress Bennett, and spoke of your kindness to him and my brothers."

"Your father?"

"Aye," Marisa answered the woman's question. "The Earl of Derran."

The woman's eyes bulged slightly in shock. "You be the good earl's child?"

Marisa nodded proudly. "I have the honor to be his daughter."

"He was a fine man, my lady. I was sad to hear of his passing."

"I thank you for that, Mistress Bennett."

Jean waited patiently to show them the way.

"I will send you something to drink whilst your meal is prepared. One of my best bottles of wine." Mistress Bennett said. "Go you and rest."

"I would rather ale," Cam insisted. "You may bring wine for the countess."

"Then I will take ale also, Mistress Bennett," Marisa said, tilting her head towards her husband, fixing him with a smiling glance.

Cam responded with a slight nod of his head.

"Ale it shall be," Mistress Bennett replied.

Cam and Marisa followed Jean's swaying hips as she lead them down a hall to a large, sunny room. It smelled sweet, with crushed herbs scattered in bowls, their scent permeating the room. To one side stood a table and chairs. A fire burned low in the hearth.

Jean bobbed a curtsey and announced, "I'll be back with your drinks quickly."

Marisa pulled off her kid gloves, dropping them onto the small table near the window. A large silence hung over the room. What to say to him now that they were alone? She searched her mind for a conversational gambit. "Will his Majesty expect you to return to London for his wedding?"

Cam, sitting in a large, comfortable chair, watched his wife pace nervously about the room. "No," he responded. "His Majesty knows full well that I do not wish to be a part of the public circus which must attend his wedding. Life at court holds no interest for me." He added, his voice low, laced with weariness, "Once, when I was a youth, I sought that life. Now it holds nothing but emptiness for me."

Marisa spun around to face him; what she was about to say was interrupted by the arrival of

Jean, who entered carrying two tankards of ale.

"Mistress Bennett said to tell you that the meal will be along shortly. If you've need of somethin' else, be pulling that bellcord over there." Jean pointed to a thick length of rope by the smaller window.

"My cousin will be arriving ere long. Show her to us," Marisa instructed. Before the servant could leave, Marisa asked, "Have you any mead?"

"Aye, my lady."

"Good. Bring that when you escort her."

"Very good, my lady," Jean said, leaving them alone again.

Each took a long draught of the cold ale. Finally, Marisa broke the quiet that surrounded them. "I am at a loss as to what to give to his Majesty for a wedding gift," she announced. "What would you suggest, husband, since you are well acquainted with the king's taste?"

"'Tis sometimes difficult to fix on one thing for the king since his interests are so varied," Cam admitted. "He likes the rare and the unusual; anything of a scientific nature intrigues him."

"What of the Portugese princess, Catherine?"

"I am told that she is very religious," Cam answered.

"You say that as if 'twas a fault," Marisa observed.

"What may be a virtue in Portugal may prove a hindrance in England," Cam said in a wry tone. He directed a penetrating look at his wife. "I fear she will likely prove far too devout and circumspect for Charles's bed."

"Meaning?"

"That a man as lusty as Charles will seek companionship elsewhere."

"Barbara Castlemaine?"

"Amongst others," Cam noted. "Charles has never been a man to ignore the possibilites."

"And, as king, his *possibilities* are without number," Marisa stated.

"Precisely," he agreed.

The sound of a coach and horses interrupted their discussion. Marisa leapt to her feet, making for the window. "They've arrived," she said needlessly, feeling as though their conversation had entered dangerous waters. Had her husband once been a man like the king, experienced in many bedchambers? A man of such appetites that one woman's bed would never be enough?

Jean entered, carrying a bottle of wine and a glass on a hastily polished walnut tray, followed by Brianna. "Mistress Bennett would know if you be ready for the meal, my lady?"

Marisa sliced a glance at her cousin. "What say you?"

"I am famished," Brianna responded.

"Jean, pray inform Mistress Bennett that we shall enjoy our food now."

Replete, having finished the simple, well-cooked fare that Mistress Bennett provided, the Earl and Countess of Derran, along with their party, set out to continue their journey.

Marisa cast a fond glance at her maid, curled in the corner of the carriage, asleep. They had been on the road for almost an hour, eager to make for their next stop. She'd chosen to ride inside for this leg of the trip, anxious to talk to her cousin, yet not sure how to broach the subject. Surely Brianna could shed some illumination on the marriage bed. Marisa knew her cousin was a pious woman, far more so than she was herself. Had that piety carried over to the bedchamber? She disliked asking Brianna, for she was well aware of her cousin's reticence when discussing her marriage. Marisa assumed it was because Brianna had been devastated by her loss. She respected her cousin's mourning, fearing that perhaps her questions would dredge up painful memories best left private.

Looking at Brianna's calm, serene features, Marisa decided not to pursue her inquiry. 'Twould be better, she decided, to question her grandmother, a woman known for her plain speaking.

"Marisa?" Brianna asked. "Does something trouble you?"

Marisa gave her cousin a smile. "'Tis nothing."

"I would be of help if I can."

Marisa reached out and took Brianna's hand in hers. "I know that, coz. Truly, 'tis a small matter, something that my husband said to me."

"What?"

"'Tis of little import."

Brianna shook her head. "I do not believe you. Come, please share it with me," she implored.

Marisa's eyes quickly darted to Charity; the maid was still fast asleep. "'Twas a remark about the foreign princess that the king is to marry."

"What did he say?"

"He wondered if the princess's religious devotion would render her unable to . . ." Marisa paused, a flood of color creeping into her cheeks. ". . . enjoy the marriage bed. His Majesty is a very virile man, who, my husband states, needs a woman who will match him."

Brianna's freckle-dusted cheeks grew darker with color as she blushed from the implications.

"Is it thus with all men?" Marisa wondered aloud. "Mother told me that with a man you love, the bedding ritual can be so very special." Marisa lowered her eyes. "She loved my father; he loved her. They were so happy together, though my father was not the kind of man that the king is. She showed me the last letter Father wrote to her, which she kept with her always. In his missive, he told her that he had remained faithful to her, to their vows."

Brianna wasn't quite certain how she should reply. This was the perfect chance to tell her cousin about the state of her marriage with her late husband, to explain what she had endured—the pain, the humiliation, the never-ending fear that he would once more seek her bed. Each day in her prayers, Brianna had begged for deliverence, hoping her husband's fancy would turn to another woman. She would have turned a blind eye should he have procured a mistress. But he never did. No, he once told her, he was determined to save his seed for a legitimate heir.

Brianna sighed. How much happier she would feel if she could unburden herself to Marisa. Oh, sweet mother of God, she wished she could!

"Do you fear that your husband will seek his pleasures in another bed?"

Marisa raised her gaze. "I do not know." She clasped her hands together, feeling the weight of the rings on her fingers, the responsibilities they represented. "Since he has yet to come to my bed, I am at a loss to know what he will do after our vows are consummated. 'Tis puzzling, to be sure, to wonder what will pass once we have become truly husband and wife."

"Mayhap he fears your rejection?" Brianna suggested.

"Rejection?" Marisa scoffed. "'Tis I who have reason to ponder on rejection. You know 'twas he who refused me," Marisa stated empahtically.

"What would you have done had your husband quit your bed ere he lay there?"

Brianna longed to say: *I would have built a chapel in thanksgiving.*

Marisa cursed her tongue when she saw the look of sadness on Brianna's face. "I am sorry, cousin, for my thoughtless words," she said. "Pray forgive me for my needless resurrection of memories that may be painful to you still. I meant no harm."

"I know that, Marisa." Brianna wished she could explain the nature of her pain, but the guilt she carried was still too strong to share.

Marisa bent and retrieved her sewing basket, which lay at her feet. Opening it, she drew out the pattern she had started days before. Within the wooden rack that held the material taut, Marisa examined the work she had begun. Bordered with roses, the central picture was of a pair of swans, gliding serenely along a river, followed by several cygnets.

"May I see?" Brianna inquired.

Marisa handed over her work, pleased at the scrutiny her cousin gave the piece.

"'Tis beautiful," Brianna said, her fingertips tracing the stitchery.

Flattered by Brianna's praise, Marisa glowed. "'Tis from a childhood memory," she recounted. "My grandmother gave me a pair of swans for the celebration of my ninth birthday. They were so lovely." She smiled in remembrance. "I recall telling my father that I would have the swan as my device." Marisa gave a little laugh. "Imagine the impudence, declaring that I would take the swan emblem for myself and that henceforth I would have to have my very own seal so that all would know the mark of Derran's daughter. Within a fortnight, my father presented me with a golden seal, a swan. And mama gave me six swan badges—for my own retainers, she said, all bearing the Latin motto *Audentes fortuna juvat.*

"Fortune favors the bold," Brianna translated.

"Aye," Marisa confirmed. She accepted her work-in-progress back from her cousin's hand. "An accident claimed the female swan ere two years had passed. Not long after, the male swan died."

"'Tis said that they mate for life," Brianna said.

Marisa used her small golden scissors to cut a length of thread in a brilliant shade of blue. Threading her needle, she began to ply it. "So I have been told," Marisa said, her green eyes narrowed as she concentrated on her task. "I wonder if 'tis true?"

"Be you sure that's them?" asked the rough voice.

"Look at the coach, you bloody fool," answered a second voice, pointing. "'Tis the crest we were told would mark it as the one."

"Do ye think them wenches'll be wearing lots of jewels?"

"Of course I do," the man explained, "she's a countess, isn't she? Them kind be used to parading their riches before other folk."

The first man wet his thick lips, and saliva drooled through his matted beard. "Do ye think we can sample them after we've done what we've come for? I ain't ever had me no quality woman before."

The other man scratched his crotch. He was being paid well to see that the crippled man who was traveling in the coach was killed. Then he was to get rid of his companion in the deed. He had been instructed to leave the ladies alive and to return to London with proof that the Earl of Derran was indeed dead. Nothing was said, however, about not having a bit o' fun. That stupid maid at the inn had been all too eager to help them once he explained that they had a very important message to deliver to the countess and her husband, even going so far as to tell him about a little-used path that would save him time. He snickered. Very important indeed, he thought, as he checked his pistols. She'd confirmed what he'd been told: the earl was a useless, ugly cripple. This would be easy money.

He belched. "Why not, long as we gets done what has to be." He glanced at his companion. Far be it from him to send a fellow thief to hell without the comfort of a last taste of female flesh. Hell, he could use a good roger himself; ever since he'd come down with the pox, whores avoided him.

He pulled the dirty kerchief over his nose. His companion did likewise.

"You do the coachman," he said, mounting a brown horse and drawing forth one of the pistols he carried in his wide belt. "The earl is mine."

Chapter Ten

Cam heard the pistol shot. Abruptly, he pulled the big white stallion to a halt, listening. The sound had come from behind, from the direction of the coach.

The lad riding with him did the same. "What's that, my lord?"

"Trouble," Cam answered succinctly. He reached for the pistol hidden in the folds of his black wool cloak. The only other weapon he had on him was the dirk secured in his left boot.

Damn his pride! He should have been riding inside the coach. He knew that the roads were not always safe, but he thought it for the best if he kept to himself, away from the temptation of his lady wife. Cam rationalized that by riding ahead he could both rid himself of excess energy and check the road for signs of robbers. Perhaps he should have insisted that they hire an escort. Too late now, he thought, as he turned his horse

158

in the direction from which he'd come. His only care now was that he get back in time to prevent any harm befalling the ladies in his care.

He urged his mount forward with the pressure of his legs. The big horse responded quickly, setting off in a gallop. *Sweet Jesu*, he prayed, *let me not be too late.*

Marisa heard the shot and tossed her needlework to the side, watching as her maid awoke with a start.

"Be still," Marisa urged Charity.

"Highwaymen?" asked Brianna in a whisper.

Marisa nodded. "I fear so."

Charity's eyes grew round with fear. "What'll we do, my lady?"

Marisa wished she knew. They had no real weapons in the coach. In her luggage she carried a set of pistols. A lot of good they were doing her now, she thought as the vehicle came to an abrupt halt. On the seat next to her were the scissors she had been using.

Within seconds the coach door was jerked open. A man appeared, a pistol in his grimy hand, a soiled dark cloth tied about the lower half of his face.

"Get out," he ordered.

Brianna and Charity looked at Marisa, who answered, "As you wish." She deemed it best not to provoke him.

The women alighted from the coach. Charity clung to the Lady Brianna. Marisa looked at the top of the coach, where she saw her driver slumped in his seat. The lad next to him was visibly trembling. She noted another man still seated on a lathered horse. The beast had been ridden hard. Why? Wasn't it a general rule that highwaymen waited for their prey to come to them? It appeared, she decided, noting the other sweating mount that stood cropping the grass, that they had been pursued.

"Where is the man with you?" questioned the rail-thin man standing on the ground, his pistol pointed at Marisa.

"What man?" Marisa shot back.

"Bitch!" he spat, smacking her across the face with the back of his bony hand.

Marisa reeled from the unexpected blow. Fury rose in her at the thief's gall. Her hand rose to touch the slight swelling of her cheek. No one had ever struck her. Her first reaction was to find a whip and beat him. Her second, more logical, thought was to realize that this vermin was temporarily in command of the situation.

"Marisa, are you hurt?" Brianna asked, moving to her cousin's side.

"Get back," snapped the man. "Now, my fine lady, let me ask you again—where is the man who was with you? Where is the Earl of Derran?"

So, Marisa realized, it wasn't just a simple robbery. They were after the Buchanan. For what reason?

"I do not know," she replied.

"You be a liar," the man stated, anger rising in his voice.

"How dare you question me?" Marisa demanded, calling forth all her Fitzgerald pride, stalling for time.

The bearded man on the horse moved closer. Marisa could read the lust in his eyes as he gazed at her cousin and her maid. He dismounted, removing the dirty kerchief from his face. He licked his fleshy lips, a leering grin on his mouth.

"You'd best be tellin' me what I want to know," the man who seemed the leader ordered, "else my *friend* will enjoy persuading them."

Marisa cast a swift glance at Brianna and Charity. The maid was quivering with fear; her cousin's face was drained of all color, her eyes like those of a trapped doe, unable to move. She watched as the man moved closer, saw Charity cower and Brianna remain frozen, even as he reached out a filthy hand and grabbed at the golden cross Brianna wore. He ripped the chain from Brianna's neck, snickering as he did so.

"I be wanting the black-haired wench," he said to his partner, moving closer still, putting his hand on Brianna's breast.

"Leave her be!" Marisa shouted.

The man with the pistol moved closer to Marisa. "I be givin' the orders here, my lady," he said, enjoying the feeling of power.

Marisa's voice was icy cold with contempt. "Then tell that pig to remove his hands from my cousin."

"You be hearing that, Drax?" the man with the pistol asked. "The countess here be tellin' you something."

Drax nodded, turning his head to stare at Marisa. He chortled, ignoring her words. He reached out his other hand and grabbed Brianna's bodice, a sly gleam in his eye.

Marisa made to move and the other man grabbed her arm, digging his dirty nails into her skin, halting her.

Marisa's green eyes widened with shock, ignoring the pain.

One moment Drax was standing before her cousin; the next, he slumped down, his mouth gaping open. Then he lay in the dirt, face down, a dirk embedded deeply in his back.

Charity screamed in horror.

Brianna gasped.

Both Marisa and the man holding her turned to see who had thrown the weapon.

Standing there was Cameron Buchanan, a pistol in his left hand. "Release my wife," he commanded.

The other man gave a harsh snap of laughter, putting his pistol to Marisa's head. "No," he said, feeling a trickle of sweat run down his back. He took a deep breath, his hand tight on Marisa's waist. Damnation, but he had not expected the cripple to come to the rescue. What was he going to do? His pistol held only one bullet, as did the one he had tucked into his belt. He cast another glance at his opponent. The man had no other weapons. Beneath the tilted wide-brimmed hat, he could see the black patch that covered the earl's right eye. A sneer formed on his mouth. A half-blind cripple was no match for a man like him.

Cam stood stock still, his eye focusing on the brigand who held the pistol to Marisa's temple. He had to take a gamble, else all would be lost.

Cam shrugged his wide shoulders. "So be it, then," was all he said.

The cold-bloodedness of her husband's words sent a chill racing through Marisa. She blinked in surprise, her gaze searching her husband's face for the truth. A thread of connection passed between them; 'twas as if she could hear what he was thinking: *trust me.* Marisa reacted with pure instinct, a small smile curving her mouth.

The thief shivered slightly, his confidence ebbing. He stared at the man standing only a few feet away. This was not what he'd expected.

He'd been promised a grand sum of money to kill the earl; now fear for his own life crawled through his mind.

"I will kill her," he threatened.

Cam breathed deeply. He forced a callous tone into his voice. "Do it," he said, hoping to unsettle the man enough so that he would forget about Marisa and try instead for him. "You have one shot. I, too, have one shot." He smiled. "Either way I shall win."

"Win?" the thief asked, his voice beginning to shake. He patted the smaller weapon in his belt.

"Aye," Cam said. "If you kill my wife, I shall be sorry to lose such a pleasing bedmate, but I shall be a very rich widower. Wealth can buy me other women," he stated crisply. "And you, fool that you are, will be very dead."

"You think yourself that lucky a shot?" the brigand challenged, believing that a man with only one eye couldn't possibly be an accurate shot.

Cam's smile was cold and deadly. "I do."

Marisa took the opportunity that presented itself to her when she felt the man holding her shift slightly, his attention focused on her husband. Her right hand moved slowly till she came upon the object that she had placed into the attached pocket of her skirt; her fingers closed about it, drawing it out. *Now!* her mind screamed.

The thief cried out at the pain, releasing Marisa and dropping the pistol in his panic as he looked at his blood-covered thigh. The bitch had stabbed him with a pair of scissors!

It was his very last thought as the bullet tore into his forehead.

Charity screamed.

Brianna swooned, falling to her knees, her breath coming in short gasps.

Marisa reacted, moving swiftly to her cousin's side. "The danger is over, Brianna," she said in a soothing tone, noting the abject terror still in her cousin's golden-brown eyes, feeling the small shudders that shook Brianna's body.

Brianna nodded, hating the fear that she thought shamed her. "Forgive me for my weakness," she said in a voice barely above a whisper.

Marisa closed her arms about her cousin's body. "'Tis no weakness to be afraid of true danger. I, too, was sore afraid."

Brianna smiled at her cousin's reassuring words. "Thank you for that sweet lie."

"'Tis no lie, I assure you," Marisa said, helping Brianna to her feet. Her avid gaze searched for her husband. Cam was calmly pulling the dirk from the other man's back, wiping the blood off with a lace handkerchief, which he let drop to the ground beside the man. Marisa watched as he moved slowly towards the man he'd shot.

"Charity, help Lady Brianna into the coach," she said, releasing her cousin into her maid's arms as she walked to the front of the carriage. The lad who had ridden with Cam had scrambled up to the seat, and was helping bandage the coachman's arm.

"Can you handle the team?" she questioned softly.

"I think so, my lady. 'Tis only a minor wound," he assured her. "I thank heaven that the villain was only a fair shot."

Marisa looked at his face, noting the paleness in her coachman's normally ruddy skin. "I think it best that Dickon handle the horses. I would have you save your strength, Palmer, for the morrow."

"Aye," Palmer responded, "I will do as your ladyship bids me."

"Good," she said, turning and walking back to the door of the coach. Marisa noted that her husband was once more in the saddle. The other stallion was tied to a leading rope at the back of the carriage, along with another, smaller amount. She raised her gaze to his. Words clogged in her throat. The Buchanan had saved their lives at the risk of his own. To simply utter the words "thank you" seemed such a paltry thing. Gratitude for his bravery filled her, along with a strange exhilaration that made the blood beat faster in her veins.

"What shall we do with them?" she asked.

"We leave them here, in the dirt, where offal belongs," he said. "Do you have any objections?"

Marisa dropped her gaze to the two figures. She supposed that Christian charity demanded she see to the burial of the two brigands. Her eyes narrowed in contempt. They had tried to hurt her and hers. "They may lie here till they rot and the carrion feed on them for all I care," she said dismissively.

"Then I suggest we waste no further time on them," he said. "Can you handle a pistol?" Cam moved his horse so that he was within inches of her.

"Aye, though I think with not the same skill as you possess, my lord," she answered.

"'Tis of no import as long as you can hit what you have to." He leaned down and gave her the highwayman's weapon. "Keep it within reach should we be forced to stop." Holding the reins of the horse in his gloved right hand, he reached out to touch her swollen cheek, caressing it gently with his bare left hand. "He should have died a slow death for this," he murmured. Cam sat back, his gaze focused on her face as he pulled on the matching glove. "You are a brave lass," he stated. "I dinna ken many who would have held fast when faced with death."

Was that pride she heard in his Scottish voice? Marisa felt the color creep into her cheeks. "I think no braver than you, husband," she said softly, retreating to the safety of the coach.

"'Twas no simple robbery attempt, I am thinking," Brianna stated.

Marisa settled herself in the security of the interior. "No." She placed the pistol in her sewing basket. "He asked specifically about the Earl of Derran. 'Twould seem someone wants my husband dead, at any cost." Marisa was determined to question her husband later that evening after they were settled at the inn where they would pass the night. She folded her hands on her lap, her eyes downcast, her thoughts focused on him. Had she misread the kindness she believed she saw in his face? And what about the softness of his touch? His big hand had been so very gentle on her face. The touch, she could almost believe, of a lover.

Now she was being foolish, she decided, letting her fancy run rampant. He was no lover of hers, nor ever likely to be all that the word implied. Eventually, she knew, they must mate, if only for the sake of their marriage vows, for the heirs the earldom required. It was the duty and responsibility they both shared.

Marisa's mind focused on one question that would not disappear, no matter how many times she tried to push it aside and ignore it: Would he eventually fulfill that charge in the same cold, efficient way he had dispatched the men who threatened them?

*   *   *

Cam's thoughts were dark and disturbing. He wished he'd had the chance to make both men pay dearly for the havoc they'd caused. Dispatching them both so quickly was the only way, he knew, yet it did not dampen his raging anger. Seeing his wife held captive froze the blood in his veins. He'd forced himself to push aside the panic that rose within him, instead focusing on the best way to free her. In his life, with his work for the king, he'd faced death innumerable times. It was a constant in his world of intrigue and deception. How different, and difficult, was the situation when he watched as someone he . . . What? Cared for? Respected? Aye, that was it. He respected the woman he'd wed. Marisa Fitzgerald had shown remarkable courage this day. When he'd uttered those damning words, when he played at being unconcerned, he knew that somehow he had to make her understand that it was all a charade, part of a dangerous masquerade he must play in order to win. He wasn't sure she understood until those enticing green eyes begged him for answers.

She'd trusted him. He'd seen it in those eyes, on the slight curve of her sweet mouth. In the matter of life and death, she had willingly placed her trust in him.

Cam poured the remainder of the bottle of wine into his cup. He'd dined alone in his room, leaving the women to sup by themselves in the large rooms set aside for their use. He brought the cup to his lips and drank deeply. It was a good vintage, but then, he thought with a slight smile, the innkeeper and his lady had deemed it an honor to house the Countess of Derran. If they thought it odd that the earl and countess did not share a room, they said naught. The hidden strongbox contained within the coach and its deep reserves of gold spoke most eloquently, he'd found.

He moved to the window, which he'd left open. Night had fallen, locking him once again in a prison of growing despair. Beyond this door slept the woman he'd wed. Cam imagined her sharing her night with her cousin, curled comfortably secure in her bed, exhausted by the events of the day. It was sheer strength of will that forced him to turn away from her this afternoon and remount the stallion when all he wanted to do was take her into his embrace and hold her close to him, to fill her body with trembling of another kind. To reaffirm life after facing the possibility of death. To replace bloodlust with lifelust.

Cam picked up the single candle he'd lit earlier. Holding it aloft, he strode back to the small table which contained a washbasin and bowl, and stared into the small gilt mirror which rested above on the wall. The candle's warm glow lent a softer light to his face, masking some of the scars. *The face not even a mother could love.* The one woman he believed he could truly trust had shattered his foolish illusions when she had run screaming from the Great Hall of his father's castle. His beautiful blond mother, from whom he'd inherited his looks, had taken one look at her scarred son and fled in horror, little caring what effect this had on her favorite son.

The irony that he'd been forced to make his wife accept his trust was not lost on Cam.

Aye, Marisa'd trusted him with her life; she'd had no choice.

And he, too, had no choice about what he must do.

* * *

She moved as quietly as she could about the room, determined not to rouse her sleeping cousin or Charity, who slept on a pallet at the bottom of the bed. Marisa glanced at the two women, happy to see that both were deep in sleep. She, however, was restless. She had lain in the bed, hearing the soft breathing of Brianna and the slight snoring of her maid. Unable to bear just lying there, she arose, lighting a finely polished brass candlestick.

The table had been cleared of their food; all that remained was a dish of comfits. Picking up a sugared date, she popped it into her mouth, enjoying the sweet taste. But its sweetness couldn't alleviate the bitter resurgence of memories of what had transpired this afternoon. Two men dead. Not ordinary highwaymen whose purpose would have been to steal what they could and flee. These men had been after a particular individual, her husband. For what purpose?

Marisa sank into a chair, her thoughts flying back to the turbulence of that day. She had never properly thanked the Buchanan for his timely rescue, for she was aware that had he not seen fit to risk his own life for theirs, they could all well be dead. His courage merited a reward. But what could she give?

Her mouth curved gently. Aye, she thought, it would be a gift she alone could bestow. It would show to him how much she valued his service, and that a Fitzgerald always paid her debts.

Standing, Marisa walked to the tall wardrobe wherein hung her clothes. Opening the door carefully so as not to wake the others, she withdrew her purse from a small drawer. She reached inside and drew out a small silver ring that contained several keys. Smiling, she bent, pulling out a small chest hidden in the bottom. She carried it back to the table, fit the key into the lock, and brought forth a small, sealed piece of paper. It had been a gift from her father on the occasion of her birth. She laid the folded sheet down. Next, she took a quill pen and a small bottle of ink from the wooden chest, followed by a sheet of paper, along with a seal and wax. Dipping her pen, she began to write.

Taking a chance that her husband was still awake, Marisa decided not to wait till the morning to give him her thanks. She slipped into her robe, neatly tying the cord around her slim waist. Taking up the candlestick, she opened the door and peered along the corridor. She saw no one about, so thought it safe to proceed.

She stood before the door to his room, her heart beating rapidly. Taking a deep, steadying breath, she raised her hand to knock.

When no one answered, Marisa decided that she had been foolish. He was of course, asleep. Clutching the papers in her hand she turned to go.

It was then that the door opened a mere crack. "Aye?" spoke the deep voice.

"I've come to talk with you, husband. May I enter?"

The door swung wider and Marisa slipped through. No fire burned in the grate, and there was a distinct chill in the room. "Why did you not summon a servant to rebuild your fire?" she asked, placing her candle on the small round table. It was then she saw the empty bottle of wine.

"It is of no consequence," he answered, moving to the bed. Resheathing his dirk, Cam pushed the bedpillows to the plain headboard and settled himself full length, crossing his booted ankles on the blanket, the dirk at his side.

He had her at a disadvantage, she noted, for his face was completely in the shadows, whilst she was bathed in the light given off by the sweet-smelling candle.

"Why have you come?" he asked.

"To express my gratitude for what you did this day."

"You could have accomplished that on the morrow." Damnation, had she any idea what she was doing to him by coming into his room, by standing there, surrounded by a nimbus of light? Her chestnut hair glowed with a warm fire, as did the green depths of her eyes. His left hand curled into a tight fist by his side. He could feel the powerful tug of her siren presence.

Marisa suddenly felt shy and awkward, unsure of what she was doing. She disliked not being able to see him clearly, to gauge his reaction to her gift. "I know that I could have told you," she said, her voice pitched low and soft, "at any time how much I admired your audacious courage in dealing with the highwaymen. I choose now."

"So I see."

"No," Marisa answered, walking closer, "I do not believe that you do." Darkness surrounded her as she made her way to his side. She stretched out her hand, and thought she saw a slight movement, as if he pulled back slightly. "Take them," she said, offering the documents.

He did so, and as she made to move back, Cam's fingers gripped hers tightly, refusing to let go. "What have we here?"

Marisa could feel the warmth of Cam's hand enfolding hers, his grip secure. "A deed," she mumured.

"To what?"

"An estate."

"Which estate?" he asked, caressing her wrist, feeling the smoothness of her skin, like warm, living marble.

"FitzHall, in the Wye Valley," she stated, a sigh escaping her throat. Despite the chill in the air, Marisa felt heat course through her body.

"The house you ordered rebuilt?" He remembered the plans she had shown him, the pride and determination in her voice as she spoke of what she had accomplished.

"Aye," she said. "It was mine, entailed solely to me by my father's hand." A blush crept into her cheeks. "I was told that I was conceived there. Now I deed it freely to you, as a token of my gratitude for my life."

"A simple thank you would have sufficed, lass." Puzzled by her generosity, Cam was uncertain of what more he could say. Never had he expected a gift so fine as this. In truth, he expected nothing in return for what he'd had to do.

Marisa wet her suddenly dry lips. "Allow me to decide what is fair payment for such a debt. I entrusted our lives to you, and you did not disappoint. Now," she said, pausing slightly, "I entrust my birthright to your care."

Cam gave a tug on her wrist, sending her toppling down upon his prone body. "Then shall we seal it with a kiss?" he whispered darkly, his mouth catching hers, caution tossed casually aside. Slowly, he stroked the fires of passion to life. Her fresh mouth, so innocent and appealing, beckoned him. His tongue traced the curves of her lips, tasting the flavor of her mouth. Twisting, Cam moved so that Marisa was now beneath him, one of his legs thrown across her thighs to still her. He loosed the robe, pushing it aside. The cool touch of fine linen greeted him as he swept his hand across the thrusting fullness of her breasts. He bent his head and licked the material, watching as the wet fabric clung to the bud of her nipple.

His manhood grew tight and full when he swept aside the material of her nightshift, exposing the beauty of her breasts to his sight. As his mouth played upon her flesh, sucking and licking, his left hand stroked downwards, over the curve of her belly, till he found nest of curls at the apex of her thighs. His fingertips teased and traced, molding the cotton to her body, rubbing it slowly. Cam heard the low moan coming from her throat. He kissed the widly beating pulse in her throat before moving to recapture her lips once again. This time he used his tongue to gain entrance, sweeping aside the barriers of her inexperience with his consummate skill.

Marisa was overwhelmed by the seductive mastery of Cam's mouth. Each kiss was deeper and longer than the one before, taking her on an excursion of intense sensual pleasure. Her body felt as if she were floating; the only thing keeping it anchored was the weight of his masculine form. Against her leg she could feel the hardness of his flesh. When his fingers cupped her, an ache grew deep inside her, demanding release. She moaned, moving her hips against his hand.

Her hands lifted and slid around and up his back, feeling the texture of the muscles beneath the fabric. Instinctively, Marisa dug her nails into the fine lawn shirt, raking and smoothing. It was when her left hand moved and her fingertips came into contact with his neck, with the puckered flesh of a scar, that Cam reacted violently.

He grabbed hold of her questing hand. "Get out," he said.

The coldness of his request froze the warmth in Marisa's body. She blinked in confusion, wondering what she had done to shatter the delight they were sharing.

"What troubles you, husband?" she asked.

"I want you to leave, now," Cam stated flatly.

"But why?" she questioned, adjusting the bodice of her nightshift. Suddenly shame rose within her at the way she had reacted to his skillfull touch. *Sweet Mother of God,* she thought, he must think her a whore to have abandoned herself so freely.

Tears stung her eyes. Marisa dashed at them with the back of her hands, forcing herself from the bed. "Forgive me," she said as she fled the room.

Cam forced his breathing to a more normal rate, throwing a hand over his eyes. Softly he murmured, "No, my sweet wife, you must forgive me." He had almost taken her then and there. Only a few minutes more and he would have sealed their vows completely. Only a few minutes more and he would have heard the gasps of horror, felt the shudderings of passion turn to revulsion when she beheld all his scars.

No, he could not risk that. He could not trust her.

Cam had almost lost control once again, and that, he knew, he must never allow to happen. To do so, to let her in even a little, was to court more pain than he was prepared to accept.

Chapter Eleven

"Charity, please see to our morning meal," Marisa instructed, bustling about the room.

"As you will, my lady," answered the maid, fully recovered from the ordeal of the previous day.

Brianna, who'd been awake when Marisa had come back to bed, noted her cousin's singular mood. Last night Brianna had heard the sound of tears coming from her cousin's side of the feather bed. She'd wanted to question her then, but their lack of true privacy prevented her. As soon as she heard the door close, Brianna put down the hairbrush. Turning in her chair, she addressed Marisa. "What happened last night?"

Marisa abruptly stilled her hand, a comb poised halfway through her hair. "What do you mean?" she asked, resuming her task.

"I was awake and I heard you come back into the room."

Marisa fixed Brianna with a questioning stare.

"Why did you not ask then?"

"Had we been alone, I would have," she said. "You were weeping."

"Pray forgive me for disturbing your sleep, coz," Marisa murmured, her voice low.

"'Twould not be my first night without complete rest, Marisa," Brianna stated. She stood up, coming to Marisa's side and giving her cousin an affectionate smile. "You should wear it loose," she observed, taking the comb from Marisa's hand, moving so that she was behind Marisa. Pulling the wooden comb through the thick chestnut locks, Brianna asked, "Has it something to do with the events of yesterday?"

Marisa relaxed slightly as her cousin's gentle hands worked magic on her tangled hair. "Aye, in a manner of speaking."

Brianna urged, "Will you not confide in me?"

Marisa once more felt the hot color of shame flood her cheeks with the remembered abandon of the night. "Would that I could," Marisa said.

"It involves your husband, does it not?" Brianna could see the slight stiffening of her cousin's shoulders when she mentioned the Buchanan. A coldness crept over her. Had the earl at last taken what was his by law? Was that the reason for her cousin's strange mood?

"I think 'twould be better if I put it out of my thoughts," Marisa answered.

Brianna hesitated for a moment before asking her next question, fearing the answer. "Did he hurt you in any way?" Brianna couldn't believe that the man who had placed his life in danger for them all, the man whom she'd seen gazing at Marisa in such a hungry, yearning way, would seek to hurt the woman he had so valiantly saved.

Marisa wondered how she could truthfully

answer that question. Aye, she had been hurt, though not, she was sure, in the manner her cousin believed. She'd come back to her room, aching in strange places, aching in ways she'd never before imagined. The thin material of her nightshift chafed her swollen breasts; had she been alone she would have rent the garment from her body. A dull throb lodged deep in her belly, gnawing for release. Her pride had been hurt, as had her faith in herself. Humiliation assailed her mind, lashing at her as with sharp talons. She'd been such a fool. No, Marisa thought, more than a fool. She'd glimpsed the fabled "hot blood" of the Fitzgeralds in his bed. Like a dockside harlot or a slut from the infamous London stews, she'd been caught in the alluring trap of carnal lust.

Softly, Marisa replied, "No."

"Art sure?"

Marisa nodded.

Curse their wicked family pride, Brianna thought sadly. It prevented both of them from sharing completely what troubled them. Her pride had prevented her from leaving her husband's home, for she hesitated to admit that she had made a grave mistake in her choice of a husband. Had she done so, she might have prevented what transpired.

Charity entered, bearing a jug of thick cream, followed by a slim woman who bore a tray containing two steaming bowls of oatmeal porridge, along with thick slices of warm brown bread.

Marisa realized that her appetite was as strong as ever, despite what had happened the night before.

"Shall I do your hair now, my lady?" Charity asked as the inn's kitchen maid left the trio.

"Do a simple braid," Marisa instructed, "as I

plan on riding the distance this morn."

"Is that wise?" Brianna interjected as she poured the thick cream over her portion of porridge.

Marisa shrugged her shoulders as Charity began
to plait her hair. She had meant to question the
Buchanan as to why the highwaymen had asked
for him by name. Had it something to do with his
years of service to the Stuart cause? she wondered
as she bit into the bread. Marisa was determined
to find an answer. Perhaps during their visit
to her grandmother she could approach him
for answers, despite the awkwardness she felt
around him.

"I had given thought to that," Marisa said, "and
I dispached a messenger to my grandmother, instructing that an armed escort be sent here today.
Fresh mounts will be provided for them when
they arrive so as not to delay our journey."

Brianna smiled at her cousin's efficiency. "I
should have known you would leave nothing to
chance after what passed."

Marisa finished her meal. "'Twas an oversight
on my part when we left London," she said with
a note of self-censure to her tone. "I shall not
repeat it."

Cam, riding Romulus, held the stallion in check
as a servant helped the Lady Brianna and Charity into the coach. Marisa whispered words to
her cousin before she mounted the other stallion.
Remus pawed the ground, eager to be off. Cam
thought well of her plan for an armed escort; this
time, should trouble arise, they would be prepared to handle it. He watched as the man who
appeared in charge of the group drew his horse
near Marisa's. Cam saw the flush of color in the
young man's face as he talked with the countess.

Clearly he was dazzled by Marisa. Cam could well understand why. The sun gave her chestnut hair a rich, warm glow. When she'd visited him last night, it had been pulled back away from her face with a silk ribbon. He'd found that blue ribbon this morn in his bed. It now lay tucked into his shirt, a memento of sorts from their very intimate skirmish.

He caught the sideways glance she threw in his direction. It was soft and somewhat shy, almost as if she were unsure. That thought almost caused him to laugh aloud. Marisa Fiztgerald was every inch the beautiful English aristocrat, and so much more. In his arms last night she'd been a woman coming alive, her responses pure and unaffected. Her sweet mouth and ripe curves had almost driven him over the brink, past the point of no return. Barely had he been able to pull away, his body straining with the effort. To his jaded palate, long since inured to the taste of easy virtue and rich living, she was a taste of freshness, like a bracing drink of clear, cold water from a loch.

Sweet Jesu, Cam thought, when had convenience become affection? When had love enveloped lust, changing it from merely wanting to bone-deep desire? For love her he did. Marisa was in his mind—and, he was afraid, she had crept unbidden into his soul.

She was a lady of light, wed to a prince of shadows.

He could not love her as he wished, with no barriers between them, for to do so would expose what he kept assiduously hidden, what he could never share.

So he would love her as he must.

*   *   *

Marisa was glad of the company on the ride to her family seat. Her bailiff had brought four other men, each of whom could be counted on for his loyalty to the Fitzgerald family. While talking to her bailiff, Robin de Warth, she cast a look at her husband, sitting proudly upon the back of the huge stallion. The new Earl of Derran nodded his head slightly, a mocking smile on his wide mouth. Color ran under her skin as she snapped her gaze back to her bailiff. Why did she think, if only for an instant, that his smile masked loneliness?

"My lady, are you ready to depart?" Robin asked. He was a man in his late twenties, hale and hearty of body. Son of a Dorset vicar, he had no wish to follow in his father's footsteps, and so chose another path in which to make use of his education. He was well paid for his stewardship; he had trust, position, and a loving wife and family. Robin counted himself a very lucky man. Unlike his mistress, he hadn't had to marry on Royal favor; he'd wed a woman he loved, whole and healthy, who'd given him two fine sons and a daughter he adored, with another child on the way. Aye, he was content, a genuinely happy fellow. Could the same be said of the Lady Marisa? Was she a happy woman?

"Aye," Marisa insisted, "let us go. I would see my grandmother and lie in my own bed this night." She gave de Warth a questioning look as she nudged her mount forward. "How fares my grandmother?"

"The old countess is well," Robin said, referring to the name given to her grandmother by the Fitzgerald tenants. "She is anxious to see you safe at home, especially after your message arrived.

Faith," he said, smiling broadly, "it was all I could do to talk your lady grandmother out of accompanying us. I've heard that she was indeed a fierce lioness on your behalf whilst you were in exile in Ireland all those many years."

Marisa grinned. "Aye, that she was. She is as potent a force as twenty good men-at-arms." Marisa brushed at the wisps of hair that escaped from her braid. "I love her most dearly."

"As she most assuredly does you, my lady," Robin agreed.

Pushing her horse to a faster pace, Marisa and Robin rode a bit ahead of their caravan. Within seconds, Cam had ridden to join them.

Marisa had decided to leave her cloak in the coach, enjoying the feel of the warm sun on her skin. Cam, riding on her right, envied the sun's proximity to Marisa's flesh. His imagination took flight as he envisoned her bare body gracing a thick tartan plaid blanket, her hair spread all around her, a smile of such bonny beauty that it would sear one's heart in an instant. There, amongst the rolling hills of his native lowlands of Scotland, he would whisper the words he longed to say: *Gràdh mo chridhe:* Love of my heart.

But a cloud obscured his wishful vision. Cam envied the handsome young bailiff his unblemished face, his sturdy body. Robin de Warth would easily be welcomed in a woman's bed.

Abruptly, Cam's thoughts shifted course as he recalled the unexpected gift he'd received the night before: the estate. It was obviously important to his wife, a property of significance.

Her genorosity puzzled him. Why had she made him such a lavish gift?

Marisa could well imagine her grandmother's reaction when she informed the old countess that she had willingly relinquished a part of her Fitzgerald heritage. The gift of FitzHall would no doubt force her grandmother to question her sanity. She assumed she would be in for a severe lecture. Very well, she thought, so be it. Marisa reasoned that the estate was hers to dispose of as she desired.

She hadn't told Brianna of her decision yet either. What would her cousin make of it? Would she, too, think her foolish? And, Marisa wondered, was she truly? It was a rich estate, with several farms and much livestock. The income generated by the property helped fill the Fitzgerald coffers.

Robin broke the silence that had existed for several miles. "Forgive my memory, my lady. I forgot to tell you that goods arrived three days ago from your ship, the *Fitzstar*. We now have an abundant supply of spices, molasses, and wood from the Caribbean. Captain Chambers bade me tell you that his Excellency the Governor of Jamaica was most grateful for the gift to remember his birthday."

Marisa smiled. "I rather hoped that the set of dueling pistols would find favor with him. They were one of my father's favorite sets."

Cam posed a question. "You are acquainted with the Royal Governor of Jamaica?"

A slightly mischievous look came over Marisa's face. "In a manner of speaking. Lord Percy Hampton was once my grandmother's lover, though the affair ended about twenty years ago."

"Percy Hampton?" Cam recalled meeting him once in France. By his reckoning, the man would now only be about forty-five or thereabouts.

"You know him?" Marisa asked.

"I suppose it must have been his son I met in

Paris at his Majesty's court-in-exile."

Marisa shook her head. "No, Lord Percy's father died when he was a child."

At her husband's perplexed look, Marisa smothered a laugh. "When you know my grandmother, you will not find it difficult to understand why a much younger man would have found her enchanting."

"She must be a remarkable woman, gifted with beauty and charm beyond measure," Cam said, mentally adding, *as is her granddaughter.*

"She is that and much more," Marisa stated.

Barbara Elizabeth Tremaine Fitzgerald, Dowager Countess of Derran, sat in her rooms reading a rather long letter from her daughter-in-law, just received this morn from Ireland. She laughed with a deep glee at an observation written therein. Her eyes shifted from the page to the portrait that hung on the opposite wall. It showed a boyishly handsome man in his prime, with reddish-blond hair and laughing blue-gray eyes, a wicked smile curving his wide mouth. Underneath the painting, carved into the wood of the frame, was the name *Robert Hugh Fiztgerald.* Her beloved husband Robin. He'd died just weeks after the portrait was completed, leaving her alone with a young son. In her grief, she had lost the child she was carrying, another son. Lady Derran's green eyes misted with memories of happy days spent in this, their nuptial bed. It had been there that she'd learnt from a master the art of lovemaking, of the unparalled joy to be found in the exploration of her passionate nature. With his tutoring, she'd discovered the depth of her capacity for pleasure.

A miniature portrait in a gold frame rested on

her writing table. The countess picked it up, looking at the young woman. She could see Hugh's smile and her own green eyes in that small picture. Had her granddaughter also inherited their intense passionate sensibilities? From her own observations, Barbara judged that she had, which was why she was so concerned about Marisa's marriage. Practicality and consideration to the crown aside, had her granddaughter wed with a man who would help her express what lurked below the surface? Or would she have to seek elsewhere for what she might need?

The dowager gave a small shrug of her slender shoulders. Passion once freed could not be ignored, she'd discovered. Though she had never again found the depth of love that she had once shared with her Robin, she'd found temporary happiness in other men's arms. Her nature demanded a physical release. Had he lived, she would never have left Robin's bed. Without him and his love, she sought only the appeasement of a hearty appetite. Had she wanted to wed again, she could have. Numerous offers for advantageous unions had come her way. It was her choice to remain *his* wife alone.

And now their granddaughter, the last physical link between them, would be arriving at any time with the man who bore her cherished husband's title.

Barbara prayed that this unknown fellow was worthy of both her grandchild and the title. At her advanced age, she feared neither man nor God; ordinary strictures no longer concerned her, so she would not hesitate to eliminate a problem should the occasion demand. Indeed, had anything befallen her Marisa she would have seen the culprits hunted down and brought to justice—*her* justice.

She reached for her new walking stick, a fine carved item of deep mahogany. How very sweet of Percy to have sent it to her. He'd been an apt pupil in her bed, responsive and clever. Now, even though he was long since wed, he would still take the time to remember her with a small token of his affection.

A loud knock sounded on her door, forcing her thoughts back to the present.

"Enter," Barbara called out, her voice not as strong as it used to be.

A woman of indeterminate years approached her. "Your granddaughter's been sighted not far from here, my lady," she said, her thin, sallow face breaking into a grin.

"Excellent," Barbara replied, rising slowly from her chair. "See to it that supper is waiting for them. We shall eat in the Great Hall tonight. I want the room ablaze with light."

The other woman heaved a sigh. "I remember, my lady."

Barbara gave a sort. "See that you do. I want nothing to spoil her return. She does not tarry with us for long, as she is anxious to see to the restored FitzHall.

"Come, give me a hand on the stairs, Maude, for I would be waiting ere they arrive."

Before she quit the room, Barbara once more gave a glance at the portrait, smiling as she did so. *The long wait shall soon be over, my love; once more I will be in your arms, this time forever. Let me see our Marisa content, and I can join you.*

Marisa rode her horse at a quick pace through the iron gates, emblazoned with a large D. The

rest of her party followed. The sound of hooves
beat upon the stones of the path leading to the
main house.

She pulled on the reins, halting her animal.
She was once again in Dorset, familiar and welcoming. Ahead of her stood a large house; each
generation had added something to it so that it
sprawled and dominated the landscape. Oak trees
surrounded it like sentinels on watch, ever vigilant. Rose bushs flourished, holding court with
their many hues.

Marisa loved this place. It was the seat of the
Earls of Derran, the Mother Earth from which
they drew their strength. Yet, much as she loved
it, it did not possess her heart. That was bound to
FitzHall, the property she had placed in the hands
of her husband.

Giving her mount a nudge, Marisa rode for the
house.

The dowager countess stood in the doorway.
The falling light cast shadows over the property, though as she looked down the lane, she
recognized her granddaughter, seated on a huge
white stallion. Behind her rode de Warth on a
plain mount, and beside him was another man,
a plumed hat covering his head, mounted on a
twin to Marisa's horse.

She watched, her eyes filled with pride, as
Marisa impulsively leapt from her horse, not
bothering to wait for a groom's assistance. Tossing decorum aside, Marisa bounded up the stairs.
Within seconds her granddaughter was once more
safe within her arms.

Marisa, though not overly tall herself, enveloped her much smaller grandmother, who stood
less than five feet high.

"Thank God that you are safe, my dear," Barbara

sighed. "I could not have born it had I lost you, too."

"Then your gratitude, as mine, must be with my husband, *grand-mère*," Marisa said, "for 'twas he who rescued me, my cousin Brianna, and my maid from certain harm."

Barbara kissed her granddaughter's sun-warmed cheek, her still-sharp eyes noting the bruise that discolored the flesh there. "Who did this?" she demanded.

Marisa answered, her voice soft. "Do not despair, *grand-mère*, for he who did the deed is dead."

Barbara smiled, keeping her arm about her granddaughter's waist.

"Now," Marisa stated, watching as her husband dismounted, and her cousin and maid alighted from the coach, "I would have you greet your new grandson, my husband."

Barbara's gaze focused on the man as he handed the reins of his horse to a groom. From the side, he looked handsome enough. It was when he turned, making for the stairs, that she saw his face fully. Her green eyes widened in shock. There, standing before her, his hat removed so that he could sketch her a bow, stood a man whose face displayed both purity and destruction, beauty and pain.

What, Barbara wondered, smothering the gasp she mustn't utter, had Charles Stuart wrought?

Chapter Twelve

"You wished to see me, *grand-mère*?" Marisa asked as she poked her head around the door to the dowager's sitting room.

"I do indeed," Barbara insisted, setting aside the book of poetry she was reading. She waved her hand toward the younger woman. "Come in," she said.

"I was planning on resting before supper, *grand-mère*," Marisa stated, "perhaps relaxing with a hot bath."

In her usual imperious tone, Barbara informed her grandchild, "You may rest after the meal," then said, "and I shall leave you enough time to enjoy the rewards of a hot, scented tub. What I want to discuss with you should not keep you long."

She fixed her direct green eyes on Marisa. "Who is this man you've wed?"

"You were told his name," Marisa answered,

ignoring the implications of her grandmother's question.

Barbara skewered Marisa with a sharp glance. "'Tis not what I meant and well you know it. What manner of man is he?"

Marisa toyed with the end of her long braid. "'Tis difficult to know how to answer your questions exactly," she responded honestly. "He appears a man of few words, though we have had a chance to converse on several occasions over a meal."

The dowager interrupted. "Over a meal?" she asked, her still-dark brows raised.

"Aye," Marisa replied. "We have been wed only a short while."

Barbara changed her tone, her voice now soft and coaxing. "Does he treat you with kindness?"

"Indeed, he is most kind," Marisa acknowledged.

"'Tis too bad about his face," Barbara sighed, beckoning with her hand for her granddaughter to come sit beside her. "How came he by that? 'Tis indeed a shame that a face of such singular male beauty was partially ruined. When first I beheld that face, I thought that I had been given a glimpse of a true angel; so lovely was he, he fair stole my breath away. Then, when he removed his hat and faced me, I was shocked to see such beauty marred."

She reached out her hand and lifted Marisa's chin, gazing deeply into her grandchild's familiar green eyes, the mirrors of her own. "Does he possess scars anywhere else on his body?"

"I do not know, *grand-mère*," Marisa answered.

Barbara dropped her hand. "You do not know?"

Marisa linked her hands together, resting her chin on them. "No."

Barbara blinked in confusion. "Have you never been curious, my dear?" Another thought flew into her mind. Was this man the kind of lover who cared only for his own pleasure, and once achieved, pulled away, both in body and spirit? Was this Scotsman selfish, without a care for his woman? Barbara knew that most men were not of the ilk of her husband or the lovers she had chosen, nor for that matter like the king. Charles Stuart was a man who loved and appreciated women, as she should have reason to judge. She could not believe that a man who had been as close to the king as had this Scotsman was unwise to the ways of the world, ignorant of the designs of the flesh.

Marisa readily acknowledged that she *was* most especially curious about what the Buchanan looked like. She had seen glimpses of his chest: did the golden hair cover his entire body? Would his man's flesh respond as had hers if she were to moisten her lips and wet the fabric of his shirt? Her innocence abounded with questions, with baffling suppositions. "Aye," she said, "I have in truth been curious."

"Then why have you not satisfied this curiosity?" Even though scores of years too numerous to count had passed, Barbara could still recall the feel of Robin Fitzgerald's lean body, of the muscles and flesh which covered the hard bone. She baldly asked, "Does he leave your bed after he takes his comfort?"

Marisa rose, walking a few paces before she turned and faced her grandmother. "We have not yet shared a bed," she admitted.

"What?" came the startled question.

With a steady voice, Marisa answered, "We have not yet consummated our wedding vows."

"Impossible," Barbara stated. "I have it on good authority that your sheets were bloodied."

Marisa narrowed her gaze. "You set spies in my household?"

"But of course," the older woman readily admitted. "How else was I to know what transpired?"

"'Tis poor value you had for whatever money was spent on this endeavor."

"I did not *pay* for information, my dear," she informed her granddaughter. "I simply inquired, 'tis all." Barbara fixed her calm gaze on Marisa. "If you and the Scotsman have not yet shared the marriage bed, then why the charade?" Barbara's eyes widened. "Is he not capable of being a true husband to you?" Her tone was calm when she asked, "Was another man summoned to fulfill his part of the bargain?" At the look on her grandchild's face, she knew that hadn't happened. Another answer sprang to mind. "Or"—she put the question bluntly—"does he perchance favor boys?"

Marisa sighed at the barrage of questions. "He is not averse to women; I have that on knowledge-able authority," she said, remembering the words of Countess Castlemaine. With terse sentences, Marisa clarified for her grandmother what had happened on her wedding night.

"So," Lady Barbara asked on a deep breath, "you are a virgin still?"

Marisa gave her a rueful glance. "Aye."

"Not of your own volition, eh?"

"I was, and am, willing to honor my marriage vows, *grand-mère*," Marisa confirmed.

"I never doubted that," Barbara stated emphatically. "You are a Fitzgerald. 'Twould appear to be your husband who lacks the fervor to do the deed." At the tell-tale blush that colored Marisa's cheeks,

Lady Barbara amended her choice of words. "Perhaps not?"

Marisa related the details of the previous night at the inn. When she finished, she took hold of the old woman's hand. "Do you think me wanton?"

The dowager gave her grandchild's hand a squeeze. "Fie, child, of course not. You are a healthy young woman, 'tis all. 'Tis long past time that you were bedded, and bedded *well*. It displeases me to think that women are brought up to deny what it most normal, most enjoyable when performed with the proper man." Barbara looked at the portait of her husband. "Your grandsire was just such a man. I, too, was a virgin when I came to his bed." A smile of sweet contentment curved her mouth. "He was most generous, willing to take the time to see that I understood what pleasure meant, what true loving entailed.

"I love him as I loved no one or nothing else on this earth, my child.

"I was most fortunate in my husband. My younger sister was not so lucky. Her husband was a brute, a slobbering pig who treated her like a brood sow. 'Tis how he saw women, as chattel to be used as he saw fit. She died in childbed, along with her baby, exhausted by all the pregnancies forced upon her. No sooner had she miscarried of a babe then he was filling her with another." A cold gleam of satisfaction chilled her green eyes. "Justice was served, in a manner of speaking: his third wife poisoned him. Oh, to be sure, she was hanged for her crime, but 'tis said she met the hangman's noose with a smile.

"Ah well, enough of that," Barbara said. "We must see to it that you and the Scotsman are—"

"No," Marisa interjected. "There will be no schemes, no *arranging* of anything." She stood

up, her chin raised, her voice firm. "This is
between him and me. I want no interference.
Promise me."

Barbara nodded her white head, a smile on her
lips. "So be it then, if that is what you wish."

"It is, *grand-mère*." Marisa reached down and
gave her grandmother a kiss. "Now I must take
my leave. I will see you at supper."

"Aye, that you will, my child. Till then," she
said, watching as Marisa made her exit. Then
Barbara rose from her couch, moving towards
the portrait. She tilted her head back to stare into
the eyes. In a throaty chuckle, she said, "'Twould
seem that our beauty has been captured by a
rare beast, my love." She dropped her gaze and
focused it on the closed door. "But who shall win
the hunt?"

Cam lay on his bed, his hands behind his head.
All politeness had been shown to him since his
arrival. Servants had brought him water for a
bath, a mug of cold cider to drink. His small
trunk had been unpacked and his clothing hung
in the wardrobe. If any thought him an oddity,
they kept it to themselves.

Cam rose when he heard the knock on his door.
He had turned the key in the lock while he bathed,
so as not to suffer any untimely intrusions. He
disliked being in a vulnerable situation. A key
and a solid lock usually prevented that from
happening.

"Who's there?" he called out.

"My name's Kendall, my lord. The old countess
sent me."

Intrigued, Cam unlocked the door. There on
the other side was a man of middle years, of
short height with a slim, wiry build. What caught

Cam's attention was the empty white shirtsleeve pinned to the man's left side. He wore plain dark breeches, white hose, and a pair of sensible shoes.

"For what purpose?" Cam demanded bluntly.

"She said you had no personal servant, my lord, and that I was to tend you whilst you was here." Kendall moved into the room, heading for the cast-off garments that Cam had left on the floor after his bath. "I shall see that these are freshly laundered, my lord," he said, plunging ahead with his tasks. "Is there anything else you wish for me to do?"

"'Twas kind of my lady wife's grandmother to send for you, but I have no need . . ."

"Have you then a man of your own?" Kendall asked, his solitary arm filled with clothes.

"Well, no, I dinna, but . . ."

"Then 'tis settled," Kendall announced, "for you do have a need of me, my Lord Derran."

"I think not," Cam stated, his mind already filling with questions. Had this man been sent to pry, to seek information and report back to his wife's grandmother?

Kendall raised a graying brow, deciding to speak plainly. "Do you fear that I will judge you less than a man, my lord, for your imperfections?" He jerked his head towards the empty sleeve. "Look at me. I lost my arm in the service of the late earl. 'Twas the same battle in which he died." Kendall's pale blue eyes closed momentarily. "In war I saw horrors beyond imagining, my lord." When he opened his eyes, Kendall saw the look of skepticism in the earl's one dark blue eye. "You may place your trust in me," he said emphatically. "Should I fail you—"

"I will kill you," Cam said softly. "On that you must have no doubt. I brook no betrayal."

Kendall nodded his head. "Then we have an understanding, my lord." He smiled his relief. "I shall see to these and return to help you dress for supper."

Cam closed the door with a firm click as Kendall left. He ran his left hand through the still damp waves of his hair, pushing it back from his brow.

Was their no end to the surprises that these Fitzgerald women could provide?

Perhaps, he decided, it would soon be time to reveal a hidden treasure of his own.

Marisa awoke the next morning refreshed, having slept till almost noon. She buried her head in the thick goosedown pillows, enjoying the smell of fresh lavender, recalling with a contented sigh the events of last evening. The meal had gone well, with her grandmother dominating the conversation. They had all devoured the fresh trout, followed by the tender leg of lamb. Supper ended with pears soaked in brandy and laced with thick cream.

Slowly opening her eyes, she saw Charity perched in the window seat, mending one of her chemises.

"What is the hour?"

Charity gave Marisa a large smile. "Why 'tis just past the noon hour, my lady. Shall I fetch you something to eat?" she asked, putting down her sewing.

"No. Though I would like some of the coffee that Captain Chambers brought with him this last voyage. Since my grandmother has a weakness for it, I know her cook will have some ready."

When Charity left to get her the coffee, Marisa rose from her bed. Today she knew she must broach the subject of the attempted robbery to her husband. That it had been well planned, she was certain. But she was unsure of the motivation. Had her husband recognized the men? Searching her memory, she couldn't recall that he had, though what passed through his mind was offtimes guarded from her. He had a way of making himself seem removed from all those who surrounded him, as if he were an observer, fearing contact.

Even in conversation around the table, he had kept to generalities, expressing only mild observations, never revealing more about himself than was necessary. The dowager countess had tried, unsuccessfully, to draw him out. He was unfailingly polite, circumventing every personal inquiry most ably.

Marisa took hold of her brush and drew it slowly from her scalp to the ends, walking towards the window. Below the window seats were storage compartments. Opening the largest one in the middle, she removed a length of taffeta. Her grandmother had informed them last evening that she had arranged a ball in honor of the wedded couple. It was to take place in a week's time, with all of their neighbors invited. This would be perfect, Marisa thought, holding the material up against her skin. Moving, she stood before the mirror, the fabric draped around her shoulders.

Aye, 'twould do quite well.

An hour later found Marisa strolling along the edges of a mill pond not far from the main house. She was accompanied by Brianna and her grandmother.

"I think that you shall like what I have to show

you," Barbara said with a smile.

"You have been hinting at something whilst we walked here. Will you not tell me?" Marisa demanded.

"And spoil the surprise?" the old countess asked, laughing. "Of course not. Lah, child," she said with great affection, "but you are so impatient. All in good time."

"Do you see how I am treated, Brianna?" Marisa said in a teasing tone, "with no regard for my tender feelings." She stopped, her hands crossed over her chest, her face filled with piety. "Woe unto me," Marisa murmured dramatically.

At that, Barbara and Brianna both burst into hearty laughter. "Mayhap you should have remained in London and plied your craft upon the stage," Barbara suggested, "for 'tis wasted upon us, I fear. We are but a poor audience for such talent."

"I am deeply wounded by your verbal arrows, *grand-mère*."

"Then I have that which will lighten your supposed melancholy, my dear." Barbara waved her beringed hand towards the water. "Behold."

Marisa spung around. There, gliding serenely through the water were two pair of swans, one black and one white.

Marisa raced to the stones that flanked the water, bending down, her wide skirt spreading all around her.

Brianna, who had been let in on the secret, pulled a slice of bread from the deep pocket attached to her black skirt. She broke the thick slice into pieces and handed one to Marisa, joining her on the large gray stone.

The swans floated to where the bread lay on the water, bending their graceful long necks to daintily gobble the scraps.

To the man on horseback who observed the pastoral interlude from his vantage point hidden amongst the trees that bordered the bank opposite, it was a scene of serene beauty. It was softness, peace, and most especially, grace, in all its forms. All that was missing was the sweet sound of children's laughter. Had his marriage been normal, he might have been enjoying the walk as well, reveling in the loveliness surrounding him.

Cam focused his good eye on the two younger women as they laughed. Each was a woman a man would count himself blessed to possess.

The sound of excited children's voices filled the air. Cam shifted the weight of the basket he carried, keeping a tight rein on the big stallion. Joining the trio, Cam saw, were a man and a woman, along with three children.

"My lady, how fare you today?" Robin asked.

Marisa stood, brushing off her skirt. "I am quite well, Robin." Marisa shifted her gaze to the figure standing next to her bailiff—his wife, heavily pregnant. "How fare you this day, Mistress de Warth?"

Robin's wife, a woman of short stature, with a sweet face, beamed. "I am tolerably well, my lady, though," she said, her hands splayed across the large mound of her stomach, "my babe is restless." As she finished her sentence, her eyes widened from the powerful kick her child delivered.

"May I touch you?" Marisa asked.

Mistress de Warth gave Marisa a wide smile of acknowledgment in return, taking Marisa's outstretched hand and placing it on the swell of her belly.

Marisa felt the vigorous movement of the babe,

wondering as she did so if ever she would ever carry life within her own body. To accomplish that, however, she must first experience a man in her bed.

Cam, having crossed a small stone bridge that spanned the water, watched as his wife laid her hand, the one that wore his ring, on the other woman's belly. As Marisa did so, Cam could see the look that crossed her expressive face, and he felt an intense ache develop deep in his gut. A yearning to plant his own seed, to see it nourished within her slim body, to see it grow, seized him. His long-denied flesh responded to the images his mind conjured, refusing to remain dormant.

He saw her bend down and lift the daughter of the bailiff into her arms. The child, one plump thumb stuck in her tiny mouth, laid her dark head trustingly onto Marisa's shoulder. A twist of longing at the poignancy of the scene made Cam wonder if Marisa would welcome his bastard daughter with as much warmth as she did the child of her steward. Would his wife shun his daughter for the stain of her birth?

Dare he trust her with the truth? With a precious part of himself?

A mewling noise came from inside the basket he held, drawing Cam's attention back from his pensive thoughts. He urged his mount towards the gathering.

Marisa, having just put down her delightful burden, turned, giving a sharp glance at the man who rode slowly into their midst. All conversation ceased. No one moved, even the formerly lively boys.

The dowager took matters into her own hands, addressing de Warth's wife and children. "'Tis my newly aquired Scottish grandson." A quizzical smile on her mouth, she inquired, "What have you in the basket, Derran?"

"Small gifts for my countess and her cousin."

Barbara rapped the elder of de Warth's sons with her gold-handled cane. "Fetch them, boy," she instructed.

The boy leaped to do the old countess's bidding, even if it meant going closer to the scarred stranger.

Cam leaned down, handing the lad the basket. "Dinna drop it," he said.

The boy, his eyes round with suspicion, backed up slowly, both in fear of the man and the huge animal, but stopped when he felt Marisa's hand on his arm.

"What have we here?" she asked, flipping aside the material that covered the contents of the basket.

"Something I thought you might take a fancy to, my lady," Cam said.

"Oh," was the one word that escaped Marisa's lips as she reached into the wicker, gently pulling out the animal inside. She handed the black kitten to Brianna, who stepped forward, then removed another; it too was black, with one white paw. Cradling the tiny animal in her hands, Marisa brought it to her face. One small paw swiped at her nose, causing Marisa to chortle at its antics.

"Wherever did you find them?"

Cam was delighted that his gift had indeed found favor. He cast a glance at Brianna, who was petting the soft black fur, mumuring in her native tongue to the creature. His wife was also pleased with the small bundle. "Whilst I was riding, I came across an old woman. She bade me take them else she would have to leave them to fend for themselves, for no one wanted them."

Robin de Warth posed a question. "Who was this old woman?"

Cam shrugged his shoulders. "I dinna know."

Mistress de Warth said softly, "'Tis most likely Mistress Buck."

The two boys spoke up. "The witch."

Barbara harrumphed. "Nonsense. Witch indeed." She shot her granddaughter a swift glance. "'Tis pure rubbish," she insisted. "Mistress Buck is a young woman—one skilled in the healing arts. No more, no less."

"'Tis said she has the sight," Mistress de Warth professed.

At that Barbara merely smiled.

Marisa turned her head and caught the sly look on her grandmother's face. Whoever, or whatever, this Mistress Buck was, Marisa knew the woman enjoyed the old countess's protection, and if she did, then she would also enjoy Marisa's.

"I find myself growing fatigued," Barbara stated. "Will you accompany me back?" She directed her question to Marisa.

"Of course, *grand-mère*," Marisa agreed, taking the wicker basket from de Warth's eldest son. She tenderly placed her kitten back into its temporary home. "Brianna?"

"I shall carry this one," Brianna said, letting the kitten tug on her finger. "I think it will behoove us to feed them promptly."

Listening to the growling noises her kitten was making, Marisa nodded her head in agreement.

Mistress de Warth spoke up before they departed, her manner diffident. "I would deem it an honor, my lady, if you would partake of a meal at our table ere you make your way to FitzHall."

Marisa answered quickly, "We would be most pleased to accept your gracious offer. I will send a servant round to let you know when 'tis most convenient."

"Until then, my lady," Mistress de Warth replied, taking her husband's arm as they chose the path that led them to their house, their children running ahead.

Lady Brianna moved to the old countess's side, talking quietly to her, leaving Marisa standing but a few feet from her husband. As they walked away, Marisa stood her ground. She raised her head, meeting her husband's cool gaze. "Thank you."

Those two simple words, uttered in her soft, silken voice, stroked him as surely as if she had taken her hand and caressed his skin. He'd even envied the kitten Marisa's ministrations moments earlier when she had glided her hand across its arching back. Would that he could feel her do the same to him, though he knew it was impossible. Still, the knowing did not stop the wanting, the hungering, the craving.

"You are most welcome, wife," Cam responded, putting his knees to his horse's sides, forcing the animal to gallop. A retreat was called for, he decided as he thundered past the old countess and the lady Brianna, lest he leap from his mount and take Marisa in his arms, plundering her mouth with his own.

A ball of blue yarn lay on the floor, the end dropped next to a bowl of cream. The black kitten, his one white paw placed firmly on the yarn, lapped greedily at the treat.

Marisa watched from her bed, the candles burning brightly in her room. The kitten was an amusing creature, bold and unafraid as he investigated everything he possibly could in her apartments. One moment he would slink, stalking an imaginary prey, the next he would be pouncing on any object that caught his interest.

A mild "meow" indicated that he was finished with his meal. Having eaten some finely chopped fish upon arrival, he was now replete and wanted attention. He padded over to the bed, cocking his head.

"I suppose you want to join me?" Marisa asked, leaning over to scoop up the soft bundle of fur. A low purr was the response as she placed the kitten on one of the thick pillows. She chucked its chin, hearing a repetition of the purring. He settled on the pillow, closing his eyes, seemingly content.

"What shall I call you?" Marisa wondered aloud. She thought about that for a few moments before deciding. "Lionheart." She recalled seeing several drawings of the big cats in an ancestor's journal when she was a child. A tawny-maned creature of the wild, powerful and male, much like the man who had given her the now-sleeping kitten.

She was lost.

Trapped.

High walls of green surrounded her.

Every path led to another wall, forcing her to retrace her steps till she could find another path in the maze to take.

The sun was high overhead, the air warm and close. Perspiration trickled between her breasts. A half-mask was tied around her eyes; she could hear vague voices in the background, laughing and talking.

In front of her loomed a stone bench. Tired, she sank down. It was then, while she was resting, that she noticed that her gown was made of the material that she had found in her trunk. A gown fit for an evening at court. Around her neck hung the Stuart sapphire.

Where was she?

With her right hand, she loosened the black mask, flinging it to the ground. Ridiculous, she thought, losing patience with the futility of this game.

Rising, she was determined to find her way out when she heard an unfamiliar sound.

She gasped.

Coming toward her was a huge golden cat wearing a collar studded with sapphires to match the necklace she wore.

She flicked her glance to both sides, realizing that there was nowhere for her to run. No escape was possible. She would have to face the beast.

The animal stopped mere inches from her body, growling deep in his throat. Strangely, she felt a calmness fall about her as a gentle breeze stirred. Instinctively, and without questioning why, she held out her hand to the beast, who laved it with his rough tongue, licking the palm. A rumbling purr filled her ears as the cat settled at her feet.

She spread her skirts and sat back down on the stone bench, a knowing smile on her face.

Marisa awoke with a start, feeling something wet against her skin. She turned her head; her hand, outstretched in sleep, was now an object of play for the kitten, who nipped and lapped.

"The basket for you," she said, getting up from the bed and placing the kitten in his temporary quarters. From her window, Marisa could see that the sun had just risen and the grass was fresh with dew. Unlatching the window, she opened it, enjoying the cool breeze against her skin.

Such an odd dream.

Marisa laughed softly. Perhaps she should consult the mysterious Mistress Buck and demand an answer.

She simply shrugged her shoulders.

'Twas only caprice.

Chapter Thirteen

"'Tis I, MacHeath. I've a message for the countess," announced the weary traveler, whose clothes were caked in mud and dirt, evidence of his long ride across the length of England and back across the border into Scotland.

"Pass on, MacHeath," boomed the voice of the guard at the gate, adding, "Will you be wantin' a wee dram of whiskey to cleanse yourself of the Sassenach dust?"

The man called MacHeath rode his lathered brown mount through the narrow gate into the large courtyard. "I'll be wanting it when I've done delivering my message to the countess." He dismounted, removing a leather pouch from inside the black cloak he wore. "Just you be seeing that there still be some for me when I've finished."

The other man laughed heartily as MacHeath continued on his way into the castle. He'd worn out several strong horses on his mission. MacHeath shuddered to think of the young laird Cameron being forced to live the remainder of his life amongst the English, having been bound by the Stuart's command to wed with one of their women. To MacHeath, it was an unfair banishment from all that Scotland had to offer, even if the young laird was getting an English earldom in the bargain.

He knocked on the thick door of the countess's solar.

A young maid of fourteen years opened the door.

"I seek the Countess of Tairne."

"Bid him enter, Janet," spoke an older woman's softly burred voice.

MacHeath moved into the room. He spotted the woman he sought, surrounded by her two daughters-in-law, one heavy with child, the other with her month-old son in her arms, and their retainers. Dropping to one knee, he handed the countess the leather pouch.

"Leave me," she said.

At the insistence of the Countess of Tairne, everyone quit the chamber. Alone, she broke the seal on the pouch, withdrawing the thick vellum sheets. She paused before she read the contents, fearing what the man she had written to had to say. *Faith, what a stupid fool she had been*, she thought as she gazed out the tower window, enjoying the sight of their herd of black Galloway cattle grazing contentedly. That her idiotic vanity had lead her to commit such a rash act, and by doing so, perhaps lose the one person she loved before all others—her youngest son, Cameron— made the countess curse her folly.

Would her proud son ever find it in himself to

forgive her her rash mistake? She had shamed
not only him, but herself by her addle-brained
reaction to the alterations a destructive bitch had
wrought on him.

She picked up one of her favorite possessions,
a highly polished mirror of silver with a border of
precious jewels. It had been a gift from Cameron,
the jewel of her heart, in remembrance of her
birthday. *Beauty deserves to gaze upon Beauty,* the
note he had sent along read. The countess lifted
it up and stared into the depths. What she saw
reflected was a still-beautiful woman who looked
more like the older sister of her sons than their
mother—a woman whom time favored, whose
blond hair still retained its deep shine and color,
whose sapphire-blue eyes still sparkled with vital-
ity. All this she had passed along to her youngest
son. His angelic male beauty was a mirror of
her own feminine features. He alone of all her
children possessed her looks.

Spoilt, willful, and cursed with a goddess's own
vanity, Alanna Maxwell Buchanan had wed the
virile Earl of Tairne when she was a lass of fourteen. Her husband had worshipped her, as did her
children. Alanna had basked in their adoration,
until that fateful night when it had all crumbled
around her slim shoulders.

If she could only recapture that one night, take
back the scream of horror which escaped her
lips. As if it had been burned into her mind the
same way the scars had been seared into her
son's flesh, she recalled Cameron's arrival that
evening. There had been no warning, no prep-
aration for the sight which greeted the family. He
had arrived without servants, having avoided the
long, dangerous ride through England, it was later learned, by securing passage on a ship bound

for Southerness in Solway Firth. From there he had procured a horse and ridden for the hills of home.

Hers had not been the only gasp when he pushed back the monk-like cowl that covered his face, before removing the dark cloak. It had, however, been her eyes he had sought with the one remaining to him—her voice that he needed to hear, her arms that should have comforted him, soothed him. Instead, Alanna had risen, frozen momentarily as her eyes locked with his solitary orb. In place of her handsome son was a scarred, crippled stranger, thin and wan. Sometimes at night, in the silence of her mind, she could hear the echo of that scream, of the horror it must have conveyed to all there. "No," she gasped at first in a faint voice. *"No!"* she had shouted, fleeing the room, taking to her bed.

It had been her husband, Angus, father to her bairns, who had finally forced her to see reason. Having shut herself off from everyone for almost a week, grieving for what she perceived was the loss of her perfect child, Alanna had reluctantly let him enter her bedchamber.

"Alanna," he had said, "Ye canna stay here forever, lass. Yer son has need of ye."

She shrugged her shoulders in response.

He slapped his hand across her table, scattering the many glass bottles of scent, uncaring that they smashed onto the stone floor. "Yer a bloody fool, woman, if you canna stop thinking of anyone save yerself," he thundered. "Yer acting as if yer bairn is dead. Well," Angus declared, "he is alive. Do ye ken, Alanna? *Alive.*" She could still feel his powerful hands gripping her as he shook her, forcing her to look at him. "De ye nae ken that it hurts me to see him this way? He is my son,"

Angus said, his voice filled with pain. "But I love
the lad, come what may. I dinna care about his
face as long as he is alive." He thrust her from
him, turning his wide back to her as he collected
his thoughts. "Did ye not think I ken that you
loved him more than Kenneth or Duncan?" he
questioned, referring to their older sons, when he
faced her once again. "You love him more than
you do me," Angus added on a sigh.

Alanna's blue eyes widened in shock. "'Tis nae
true, Angus."

"Alanna, 'tis true," he avowed. Angus's gray eyes
held no condemnation. "Dinna dispute what you
canna change, my love. That is nae why I sought
you out."

"You wish to lie with me?" she asked bluntly.

Angus gave his wife a bittersweet smile. "Aye,
lass, that I shall always want to do till they plant
me beneath this earth, but 'tis nae the reason."

"Then what?"

When Angus spoke, his deep voice echoed within the large room. "I came to to tell ye to stop
whimpering, woman. Yer his mother, the woman
who birthed him. Put aside yer own pain. Think
of Cameron, and nae yerself." He narrowed his
eyes. "De ye think ye can do that? Or is it too
much to ask of yerself?" With that, Angus left her
alone.

Her husband's words had broken through
Alanna's self-absorption, forcing her to examine
her behavior.

It had been too late to make a difference.

Cameron had withdrawn from his family. Physically, he was there, though he kept to his rooms,
preferring to eat his meals in private. He drank,
and when he did so his tongue was sharper,
colder.

Alanna sought him out. Instead of love in his blue gaze she saw only disappointment. Instead of a mouth curved in a welcoming smile, she saw only a mocking twist. She tried to explain, to seek his forgiveness.

Her son rebuffed her every attempt.

Alanna sadly realized that a part of her son had died at the hands of the woman who'd disfigured him, and another part when she ignored his agony, placing her own torment above his very real pain.

Her failure haunted her every waking moment. From her open window she could hear the eager, excited squeals of children. Her grandchildren. The sons and daughters of her two eldest boys.

He'd even tried to deny her his daughter. Alanna was well aware that her son had a bastard daughter hidden on the estate. Meg, Kenneth's wife, had informed Alanna of Cameron's affair with one of her ladies, an impoverished cousin. Cam had stubbornly refused her offer to house the woman within the castle until after the birth of the child. The bairn, no matter that it hadn't been conceived within the bonds of marriage, was still a Buchanan and deserved to be treated as such, to be part of their large family.

Alanna beseeched her husband to use his influence on their son, but Angus refused, telling her that Cam was the bairn's father, and the child was his responsibility.

She waited for Cameron, certain that he would want his child to know its family. When months passed, she confronted him, demanding to see her grandaughter. "De ye nae see that she deserves to be amongst her family? That she should know her aunts and uncles, her cousins, and her grandparents?"

His sharp laughter froze the blood in her veins, as did his harsh words. "She isna a trophy, Mother, to be displayed by you as if a battleprize. She is *my* daughter. Her mother is dead, may God grant her soul peace, so 'tis for me to see that the bairn is provided for."

"Nae," she protested, "I think . . ."

"I dinna give a tinker's damn for your thoughts, Mother," Cam stated. "Now leave me in peace."

Alanna reluctantly relented. Her vanity had cost her her beloved son and now, it seemed, his child.

The years slipped by. Even though she'd discovered that a foster family cared for the child, she respected Cameron's wishes to keep her distance. At least until she overheard him talking to Angus on the day King Charles's messenger arrived.

She had heard the servants' excited chatter about a rider wearing the king's livery. Deciding to see what it was all about, Alanna went to her husband's chambers. The door was ajar; inside sat Angus and Cameron, a chess board on the table between them. Making certain that no one was about, Alanna eavesdropped without hesitation, fearing that if she made her presence known, she would be dismissed ere she could learn anything of value.

She listened as Cam spoke to his father of the king's plans for his future. A marriage with an English heiress, an earldom for her favored son. He would have what they could not provide: power, wealth, a title of equal rank to his father's. Alanna waited, her breathing slowed. Would he take this Royal favor? Or, would he thrust it aside, too proud to accept the king's gratitude? Angus's deep voice questioned their youngest son. "Will ye accept the Stuart's offer?"

After what seemed like an eternity, Cam answered, "Aye, I will."

Alanna closed her eyes and said a silent prayer of thanksgiving.

"I must trust ye, Father, with the welfare of my bairn," Cam said. "Elsbeth has been well cared for, though should anything happen to me I would have you see to her. She is *my* child, have nae doubt about that."

Hearing the next words that came from Cam's lips was like swallowing a brew made from bitter nettles, Alanna thought as she fought back tears.

"She is a bonny lass, father. A wee version of myself when younger—and, of course," he added bitterly, "Mother."

"I shall not fail the lass, son," Angus promised.

Alanna withdrew. She waited until her son was safely away to England before she made a move. She was, after all, the Countess of Tairne, the child's grandmother. Whilst her son was in England, she set about achieving her goal: to unite the child with her family. She had accomplished her goal with coercion, half-truths, bribery, but Alanna Maxwell Buchanan had no regrets. Her grandchild now resided under their roof, despite Angus's angry grumblings. He, too, was captivated by the lass; so much so that he wouldn't return her to her foster family.

Her stomach rumbled. She had skipped the morning's meal to ride with Cam's daughter. The child was a natural rider, much as her father had been, and was. Elsbeth rode her pony like a border queen, wild and unafraid, her long blond hair, bleached pale by the sun, flowing about her small shoulders, her blue eyes—Cam's blue eyes—bright and clear as a loch.

Alanna spread thick orange marmalade on an oatcake, took a bite, then poured herself a drink of cold water from the silver ewer on her table. She realized that she was putting off reading the letter. She had put aside her considerable pride when she wrote to Jamie Covington, begging for news of her son. Not knowing if Cam had told his friend about their bitter estrangement, Alanna had volunteered only that she and her youngest son weren't as close as they had been once. She had further explained to Jamie that she and Angus wished to send gifts to Cameron and his English bride and thought he could tell them where they should be sent.

Coward, Alanna mocked herself. She had no way of knowing if Jamie had shown her letter to Cam, or if Cam had forbidden his friend to divulge any information. The only way to find out was to open the sealed document.

Angus Buchanan, fifth Earl of Tairne, considered himself a lucky man. He had a wife he loved, considered one of the finest beauties in Scotland, three strong sons, assorted grandchildren, good friends, loyal clansmen, and an estate which provided all of his family with a home and food.

His roving glance took in all of the people seated at his table in the Great Hall. Both his older sons were there, as were their wives, including several of his grandchildren. Four older lads and one lass were allowed to join the adults at supper.

Kenneth and Duncan resembled him; each man was a bear of a fellow, with thick, shaggy dark brown hair and beards, and soft gray eyes. Good, solid, dependable men.

At the other end of the table sat his lady. Angus returned the dazzling smile she bestowed on him with one of his own. These many years wed, and still he hungered for her with the fervor of a youth. Angus watched with a fond eye as she instructed her eldest granddaughter, Anthea, in how to daintily eat a game bird.

So much did he still love her that he could refuse her nothing. Angus had never been able to deny Alanna anything she desired. His big heart accepted her as she was, with no regrets. Well, perhaps one: the night that Cameron had come home to them. Her outburst had wounded their youngest beyond the repair of mere kind words and a simple "I am sorry." She who revered beauty had been forced to confront the destruction of that which she considered perfect. Unable to bear the sight of her beloved son, she had fled. It was the only time in his marriage when he had considered beating Alanna. For that, for the bleak look she placed into their son's remaining eye, he would never forgive her. No matter that he loved her beyond reason, Angus thought, he could never forgive Alanna that mistake or forget Cameron's pain. He'd forced her to see that it had been a grave error in judgment on her part.

Before their evening meal, she had come to him, asking for his help. Angus was secretly amused that Alanna would play the role of humble wife, seeking aid. She hadn't sought his help when she decided to remove Cameron's wee lassie from her foster sanctuary, though he was right glad she had, for Elsbeth was a delight. 'Twas as if time had turned back the years and a female version of his youngest son stood before him. Or, truth be told, Alanna as a child.

"I have something to say," Angus announced.

Instantly, all activity at the table ceased. All eyes focused on the Earl of Tairne.

"Today my wife received news of Cameron."

Voices spoke loudly, demanding answers to diverse questions. "Where is he?" "Is he safe?" "With whom has he wed?" "Does he return to us soon?"

Cam's abrupt departure for England's capital had left his family filled with questions. The king's letter of command had not specified whom he was to wed, only that a suitable bride, a rich woman of noble birth who would bring her husband an earldom, had been found. His family knew that Cameron Buchanan's loyalty to the Stuart king was unshakable and that he would bend to the king's will, whether it was his choice or not.

The Countess of Tairne answered their queries as best she could. "Cameron was wed in Whitehall Palace with the king in attendance. The lady that King Charles chose is the only surviving child of the Earl of Derran, Marisa Fitzgerald. With their union, Cameron was granted the title Earl of Derran."

Conversation buzzed around the table.

Kenneth demanded, "Our brother Cameron now wears an English coronet?"

Angus answered his firstborn. "He does."

"Then," Kenneth said with a wide grin, "here's to the best kind of English earl, a true Scotsman born." He stood up, raising his silver wine goblet. "God grant good health and long life to the Earl of Derran and his lady."

"Aye," Angus responded, lifting his own glass

to his lips and drinking deeply.

"Will Cam be returning to us and bring his countess?" asked Duncan.

"I dinna think we shall see our Cam return to Scotland for many months," Alanna said, adding sadly, "perhaps years. The estates of the Fitzgeralds are vast and are scattered throughout England. 'Twould seem that some were destroyed during the usurper Cromwell's time." She folded her hands, directing her glance to her husband. "'Tis why Tairne and I have this day made up our minds to journey to England."

"What?" was the simultaneous question from her sons.

"You dinna have anything wrong with your hearing, my lads," Alanna said with a bemused smile.

"Aye," Tairne agreed. "We may not be as wealthy as the Sassenach woman Cameron now calls wife," he stated, "but we can still provide proper gifts for the celebration of his marriage."

"Aye, that we can," Kenneth chimed in, exchanging glances with his sibling. "We will show the English just how we Scots can honor one of our own. When do ye expect to leave?"

Angus spoke quickly. "Within the week."

Meg asked, "What about Elsbeth?"

"She comes with us," Alanna affirmed. "The bairn belongs with her father."

Angus knew how difficult it would be for his wife to give up custody of her grandchild now that she had found her, especially as Elsbeth was such a potent reminder of Cameron. The child represented the last true link to their son; relinquishing her meant losing Cam once again.

Duncan asked, "What if his wife decides otherwise?"

"I dinna know," Alanna said. "We must trust that Cameron will do what he believes is best for his daughter."

Chapter Fourteen

Marisa, riding Remus, raced her mount across the green Dorset hills. The day was beautiful, warm and sunny with puffs of white clouds floating overhead. This would be one of her last opportunities to ride as she pleased. Tonight was the ball in honor of her marriage, with the local gentry invited. She couldn't believe the number of invitations her grandmother had sent.

Her husband had merely accepted the announcement of the affair with what she thought was good grace. That surprised Marisa. She would have thought that he would have nothing whatsoever to do with a function where he would be on public display.

On further reflection, her Scottish husband seemed a man of surprises, from the delightful gift of the kitten to the incorporation of her device of the swan with his of the stag on a new seal he'd ordered made for the earldom. The gesture had touched a responsive cord in her heart. As a way of expressing her appreciation, she embroidered two very special handkerchiefs for him. This morning she gave them to his new manservant, Kendall, with instructions that he present them to the earl as he dressed for the ball. She'd been glad to see Kendall again, for he was another part of the treasured past, another link to her father.

Marisa's time had been spent going over plans for the rebuilding of FitzHall and talking to her grandmother, so she hadn't yet had a chance to question her husband about the highwaymen who had attempted to rob them. Whilst they tarried here in Dorset, there had been no more incidents, no further trouble.

Ahead of her on the path, to the right, loomed a stone cottage. Marisa brought her stallion to a halt, pondering whether or not to proceed. 'Twas the home of Mistress Buck. Her curiosity had been roused since first she heard of the woman, so when she set out this morning, she decided to ride by and take a look.

No sooner had she stopped than the door to the cottage creaked open. Out stepped a woman who could have been anywhere from twenty to forty. Marisa had been expecting a crone, bent and haggard. Instead, the woman appeared vital and strong.

"I have been waiting for you." The woman's clear voice carried over the short distance.

Marisa froze. Mistress Buck was clearly addressing her. Marisa hesitated for a moment, weighing the options open to her. She could ride away, pretending that she had never heard the woman's words, or she could ride forth, accepting the invitation.

With a smile on her face, Marisa urged Remus forward.

The large cottage was surrounded by a fence made also of stone. Grazing behind the house were one placid milk cow and three big sheep, a ram and two ewes.

"Good day to you, countess," Mistress Buck said as she watched Marisa ride up, opening up the wooden gate. "Please, do come inside," she urged. "'Tis not what you are used to, perhaps, though I think you will find it pleasant enough."

Marisa slid down from her seat atop the big horse, wrapping the reins around an iron post. "You said you were expecting me?"

"Indeed," Mistress Buck responded, casting an admiring glance at the white stallion. She produced a carrot from the pocket of her plain white apron. "With your permission, countess?"

Marisa nodded her head.

Mistress Buck patted the stallion's neck, murmuring soothing words to the horse while she feed him the treat. Remus quickly gobbled the offering. "He has the heart of a champion, my lady."

"Aye," Marisa agreed with pride, "he does that."

"Would you care for something to drink?" Mistress Buck asked as she made her way back to her open door.

"I would, thank you," Marisa answered as she followed the woman into her house.

Marisa hadn't known what to expect of the house, nor of the woman. Both appeared tidy. There was a smell of spices filling the air as she entered. The wooden furniture was simple and spare. In the hearth a caldron was hung. Marisa watched as Mistress Buck went over to it. Taking a wooden ladle, she stirred the contents of the iron pot.

"'Tis only my midday meal, I assure you," Mistress Buck announced. "I know what many of the folk around here think, that I'm a witch, a worshipper of old Nick." She straightened, facing Marisa. "'Tis not so, my lady."

"If I believed you were I would not be here," Marisa said, then added with a smile, "nor would you."

"I practice the healing arts," Mistress Buck admitted. "To some, them that don't understand, that makes me different, suspect. Others, like the old countess, accept me for what I can do, the services that I can provide. Your grandmother is a wise woman, my lady. Life has dealt her many cruel blows, though still she survives." Mistress Buck fixed Marisa with a direct glance, her eyes the palest blue that Marisa had ever seen. "You are much like her in that respect, I would wager."

"I count that as a compliment," Marisa said.

"As well you should, my lady." Mistress Buck walked to a near corner and lifted the lid off a crock. Taking two wooden cups, she plunged each into the crock and set them on her scrubbed beechwood table. "'Tis not the fine wines you are used to, my lady, but it be good."

Marisa pulled out the sturdy chair and sat down. She lifted the cup, tasting the contents. It was fresh, cold milk, thick with cream.

"Would you share a meal with me?"

Marisa surmised from the slightly hesitant way that Mistress Buck broached the question that she wasn't used to entertaining guests at her table. Her reputation no doubt helped keep many from her door. Marisa, having spent years in Ireland, was familiar with women who practiced the healing arts. Such women were respected, given positions of importance in a village or household, especially in her cousin Killroone's castle. And, if this woman did possess the sight, much honor would be accorded her.

Marisa had met an older woman once who was blessed with the ability to see. 'Twas when she was newly brought to Ireland, smuggled out of England via Wales by her other kinsman, the Earl of Ravensmoor. She was a child, wary of strangers. The old woman was great-aunt to Killroone's countess, a member of his family. One day, perhaps a month after her arrival in Ireland, Marisa was playing with one of her cousins in a mock archery contest, when the old woman came upon them. She watched the children for several minutes before she beckoned the young Marisa to come to her. Marisa did so; the woman took Marisa's hand in hers, closing her eyes for several moments before she snapped them open, intoning, "You will be cherished daughter, adored wife, and loving mother to one name; love from love will spring. Much will be asked, though the rewards are worth the struggle."

Marisa shivered. It had been a long time since she had thought of that. *Adored wife. Loving mother.* Would either come to pass?

"Something troubles thee?" Mistress Buck asked as she placed a bowl of thick rabbit stew before Marisa.

Marisa snapped her head up, removing the riding gloves she wore. "No. 'Twas just a memory from when I was a child. Being here brought it back, 'twas all."

"From the look your face wears, I would say 'twas not a sweet memory."

Marisa steepled her hands, bracing her chin against them. "Not unpleasant so much as puzzling."

Mistress Buck did not press Marisa further for details. Instead, she bowed her head and spoke a prayer of gratitude for her bounty.

The stew was filling, with a savory taste. Marisa was surprised by how comfortable she felt in this stranger's house, eating her cooking, enjoying the quiet moments. She couldn't explain the sudden realization that she felt she could trust this woman.

Mistress Buck cleared away the bowls, setting them aside. "You were curious about me, were you not?"

Marisa was pleased by the bluntness of her hostess's question.

"Aye, that I was," Marisa responded, her voice just as direct. "Since I am the last of the Fitzgeralds and am made by the king himself Countess of Derran in my own right, I must needs keep a keen eye on all who live on my lands, especially those who live within the borders of my seat."

"And most especially those about whom there is much talk," Mistress Buck declared.

Marisa smiled in acknowledgment. "Just so."

"I have nothing to hide, my lady. I can assure you that what I do has harmed no one. 'Tis my only wish, my only desire, to help where I can." Mistress Buck stood up, her mass of fine curls falling about her shoulders. "My skill is a gift from God, my lady."

"And what of your gift of sight?" Marisa asked, "Is that also a divine boon?"

GET YOUR 4 FREE BOOKS NOW—A $19.96 Value!

Mail the Free Book Certificate Today!

Get Four Books Totally FREE— A $19.96 Value

▼ Tear Here and Mail Your FREE Book Card Today! ▼

PLEASE RUSH
MY FOUR FREE
BOOKS TO ME
RIGHT AWAY!

Leisure Romance Book Club
PO Box 1234
65 Commerce Road
Stamford CT 06920- 4563

AFFIX
STAMP
HERE

Mistress Buck managed a sadly sweet smile. "To answer in truth, my lady, I must say that 'tis often both a blessing and a curse."

"How so?"

"'Tis a blessing when I can be of aid to someone, to deliver tidings of joy; a curse when I see but cannot change. Much as you have wealth and power, my lady," she pointed out, "and can promise comfort and security, though it cannot keep your family safe from harm or hurt, should that be their fate."

That thought gave Marisa pause.

"Can you do this at will or is it merely chance?"

Mistress Buck shrugged her shoulders. "I cannot summon the sight. 'Tis either there or not." She moved closer to Marisa, taking hold of Marisa's slender hand. "You have many questions for which you seek answers."

Marisa could feel a gentle warmth in the hand holding hers. She studied the intensely pale blue eyes of Mistress Buck. In those eyes she saw a calm honesty that she could rely on.

"Aye, that I do," Marisa answered.

"Then we shall have to find your answers."

"Now?"

"No," Mistress Buck responded. "I will come later this day to you—with your permission?"

"Granted," Marisa stated.

"And the Dark Lady must be there also."

"The Dark Lady?"

"You have a kinswoman, do you not, who shadows your path and shares your homecoming?"

"Aye," Marisa replied, "my cousin, the Lady Brianna."

"'Twould be best if she were there also. I cannot promise the sight, though I will try my best." Mistress Buck released Marisa's hand. "I shall be gone ere your guests arrive."

Marisa stood up. "Then I shall expect you, Mistress Buck." She made her way to the door, pulling her kid gloves back on her strong, slender hands. With her hand on the latch, Marisa said, "My gratitude for your hospitality this day."

"And mine for your clarity of thought, my lady."

At the sincere compliment, Marisa's mouth curled into a soft smile. "I bid you good day."

Once outside, Marisa released Remus from his temporary restraint, climbed onto a sturdy mounting block and lifted herself into the saddle, adjusting her long skirt. Instead of leaving as she had come, Marisa backed her horse up and then urged him to take the fence.

He sailed over it as if the legendary Pegasus was his sire, a jubilant Marisa on his back.

Cameron rode Romulus through the cobbled streets of the small village of Fitzpemberton, looking for the Crown and Star Inn. Just two hours ago he had received a message from Jamie Covington, asking for Cam to meet him there.

As he made his way down the narrow street where the inn was located, Cam took note of the reaction of the villagers. He seemed to be the focus of their collective attention, with some folks outright gaping at him. He knew that he could expect more of the same at the damnable ball being held this night. Why had he consented to be a part of it? To humor his new grandmother? Perhaps. Or to take back some measure of respect for himself? His marriage had plunged him into a world he had thought never to inhabit again. Now, perforce, he could no longer maintain his place in the protecting shadows. The mantle of the Earl of Derran demanded that he be seen, even if only occasionally.

These past few days had forced his hand, as the demands of his new earldom necessitated his personal involvement. An added bonus was that he was often in the company of his wife and her—*their* he corrected himself—bailiff, Robin de Warth. Each had a chance to gage the mettle of the other. It had been an education of sorts for himself, he thought, as he learned just how much work was involved in the running of vast estates; being the third son of a family with only one entailed property, he never had to concern himself with Tairne affairs, and as agent for the king, he was involved with court business in only a minor manner. But from his experiences there, and with other lords of the realm, Cam realized that his wife was, even amongst men, unique. She was loyal to her family name and loyal to the responsibilites that name carried. As long as estates provided them with a steady income, most nobles, he had observed, cared little for daily involvement in their maintenance.

The Crown and Star was visible at the end of the lane. Cam was deeply puzzled by Jamie's sudden appearance. He had dispatched a messenger to Jamie after the attack on his wife and had been waiting eagerly for Jamie's reply. 'Twould seem that whatever information Jamie had found out could not be trusted to a courier.

A lad emerging from a baker's shop with two loaves under his arm paused when he saw the man attired all in black atop the huge white stallion. He blinked several times before yelling out, "A good day te ye, yer lordship."

Cam swung his head to the left side, catching the welcoming grin on the boy's face. "And to you, laddie," Cam responded before continuing on his way. That single friendly gesture did much to lighten Cam's mood as he rode into the yard of the inn. He dismounted, tossing the reins to a groom of middle years.

Entering the establishment, Cam searched the premises quickly for his friend.

A tall, thickset, balding man approached Cam. "Can I be of help?"

"I am to meet someone here," Cameron said "James Covington."

"Be you then the Earl of Derran?" the man inquired politely.

Cam nodded. "I am he," he stated simply.

The innkeeper apologized. "'Tis sorry I am that I did not know you, my lord."

"'Dinna trouble yourself," Cam insisted. "Now, where is my friend?"

"He has engaged a private room, my lord. If you will be so kind as to follow me." The innkeeper made his way to the winding stairs.

Cam followed the innkeeper slowly. He knew that he must conserve what strength he had in his leg for the dance later. If any one good thing could be said to have come from his limp, he thought ironically, 'twould be that he no longer had to partner all and sundry. He could stand at the sidelines and merely observe. Cam had never enjoyed the formal dances of the court-in-exile. Back then, he'd had too many other more pleasant ways to pass his time.

The innkeeper knocked on the door.

It swung open, revealing a weary-looking James Covington.

"Jamie," Cameron said happily.

"Will you be wanting anything, my lord?" the innkeeper asked.

"I took the liberty of ordering some ale for us, Cam," Jamie stated.

"Then 'tis fine with me, Jamie," Cam answered as he strode through the doorway, removing his plumed hat and cape.

"I shall take my leave of you," the innkeeper announced. "My Lord Derran," he said with reverance in his tone, "Good sir," he directed at Jamie.

The two men embraced when the door closed. "What brings you to Dorset, Jamie?" Cam asked. "I had thought to have only a paper communication from you."

"I was most disturbed when your letter reached me," Jamie insisted, handing a cold tankard of ale to Cam. "'Tis most fortunate that the countess and the lady Brianna were unharmed."

"Aye, I agree." Cam took a seat in a thickly padded horsehair chair. "I regret that I had to kill the whoresons swiftly, for I would have enjoyed getting the information I needed from them." He took a long drink of the ale. "Speaking of information, what have you found out?"

Jamie took a draft of his ale. "Nothing, I am afraid."

"Damnation!" Cam exploded, slamming the pewter tankard down on the small table next to his chair, sloshing foam on the wood and on his gloved left hand. "There was truly nothing?"

"I tried my best, Cam."

"I dinna have a doubt of that, Jamie."

"I set my most trusted men on the assignment," Jamie explained, "since I knew that 'twould not be prudent to have this attack upon the newly created Earl of Derran bandied about the court. Nor," he added, "did I inform his Majesty, as per your wishes.

"And you are certain, Cam, that the men who attempted this crime indeed sought you?"

Cam, momentarily mollified, responded, "Aye. I heard one of them demand of my wife the whereabouts of the earl. They were not mere highwaymen taking a chance on a rich bounty. They rode from behind, not ahead. We were hunted like prize stags in the Royal forest." He mopped up the spill on his glove with a handkerchief pulled from the inner pocket of his doublet jacket.

"You must face the fact, Cam, that we may never know who hired the unknown assassins," Jamie said sympathetically. "Whilst you were in the king's service you made many enemies. Mayhap one sought revenge. I would imagine the list would be long should you decide to compile one."

Cam shrugged his broad shoulders. "Aye, long and dangerous," he said. "I dinna want to spend the rest of my life looking over my shoulder, Jamie, waiting for the knife, the sword, or the bullet. Nor," he added with emphasis, "do I wish my wife to live like that." Cam stood up, walking to a small window that overlooked the back alley. "I had thought that all a part of the past that was long since buried. 'Twould seem that my sudden reappearance in London has disturbed someone greatly."

Jamie said, "Then I suggest that you hire men to watch over you and your family."

"I have seen to keeping my wife and her family secure. The Fitzgeralds are well loved in Dorset, so it was not difficult to convince de Warth, my wife's bailiff, to help me find men who would have a care for my wife and her family. Were this a hundred or more years ago, the earldom would have had a private force at its disposal. She and hers are safe as long as we remain here."

"But I thought you were to leave for another of the countess's estates?"

Cam turned back to face his friend. "We are set to quit this place ere the week is over."

"You could not dissuade your wife?"

Cam's mouth curved into a sardonic smile. "My English wife has a strong will, Jamie. When she is set on a course, 'tis hard to put her from it. This place, FitzHall, is very important to her."

"What about you, Cam? Are you important to her?" Jamie inquired.

"I dinna know, Jamie," Cam answered honestly.

Jamie glanced at Cam. He knew that this was no moment to press Cam for answers. Perhaps that would come later. In lieu of examining Cam's reply, he said, "You asked me earlier why I had come. Several reasons in truth. The first being to tell you that a messenger arrived the day you left for Dorset."

"A messenger?" Cam asked. "From where?"

"Scotland."

"My daughter?" His voice was a stark whisper. "Has something happened to her?"

"No, 'tis nothing to do with Elsbeth."

"Then who sent the courier?"

"Your mother."

The two words chilled the room. Cam's features were taughtly drawn. His nostrils flared in anger.

"What does the Countess of Tairne have to communicate to you?"

"She sought information about you and your bride."

"How dare she?" Cam demanded.

"She is your mother, Cam."

"She is the woman who gave birth to me, Jamie." Bitterness underscored each word.

Cam had never spoken of his return to Scotland save for the birth of his daughter. Jamie was aware that something must have happened, for whenever he mentioned Scotland Cam grew taciturn.

Jamie probed the raw scar. "What caused this breach between you?"

Cam fought the rising tide of hurt that welled inside of him even now. If he closed his eyes, he could bring the scene fresh to mind. He—*the favored child*, she had often called him—standing there like a prisoner awaiting his sentence. She could never rebuff him, or so he had foolishly thought. She loved him. Her love might help ease the interminable anguish.

Then, the unthinkable. His beautiful mother had run screaming from the sight of her flawed son.

Did he want to confess this to Jamie? See the pity that would surely flare in his friend's eyes? *No!* He could not. He was a man who needed no one's solace or charity.

"I canna speak of it."

Jamie understood that it would be futile to press Cam further when he chose not to speak. "As you will then, Cam."

Cam manuvered a change of topic. "You said there were several reasons for your journey here?"

"Aye. 'Twould seem that messengers are now making my once quiet house a regular stop. At times I feel as though I am on the pilgrim trail with so many seeking my blessing," Jamie said with a spark of humor in his brown eyes. "Just three days after your letter reached me, I had one from your lady wife, inviting me to attend a ball in honor of your wedding."

"Marisa sent you an invitation?"

"In her own hand."

"She said nothing to me."

"She bade me keep it a surprise, though she was not to know that you had already contacted me after the incident with the highwaymen. 'Tis why I rented rooms at this inn instead of coming directly to you."

"Then you shall not disappoint my lady, Jamie." Cam took hold of his hat and cloak. "I must return ere someone gets suspicious.

"Until later." Cam paused, adding, "I promise to be properly surprised by your sudden appearance at the ball." He adjusted his black plumed hat upon his dark blond hair. "'Twas considerate of my lady to ask that you be present. Quite considerate indeed," he repeated softly to himself as he closed the door behind him.

Chapter Fifteen

Marisa searched through her jewel casket, looking for just what she should wear to this evening's ball. Charity had finished arranging her long chestnut hair into an artfully composed coiffure, and she wanted a pair of earrings that would dazzle. Tonight she was determined to enjoy herself to the fullest.

At last she found what she was looking for. Pearls and diamonds. A perfect choice, she thought, for the dress she would be wearing.

She rummaged through a small porcelain box that contained the black patches frequently worn by women to enhance a particular feature. She placed a small round one near the curve of her lower lip. It remained there for a few moments before she hastily removed it. Every woman who came this evening, she was sure, would be following the accustomed style. She would not.

Marisa cast a glance at her bottles of perfume, wondering which scent to use. She wanted something that would have an impact, something that would leave the impression she desired. She sniffed each bottle in turn, coming back to the fragrance contained in the small, hand-painted china pot. It was more of a cream, blended carefully and exclusively for her in France. What had the king called her? "An English rose." Dipping her middle finger into the pot, Marisa stroked the sweet smelling potion across her left wrist, along the stem of her throat. She closed her eyes for a moment; her imagination conjured up another hand, larger than hers, masculine, with a long, supple index finger, slippery smooth with the creamy scent, sliding between her full breasts, leaving a hot trail of sensation behind. Her nipples burst into tight buds against the silk of her chemise.

A repeated knocking on her door abruptly ended the flight of fantasy that her mind had taken.

Startled, Marisa opened her eyes and caught a glimpse of herself in the wide gilt mirror that hung on the paneled wall. Her nipples were indeed visible through the silk fabric. Experimentally, she took her own hand and cradled her breast, feeling the taut proof of her excitement. As before, when she was with Cam in his room at the inn, she felt a deep throbbing tingle between her legs that she didn't comprehend.

The knocking persisted.

Marisa, clad only in her chemise and silk petticoat, opened the door slightly. When she saw it was her cousin, she welcomed Brianna in.

"Why ever did you do it?" Brianna asked as she marched into the room.

Marisa gave her cousin a quixotic smile. "'Twas an inspiration," she confessed. "When I saw the fabric, I knew no one could wear it save you."

"You flatter me, coz," Brianna said, "as you well know that the material would have suited you, too." Brianna moved restlessly about the room. "Have you forgotten that I am still in mourning?" Brianna asked.

"I did not forget, sweet cousin," Marisa said, defending her actions. "I thought only to give you a respite from the continual bleakness of your costume. 'Tis for this night only, and I would have you bask in the attention you so deserve."

"I cannot," Brianna insisted.

Marisa decided to try another tactic. "Will you not do it just to please me?"

"Why is it so important to you?"

"Because," Marisa explained, "you are the sister I did not have." She drew her cousin to the window seat, where the late afternoon sun glinted through the mullioned windows. "Much as you try to hide it, Brianna, I do see the sadness in your eyes. I thought that the gown would give you joy, if only for a night. Was I wrong?"

Brianna could not give voice to another lie, for there were far too many on her soul. The gown truly was most beautiful, fit for a queen. Brianna hadn't been able to resist running her hand over the fabric, touching the trim that surrounded the bodice and the sleeves. "No," she admitted reluctantly, "you were not wrong, coz. The gown pleases me beyond words."

"Then you must wear it. Tonight will be a special occasion. Treat it as such. For me." Marisa added softly, "And most especially for yourself."

Brianna gave in to her cousin's persuasion. It seemed to matter so much to Marisa; besides, she intended to remain silent and unobtrusive. As a widow, she would not be expected to participate in the evening's dances. This night was for Marisa and the stranger who was her husband.

"You win, coz," Brianna conceded.

Marisa laughed. "I do not consider this a victory, Brianna, merely good judgment on your part." Now was the time, she decided, to tell Brianna about her visit to Mistress Buck. "You should have ridden with me this day, for I made the acquaintance of Mistress Buck."

"And what did you think?"

"That she is no witch."

"Had she been," Brianna wisely pointed out, "the old countess would not have harbored her. Your grandmother would do nothing to jeopardize your position as the Fitzgerald heiress."

"Nor would I," Marisa admitted. Marisa drew her legs up, wrapping her arms about her knees and resting her chin upon them. "Mistress Buck is a most interesting woman. Like no one I have ever met."

"However so?"

Marisa pondered her answer for a minute. "She was very friendly, without a false face." Marisa searched for the word that she wanted to convey her impression. "I felt comfortable with her, as if we had somehow known each other for many years, not merely moments." She threw Brianna a questioning glance. "Do you think that odd?"

Brianna shook her head. "Not at all, Marisa. 'Tis what I felt when first we met."

"She did confess to me that she has the sight."

Brianna took a deep breath. "Did she tell you aught?"

"No. She said that her ability couldn't be commanded at will, that she could but try." Marisa sliced another glance at Brianna. "Mistress Buck should be on her way here as we speak."

"She is coming here?"

"Aye. And she told me that 'twas important that you be present during visit."

Brianna's face went paler. "Why me?"

"I do not know." Marisa neglected to mention that Mistress Buck had named Brianna the "Dark Lady."

Fear hit Brianna square in the shoulders, like a heavy weight almost crushing her. What did this woman want with her? Could Mistress Buck see into the secrets of her heart? Would she expose Brianna? Announce to all her guilt? Would the wounds Brianna kept carefully buried be brought out into the open?

Marisa saw the sudden look of panic in Brianna's golden-brown eyes. "Is something amiss, Brianna?" she asked, concern for her cousin rising within her.

"No," Brianna lied. Once more she was forced to deny her cousin the truth.

Marisa extended her hand, taking notice of the short, bitten nails on Brianna's hands. It was the first time she had noted that her cousin's hands were less than perfect. "You can tell me anything, coz. Knew you not that ere now?"

"There is naught to tell," Brianna whispered, pulling her hand away. "I find that I am quite tired. If you will excuse me, I will take my leave of you now to rest." Brianna rose from her seat and began walking away. She took a few steps, her black skirt trailing the floor. She had lost some weight recently and her clothes were loose on her already slender frame. "I do thank you, sweet coz, for your kindness, for all your kindnesses to me. Tonight I will wear your gift proudly."

Marisa watched her leave, and as she did, she wondered what could be weighing so heavily on her cousin's mind. Had Brianna's grief sucked the very joy from her spirit like a blood-hungry leech? Had loss of love caused this? And if 'twas so, Marisa wondered, did she want any part of something that left you so devastated when your beloved was gone?

Brianna had been very different before her marriage. Killroone's sister was bright and full of life, with a constant sparkle in her eyes and a ready smile on her lips. She and Brianna had talked for hours, enjoying each other's company. It was to Marisa that Brianna confided when Donal MacBride informed Brianna that he wanted her for his wife and would put his suit before her brother. Brianna's happiness was overwhelming, especially the day that she wed the handsome Donal. Marisa remembered that she thought the romance between her cousin and Donal straight out of the troubadour tales. Then, when next she saw Brianna, her cousin was a widow swathed in black, her brown eyes haunted and tear-stained.

Was this the price of love?

Mistress Buck walked up the long path leading to the entranceway of the Fitzgerald house. Her heart was heavy. She hadn't told the Countess of Derran that already she had seen glimpses, flashes of fragmented visions, involving her. There was danger surrounding Marisa Fitzgerald. An unknown dark force intent on destruction. No clear sight arose—only vague sensations. Mistress Buck knew that she had to warn the countess, but what could she say? Would Marisa Fitzgerald think her mad?

And what of the man she saw locked in darkness? Trapped in agony? Who was he? What had he to do with the Countess of Derran? Mistress Buck was certain that he was not the enemy. His cry of pain, like that of a wounded forest creature, nagged persistently at her.

Her mind was crowded with the fleeting visions, all eager to be released. Pain throbbed across her skull. She could feel the suspicious glances of the estate workers as she moved toward the entrance. A chill settled around her shoulders even though what remained of the day was warm. Soon night would fall—and with it, she sensed, would come turmoil.

She picked up the brass knocker and rapped upon the heavy door.

A woman opened it, giving her a skeptical glance. "What do *you* want?"

Mistress Buck stood straight, refusing to back down under the quelling stare. In a clear voice she said, "I have business with the countess."

The thin woman narrowed her eyes. "What business?"

"'Tis naught of your concern," Mistress Buck stated. "If you would please tell Lady Derran that I am here."

"Wait here," the woman said and shut the door in Mistress Buck's face.

It would seem that the woman was afraid even to allow her to wait inside the house. A bittersweet smile curved Mistress Buck's mouth. Had she truly been what some deemed her, she would have made the woman pay for the insult. As it was, she would have to accept it with a calm grace and hold her tongue. Memories of her mother's trial and execution as a witch at the hands of a few self-righteous Puritans were never far from her mind. Had it not been for the old countess, she too would have met a similar fate.

The door slowly opened again. "The countess will see you," the woman announced, her voice reflecting her disbelief that the mistress of the house would request that Mistress Buck be granted a private audience in the countess's chambers.

"This is Charity," the woman said, "the countess's personal maid. She will show you to her ladyship."

"Thank you," was Mistress Buck's reply as she followed the maid up the wide staircase.

Charity gave a quick knock before she entered Marisa's sitting room. "My lady, 'tis Mistress Buck." Having made her announcement, Charity withdrew.

Marisa, who sat on a low couch, stood up, beckoning Mistress Buck. "Come. Have a glass of sherry with me."

Mistress Buck walked to the couch, taking a seat. In front of the soft couch was an oval cherrywood table; on it rested a silver tray, a bottle of Spanish wine, and two small silver goblets.

Marisa poured the rich ruby liquid into the goblets, offering one to her guest. "Have you ever tasted sherry before?"

Mistress Buck replied, "No, my lady."

Marisa gave her a wide smile. "Then you are in for a rare treat. 'Tis a bottle from one of the finest vineyards."

Mistress Buck took a tentative sip of the wine, finding that she liked the slightly nutty taste. "'Tis good indeed," she pronounced.

Marisa, clad in a soft *robe de chambre* of a deep wine color, swallowed her drink, anxious on one hand to hear if Mistress Buck could summon her sight, nervous that she would.

Mistress Buck placed her glass back on the tray. She lifted her eyes to Marisa's face, looking deeply into the other woman's green eyes. "You are surrounded, my lady, with great love, and yet," she cautioned, "there exists also envy and hatred."

"Hatred?" Marisa asked. "From whom?"

"That is not clear, my lady." Mistress Buck clasped her hands together on her lap. "My gift can at times be only a feeling, with no clear image."

"Is it someone close to hand? Can you tell that?" Marisa demanded.

Mistress Buck closed her pale blue eyes, concentrating. "No, my lady, 'tis from no one here. It follows you like a relentless hunter, one who will not be satisfied until he has drawn blood."

Marisa shivered at this information. "There was an attack on my coach after we left London," she said flatly.

"While you are here you are safe," Mistress Buck said. She took hold of one of Marisa's hands, the one that wore the gold ring of marital union. She raised her eyes to Marisa and once again gazed deeply into the countess's. Mistress Buck knew without question that the bond of marriage had yet to be consummated. The countess was a virgin bride who had yet to experience carnal pleasure. "You will know love stronger and deeper than you have ever imagined," she told Marisa. "You must trust your heart, for it will guide you when reason fails."

"Are you certain?" Marisa inquired. Where would she find this *love* that Mistress Buck spoke so convincingly about?

Or did the woman merely mouth what she thought Marisa wished to hear, not being privy to the truth of her wedded state?

"As much as I can be, my lady." Mistress Buck's face was composed. "There are reckonings to come; each will be a test of courage, and only the valiant heart will prevail." She let go of Marisa's hand. "I wish that I could tell you more. If only I could see a face, or put a name to the hatred, but I cannot."

"'Tis no matter, for I shall maintain a vigilant guard."

"Yet I sense some doubt."

"Perhaps," Marisa admitted honestly.

"I cannot force acceptance. 'Tis there or not."

"Oh," Marisa said, "I do accept what you say."

With a skeptical smile, Mistress Buck added, "What about *believe*?"

"That is another matter."

"What you unknowingly seek, my lady, you shall find, for 'tis close at hand." Mistress Buck stopped for a moment, a quiet contentment flooding her with warmth before she continued. "Journey's end comes anon." She stood up. "I will leave you to finish dressing." Mistress Buck paused. "Where is the Dark Lady?"

Marisa's lips curved into a smile at the sobriquet. "The Lady Brianna is resting in her room. I could convey whatever you have to say to her."

"I do not dispute that, my lady, but 'tis important that I myself see her."

Marisa explained, "My cousin is recently a widow who still carries much grief with her." Marisa rose also. "I do not think she will receive you."

Mistress Buck gave a deep sigh. "I can but try, if you will allow it?"

"Her rooms are down the hall, to the left."

"I bid you good-bye and God-speed, my lady."

"And I you, Mistress Buck."

Brianna, her head bowed, finished her prayers, a mother-of-pearl rosary clutched in her hand. As a Catholic in a Protestant country, Brianna kept her religion private. Her cousin was a peeress of the realm, and Brianna respected that. She knew that the English King Charles was tolerant of all faiths, though many of his subjects weren't. In London, Marisa had managed to arrange for a priest to visit Brianna. Here, it had proved difficult.

Mayhap, she thought, 'twas just as well. For even in confession she couldn't bring herself to speak of her sins, or betray the memory of the woman who had so loved her that she had broken God's holy commandment and murdered Donal MacBride. His death had been judged an unfortunate accident, though Brianna knew otherwise. Her servant, Bridget, had helped mend her after the disaster of her wedding night, had dried the copious tears she had shed after each nuptial visit, had witnessed the bruises from Donal's careless handling, had heard his incessant bragging of his skill as a lover. Bridget had begged her to leave, to return to her brother Killroone's castle.

Brianna thought how foolish and prideful she'd been. Had she chosen to seek her brother's aid, both Donal and Bridget would be alive. Well, she ammended, Bridget would still be alive. Her brother, she knew, would have killed Donal, though the fight would have been fair. Killroone would not have let the insult to his younger sister go unpunished.

Donal had been drinking that last night. She had been unwell; a severe ache in her head made her seek her bed early. Within the hour, her husband had come to her room, forcing his way in, shoving out Bridget, who had brewed her mistress a comforting herb drink. Brianna had begged him to leave her; he laughed, unfastening his breeches. She screamed in pain as he thrust into her dry body. She heard Bridget at the door, pleading to be let in, and her husband's shouts of, "Get you gone, crone. My wife and I do not wish to be disturbed."

When he finished, seconds later, he belched, swaying as he stood up. "More wine. I need more wine." Those were his last words to her as he threw back the bolt on her door, opening it so that it banged against the wall.

Brianna lay there, her skirt pushed up to her waist, her legs splayed and sore, the sticky evidence of his seed on her and the bed. Bridget had rushed in. Brianna held out her hand and Bridget had come, pulling down the silk petticoat and the striped satin skirt, tears in her eyes. "He musn't be allowed to continue to use you like a whore," she had said. Brianna recalled the determined, angry look on Bridget's face as the woman turned and left the room.

Fearing the old woman would do something that would get her punished, or perhaps even banished, Brianna forced herself from the bed. She had made her way to the hall when she saw Bridget come up behind Donal on the staircase, her arms outstretched.

"No," escaped faintly from Brianna's lips.

She had been too late. Bridget had given Donal a mighty shove, helped by the fact that Donal was drunk. Her effort had cost Bridget her life as well, for she lost her balance and fell tumbling down the stairs after him.

Brianna would never forget the sight of the two crumpled, bloody bodies in a heap at the bottom of the stairs. She had clasped her hands to her mouth to stop from retching.

She had screamed loud enough to rouse the household, then collapsed at the top of the stairs. When she awoke hours later, Brianna recited the story that would be her truth—that Bridget had died while trying to save her husband from falling. Donal's memory meant nothing to her; 'twas for Bridget's soul that she lied. Bridget would have been denied burial in consecrated ground if she was deemed a murderess.

Brianna stared at the gown her cousin had provided for her to wear to this evening's ball. She brushed her hand across the material. The glow of the candles that lit her room intensified the color of the taffeta material. It was a deep reddish-bronze, with white lace across the bodice. The underskirt was made of white satin. Her finest lawn chemise would be worn under the dress so that its lace sleeves would peek generously from beneath the puffed sleeves that ended at her elbows. Marisa had lent her the O'Neill Rubies to wear with the gown.

Her new maid, a sweet-faced country girl, was elated with her elevation in status. In Brianna's heart, the girl, Edyth, would never replace her beloved Bridget, but Brianna knew that she had to find a maid of her own, for she could not continue to borrow Charity from her cousin. It had been Charity, however, who had skillfully styled her hair, with Edyth in attendance, observing.

Once, Brianna remembered, she had loved to dance. A lively galliard had been her favorite. She and Marisa had been keen pupils of the French dancing master her brother had hired.

A polite knock on her chamber door captured Brianna'a attention. Since her maid was below, fixing her a selection of food that would cut the pangs of hunger till she could eat later that night, Brianna perforce had to open the door herself.

She did so, and the unknown woman who stood there, her pale eyes focused directly on Brianna, startled her. She knew without being told that this was Mistress Buck.

Brianna attempted to shut the door.

"Please, my lady, I must speak with you," spoke the soft voice.

The door was mere inches from being closed. Brianna, both hands resting on the solid wood, had only to give it a final push and it would be a barrier betwixt herself and the other woman.

One hand falling limply to her side, Brianna used the other to swing back the door. In her gentle, Irish-accented voice, she said, "I bid you enter."

Mistress Buck did so. She stood, her hands at her sides, waiting, as Lady Brianna moved to put some distance between them. Then Brianna, seated at her writing desk, turned to face the other woman. "And what will you be wanting, Mistress Buck?"

Mistress Buck could feel the sorrow that enfolded this woman. It was in the depths of the golden eyes that looked at her, in the stiff manner of her carriage.

"To ease your pain, if I could."

Brianna lowered her lashes, pretending to find a piece of paper on the desk more interesting. "Of what pain do you speak?" she asked in an overly calm voice.

"Guilt."

Brianna's head jerked up in reaction. She swallowed, forcing herself not to blurt her next words. "What do I have to be guilty about?"

Mistress Buck walked to where Brianna sat. Bending down, she knelt on the floor at Brianna's slippered feet. "The deaths of your husband and your servant."

Brianna's gasp could be heard in the room. "How do you know?"

Mistress Buck was glad that the Lady Brianna did not deny her statement. The mask of control the Irish noblewoman wore slipped. "'Tis as I told the countess, I see things. Sometimes clearly; offtimes 'tis just a sense of something." Without objection from the Lady Brianna, Mistress Buck took hold of her hand. "For several nights, a dark lady has haunted my dreams. In these dreams I have heard cries of sorrow and anguish. Blood ran down a winding staircase. 'Twas only later that I saw the bodies of a young man and an older woman. When the countess visited me this day, I sensed the dark lady of my dreams was near."

Brianna pulled her hand away, preferring to gather her hands together in her lap. In a voice scarce above a whisper she asked, "What do you intend to do with this information?"

"Nothing."

Brianna repeated, "Nothing?"

"Aye, my lady. It serves me naught. 'Twas only for your sake that I mentioned it."

"How so?"

"To tell you that you must banish the guilt you feel. For if you cling to it, you will not accept the life that awaits you."

Her eyes welling with tears, Brianna managed to ask, "What do you mean?"

"'Twas not your fault. What happened was meant to be."

"You do not understand," Brianna said through choked-back tears. "I could have prevented the tragedy had I not lacked courage." For some unknown reason, Brianna trusted this stranger.

"No, my lady. They chose their paths, as you must now do." Mistress Buck rose. "Lessons offtimes come with a bitter price." She cast a glance at the gown that lay across the bed and smiled. The man who waited would be pleased, Mistress Buck thought. "Happiness lies ahead of you, my lady, if you will banish the past."

Darkness crept into the room as lingering shadows filtered through, devouring the light.

"I must leave now."

Brianna, her eyes flooded with moisture, remained silent as Mistress Buck departed. When the door clicked shut, the tears that she had been holding at bay burst out. She sobbed deeply, her shoulders shaking with the force of her exposed pain.

The horseman saw the lone female figure walking down the lane as his galloping stallion was just about upon her. He pulled back on the reins, bringing the big horse back on his hind legs as he reared in the air. Calming the beast, Cam shouted angrily, "Are you daft, woman? You could have been killed!"

The woman, startled for a moment by the huge animal, twin to that the countess had ridden earlier, raised her head. As she did, she saw the face of the man.

Cam recognized the wide-eyed stare. His mouth curled into a mocking twist as he said, "Forgive me for frightening you."

His voice penetrated her with the force of a sharp dagger thrust. She recognized it, and him.

Mistress Buck took a deep breath before she responded. "You did not frighten me, sir. I was merely . . . startled." And she was, for this was the same voice she had heard crying out in agony. "The fault was mine. My thoughts were not on where I was going."

"'Tis obvious, madam. You'd best be more watchful."

An almost overwhelming awareness of pain flooded her, scorching hot, as if her skin were on fire. So intense was this feeling that she swooned.

Cam leapt from his horse. He knelt beside her, removing his glove so that he could feel her skin. The smooth flesh was warm. Her pale eyes fluttered open.

Cam saw a stable lad and bellowed, "Get me some water," in the boy's direction. "Dinna move yet, lass," he said, cradling her in his arms.

Mistress Buck lay still, savoring the feel of the man's strong arms about her. Even in the dim evening light, she could see the traces of scars on one side of his face. One blue eye was covered with a black patch, hiding what was beneath. This was a man who had known suffering beyond most people's endurance. A man condemned through pride and circumstance to a dark, tormenting world.

The boy returned with a bucket of water. He held out the ladle to Cam. "You be wanting me to get someone else, my lord?"

My lord. Mistress Buck knew now who this disfigured stranger was. This was the Earl of Derran. Marisa's recently wedded husband.

"No," Cam answered the boy, who ran off. "Here, drink this," he said to Mistress Buck.

She did so. The water refreshed her, restoring her spirit. "Thank you, my lord."

"Are you able to rise? Do you need help?"

"I can manage, my lord."

Cam moved carefully to his feet, standing. He extended his left hand to help her up.

When she was on her feet again, Mistress Buck managed a small smile. "My Lord Derran," she said simply, introducing herself, "I am Mistress Buck."

"Your reputation as a healer precedes you, madam."

As his anguish preceded him, she thought. Where before she had been able to approach the countess and her cousin to share her visions with them, this man was different. Walls as solid as those of the greatest fortress surrounded him; only a love strong and deep would heal the wounds of his soul and crumble the fortifications that kept him a prisoner.

"If ever I can be of service to you, my lord, you have but to ask."

Her gesture seemed genuine to Cam. "God speed, mistress," he said as he gathered Romulus's reins. The stallion snorted, stamping his feet. "Easy," he crooned in a soft voice to the animal.

Mistress Buck shivered. That seductive Scottish voice, when used on a woman, would warm any maiden's heart, however reluctant. 'Twas like a haunting melody that lingered in the senses.

This was a man worth whatever effort love demanded.

He was somehow involved with the danger that threatened the countess, for Mistress Buck saw a figure emerge in her mind. 'Twas that of a woman, though her face was obscured. She tried to see more clearly, but the vision faded as quickly as it had come.

Her parting words to the earl were, "Have a care, my lord, for the past is not yet done with you."

Chapter Sixteen

As he dressed for the ball, Cameron gave a thought to the parting words of Mistress Buck. *The past is not yet done with you.*

What the hell had she meant?

He stood still as his valet adjusted the flounce of his white lace-edged shirt over the top of his black doublet. Glimpses of silver could be seen through the slashed sleeves. Silver ribbons decorated the waist and sides of his black petticoat breeches. His hose was also black, with wide canons at the knee, edged in silver.

"You look very fine, my lord," Kendall said. "Her ladyship should be well pleased." He stepped back to admire his handiwork.

"You think so?" Cam arched a dark blond brow.

"Aye, my lord, that I do."

Faith, Cam thought, his man was a bloody fool. And, as for that, so was he, Cam decided. It *was* for her good opinion that he had hired the village tailor, instructing the man in just how and what he wanted. Cam found out that the patronage of the Earl of Derran meant much to the merchants of Fitzpemberton. Nothing was beyond them in seeing the earl's wishes hastily carried out. For the handsome fee he paid, they would even overlook his physical flaws when dealing with him. He was aware that they pretended not to notice the slight limp, the mangled bones of his right hand, the black eyepatch. No doubt they mocked him behind his back; no man alive mocked Cam to his face.

Cam moved to the small gilt mirror he permitted in the room. His freshly washed dark blond hair hung in thick waves to his broad shoulders. Slowly, he raised his right hand, covering half his face. He stared at the image before him. His left hand curled into a fist, fingers digging into the skin of his palm with intensity. How he longed to smash the glass, to erase the living portrait that was reflected there.

His fist uncurled; his right hand dropped.

Aye, the past would always be with him; he could never escape it, for he wore it as a daily reminder.

Tonight would be a test of fortitude. Cam assumed that everyone who was to come to this evening's entertainment had already been advised as to the physical character of the man that Marisa Fitzgerald had wed. Gossip, he had found, had swifter wings than any Royal courier service.

Let them have their damnable look, Cam decided as he gave the man in the mirror a parting glance. An invisible mantle of pride swept round him. He was Cameron Alistair Buchanan, the Earl of Derran, empowered by

Charles II with wealth and position. So be it.

"You have forgotten something, my lord," Kendall said, his eyes twinkling in anticipation.

"What, pray tell?"

"This," Kendall announced, producing a parcel wrapped in sky-blue velvet for his master's inspection.

Cam pulled the white silk ribbon that held it closed. Within the folds of the velvet lay two handkerchiefs. He lifted one out, handing the other in its velvet container to Kendall. It was skillfully worked, the intitals of F and B interlocked.

Fitzgerald and Buchanan.

Soon, Cam vowed, their bodies would intertwine as well.

Marisa was nervous.

An anticipatory tingle feathered along her nerves. "Do hurry, Charity," she told the maid.

Charity gave her mistress a wide grin, knowing that tonight the usually calm countess was fretful. She pulled the laces tighter on the gown, which caused the bodice to push Marisa's breasts even higher over the crisp white lace of her chemise. Finished, Charity stepped back to adjust the skirt, pinning it back with jeweled fasteners to show the silver satin underskirt. She moved to fetch Marisa's slippers of white velvet dotted with tiny seed pearls and diamonds.

Marisa could hear the musicians assembled in the gallery, the melodic blend of the virginals and viols. Many of the guests, Charity informed her, had arrived. Her grandmother would be holding court below, biding her time till she could present her grandaughter and her grandaughter's husband to the special gathering. Marisa was glad now that she had thought to invite Jamie Covington. She imagined that being on public display would be very difficult for her husband. He would need a friend there whom he trusted.

Just why that was so important to her she declined to investigate further.

Marisa stared at her reflection in the mirror. Her cheeks flushed a becoming shade of rose when she saw just how well the dress fit her. On each wrist she wore a thick band of pearls, fastened with a diamond clasp. Around her throat was a collar of pearls. In her ears pearls and diamonds glowed.

"You look ever so lovely, my lady," Charity said on a sigh.

"Thank you," Marisa replied. "Have you seen my fan?"

Charity nodded. "Here it is, my lady," she said as she picked it up from the bed.

Marisa snapped it open. Though the night was cool, she still felt a need for it.

"You may inform the earl's man Kendall that I await my husband's pleasure so that we may descend the stairs together."

"I shall, my lady," she said, quitting the countess's chambers, a wide smile on her face. Her ladyship would most certainly find favor with the master this night. Charity thought it passing strange that they did not share a bed, even though they were properly wed. At times, when each believed no one saw, Charity observed sly glances passing bewixt them, fleeting, sharp glimpses that she didn't always understand.

In truth, his lordship, to her eyes, was not the most amiable-looking man, what with his scars and all, but he wasn't a hard taskmaster. Nor did

he try to sneak a fondle with her or any of the
other servants. From what she could observe, he
kept to his wedding vows with a single-minded
devotion. That pleased her because Charity was
quite fond of her mistress. In London she'd heard
stories about the wild ways of the court, the rakes
who roamed the city looking for fresh conquests.
Charity knew that as a servant, she, and all like
her, were considered fair game by most men of
rank. That she remained a virgin, by her choice,
was purely good fortune in a world that little
cared.

Kendall answered the door. Charity flashed him
a smile; his lordship's man was well known to
her, another Dorset native. His small, wiry body,
inherited from his Irish mother's family, barred
the entranceway. "Aye?"

"I bring a message from her ladyship," Charity
announced with importance.

Kendall, giving the lass a cocky grin, raised a
brow. "Aye?" he repeated.

Charity stated, "The countess awaits her husband."

"Then," spoke the deep Scottish voice from
behind Kendall, "we should not keep my lady
wife waiting, should we?"

Jamie Covington observed the gathering of people in the large room. Men and women laughed
and chatted, their glances continually straying to
the wide staircase, waiting for the show to begin.
For show it was, Jamie concluded. His friend
would be, once more, the cynosure of all eyes, as
would his lady wife. What would these country
folk make of Cameron Buchanan? Jamie's hazel
eyes scanned the room, taking the measure of
those assembled. 'Twas hard to judge.

A slim, dark-haired woman on the other side
of the crowded room caught his eye. His breath
caught in his chest for an instant. When she turned
her head, saucy black curls dangling about her
bare shoulders, he recognized her. Odds fish, but
she was lovely! 'Twas the Lady Brianna O'Dalaigh
MacBride. Tonight she had abandoned her black
widow's garments, favoring instead a gown of
bronze. Her skin seemed to glow, he thought.
Adorning her neck, wrists, and ears was a stunning collection of priceless rubies.

Jamie found himself moving in her direction,
anxious to get closer to her. The physical stirings
he'd felt when he was in her company in London
were stronger now. There was something about
this quiet beauty that drew him to her, like a man
who'd been blind and suddenly saw the power of
the light.

"Lady Brianna," Jamie said softly.

Brianna, who'd seen Jamie walking in her direction, tilted her head back, looking him full in the
face. Her initial unease vanished when she met
the warmth of his gaze. "Mr. Covington," she
responded, warmth echoing in her voice.

"Jamie, please," he insisted, sketching her a
slight bow.

"As you will, Jamie." Brianna noted, and
approved, that like many other men in the
room, he chose not to wear an elaborate wig or
a fancy hat. Court fashion, mainly in the French
style, was slow to take hold in the country. "'Tis
indeed a most pleasant surprise to see you here
in Dorset. A friendly face is most welcome." In a
nervous gesture, Brianna's fingers toyed with the
fan she held.

Jamie, with a sudden, shocking clarity, knew
that he wanted this woman for his wife, for his

lifetime companion. Like no one he had ever known, she seemed to have entered his heart, filling it with quiet delight.

Jamie gave Brianna a deep smile. "I am thankful that Lady Derran saw fit to invite me to this occasion."

"As am I," Brianna mumurmered softly.

"I would have you save a dance for me, Lady Brianna," Jamie requested.

A dark flush stole over Brianna's cheeks. She lowered her eyes, saying, "I will not be dancing tonight."

"My God, how clumsy I am," Jamie said, apologizing. "I forgot that you are still mourning the loss of your husband. Forgive me," he beseeched her.

Brianna wondered what Jamie Covington would say were to she to confess that rather than mourning Donal MacBride, she was relieved that he was dead, for it meant that she would never again be forced to share the bed of a man who repulsed her. She was, she knew, in her own way responsible for the tragedy by failing to leave her husband. Would anyone understand that she'd felt she had to stay? Brianna had been taught to respect the vows she made before God, that she was to be an obedient wife to Donal in all things. Her religion forbade divorce. She'd submitted to Donal's clumsy attempts at lovemaking with stoic determination. Not once had he touched her in a loving way. The easy closeness she had seen between her brother and his wife, the touches, the caresses, were completely absent from her own marriage.

Brianna realized how much it hurt to have to spurn Jamie's offer of a dance. She would have loved to accept, for she missed dancing. Guilt and pride held her in check. "I humbly thank you for your most kind offer, Jamie. Would that I could."

What a complete ass he had made of himself, Jamie thought. "I understand, Lady Brianna. Pray forgive my unseemly lack of manners." He had only wanted an excuse to be with her once again. Perhaps life in the capital city had given him a cynical perspective. There, he'd seen widows scarce a few days in mourning quickly and eagerly doffing their black garments for clothes designed to attract a rich protector. Others, he knew, shed them with reluctance. They were the women who had loved their husbands, but realized that they had to marry again in order to maintain the ordered path of their lives.

Brianna gave him a bittersweet smile. "You are, of course, forgiven." She slid a sideways glance at the people in the room. "And what do you think *they*"—she emphasized the word with a small, discreet wave of her fan—"will be thinking about my cousin and her husband?" she asked.

Jamie removed a glass of wine for each of them from the silver tray held by the liveried servant. He handed the delicate glass to Brianna. Their fingers briefly touched, sending a shimmering spark between them, which neither openly acknowledged. "I wondered about that," he admitted, sipping the wine. "I am inclined to think they'll be most puzzled."

"Do you mean that they will wonder why my cousin wed with the Buchanan?"

"Precisely," he said. "And they will undoubtedly reach all the wrong conclusions."

Brianna tilted her head back. She was glad that Jamie wasn't as big and intimidating as Donal had been. "What are the correct conclusions?" she inquired.

"That 'twas a bond brought about by honor, and for the sake of loyalty." He lifted the glass to his lips once again. "If only . . ."

"What?" Lady Brianna probed.

"If only," he finished, "they would look beyond Cameron's face."

"As Marisa has done," Brianna said.

"Has she?" Jamie demanded. "Truly?"

Brianna bent her head with a nod. "Would you be thinking that Marisa is lacking in compassion?" Brianna asked. "I have seen how she looks at her husband," she confided, "and 'tis not with loathing, nor with fear."

A hush fell over the crowd. The musicians in the upper gallery stopped playing their instruments. Jamie and Brianna ceased their intimate conversation.

All eyes were focused on the wide staircase. At the bottom of the stairs stood the dowager countess, her face wreathed in smiles. Her green eyes glowed in triumph. This night Barbara wore her most extravagant collection of emeralds—necklace, bracelets, earrings, and jeweled combs fixed into her hair. Her gown of gold drew admiring glances from both men and women.

"I bid you all welcome in the name of the Earl and Countess of Derran," she began, basking in the good will of the company. "I have asked you all to come this night to share with me in the great happiness that I feel that my beloved grandaughter has been returned to me, and to England, to resume her rightful heritage.

"This night we celebrate both her restoration and her recent marriage.

"I have tried, in her absence, to maintain her inheritance as best I could," Barbara stated, her strong voice slightly wavering with emotion, "to keep faith with the wishes of my son, her father." A clock in the background signaled the hour.

"For too long, I have been without the comfort and love of the last of my family, for which I curse that bastard Cromwell; may God damn his filthy soul to hell for all eternity!" she declared vehemently.

"But I digress," Lady Barbara said, her tone softening, "when all I want to do is have you join me in bidding Marisa and the man she has wed, Cameron Alistair Buchanan, a very gracious welcome." She nodded her head slightly, the signal for the musicians to begin playing again.

As they did so, Marisa and Cameron made their descent down the stairs. Marisa's arm was linked with Cam's. The room was quiet save for the sounds made by the instruments. Talk ceased as the men and women watched as the Earl and Countess of Derran reached the bottom stair and the old countess. Marisa gave her grandmother a loving glance, kissing her cheeks warmly. Cam, to the utter surprise of both Marisa and Barbara, did likewise.

Brianna and Jamie, both watching from the side of the room, exchanged glances.

"I would have you all join me in saluting the marriage of Lord and Lady Derran," Lady Barbara insisted as servants hurried to refill the glasses of the guests. She raised her glass in tribute. "To the earl and the countess," she said.

"To the earl and the countess," was the repeated refrain from the mouths of the guests.

Marisa decided that she needed to publicly acknowledge her grandmother, and this was the proper time to do that. She stood beside the older woman, clasping Barbara's hand tightly in hers. "I, too, would have you join me in a salute. This is for my grandmother, Barbara Tremaine Fitzgerald, Dowager Countess of Derran, whose love and support have meant more to me than she could ever know. If not for her, I doubt that I would have had anything of value to return to. She bravely kept my inheritance secure, against even the forces of the Commonwealth when the need arose.

"Please raise your glasses to her." Marisa squeezed her grandmother's veined hand. "*Grande-mère*," Marisa said with a proud smile on her face.

Echoes of the words sounded in the room, along with sustained clapping. Barbara beamed, loving the attention.

Cam, standing next to Marisa, chose to make a gesture also. With his deep, mellifluous voice, he instantly commanded the attention of the entire room. "A health unto his most gracious Majesty, Charles II, by the grace of God, our king; and," he added, recognizing the recent wedding of the King of England to the Portuguese princess, "to our new queen, Catherine."

Cameron quaffed the wine in his glass, his gaze searching the room for Jamie. He saw his friend standing but a few feet away, with Lady Brianna at his side. Cam observed that Jamie appeared relaxed and happy. Could his friend be falling for the Irish widow's charms? With the eye of a connoisseur, Cam rated Brianna a beauty, a woman of grace who could be just what Jamie would have need of in a wife, as he could be what she needed in a husband. Cam could vouch for Jamie's character, his sense of responsibility. Perhaps he should discuss the matter with Marisa.

That thought brought a trace of a smile to his face.

Marisa.

His wife.

Tonight, he thought, his countess was beautiful beyond compare. Her thick chestnut hair was a mass of curls around her slim neck. His mind skipped ahead to a vision of her later tonight, ready for his kisses, eagerly waiting for his love-making. How much longer could he wait till they were one?

He turned his head, drinking in the sight of his wife. Her gown was silver satin, with an underskirt of cream silk, giving her skin a shimmering radiance. Diamonds and pearls adorned her wrists, ears, and throat, even adding luster to the shoes she wore. Along the walls upstairs were portraits of her ancestors. Peter Lely should be commisioned to paint her, Cam mused, for only a master painter could render her justice. A study of beauty captured for all who would follow, a permanent record of how she appeared tonight.

A smile curved his wide mouth. He would need no reminder; the memory of Marisa, tonight, would stay with him all the days of his life. When he was old, he would pull it from a drawer in his mind, mentally savor the sensual remembrance before he locked it away, saving it for another time when he needed to feel once again the pulse-quickening thrill of sexual excitement.

The guests waited for a signal that would allow the dancing and general merriment to commence. The dowager gave her grandaughter a quick look.

Cam, too, interperted that silent request, sending out one of his own. Custom dictated he and his wife open the dancing; cognizant that he could no longer perform the steps required of any dance, he needed a substitute.

Jamie read the entreaty on Cam's face. Without hesitation, he responded to Cam's plea, hastening from Brianna's side to join Cam and Marisa. "May I have the supreme honor of this dance, my lady?" Jamie asked politely, sketching a short bow.

Marisa, her hand resting on Cam's left arm, tilted her head towards her husband. "Have I your permission, my lord?" she inquired, understanding just what she was asking of him.

"You have, my lady," the Buchanan responded, lifting her right hand in his, saluting the soft flesh with the warm touch of his mouth.

How right it felt to have his lips on her, Marisa thought as she met his eye with her own. That she should think so momentarily shocked her. Yet it was the truth. The pull of unspoken passion rose between them. There was no use denying it. Even with her lack of experience, Marisa intuitively realized that some strong bond connected them.

In a slightly husky tone, Marisa said, "Thank you, Cameron," accepting Jamie's hand as he led her to the open space on the floor so that they could begin the festivities.

Cameron. She had finally uttered his name in conversation, willingly. The force of that one word shot through Cam's body, jolting him. No longer the distant and formal "my lord" or the chillingly polite and respectful "my husband." Cam heard his name as if 'twere spoken for the first time, fresh and clear. To think that one could hear one's name throughout one's life and never know the true joy of it till one's beloved articulated it. Scarce a month ago he would have chided anyone who said such a thing to him. His cynical humor would have denounced the speaker quickly as foolish, completely lacking in wisdom.

Damn her! Marisa had uncovered an unknown chink in his armor, one that he hadn't been aware of, all because she had said his name.

As they made their way through a dance known as a pavane, Marisa stole a glance in her husband's direction.

"'Twould seem that your mind is not quite on the dance," Jamie commented after catching the direction of her eyes.

"Have I been so lax a partner?" she asked. "If I have, I beg your forgiveness," Marisa insisted, dragging her gaze away from its compelling object. What was it that drew her to him, even from across a crowded room, as if all others ceased to matter?

"No, my lady, you have been perfection itself," Jamie assured her, "though I would add honestly that you seem distracted, as if you wish to be elsewhere. Do you? Or," Jamie continued, "is it that you wish that I were someone else? Cameron, perhaps?"

"Nonsense," she vowed.

"Is it?" he persisted.

Marisa lifted her chin. Her direct glance met his questioning glance. "No," she answered.

He spoke softly, so that only she could hear his words, "I can be trusted, my lady."

The music changed to that of a country dance. Marisa and Jamie focused on the complicated steps, continuing their conversation sporadically.

Marisa believed him. "I think that you can," she told him. She gave Jamie with a true smile that came from her heart. "Now is the time to tell you of my gratitude. I would thank you for responding to my invitation."

"I was most happy to," he insisted.

"Still, I know that your work in London for his Majesty is important."

Jamie inquired, "If I may share a confidence with you?"

"Of course," Marisa responded.

"I grow weary of the life I lead there." Jamie's hazel eyes were direct. "When I began, I had a purpose, one I shared with Cameron—to see Charles Stuart on the throne of England, as was his birthright. That now having been happily accomplished, I find that I tire of the court. What was once an intriguing game has lost its interest for me. Which isn't to say that his Majesty does not have enemies; he does, as will any monarch. But there are others now who would willingly shoulder my responsibilites." He paused as they executed a complicated step. "I have no family, no wife nor children with whom to share my life."

Marisa recognized that his was a confession of loneliness. "And you wish to change that?"

"Yes," he answered. "I would have what I see about me. A wife. Someone to share my bed."

Marisa raised one eyebrow. "One can have that readily without the necessity of a wedding."

"'Tis not what I seek," Jamie explained. "For if it was, I could have well had my fill in London. I seek a wife, not a temporary mistress."

"Have you a woman in mind?"

He decided to be frank. "A woman like your cousin, the Lady Brianna."

Jamie didn't really know what to expect when he made his pronouncement. What he hadn't counted on was the delighted look on Marisa's face.

"I believe that you and my cousin would suit well," she said.

"You do?"

"Yes," Marisa responded, snapping open her fan as they ended the dance. "Though you may have a difficult time persuading her."

"You will erect no barriers?"

Marisa shook her head as they made their way back to where Cam sat, flanked on either side by the dowager and Lady Brianna. People halted them, offering felicitations, wishing her well on her marriage.

In a low tone, so that her words would be heard by him alone, Marisa asked, "Can you stay with us awhile?"

Jamie cocked his head. "Why?"

"It will be good for Cameron to have a true friend about, especially as we leave soon for FitzHall." Her green eyes were suddenly alight with merriment. "Besides, how can you woo my cousin if you return to London?"

"I am persuaded by your cunning arguments, my lady," Jamie answered. This was indeed the best solution. He could keep an eye on both Cam and the countess while still maintaining his contacts in London. His network would continue trying to discover who was responsible for the attack on Cam and Marisa. His heart ached for the terror that must have gripped the women, even though Cam steadfastly praised the bravery of his wife. Jamie hadn't been able to prevent what had happened to Cam years before. Remorse for that still haunted him. He owed it to his friend to try with all the resources at his disposal to prevent a recurrence.

"I will inform my man Bridge so that he can see to arranging for some more clothes, as what

I brought with me will not suffice."

"You may have use of one of my messengers," Marisa added. "I will see to it that one is placed at your disposal.

"Now," she said, her voice sparkling and light, "shall we rejoin Cameron and Brianna?"

Chapter Seventeen

The garden would provide the escape that Marisa required. She had had enough of polite conversation, insincere compliments, and hints that she would perhaps regret having permitted the king to arrange a marriage for her. One sly comment was the final straw. Marisa overheard it as she made her way down a hallway, past the library, the door of which was slightly ajar. "If this be a sign of the king's favor, then 'tis well to do without it. Imagine facing that in your bed."

The person receiving the confidence was also female; her reply was blunt, bringing a deep blush to Marisa's cheeks. "'Tis to be hoped that the countess keeps the candles snuffed. Perhaps the length of the new earl's staff is worth the pain of suffering the face. I have heard it said that deformities can be balanced elsewhere by great rewards."

Giggles of snide laughter floated through the open door.

Marisa pushed it aside, entering the room. Her spine was rigid, her hands clenched at her sides. "How dare you?" Ice formed in her green eyes. A wise person would have read and heeded the message there.

The two women rose abruptly from the couch. They had the grace to flush at being discovered by the very woman about whom they were gossiping.

One of the women replied haughtily, "We only say what a lot of those invited here tonight think."

"That is your sad excuse?" Marisa demanded.

"We sympathize with your plight," the other contended.

Marisa's voice was cool. "I have no need of your *sympathy*," she stated unequivocally. "Leave my house now."

"You cannot change the opinion of others," the first woman challenged.

"You cow-faced bitch," was Marisa's response. "Do you think that I care a damn about your opinion?" She laughed without a trace of mirth.

"'Tis well you should," said the first woman in a waspish tone, still reeling from Marisa's barbed comment. "This is not fashionable London, my lady, where you no doubt were the darling of the court," she sneered, "along with your papist Irish cousin, who thinks herself better than we God-fearing people."

"You mealy-mouthed hypocrite," Marisa said slowly, enunciating each word. "Get out before I have you tossed out in front of all the other guests like the contemptible trash you are." She stood at the door, waiting.

"'Tis just as well," the first woman said with false sweetness. "Mayhap we were too hasty with our concern," she went on, shrugging off her friend's hand as the other woman tried to pull her away. She was eager to deliver what she felt would be a telling blow. "'Tis rumored that the Fitzgerald blood breeds only whores, so it could well be that we should have reserved our concern for your pitiable mate."

"Rowena," the second woman begged. "For pity's sake, shut up!"

"Better an honest whore, madam, than a miserable drab for whose services a ha'penny would seem an exorbitant payment." Marisa lifted one chestnut brow, looking down her nose as if contemplating a particularly unsavory form of pest. "Faith, I would hazard a guess that they would have to bribe someone to have you."

Marisa warned them both. "Think well before you repeat any of your slander. I have the king's"—she paused deliberately—"ear." Let them make of that what they will, Marisa thought.

Marisa watched as they scuttled down the hallway. But the satisfied smile on her lips was soon replaced by a cold grip on her heart. She shut the door on her way out, continuing on her way to the garden.

It was there, strolling through the fragrant flowers, alone, that she found a respite from the activities within the house. So much of her time was spent with others that she missed the quiet times she had enjoyed in Ireland, walking along the rugged shore, smelling the crisp ocean air, or exploring the countryside. But she had been a girl then, free from real responsibility. She was a woman now, with the weight of her name, and another's, fully upon her shoulders.

Her steps led her to the rose-covered summer-house. Marisa entered the wooden structure, cupping one large white rose in her hand as she passed it. She had played here as a child when her father was in residence. It was a place of magic in her memory.

A marble bench in the shape of an S dominated the interior. Marisa arranged her skirt and sat down to think. Had everyone who attended this night formed the same opinion as the two shrewish bitches? She recalled the looks on several faces when she and Cam had walked down the steps. Disbelief. Shock. Pity. Fear. They saw only the limp, the broken hand, the distinctive black eyepatch. They did not see what she had come to see: the man who risked his life to save Brianna and herself; the man who gave valuable service in the cause of his king; the man who braved London's fashionables in the midst of a theater; the man whose touch contained some wild form of magic, that with the simplest of gestures he released something unexplored buried deep within herself.

Footsteps sounded on the stone path. Marisa tensed until she also heard the tap of a walking stick. Her heart beat faster, for she knew whom the noise heralded.

Cam stopped. Marisa was easy to spot with that dress of silver. An angel in the night, offering a different form of salvation. An unschooled seductress, an untutored siren who beckoned him hither to her rose-covered bower.

He took a deep breath, drawing in air to his suddenly starved lungs. The blood in his veins coursed with a definite heat. His heart raced. His hand tightened on the gold head of the cane. He had wanted to be the one who led her onto the floor, to show her off. *She is mine,* he longed to shout to all assembled, *as I am hers.*

Cam moved slowly so as not to frighten her, joining her on the marble bench, sitting with her there for a few moments in companionable silence.

"Say it again," Cam demanded, a husky tone to his deep voice.

Marisa turned her head to the right just slightly. "What?" she asked, savoring the smell of spicy scented soap he'd used.

"My name. Say it," Cam intreated her, his voice a darkly seductive force.

Marisa wet her lips. "Cameron," she whispered in the darkness surrounding them.

Cam leaned so that his mouth was close to her throat. He blew softly on her earring. "Remove it," he instructed her, wrapping one of her many curls around his lean finger.

Her hands trembling slightly, Marisa pulled the jewel from her ear. As she did so, his lips fastened onto the lobe, gently pulling it into his mouth. Her head fell back as he nibbled on the flesh.

Marisa gasped as she felt a rush of warmth infuse her body. With deft fingers Cam managed to unlace the tight fastenings of her gown so that the bodice slipped lower. His strong left arm encircled her with its power. Slowly, he moved his hand upwards, till it pushed aside the stiff bodice, seeking the soft fabric beneath, molding her left breast. Her nipple stiffened as he rubbed his thumb rhythmically over the crest.

"Cameron," she sighed as his lips brushed across her shoulders, feathering her skin with their provocative contact. Her breath came faster as strange, potent longings assailed her.

Cam knew that he could take Marisa, push her past the limits to total abandon. For a former rake, with his arsenal of skills to draw upon, it would be so easy. But not here, he thought. Not now, even though his body was ready and eager to instruct hers. This summerhouse was not the most private of places, nor the most comfortable, for either of them. He knew of a place that would be. Safe and secure, away from the curious eyes of her family. Where he could be in control of the situation.

His hand cupped her head, turning her ever so gently so that his tongue could trace her full mouth. Marisa opened her lips to him and Cam took command, deepening, intensifying each kiss. He loved the wild innocence of her mouth, the taste of wine lingering on her tongue. He could drown in the delight of exchanging kisses with her, coaxing and teasing until she responded with her own fervant ardor.

Marisa's hands clutched his back, holding onto the velvet of his jacket, pulling him even closer to her, as if afraid that he would somehow vanish if she let go. What a wondrous feeling this was, this action of mouth mating with mouth.

Cameron, her mind screamed in pleasure.

He broke contact with her lips, taking deep gulps of air. His manhood strained against the confines of his breeches; it was an intense, throbbing ache that craved relief, that hungered for the ultimate joining. He had to call a halt now or else all would be lost. His control was strained enough as it was; any further exchange of intimacies with Marisa would break down his resolve.

He shifted slightly. Her eyes fluttered open, huge and questioning. Her mouth was swollen from his kisses. Her breasts rose and fell with the deep breaths she took, the nipples stiff points against the material of her chemise. Marisa looked like a woman ready for the final culmination of lovemaking. In his earlier years, he'd had only one virgin, preferring to be with women who were experienced, who knew the game of love for what it was, with no illusions. It was less complicated that way. Better for all concerned, especially him. Virgins, he had once decided, were a chore best left to someone else.

Now, Cam realized, he prized what once he had scorned. No woman's mouth had ever stirred him like Marisa's. No woman's tender touch had ever brought forth such an instant response in his body as had hers.

He arranged her bodice carefully, pushing it back into place, trying as best he could to tighten the laces he had loosened.

Marisa found her voice at last, shaky with passion as it was. "What are you doing?"

"I should think it obvious, my lady," he said, forcing a smile onto his mouth as he completed his task and rose, "helping you reclaim your composure."

"You fear discovery here, is that it?"

Cam was silent, not knowing what to tell her.

"Do you not wish to lie with me?" Marisa inquired boldly, her head bowing slightly, momentarily afraid to read the answer on his face. It was then that she recalled the question her grandmother had asked. "Or is it that you cannot?"

Cam was nonplused for a few seconds. He reached forward with his good hand, lifting her chin. "Dinna think, lass," he stated, "that I canna finish what I start. 'Tis just that I choose not to now."

"Why?" she demanded, a stubborn look fixing her features.

"Because your first time will nae be on the cold ground, and 'twill nae be tonight," he declared.

"Tomorrow," Cam promised, his voice rough with passion. "I will bid you come to me."

When he withdrew, leaving her alone in the summerhouse, Marisa was bereft, suspended between heaven and hell, between virtue and knowledge.

He had said he would bid her come. She could refuse, her mind reasoned. She was no serving wench to be summoned for her master's pleasure.

But she would not refuse, she knew. Her soul would obey, for she had already made her choice. She could not turn her back on what they had shared this night, and what they could share on the morrow.

Kendall wiped the shaving soap from Cam's face early the next morning. It was an unexpected luxury that Cam had gotten used to these past weeks. He had shaved himself each morning since his disfigurement; now, to indulge himself once more by permitting someone else to handle the task, was a pleasure.

"Have you seen to all that I asked?"

Kendall, his wiry body moving nimbly about as he rinsed off the sharp razor and set it inside a special sheath, replied, "That I have, my lord. All awaits you."

"You forgot nothing?"

Kendall gave his master a wry look. "What you required has been taken care of. It lacks only you and her ladyship to be complete."

Cam rose from the thickly padded chair. "Excellent." Kendall helped Cam into a long doublet of blue wool. There were knee breeches to match, with plain wool stockings and serviceable shoes. Last night he had played the court gentleman, dressing the part. Today, he was the unobtrusive country squire. He walked to the wardrobe, removing an item from an inner drawer. In his large hand he held one of the handkerchiefs that Marisa had made him. Tucking it into the waistband of his breeches, he turned and faced Kendall. "You know what you must do?"

Kendall nodded, repeating back to Cam what he had been told the day before. "I am to wait until you've been gone at least an hour and then place into the countess's hands the note you have left for her."

"Remember, no one must know where I've gone," Cam said as he crossed the room. He pressed a panel in the wall beside his bed. A hidden door sprang open. It was an old escape route, with stairs leading down to the cellar. "When my wife leaves, wait till later in the day to inform the countess's grandmother and her cousin that she will be spending the night with me." Cam stepped through the passageway. "We shall return on the morrow."

"Yes, my lord," Kendall said as he closed the door behind Cameron. Kendall found his master's elaborate plans both amusing and touching. As the earl's man, he was well aware that the Earl of Derran and his countess had not shared a bed since he began his duties. Kendall did not care to speculate on the reasons and went about his duties to the best of his abilites. The old cottage, which the earl had discovered on one of his frequent rides over the estate, had been cleaned up by Kendall. Normally, he wouldn't have been required to do such a menial task; however, the earl had charged him with secrecy, so he'd decided it would be best if he took care of it himself. He'd restocked the small stone house with food, linen, and wood. It was a perfect place for lovers, nestled amidst a thick grove of trees.

"Luck be with you, my lord," Kendall whispered, "for I'm thinking that you'll be having need of it."

Marisa, who'd surprised herself by falling to sleep as soon as she crawled beneath the soft linen sheet, woke refreshed, eager to have at the day. She tossed the sheet aside, rising naked from the comfort of the bed. Her robe lay on a chair; she picked it up and belted it around her waist.

Walking to the window, she saw that the sky was a dull shade of gray. The air was cooler this morn than yesterday, with a hint of the rain she was sure would come.

She had no need to close her eyes to bring the kisses she had shared last night with her husband to mind. She touched the fingertips of her right hand to her mouth. In Cameron's arms, she had felt as if nothing was beyond her power to achieve. 'Twas odd, she mused, that surrendering to the powerful lure of the senses could make one feel like a conqueror.

Charity opened the bedroom door, a cheery smile on her face, and seeing that her mistress was awake, entered, carrying a tray with a small pot of coffee and a cup. "Good day, my lady," she said as she plced the tray down, pouring Marisa some of the strong brew. "Shall I bring you something else?" she asked as she handed Marisa the cup.

"The coffee itself will be fine, thank you," Marisa replied. Sipping the beverage, she smiled at the thought that her ships provided a good portion of the coffee drunk in the coffeehouses of London. The part of her family's fortune that stemmed from commerce was something she would have to share soon with Cameron. Little by little she had given him glimpses into the far-flung interests of the Fitzgeralds. "Has my husband risen yet?"

"Yes, my lady, I believe that he has, since I saw Kendall bringing hot water to shave the earl."

"When was this?"

"Less than an hour ago, my lady. I was in the kitchen when Kendall came down the back stairs to fetch the bucket."

Excitement snapped through Marisa's body with a force of its own. She hugged the secret of Cameron's promise to herself, impatient for its call.

"Your grandmother wishes you to join her below, my lady, for breakfast, if you can spare her the time."

Marisa's mouth kicked into a smile. Charity had stated it so diplomatically. A *request* from her grandmother was tantamount to a royal summons.

"I find that I am quite famished this morn," Marisa said, finishing the coffee that remained in her cup and holding it out for more. Indeed, Marisa was ravenously hungry, and for far more than just food. It was for a repetition of her experiences from the previous night. For the touches that left fire in their wake; for the demands of Cameron's mouth on her own. It was, Marisa decided, a strong appetite for all life could provide. So many new possibilities; so many new challenges to be faced.

"Please go tell my grandmother that I will be with her shortly. And what of my cousin, the Lady

Brianna?" Marisa asked as she shifted through her clothes, wanting to select something she thought would please her husband.

"She has risen also, my lady, and is with the old countess."

Marisa wished that she could share some of her newfound feelings with her grandmother and her cousin; but they were still too fresh, too fragile to expose to another's examinations. They each had experienced the teachings of love that she had yet to face.

Charity watched as the countess stood as if lost in thought, her green eyes contemplative. "Shall I fetch the hot iron for your curls?"

"No," Marisa shook her head, "not today. I shall wear it loose."

"Loose?" Charity was puzzled.

"I have my reasons," Marisa assured her maid.

"Very good, my lady," Charity answered, shrugging her shoulders. "I will deliver your message to the old countess and be back to help you dress."

"Yes," Marisa answered her maid, her mind drifting away from thoughts of everyday concerns to the sensual unknown. "Do that," she said and waved her hand in a dismissing gesture.

"All in all, I think our gathering was a success," the dowager stated, sipping her third cup of morning coffee.

"It did appear that way," Lady Brianna agreed.

"What do you think, Mr. Covington?" Barbara asked of the newly arrived guest.

Jamie, who had come by to see Cameron, only to be told by Kendall that his lordship was unavailable, was invited to join the ladies for their morning meal. "I'll wager tongues are still wagging over the details this morning."

Barbara gave him a dazzling smile. "I should hope so," she said.

"You hope what, *grand-mère*?" Marisa asked as she walked into the room, coming over to give her grandmother a tender kiss on the cheek, before taking a seat next to her cousin. She glanced at the empty chair at the end of the table. She had thought, and fervently hoped, that Cameron might be taking his meal with her family.

"That the ball would elicit conversation, my dear," Barbara offered. "I should think that it has, don't you agree?"

Marisa turned he attention back to her grandmother. "I'm sorry, what did you say?"

"You seem distracted, Marisa," Barbara observed. "Is something wrong?"

"No," Marisa assured the older woman. "'Tis nothing." Where was he? she wondered. His friend was here, sharing their meal. Cam had faced down a crowd last night; surely sharing breakfast wasn't so daunting a prospect? "Forgive me," she said. "Now, of what were you speaking?"

Lady Brianna responded. "Your lady grandmother declared that she was happy to think that the people who came last evening were still talking about the ball."

"Had you heard anything?" Marisa questioned, recollecting the disagreeable comments of the two women. If they had spread their filth . . .

"Only that it was good to see the daughter of the house restored to her proper position," Barbara asserted.

"Did anyone say aught of my husband?" Marisa demanded, helping herself to a thick chunk of wheat bread, spreading warm, thick orange marmalade over the top.

Barbara gave her grandaughter an indulgent smile. "He is a stranger to them, Marisa, and a Scotsman. They are naturally cautious. Give them time to accept him."

"That is not why I am concerned," Marisa explained.

Barbara's green eyes shone with love. "You speak, of course, of his injuries." She sighed. "No one was foolish enough to insult the earl in my hearing, for I would have boxed the ears of any to do so," she insisted. "Granted, his face and form are shocking at first, such beauty side by side with scars, though I think far too much is made of it. In my time I have seen wounds from battles, duels and accidents, as have many people who were here last night. 'Tis life," she said with a small shrug of her shoulders, "and what cannot be changed must be accepted."

"Thank you, *grand-mère*," Marisa said fondly.

"For speaking the truth?" Barbara queried.

Jamie put in, "That would be considered shocking in some circles, my lady."

Barbara chuckled, giving Jamie a flirtatious glance. "How well I know, though that has never deterred me."

"As we were speaking of my husband, has anyone seen him this morn?"

Jamie replied. "I had come early to talk to him regarding some unfinished business," he disclosed, "and was told that he had already left."

"He is gone?" Marisa asked, laying the bread aside and wiping her hands on a square of linen.

"'Twould appear so, my lady," he said.

"Had you made plans?" Lady Brianna questioned.

Marisa folded her hands into her lap. "I believed so," she said, concerned that her husband was playing some kind of perverse game.

A discreet knock sounded on the door and Kendall entered. "Forgive the intrusion, my lady," he said as he addressed Marisa, "but I have a letter for you from the earl. He bade me deliver it into no other hands but your own."

"Then please do so," Marisa insisted, rising.

She took the paper from his hand. Turning it over, she saw the newly made seal Cameron had ordered. She broke the wax that held the folded sheet of paper together and quickly scanned the words.

My dearest wife:
I bid you come to me.

It was signed with a bold C. Marisa noted that there was another line scrawled on the bottom.

Kendall will tell you where. Trust him. Trust me.

Marisa looked up from the paper held tightly in her hand, her eyes locking with Kendall's. "You know?"

"Yes, my lady."

"Marisa, what has happened?" the dowager demanded. Her granddaughter's face had metamorphosed from pensive to elated in a matter of moments.

"I must attend to something most urgent and important, *grand-mère*," Marisa responded, her heart giving a skip of joy in her chest. Cameron had kept his promise.

Marisa quickly left the room. "Follow me, Kendall," she intructed as she walked past the manservant.

"Marisa, where are you going?" her grandmother's voice called after her.

After what I want, grand-mère, Marisa longed to shout. Instead, she paused in her rush up the stairs to fetch her cloak. Barbara stood at the bottom, a perplexed look on her face, Brianna and Jamie behind her.

"Why, to solve a most pressing problem, of course," she said, a tinkle of laughter floating down the steps in her wake.

Chapter Eighteen

As she strolled along the walkway towards the pond, holding a napkin filled with bread crumbs to feed to the black swans, Lady Brianna wondered what problem beset her cousin that she had to dash off before finishing the morning meal.

A rumble of distant thunder echoed in the sky. She lifted her head, staring into the grayness above. Rain would soon come. Would that it could wash away all the sorrows and the pain, all the regrets and the follies of her life, cleansing her soul. But it would not; could not. She was—Brianna waxed philosophical—who she was.

One regret that she allowed herself was that she had not joined in the dancing last night. How wonderful it would have been to have accepted Jamie Covington's offer, to have stood up with him, to have danced once more, to have experienced the pleasure of moving to the music.

She had watched with envy as her cousin danced the *bourrée* with Jamie, her feet tapping silently along as she sat in her chair, watching. When the lively country dance was played, she listened to the dowager countess's conversation with only half an ear as she stole glances at the participants, most especially Cameron Buchanan's good friend. It was during one of these stolen glimpses that she caught the rather direct look which Jamie Covington threw her way.

How very different he was from her cousin's intense, ofttimes brooding, husband. Jamie was kind. About Marisa's husband she sensed a barely leashed power held in tight check; with Jamie she saw only a pleasant, even-tempered man.

Yet, Brianna also recognized her interest in Jamie as a man. It had flared to life suddenly and without warning. After Donal, she was mistrustful of that impulse. She had been fooled once before, mistaking her young girl's pleasure in being courted with true love.

She had to admit that Jamie was nothing like Donal.

But, a nagging voice asked her, how could she be so sure? Donal had not revealed to her his true nature until after they were properly wedded.

Brianna did not question how she knew, she merely accepted that Jamie Covington was not another Donal MacBride. Perhaps because of what she had seen there last evening in his hazel eyes, eyes that had looked at her with what she deduced was a glow of admiration. Donal's eyes, Brianna recalled, were selfish, lusting only for his own satisfaction.

She bent upon the grass, tossing the morsels

towards the placidly swimming swans. How beautiful they looked, she thought, a smile curving her lips. So peaceful and serene.

How beautiful she looked, Jamie thought as he came upon her. She appeared tranquil, almost swanlike in her black widow's garb. The lady of the lake, lost in her own private sorrow, locked tightly inside her shell of grief.

With each day he discovered himself falling more and more in love with Brianna: her gentle smile, her quiet laugh, her sweet nature.

He took a deep breath. Obstacles blocked the path to his love. How did she feel about him? That was his first consideration. He was a Protestant Englishman; she an Irish Catholic. She was the daughter and sister of an earl, related by blood to two other powerful noble families; he was without title, little caring for the added burdens and trappings of rank. He had no family. His was a modest fortune, well able to support a wife in reasonable comfort; but would that be enough for one used to wealth above his means?

And could another man replace the love she must have felt for her dead husband? He saw first-hand that she honored MacBride's memory with her close keeping of her mourning. Perhaps no one could ever supplant MacBride in her heart. Or, if not that, then could another man, could *he*, at least bring some measure of happiness into her life? He would willingly accept a smaller part of her heart if that was all she had to give.

"Lady Brianna?" Jamie spoke softly.

Brianna was startled, her head snapping to the side. She had believed that she was alone, save for the swans and an occasional duck.

There he stood, the man who had somehow become an important part of her life in just days. He had taken residence inside of her mind, and, she was afraid, within her heart. Was he the love that Mistress Buck foretold? Or had she simply misread his kindness for more than it was?

Blushing at her wayward thoughts, Brianna started to rise. Jamie's hand was before her, offering its strength. She accepted. Holding his steady, blunt-fingered hand, she felt suddenly safe. Jamie possessed hands capable of comfort. Donal's hands had been big and clumsy, prone to hurt.

"We had little chance to talk at breakfast," he said.

"I know," Brianna agreed.

"How are you?" he asked, still holding her hand. It was warm and soft. How right it felt resting in his.

"Tolerably well," she insisted, feeling suddenly shy in his presence.

Jamie cursed himself at that point, wishing for just this once that he had some measure of Cam's skill with words, and with women. Damn, Jamie swore silently, he felt awkward. His experience with women was minimal. In London he lived in a world of easy conquests and casual exchanges; he found that life contrary to his nature. Brianna's late husband had probably been a very skilled and sophisticated lover, practiced in the arts of wooing and winning a woman, much like the king was and Cam had been. What could he offer a woman who had been used to an exciting man? He knew himself to be quiet, given to reading and playing chess. He had long ago accepted the sobriquet of *The king's Puritan*.

Yet he wanted the Lady Brianna for his life's companion.

Would she think that he was reaching above his station? Would she ridicule his intent, believing that he served only his ambition instead of his heart?

Again thunder cracked, closer this time.

"We must return to the house," Brianna insisted.

Jamie, his hand still holding hers tightly, pulled her along with him as they dashed for safety.

Before they could get back to the main house, the rain came. They were soaked, their clothes clinging to their bodies. They made it as far as the summerhouse, where they sought shelter.

"We can stay here for a while, wait and see if the storm will calm," Jamie said, brushing back the wet hair from his broad forehead.

Brianna, who had finally released his hand upon entering the summerhouse, was cold and out of breath. Her black dress was heavy with moisture, molding her slender body. To a man used to the women of the king's Court, with their brightly gowned, voluptuous beauty, Brianna thought she must look like a half-drowned crow, thin and dark.

She began to shiver.

"If you will permit me," Jamie asked, and removing his doublet, he placed it about her slim shoulders.

Brianna was grateful. Even though the material was wet, it still provided her with extra warmth. "Thank you," she murmured.

The rain still pelted the earth around them. Within the summerhouse, Brianna and Jamie snuggled closer to each other. They sat on the marble bench, watching and listening to the force of the rain, sheltered by the wood and the roses, the scent of which hung heavy in the air.

Brianna sighed, basking in Jamie's companionship. The rain mattered little now. All that seemed to matter was the comfort she was drawing from the closeness of this particular man.

Jamie reached out his hand to smooth the tangles of damp hair from her neck, stroking the glossy black strands. Grasping a fistful, he lifted it to his mouth.

"What are you doing?" Brianna demanded, shifting in her seat so that she faced him.

Jamie let the hair slip through his fingers, interested now in the smooth curve of her mouth, in the heavy-lashed, golden-brown eyes, which blinked in bafflement. He lowered his head until his lips touched hers.

Brianna was taken by surprise, shocked to feel Jamie's mouth on hers. She sat still, expecting to feel his lips grinding into hers, drawing blood, savaging the flesh, as Donal's had done on those infrequent occasions when he had assaulted her mouth before he had assaulted her body.

Jamie's mouth, in contrast, was sweet and gentle. There was no threat in it.

Brianna relaxed, giving herself up to the tenderness of the moment.

Jamie pulled Brianna closer into his embrace, unable to believe that he was holding the woman he loved within his arms. Emboldened, he deepened the kiss.

Panic filled Brianna's breast. She could feel herself unraveling like a spool of tapestry yarn, unwinding in Jamie's hands. Brianna pushed him away. Oh, sweet mother of God, what must he think of me? she wondered, her hands flying to her face. "Forgive me," she muttered in a husky tone, and before Jamie could react, Brianna had fled the enclosure, his doublet dropped in her haste.

A very confused Jamie watched her run. What had gone wrong?

Cam could hear the steady beat of the rain as it struck the roof of the crofter's cottage. He opened the door, peering out, searching for Marisa. He thought she would have been here ere now. The cold dampness of the day filtered through the thin shirt he wore. Closing the door, Cam walked to the fire, standing before it to capture some if its warmth.

What if the weather had changed her mind?

What if she had simply refused to heed his command?

He cast his eye around the interior of the cottage. It was neat, scrubbed clean of the neglect he'd first encountered weeks ago. Kendall's hard work showed. Cam acknowledged that he owed his manservant a reward. A bed dominated one side of the room, the headboard made of entwined branches tied securely together. A fresh feather mattress and clean white sheets, as well as several plump feather pillows, beckoned.

Cam picked up a large, colorful piece of folded cloth. It was the Buchanan tartan, a potent reminder of his home and his family. He lifted the material to his nose, smelling the familiar fragrant scent of the heather. It brought back strong memories. Though England was now the land he called home, Scotland would forever be his heart's chosen place, the bonny land of his birth. He shook the twilled woolen fabric and placed it on the bed.

It was fitting, Cam decided, for the bridal bed of a Buchanan. The tartan served as a visible reminder to him of who he was. Pride in his heritage was deeply ingrained in Cam's soul. He vowed that his heirs would also know that pride, no matter that they were born on English soil.

He poured himself a measure of the hot, mulled wine into one of the matching pewter goblets, taking a deep drink. A large canvas knapsack lay on the pine table. Cam undid the strap that secured it, lifting out a long, thin scarf of the same tartan as the blanket. He ran his left hand across the material, the soft, well-worn texture pleasing to the touch. Perfect. He removed another item from the knapsack. It was a dirk. Sliding the long, razor-sharp blade from its sheath, he made a slight cut in the scarf. With his bare hands, he rent the material into halves. Now it would serve his purpose.

Marisa sat atop her big white stallion in her borrowed disguise. The surrounding woods were dark and heavy with mist. A sense of enchantment loomed; she could feel it all around her, as real as the boy's clothes she wore. Before her, less than half a mile away, stood the crofter's stone cottage. Smoke curled from the chimney. At least it would be warm and dry inside.

But was that all she was expecting? All she was looking for?

She could leave before he was the wiser. Go back to Graywood as if nothing out of the ordinary had occurred. Disregard the note. Ignore his dictate.

Remus pawed the muddy ground, tossing his head impatiently.

Giving the stallion his head, Marisa obeyed her heart's prompting.

Not for king, nor policy.

Not for duty, nor dynastic obligations.

Not for vows, nor lust.

For love alone, she went to him.

She *loved* Cameron Buchanan. With all that was in her, with all that she possessed, she loved that man. *Her* man. Slowly. Deeply. Intensely. Irrevocably.

He was the partner of her heart, her soul, her mind. And now he would become the partner of her flesh.

He heard the sound of the horse's arrival. She'd come, at last.

Cam rose from his seat at the table, confident that the moment he'd waited for was indeed at hand. Opening the door, he saw a slim figure in a dark cloak and a plumed hat emerging from the small stable. He narrowed his good eye. It appeared to be a youth making his way across the space that separated the two buildings.

With a gloved hand holding his hat in place, the youth dashed for the door, the rain's tempo increasing to a heavier downpour. Safe inside the warm building, the youth kept his back to Cam, unaware of the cool stare from the man in the doorway.

"You'd best be shutting the door, my lord earl," spoke the youth in an Irish accent, removing the wet wool cloak with a slight twirl of the material, shaking off the droplets of excess water and placing it over a chair, "lest we be drowning."

Cam, his mood shifting to one of bitter disappointment, asked, "Have you a message from my wife?" Damnation! he swore silently. All his plans for naught.

The youth pulled the hat from her head,

sending the waves of chestnut hair tumbling around her shoulders. Her green eyes were alight with mirth when she turned around. "Aye," she replied.

"Marisa!" Cam exclaimed in surprise.

With an elegant sweeping bow, Marisa, dressed in her borrowed boy's garb of breeches, hose, shoes and shirt, said with a touch of the brogue, "Sure and 'tis the same, my good lord."

Cam let himself take a long, slow journey over the woman standing, arms akimbo, before him. In candlelight and fireglow the curves of her body were revealed. Marisa wore a slightly damp shirt of white cotton, beneath which her bare breasts rose and fell with her steady breathing. The wool breeches clung to her legs, ending at her knees. Her legs were covered in mud-splattered white hose and black shoes.

His keen glance forced her to drop her gaze. A warmth flooded her face even as a chill took hold of her. Marisa bent towards the fire, slipping off her wet shoes in the process. She sat down on the thick sheepskin that lay before the hearth. With a casual gesture, she ran her hand over the texture of the fleece, finding pleasure in the feel of it sliding through her fingers.

Cam found his blood beginning to heat at her unconsciously sensual gesture. Would that her hands were doing the same to him. He crossed the room and took a seat next to her on a pine chair of plain and simple design. "Give me your foot, lass," he said.

Marisa turned her head, looking up into his face. Her own glance was puzzled.

"Your foot," Cam repeated, tapping his left thigh with his hand.

Marisa moved her body so that she was now

facing him. Leaning back on her elbows, she lifted her right leg to him.

Cam captured her leg, smiling at her pose. From his vantage point he could see the rosy points of her nipples thrusting against the embroidered lawn of her shirt. He placed her foot in the cradle of his thighs, close to the hardening proof of his desire. Cupping her calf with his broken hand, he reached over and undid the button that fastened the stockings to her breeches at the knee. With skill, he slid the hose slowly down her leg, caressing the smooth skin as he did so until at last he pulled the material from her foot, tossing it to the floor.

Her toes curled slightly as Cam ran his index finger along her heel and Marisa moved her foot in response, coming in contact with the bulge of his masculine body as her foot rested on the evidence of his sex. Shocked, she pulled her foot away.

Had she been more experienced, Cam thought with a sigh, Marisa might well have kept her bare foot in place and rubbed against the swelling inside his breeches.

"Now," he said, his voice taking on a huskier tone, "give me the other."

Obeying, Marisa did as he requested.

Cam ministered to that leg in the same manner as before, chasing away the chill and replacing it with a spreading warmth.

Marisa swallowed, her eyes locked with his gaze. What, she wondered, did she see there? Lust? Certainly, she decided. Her husband was a man, with all of a man's wants, moreover one with a reputation as a rake that equaled that of the king. Being with a woman was no new experience for him. It did, however, give her a measure of satisfaction to think that even as unschooled as she was in the arts of physical gratification, she could make him want her. She blinked and looked again. Pride, a trait they shared, was also apparent to her. And patience. She saw that there, too. As if time itself had no place in this cottage. She somehow understood that this would be no hurried coupling.

Her throat seemed suddenly dry. Breaking eye contact with him, Marisa noticed the copper pot that rested on the table.

"'Tis mulled wine," Cam said. "Do you wish some?"

Marisa replied, "Yes."

"It should still be warm," he said.

Marisa laid her hand tentatively against the copper pot and found it still retained some heat.

"Do you wish it hotter?" Cam asked.

"No," she answered, "this will suffice." She poured herself a small amount in the pewter goblet, relishing the sweet taste of the blended spices and wine. After draining the contents, she felt more relaxed. Restless, she walked towards the bed. It presented an invitation with its piles of fluffy pillows and the colorful woven cloth that lay across it. Marisa picked up the material. Yellow, green, and red blended into a distinct pattern. Marisa swiveled slightly so that she could see Cam. "Yours?" she asked.

"Aye," he responded. "'Tis the Buchanan plaid."

"Then those colors are now mine," Marisa stated firmly, replacing the tartan on the bed. She drew in a deep breath, and said, her clear voice carrying to his ears, "As I am now yours." For her, there was no turning back. Her hands moved to the buttons that fastened the breeches. Undoing them, she pushed the breeches down past her hips. They pooled at her bare feet and she kicked them to one side. She stood there in her borrowed shirt. Her hands were trembling as she touched the fabric and lifted the hem.

Cam watched in silence as his wife discarded her breeches, the blood drumming in his ears. The exposed lithe limbs tantalized him; the shirt, barely covering her bottom from his view, slowly lifted. He drank in the sight of her slim back, the white skin that looked as smooth as silk. Her only covering was now her lustrous chestnut hair.

Scraping back his chair, Cam rose.

Marisa pivoted slowly. She faced him, unafraid, though nervous.

Cam reached out his left hand, gently pushing aside the strands of her hair, exposing one full breast. He inhaled deeply, as if the air had been forced out of his lungs. Stepping back, he dropped his gaze. In a leisurely, unhurried manner, he swept his glance from her feet, moving it along her legs, past the nest of reddish-brown curls that gathered at the apex of her thighs, lingering there for several seconds, to the indentation of her waist, rising to encompass the ripe maturity of her bosom.

"Beautiful," he pronounced with an engaging smile on his lips even as he wished with all that was in him that he could face Marisa in the same way—flesh to flesh. But he couldn't ever risk the humiliation, the damnable hurt that would certainly follow. The emptiness of that thought scorched his soul.

Yet he wanted her, craved her with an unending hunger—and she was here.

"Cameron." It was a plea, a question, a command.

Cam bent his head, his mouth seeking her own.

This time her mouth responded eagerly, opening beneath his. Marisa's arms lifted and encircled his neck, her hands feathering through the thick old-gold curls.

His hands slipped around her waist, the softness of her skin like the most expensive satin, drawing her closer to his body, molding her curves to him. Calling in all his reserves of strength, Cam bent slightly and lifted Marisa into his arms. With his good leg, he leaned on the bed, laying her gently down.

In his wife's green eyes he saw trust—and concern. What he couldn't bear to ever see there would be pity or revulsion. From her eyes, he recognized, it would be a mortal wound. He said a silent prayer that she would someday understand and forgive him for what he would have to do.

Cam shifted off the bed, standing. He walked to the door, thowing the bar, locking the world outside. He carefully removed the soft kid boots he wore, his gaze on his waiting wife.

"Cameron," Marisa murmured softly, "the bed is empty without you. Please come back."

This was an invitation he could not refuse.

Again, he succumbed to the temptation to sample her mouth. Her lips, he found, were like the finest wine, completely intoxicating.

Marisa's hands roamed over his back, her fingers feeling the play of sleek muscles beneath the fabric of his shirt. She welcomed the weight of his lean body on hers.

Cam reached into the pocket of his breeches as his mouth kept passionate possession of hers. His fingers tightened around one of the strips of tartan. Extricating it, Cam broke the kiss. As Marisa blinked in surprise, he placed his lips along the column of her throat, moving them across her shoulder, nipping the flesh lightly. His right hand held her left arm to the bed as his mouth traveled the length of her other arm, nibbling and kissing. He put his mouth to her palm, his left hand looping the already knotted fabric around her wrist.

Marisa, her attention focused on the trail his lips were taking, did not, at first, feel the material until the noose was tightened. She flung her head to the side and saw the long strip of plaid fastened to her wrist. "Cameron, what are you doing?"

"What I must," he answered. He forced her arm backwards, keeping her bucking body pinned under his by the sheer force of his weight. He managed to finally tie the other end of the ragged strip to one of the branches forming the headboard.

"Let me go!" Marisa screamed.

"Never," Cam said, taking her mouth yet again for a brief, deeply intense kiss.

"You must be mad," she gasped, fighting back the fear that rose within her.

"Nae, my bonny lass," he whispered, "only determined." Cam forced her head still, his hand cupping her stubborn chin. "Dinna fight me, for I will nae hurt you, Marisa. You must trust me. 'Tis all I ask."

"*Trust you?*" she challenged, thinking that she had plunged into a wild nightmare. She was alone. No one except for Kendall knew where she was. "Why should I?" she demanded.

Because I love you, Cam wanted to say, though he knew he couldn't utter those words to her now. Maybe he could never say them to her. Determined to continue on his chosen path, he bound her other wrist, ignoring her question.

Satisfied that she was secure, Cam lifted his body off hers. He lay on his right side, forcing his mind to disregard the pain in his leg, focusing instead on the slender body beside him. His left hand moved along the delicate bones of her shoulder, skimming across the smooth flesh, dipping into the valley between her breasts. Cupping one breast, Cam molded his hand around the fullness. His thumb danced around the rosy nipple; it stiffened in response.

When his lips touched her breast, worshipping it, Marisa gasped. His mouth sucked on the tender flesh, his tongue licking circles around the pointed crest. A moan erupted low in her throat; before she could stifle it, it burst from her mouth. Her healthy young body was responding in spite of the circumstances. Fear ebbed, replaced by the spell conjured by Cam's mouth and hand, by those delightfully dexterous fingers.

Cam stroked his hand over her body in a sweeping caress, getting to know each inch of her skin, each rib, each bone. He followed his hand with his warm mouth, tasting her skin. It still retained the scent of her perfume. He traced the shape of her belly, dipping lower with his fingertips. If Marisa were other than a virgin, he wouldn't have hesitated to bend his head so that he could savor the complete taste of her. That, he promised himself, would come later, when she had abandoned any lingering inhibitions.

Those chestnut curls continued to beckon him.

Marisa had tried, unsuccessfully, to divorce her mind from what was happening to her body. It was impossible when with every touch, Cam stirred to life acute feelings she hadn't even known herself capable of. Warmth licked at her insides, flaring hot and vital.

The insistent demand of his mouth, coupled with the teasing motions of his fingers, caused Marisa to writhe. She couldn't escape his tender assault. As his tongue duelled with hers, his exploring fingers found the heat they sought. Slipping past the chestnut curls, he probed and delved until Marisa thought she would faint from so intimate a touch. Stars exploded behind her closed lids as she strained against her bonds while he worked magic with his hand. Her breasts rose and fell with each ragged, rapid breath.

Cam watched as Marisa slipped over the edge from his ministrations. Then, when he was certain she was ready, Cam quickly unbuttoned his breeches, freeing himself. Rising slightly, he slid into her body, stopped by the barrier of her maidenhead. Bracing himself, Cam began to push, trying to ease his way past the proof of her virgin state.

Marisa's eyes flew open. Cam was between her legs, still clothed, the wool of his breeches rubbing against the inside of her thighs. Her legs were nudged wider as she felt the hard, probing length of him testing the impediment of her maidenhead. Splinters of pain shot through her. Marisa tried to move her body, but still he continued the rhythm of pushing in and out.

Cam reached a decision. He withdrew from her body for a moment, then thrust deeply. Marisa's cry of pain tore at his heart as he let his body take over, moving inexorably toward the ultimate conclusion. The tight grip of her flesh, her movements now instinctually matching his own, welcomed him. Buried deep within her body, Cam could hold back no longer. He exploded, his seed filling her.

Their shattered cries echoed throughout the room.

Cam lay spent at Marisa's side. He closed his eye, taking in gulps of air. Sweet Lord, he thought, no climax had ever shattered him as deeply as this. His mind and body had soared, pushing him higher, taking him further than ever before. He'd completely abandoned himself and discovered that there was a lesson to be learned. With Marisa he'd unlocked a door to himself he hadn't know even existed. The pleasure and satisfaction he'd known from countless other women dissolved against the pure fire of their joining.

Love, which had been missing from his earlier liaisons, had transformed the merely physical act of sex into the most powerful, potent force. As he had claimed Marisa, so had she claimed him. He would be her man alone for all the days of their life, and beyond.

Marisa awoke. She saw that she was alone in the bed, her hands were unbound, and the tartan had been thrown over her body. Mixed with a decided soreness in her limbs was an awareness of being very much alive.

The last thing she recalled was the impact of Cam's penetration of her body—as if even bound, she was freer than at any other time in her life. So intense was the feeling that she had lost her hold on her emotions, crying his name as she spun out of control. She opened her eyes moments later, only to give in to the need for sleep, so exhausted was she.

But why had her husband deemed it neccessary to use the bonds? Her eyes had locked with his when they joined; she had seen no hint of madness, only surprise.

She shifted her body, looking around the room. She was alone, with no sign of Cam. Had he taken what he wanted and left her?

The damp gust of air shot through the room when the door opened. Marisa pulled the tartan closer to her body as Cam entered, carrying a wooden bucket filled with water. She met his glance, her fists clutching the material. A voice inside her mocked her for her sudden shyness. Hadn't he seen all there was of her to view?

She was so incredibly beautiful, he thought. The light of the numerous candles illuminated her skin, giving it the rich sheen of a pearl. "Did I wake you?"

"No," she answered, her green eyes wary. His voice sounded formal to her ears, as if they had not recently shared a bed—and their bodies.

"I fed the horses," he said, placing the bucket on the table. Cam removed the cloak he was wearing. What he wanted to do at that precise moment was to join Marisa in the bed, exploring further the realms of the senses. He desperately wanted to feel her hands on his body, her mouth on his flesh, *all* of his flesh. He wanted to to teach her how to pleasure a man.

But to do that, he would have to let her see the malicious handiwork of another woman. And that, his pride would never, ever allow. Better, he concluded, for her to feel anger rather than pity. Better for her to question than to know.

Picking up the embroidered handkerchief, her gift the day of the ball, Cam said, "I have not had the chance to thank you for yet another lovely gift. I do so now."

Marisa answered automatically, "You are most

welcome," thinking it strange to be having this conversation, especially now. Each was avoiding talking about what had happened.

Cam dipped the linen into the bucket, squeezing out the excess water.

Marisa, her green eyes wide, watched as he approached her.

He sat on the edge of the bed, his good eye locked with hers. "I willna hurt you lass, I promise."

Marisa believed him. It was beyond logic, and she accepted that fact. His damaged right hand moved over the tartan, pushing it slowly away from her body. She blushed and dropped her gaze, wondering at the impulse that leapt within her to beg him to take her once again. The pain she'd experienced upon his breaching of her maidenhead had dissolved, replaced by a sense of wonder, of rapture so complete she couldn't ignore its allure.

Cam placed the wet linen against her skin, wiping away the traces of blood from her thighs and between her legs. Marisa gasped at the cool feel of the cloth, at the touch of his hand in intimate contact with her body. Her legs splayed slightly and Cam, unable to resist the temptation, bent his head, his mouth barely touching the reddish-brown curls before he withdrew.

He stood up, curbing the deep ache in his heart and in his body with maximum control. Much as he yearned for Marisa, and for a repetition of the glorious time that they had shared, Cam recognized now that it was impossible. He'd come too far, and there was no turning back. His grand scheme to make love to her on his own terms had met with an unexpected problem: because he loved Marisa, he couldn't continue to act the thief and steal moments when he wanted hours, to hobble her body in exchange for his freedom.

This day had been their first as lovers; it would also be, he vowed, their last.

Chapter Nineteen

A thick, uneasy silence hung about the room. Both the man and the woman kept their own counsel, each wondering when, or if, they should speak. The rain had ceased, and the evening was cool. Cam had opened a small window, letting in some fresh air. A grim smile touched the corners of his mouth. Sitting in an increasingly uncomfortable chair was hardly the way he'd envisioned spending the rest of the evening. Instead of enjoying the delights of his wife's body, he was trapped alone with his own damnable secrets, unable to offer an explanation.

Perhaps it was just as well. He doubted that his wife was in a good humor. He'd witnessed the confusion on her face, the questions in her green eyes.

Hunger gnawed at his stomach, interrupting his flow of thought, for he had not eaten since early this morn. Courtesy dictated that he include his wife, no matter the circumstances. Cam levered himself from the chair, taking hold of his gold-tipped cane to steady his aching right leg. Turning, he saw that Marisa was awake. She lay on the bed, the tartan still her only covering. In his most polished court voice, he asked, "Will you join me for supper, Marisa?"

Marisa nodded her head in agreement. "Yes, I will," she answered. She had lain awake, trying to come up with answers, but to no avail. How completely unorthodox this situation seemed. Cameron had withdrawn into silence, keeping his distance from her, and she had no idea what to do.

So she remained calm, pondering what the future held for them.

Cam placed his cane on the table and turned around to fetch a sturdy open basket, a large square of cloth covering the top, from the corner of the room. He brought it back to the table and deposited it on the well-worn scrubbed surface.

Marisa, the Buchanan tartan still clutched to her body, rose from the bed, grabbing the discarded breeches and shirt from the stone floor. It felt cold to her bare feet. Spinning around, she draped the cloth over her shoulders as she pulled on the breeches. Dropping the tartan, she pulled the shirt over her head.

Cam stopped what he was doing, unloading the basket of foodstuffs, and watched. His loins ached with wanting her. He yearned to slide his hand along the curve of her back, following it with his mouth, tasting all the while. Pulling his wayward thoughts back into line, he continued his task, removing two loaves of fresh-baked bread, several varieties of apples— he had been told by Kendall that the cook insisted they were the best she had, and had just come from Kent—and cherries and peaches. A small ham and three wedges of cheese followed.

Marisa, feeling more in control now that she was fully dressed, paused as she tugged on her hose, slicing a wary glance at her husband as he wielded the sharp knife. Though not born left-handed, he used the knife with skill and dexterity. His wrist was strong, his fingers flexible. The breath caught in her throat. She had firsthand knowledge of the power and beauty that that skillful hand was capable of.

Sitting opposite him, Marisa accepted a pewter plate piled with ham, cheese, and fruit.

"Wine?" he asked, holding the bottle.

"Yes," she said. Then, when she had taken a drink and placed the goblet on the table, it was her turn to pose the question. "Why?"

Cam met her gaze with his own. "I canna say," was his response.

"Cannot or will not?"

Cam's answer was to shrug his broad shoulders.

Her green eyes darkened with anger. "You cannot tell me what happened between us was how it should be?"

Cam countered her question with, "What do you know of how it should be?"

"You had no need," she protested.

"I had my reasons," he stated, taking the opportunity to have another drink.

"Then help me to understand what they are," she pleaded.

"'Tis no concern of yours."

"Liar!" she said vehemently.

Cam's single blue eye darkened. "Heed your tongue, lass."

"I am a Fitzgerald—we do not bow to threats."

Cam stretched out his hand and grasped her slender wrist. "You are a Buchanan now, my lady. In name, and in deed."

"Who came willingly to you," she countered.

"I know that," he admitted, releasing her hand.

"Then why truss me like a plucked foul?"

Cam ignored her question; instead, he began to eat.

Marisa, vexed by his unwillingness to answer her questions, sank her teeth into the flesh of an apple, enjoying the satisfying crunch. With her hands free she could help herself to whatever she wanted. Several hours past, she had wanted to hold her husband in her arms, to feel his skin under her fingers, to explore his body as he had hers. She remembered how it felt when she had touched Cameron in the summerhouse and in his room at the inn when she had come to deliver her thanks for saving her life.

Sweet mother of God, Marisa thought, looking at him as she dropped her hand with the fruit to the table. She believed she knew why it was that he had bound her. It was to *keep* her from caressing him.

"You did not want me to touch you, did you?" she asked in a direct tone.

Cam's face was impassive; the only hint that her inquiry touched him was in the tightening of the muscles in his face.

Marisa had her answer.

He should have known she would guess. Marisa was far too clever and intelligent to be fooled for long. Yet, still he couldn't admit the truth. A lie of sorts would protect him, he decided; it would keep her a safe distance from his heart.

"You are determined, my lady wife. I shall grant you that." Cam laughed harshly. "Aye, I have my reasons. The most important being an heir from your body." His voice cut through her with the cold precision of steel.

"A child?"

"Aye, a bairn. A son, I would hope."

"That still does not explain . . ."

"My God," he interrupted her, "must you make me say all the words?"

"Yes," she urged, believing that he would finally confide in her.

"I took the only part of your body that I wanted, that I had a need of," he stated bluntly. "I dinna need clinging arms or clumsy hands."

The blood drained from Marisa's face. The sight and smell of the food made her want to retch.

"Whilst I rode you, I thought of the woman whom I love," Cam said. "'Twas her arms I craved about me." He spoke the truth—though Marisa didn't know it—for she was the woman.

Then he added, "If I could nae have her, than none other would do."

Humiliation burned Marisa's skin. She been a damnable, lovesick fool. Her husband was in love with another woman. "You loved this other woman, yet you wed me?"

"I am a loyal subject of his Majesty. Marriage to you brought me more than I ever dreamed possible." Love was her richest dowry gift to him.

"As am I," Marisa said flatly, referring to her own loyalty. "I pray your seed takes root so you may be spared from seeking to perform your onerous *duty*."

Cam pushed the words out of his mouth reluctantly. "I need not love you to bed you."

I need not, but I do remained unspoken.

"Excuse me," Marisa said, rising from her chair. "My appetite has failed me." She was determined that Cameron would not see her cry. She made her way to the door, walking proudly outside before the tears stained her cheeks.

Cam, too, had lost his appetite. He had forcibly cast aside the one woman he wanted close. Containing the scream that threatened to erupt from his throat, he stood up, giving the table a mighty shove, upending it, scattering the food all over the stone floor. He shifted his gaze to the door. There was still time. He could tell her . . .

No, for him time had run out.

Marisa fled to the small storage barn, tears scorching her eyes. Anger and hurt rose within her at Cameron's revealing words and his subsequent actions.

Romulus and Remus gave her a friendly nicker when she entered the stone building. Looking around, she saw the two saddles piled to one side of the structure. Untying Remus, she lead the big horse from the stall he occupied. Throwing the saddle upon his back, she fastened it securely. Marisa knew that she couldn't remain here any longer. She would take her chances riding back alone rather than stay there. Standing on top of a wooden barrel, she mounted her horse. Ducking to make it through the door, Marisa touched her heels to Remus's sides and the animal took off in a gallop.

Cam heard the excited whinny of one of the horses as he made his way to the door. Opening it, he saw one of the white stallions, with Marisa on his back, tearing off into the darkness.

He couldn't blame the lass. He half expected that she would have grabbed his dirk had it been nearby and stabbed him with it if she could, such was the look of raw pain he saw in her green eyes. If he saddled Romulus, he might still be able to catch up with her and force her back.

But to what?

For what?

Cam closed the door, deciding that it was better to let his wife lick her wounds in private. He surveyed the results of his wrath—the scattered foodstuffs, the wine, spilled like so much blood upon the stone floor, the table lying on its side. His glance fell on the empty bed. It was then that Cam realized that he, too, could not stay here.

He grabbed his knapsack and walking stick from the floor. Removing the tartan from the bed, he stuffed it quickly into the canvas bag, along with the still damp handkerchief.

Cam paused in the doorway, giving the cottage one last look. Then, with a savage gesture, he slammed the door as he left, shutting away the memories, though he could not shut the door in his mind quite so firmly.

Marisa lay soaking in a warm tub, having returned to her home. Her bedraggled apearance was noticed by several of her household staff, who prudently refrained from mentioning it. Charity had kept her questions unasked when Marisa threw her a quelling glance. Having caught sight of herself in the mirror when she entered her bedroom, Marisa shuddered. She looked like some wild, windblown waif. She ordered a bath brought to her immediately.

It was easy to wash the traces of Cameron from her body; not so easy to wash him from her mind. The water soothed her, relaxing the soreness she felt in her thighs. A hard ride over the hills, astride, after her initial experience at lovemaking, had pressed her body almost beyond its limits.

The water had cooled, as had her mood. Standing, she stepped from the tub, wiping off the moisture with a soft cloth towel. Her hand slid over the flatness of her belly. Marisa wondered if Cameron's child could have taken root within her body so quickly.

Before she could grab an article of clothing to cover herself, the door to her room flew open. Marisa spun around to see the dowager countess standing there.

Her grandmother shut the door with a snap.

"What's amiss?"

Marisa gave her grandmother a blank, slightly vague look as she bent to pick up the kitten, Lionheart, from the floor where it had been playing with an unraveled ball of tapestry yarn. She stroked the kitten's black fur as it meowed its enjoyment.

Barbara was not fooled. "Something *is* wrong," she insisted. "I was informed by Kendall earlier this day that you and the earl would be spending the night at a cottage on the property. That I was not to worry, for 'twas of your choice. Then I hear that you have returned from Maude, who had it from one of the kitchen girls, who said you had returned alone, looking like a disheveled boy." Her brows rose with her next statement. "'Tis barely gone eight of the clock."

"I changed my mind."

"Did you? Or was it changed for you?"

Marisa returned the kitten to the floor and walked to the trunk at the foot of her bed, removing a robe of white lawn edged in lace from inside. Slipping it on, she tied the belt securely around her waist.

Her grandmother had moved and taken a seat in a low chair, her eyes focused on her grand-daughter.

Marisa recognized the need she felt, at that moment, to confide in someone. Who better than her grandmother, with her own mother in Ireland? She could trust her grandmother, who was a woman of great experience. She joined Barbara, sitting at her feet, her head resting against her grandmother's leg.

Barbara reached out her hand and stroked her grandchild's flowing chestnut tresses. At times, 'twas like looking into a mirror, with the years washed away, when she beheld Marisa. "Tell me," she demanded softly.

Marisa spoke low and clear. "Cameron left me a message, asking me to come to him. I did. After last night . . ."

"What happened last night?"

"I left the company and went walking in the garden. Soon, I found myself at the summerhouse. Cameron followed me there."

"Ah," was all the older woman said, but it was invested with a wealth of meaning.

"We kissed."

"A good beginning."

"I thought so." Marisa raised her head, her green eyes meeting her grandmother's.

"Answer me this—do you love him?"

Marisa seemed reluctant to give her grand-mother a response.

Barbara repeated her question. "A simple yes or no will suffice, child."

"Yes, I love him, *grand-mère*," Marisa acknowl-edged. "More than I believed possible."

Barbara gave her grandaughter a sage smile. "'Tis the curse and the salvation of the Fitzgeralds," she said. "'Twas evident to these old eyes that you cared deeply for your husband."

"I realized just how much when I answered his summons."

The old countess gave a long sigh. "With our ilk, 'tis all or nothing." She saw the sheen of tears in her grandchild's shimmering green eyes. "Did he hurt you?" Barbara asked sharply.

Marisa bowed her head. "Not in the way you think, *grand-mère.*'Tis a wound to my pride—and to my heart."

"Explain yourself."

"I wanted my marriage to be real."

"In the physical sense?"

"Yes," Marisa confessed. "'Tis been postponed for far too long—but now I was ready, and I thought he was too."

"He did not take you?" Lady Barbara lifted Marisa's chin with her hand.

Marisa blushed.

Barbara had her answer. "What went wrong?" Perhaps, she reasoned, the Scotsman was too vigorously earthy, too seasoned a rake for her grandchild. Marisa possessed passion, that Barbara could well see, though her granddaughter was an innocent. Marisa was a woman to be wooed and won, not trampled under some petty male conceit.

Marisa wondered how she should begin her tale. Shrugging her slim shoulders, she decided to be blunt.

"Before he made me his wife, he tied me to the bed."

"He did what?" Barbara blurted out. She thought it was a trifle early in their marriage for that particular variation.

"He took hold of my hands and tied them with a cloth," she said slowly, "his clan colors, actually, to the head of the bed so I could not touch him or hold him.

"I begged him to tell me why. At first he refused, then, reluctantly, he told me he loved another woman, and that his purpose was to get me with child. An heir for the earldom." Marisa paused and took a deep breath. "If he could not be in the arms of the woman he loved, then he wanted no others about him. While he was claiming me as his bride, he was thinking of another woman," Marisa said, her voice raw with emotion.

"So that is why you came back here?" Barbara asked.

"I could not stay there," Marisa explained.

"Because you felt betrayed?"

"Yes," Marisa stated succinctly.

"You say that he admitted to loving another woman before you?"

"Yes."

"Then, my dear," her grandmother scolded, "'tis up to you to change his mind."

Puzzled, Marisa asked, "What do you mean?"

"Fight for your husband with the weapons of a woman. You are Marisa Fitzgerald. Flesh of my flesh!" the older woman emphasized.

"How?" Marisa was intrigued.

"Were you averse to the act of making love?"

Color rose again in Marisa's cheeks. "No," she stated.

Barbara probed further. "Did he touch you?"

"Yes."

"Where?"

Marisa shot a surprised glance at her grandmother. "Why must you know that?"

"Allow that I am not satisfying a prurient motive. I would know whether he took the time to arouse you before taking his own pleasure." Barbara gave her granddaughter an encouraging smile.

"His hands were most clever, *grand-mère*. He covered all of my skin," Marisa said.

"You liked it?"

Like, Marisa thought, was too tame a word for what she had felt when his sorcerer's fingers had caressed her past all reason. "Beyond measure," she answered.

"What about the pain?"

"It mattered not," Marisa responded honestly, "for it meant that I was indeed a wife."

"Afterwards," Barbara asked, "was there joy?"

Marisa smiled in remembrance. "Like nothing I have ever known. At one point," Marisa confided," I thought I had died, *grand-mère*. I felt as if I were floating away."

"That is good," Barbara insisted. She rose from her velvet seat. "Fitzgeralds never surrender," she said, smiling, "unless we chose to when it suits our purposes." She walked to the door. "I have something that will open your eyes to possibilities. And a woman should always be aware and take advantage of all the possibilities. I shall return."

Barbara made good on her promise, coming back less than a half hour later carrying a book for Marisa. It was in plain, worn leather, with a lock of gold. She placed it into her grandchild's hands. "Your grandfather found this in a shop in Paris." Barbara smiled wickedly. "He knew that I collected illuminated manuscripts and when he saw this, he had to purchase it for me. 'Tis said to be based on a book from the East. 'Tis written

in French and involves the adventures of a knight
and his lady.

"I will leave you now. Enjoy," she said, placing
a kiss on Marisa's cheek.

Marisa waited until her grandmother was gone
and carried the book to her bed, along with a
branch of candles that she placed on the table
by her bedside. With a quick glance, she made
sure that the kitten was in his basket. Climbing
in, she plumped up several of the goose-down
pillows and turned the key in the lock, opening
the book.

A richly colored, lavishly decorated title page
declared that this was *La vérité d'Amour*. The truth
of love.

She glanced at the text, skipping a few pages
ahead. It was then that Marisa found the artwork
that accompanied the poetry and prose. There
were pictures of a man, a half-dressed dark knight,
and a blond gentlewoman of centuries ago, clad
only in a curtain of hair. The knight's wide naked
back was to the reader, his stance half shielding
the woman; his palm rested against her breast,
cupping it, his mouth on hers.

Had she looked quite so lost when Cameron
had kissed and caressed her?

Marisa carefully turned the page, her eyes widening.

In this picture, the knight was now also nude.
The woman's thighs were wrapped around the
knight's slim hips. He supported her with his
large hands, his equally large and rigid staff now
a part of her body, his mouth on her breast.

So detailed were the paintings that Marisa could
almost see the sheen of sweat on their bodies.

Her hand shaking, she turned another page. The
couple were now on the floor, a fur pelt beneath

their bodies, the knight between the woman's legs. His expression was fierce; hers rapturous. In ecstasy both were the victors, their shared triumph for all to witness. Marisa blinked. She read the poem on the page following. It was lush and lovely, the images both potent and tender.

Unable to resist, Marisa continued to satisfy her curiosity.

The knight and his lady were ensconced in a magnificent bed, whose carved posts depicted, Marisa noted, men and women engaged in love-making. The blond gentlewoman lay on her back—her legs bent at the knees and splayed as the knight pressed his tongue to the spot where before his manhood had entered.

Marisa, her imagination rearranging the picture when she paused and closed her eyes momentarily, saw herself there, with Cam's wide mouth at the juncture of her body, finishing what he had only before hinted at.

What was she thinking?

The next picture depicted the knight now on his back, his hands reaching up to capture the woman's breasts as his lady mounted his rigid member, her head thrown back, her hair rippling over their bodies.

Had Cameron done that with other women? Marisa wondered, recalling how smug Barbara Castlemaine had been with her tales of Lady Mc-Donald, the supposed one-time mistress of her husband.

In the succeeding illustration, the lady lay languidly draped across the knight, his manhood in her mouth, a beatific glow in the woman's eyes.

Marisa closed the very intriguing, very erotic book with a snap. Securing the lock, she leaned over and placed it on the floor. It had certainly given her something to think about. Her husband had been part of the king's inner circle; no doubt he had sampled all that that life had to offer, whilst she was a country virgin. Her grandmother, Marisa realized, had been trying to help her by showing her the book to use as a guide.

Indeed, it conjured up images, some of which would remain tucked away in her mind, stored for reference. However, it would not be the only point of her determined game of love. She would woo her husband in her own way, on her own terms.

On her hand was the proof of her married state, her wedding ring. It symbolized her word, pledged before God and her king; now it also symbolized her love, pledged between God and herself.

The women who went before were of no import. They were in his past.

She was Cameron's wife.

Chapter Twenty

"What do you mean the Buchanan still lives?" Faith's voice rose hysterically.

Roger Hartwelle rolled his eyes. Was the bitch stupid as well as a common slut? "In court the talk is all of the attempt made on the life of the Earl and Countess of Derran, and how he foiled the robbery by dispatching both of the highwaymen. 'Twould appear that once again the Scotsman has cheated our plans for him. The bastard has the devil's own luck."

Faith digested this news. The bloody fool Hartwelle had bungled yet again.

"With so much attention on him, I think we'd best wait a while before we strike again."

"You're scared," she said with contempt.

Hartwelle grabbed her wrist and gave it a rough squeeze. "I am no fool, Mistress Bellamy," he said through gritted teeth. "The king has sent some of his personal guard to see that Buchanan and his wife arrive safely at their next destination. It would be folly to risk another attempt on the earl's life at this time. In a few months when . . ."

"A few months?" Faith demanded. "Jamie Covington's men have already begun their investigation. I was forced to change my address for fear that I would be found out."

"Then I suggest that you leave London."

"With what?" Faith would never admit to this loathsome creature that she had carefuly stashed away a goodly sum of coin. It would remain her secret.

Hartwelle sipped his glass of malmsey wine. The dank, dark atmosphere of the dockside tavern suited their purpose well. "I suggest you find a dupe who will pay your way, my dear," he said, dismissing her. "I have problems of my own to solve." He finished his glass, slurping the contents.

Greedy, incompetent pig! she thought.

"And do not let it enter your head to threaten me ever again," he stated, his pudgy fingers stroking her cheek. "I will give you credit for your safeguarded letter. I did not really think you had quite the foresight for that, my dear," he said in a condescending tone. "However, you dare not accuse me, as I dare not accuse you, for we both have too much to lose. Especially you," he said, "should the Buchanan ever discover you alive." He gave Faith a smile, revealing his yellowing teeth. "Unless 'tis urgent, do not contact me.

"Now," Hartwelle said, rising, "I must go before I am late. There is to be a fancy masque at court tonight. Ah," he sighed dramatically, "it has been a busy time there what with all and sundry giving either dinners or balls, sometimes both, in honor of our new queen. 'Twould appear that our King has picked a stubborn pigeon, much to the consternation of the king's whore, Castlemaine."

Faith watched him leave. Having bedded one of Hartwelle's young footmen, a pimply-faced boy, she possessed certain information that Hartwelle thought unknown to her. It seemed that he had abandoned plans, at least for the time being, of wedding the Fitzgerald heiress and was intending to marry instead a smaller prize, the dowdy daughter of a prosperous sheep farmer. Faith had no doubt that the woman would not survive her marriage vows by many months, so greedy was Hartwelle for money.

She knew Hartwelle was capable of betraying her to the king's justice. She had seen it clearly in his eyes tonight. So she would have to adopt a plan of her own. He was as ineffectual as his useless member, unable to rid them of the threat of Cameron Buchanan.

Panic raced through her veins. She couldn't risk the damned Scotsman discovering her whereabouts, nor Hartwelle using her as a bargaining device to save himself.

Faith concluded that she would have to rid herself of both Hartwelle and Buchanan without delay. She watched, from the corner of her eye, the antics of the newly arrived sailors as they attempted to barter for the barmaid's favors. The buxom woman was leading them a merry dance, angling for the man with the richest purse. They looked desperate to bugger anything, as long as it was female—all save for the quiet man drinking at a table by himself. Faith could tell by his clothes that he, too, was a man of the sea. Pulling her hood closer over her face, she made her exit from the tavern.

Slipping through the dark alleys, a small pistol clutched in her hand, she reached the safety of her newly rented house. Closing the door, she breathed a sigh of relief. Getting a man to kill Hartwelle would be easy; Buchanan was a risk, but she could no longer trust anyone save herself to see the deed done properly. His death would free her, both from her fears and her memories.

Faith Bellamy was furious, though she hid it from the man who lay beside her, his breathing labored. With him, she was coquettish and sweet, knowing that he would not take long. A few grunts and thrusts was all that he would need before getting his pleasure. She hadn't even needed to disrobe, so great was this fool's hurry.

She closed her eyes, pretending to enjoy the ineptness of her bedfellow. He would expect a few moans, so she obliged him as best she could. He was far from the brightest of men, which was just what she was looking for. She had carefully engineered their first "accidental" meeting, after observing him coming and going from a local tavern. Faith had played the part of a widowed gentlewoman to the hilt, manipulating him so skillfully that he hadn't had a chance once she'd decided on him.

He'd relished playing the helpful cavalier to her damsel in distress. A pretended twisted ankle worked well in capturing his attention. Her genteel flinch of pain, her brave determination to carry on and get back to her house in the face of such an obstacle won him over. He helped her, his beefy arm about her waist, to her modest home. So grateful was she that she insisted that he call in two days to share a meal so that she

could show him her gratitude. He accepted with
alacrity.

Her scheme was simple. She would reveal, little
by little, her sad tale, drawing him closer and
closer to her so that he would be unaware when
she sprang her trap. This evening, when she had
finally broken down and wept, spilling out the
details of the horrid position she was in, he was
properly outraged that such a fine woman as she
would be forced to endure what she had.

Faith wished that she could blush with maid-
enly modesty as she relayed her tale, but she had
never blushed, and as she wasn't either modest,
or a maiden, it was beyond her limited repertoire.
Instead, she had told him, through lowered lashes
and with folded hands, that her beloved husband
had been killed by a powerful man who wanted
her. It had all happened when she had rebuffed
the man, she explained. "He wanted to take me
as his mistress, and I of course refused such a
base offer." She paused for dramatic effect. "I
loved my husband." It was then that Faith managed a sniff, as if holding back the tears. "Two
days later, my husband was set upon by brigands, who robbed him of what little money we
had. That night the foul monster came to my
house, insisting that since my husband was gone,
I would need a protector. I slapped his face," she
said with conviction, "but it was no use. He was
stronger than I was."

"The man forced you?"

She managed a small shudder. "Please, do not
make me talk about it. I am so ashamed." She rose,
putting her back to him as she brought a handkerchief to her dry eyes. Perhaps, she thought, she
really should go on the stage.

She considered that enough time had lapsed

that she could continue. "He came back again and again. No matter how often I move to avoid him, he always finds me, till I fear that I shall go mad. I have only a small pittance that I earn from my work as a seamstress, enough to pay my rent and buy what cheap food that I can. Oh," she moaned, "what I would not give to have this man gone from my life."

He responded as if on cue, coming to her side, putting his arms around her and pulling her to face him. He kissed her and whispered that he would help her.

"You are so good, so kind," Faith said, happy that her plan was working, "how can I ever thank you?"

"Let me love you," he begged in desperation.

"Yes," she agreed, as if overcome with emotion, letting him pull her to the planked floor.

Within a few minutes it was all over. Faith supposed that this sailor thought that he was a man among men, a lover for the ages. She stifled the yawn that rose within her as he rolled off her body. When she persuaded him to leave her, she would have to take matters into her own hands to find some solace, for his quick coupling left her unmoved. Now, while he was relaxed, she would work on him. "I never knew it could be like that," she said, taking a deep breath, hoping he would accept her lie as truth.

Silly ass! Faith thought when she saw his contented grin.

"You said that you would help me," she said, facing him, pretending to forget that her skirt and petticoat were still hiked over her thighs, exposing her legs. "He will never leave me alone whilst he draws breath."

"You want him dead?" the sailor asked, unable

to resist touching her knee.

"'Tis the only way," she said, putting her hand on his shirt, noticing the stains on the coarse linen. "If not, I shall be forced to kill myself to stop the humiliation. I can endure no more," she stated emphatically.

"Leave it to me then, Jane," he declared, moving his hand higher beneath her skirts.

"Oh, Titus," Faith murmured, rewarding him with a passionate kiss, thankful that she had thought to give him a false identity, for should anything untoward happen, he knew her only as Jane Reynolds. "You are truly a wonderful man." She reached between their bodies and stroked his small, flaccid member back to life. She implored him, "Help me forget his evil ways."

Titus was more than willing to oblige.

Almost a fortnight after her meeting with Hartwelle, Faith was ready to put her scheme to dispose of him into play. Titus Fielding was her willing accomplice, believing he was saving a poor widow from an evil tormentor. Little did he realize that he was being used by a past mistress of intrigue, a woman skilled by years of practice in controlling men.

She'd promised him that she would consider his offer of marriage and a new start in the Colonies. His next voyage was to Virginia. There, cheap land could be had, along with the chance to put the past behind them.

Faith laughed to herself. As if she would ever consider leaving England for a stinking colonial backwater. But she shrugged her shoulders as she penned the note to Hartwelle, leading him into her trap; Titus Fielding didn't have to know that. Sanding the paper, she blew the excess off with a puff of breath. Admittedly, she would miss Hartwelle's money and the information he could provide her with, but one had to look after one's own interests in the end. And Faith Bellamy had always been good at that.

Hartwelle was tired of waiting for the stupid strumpet. Her letter begged him to meet her at the dockside tavern as she had important information regarding Buchanan. Well, that meeting was to have taken place over an hour ago. Where the hell was the bitch? He pulled out his pocket watch, noting the time. He would give her only ten minutes more and then he would leave. Whatever she had to impart would have to wait till he returned from his wedding trip. Though the girl he was to marry would enrich his coffers only slightly, he was almost completely out of funds and he needed her dowry. Besides, it did not have to be a *long* marriage.

Titus Fielding clung to the shadows outside the tavern. He tightened his grip around the pistol in his hand. His palms were sweating. He'd never killed a man before—at least not in cold blood.

To banish those worrisome thoughts, he focused on the woman for whom he was doing this. He couldn't believe his luck that fate had given him a woman like Jane Reynolds. He'd fallen under her spell as soon as she crossed his path that first evening. She'd made him see that by helping her, he was righting a great wrong done to both her and her murdered husband. It was justice, the only kind she could have, she'd told him.

Titus spied the man leaving the building.

It was time to make the bastard pay for his crimes.

*   *   *

Faith poured herself a drink of brandy. Anticipating the outcome of this night, she sipped the expensive liquid slowly, her smile widening. After tonight, one of her problems would be solved, eliminated entirely. That left only one more—Cameron Buchanan, that great blond stud. The man whose body she could never forget, as she'd made sure he would never forget her.

Foolish Scottish bastard, her mind screamed. If only Buchanan hadn't been so damnably strong-willed. He should have told her what she wanted to know. In not doing so, he had forced her to act.

It was warm inside her house. She hated the night air, especially the foul smells that this part of London brought her way, so all her windows were secured. It certainly wasn't the beautiful Derran House in the Strand. She'd paid it a visit yesterday, inquiring about the Countess of Derran. A liveried servant had looked down his nose at her, briskly informing her that the countess was not at home and would not be for several months. Faith bit her tongue and smiled sweetly at the servant, insisting that the countess wanted to know about her charitable work with orphans. The servant repeated that the countess was gone away. Faith asked if there was somewhere that she could write to Lady Derran with her news. The servant told her that by now the countess would surely be at her estate in the Wye Valley, FitzHall. A message would likely reach her there. Faith thanked the servant in as prim a manner as she could possibly manage, gleefully rubbing her hands together.

And, whither the countess went, so would the earl.

Noting the time on the small clock, she prepared to show her gratitude to the sailor. The small bed had already been turned down. The sheets were perfumed so that Titus's scent wouldn't overwhelm her nose. Loosening her robe, she dabbed a touch of color to her nipples.

She heard the furtive knock at her door. Closing the robe, she ran down the stairs to the door.

"Did you do it?" she asked, trying to keep the excitement from her voice.

Titus nodded his head, walking in.

"Then at last I am free," she said.

"He will bother you no more, Jane," Titus uttered wearily.

"You are sure?" she demanded.

"A man with a bullet in him resting at the bottom of the Thames does not tell tales." He dropped into a chair. "I have proven that my love for you is true."

The smile on Faith's lips was pure malicious satisfaction. "Oh, my darling," she crooned, "let me prove mine to you." She reached out and took his hand, leading him up the stairs to her bedroom. A bottle of brandy and two glasses waited for them on an ordinary pine serving table. Faith poured him a healthy measure before getting her own. "To a new life," she proposed.

Titus swallowed the strong drink quickly. "Aye, my lovely, to a new life far away from bitter memories." He held out his hand for a refill.

Faith obliged, feeling most clever. Removing her robe, she stood before him, naked. "Let me prove my love for you, dearest Titus," she proclaimed. Reclining on the bed, Faith parted her legs and held out her arms, giving a quick glance at the clock, calculating the time it would take him to strip off his clothes and climb upon her body. If she feigned sleep, perhaps he would leave her early.

Titus joined her, sinking into her flesh as fast as he could, using her body to wipe away any lingering doubts.

Faith screwed her eyes shut, as she muttured the appropriate sounds, wishing that instead of Titus Fielding, it was Cameron Buchanan who rode between her thighs with his mighty weapon plunging in and out of her body. He'd known how to make the ride worthwhile. This oaf managed only a few grunts and thrusts before collapsing on top of her, exhausted.

His snores, moments later, were annoying. Faith slid out from under his body. He'd never even noticed her berry-stained breasts.

With a disdainful look in his direction, she poured another glass of the brandy and lifted it in a mute toast: *To Cameron Buchanan, the beast I created, the beast I shall destroy.*

Part Two:
Soft as Candlelight

Chapter Twenty-One

Marisa couldn't concentrate. She'd pricked herself with the silver needle for the second time in the last ten minutes. Laying her needlework aside, she rose from her comfortable chair, putting the injured finger to her mouth.

She paced around the confines of the small sewing room. This room was to be her sanctuary, the one place where she could be truly alone whenever she needed.

Or so she had thought.

Even here, alone, she was surrounded by people, and one in particular plagued her memories. So much had happened in the weeks since their arrival at the newly constructed FitzHall in the beautiful Wye Valley.

Between herself and Cameron, there was a chillingly polite distance. The distance had been of his making, Marisa acknowledged. She had responded to her husband's remoteness with kindness and calm, vowing to make him forget the other woman. Now she believed her grandmother's repeated references to the passionate blood of the Fitzgeralds. It was up to her to make Cameron never regret what he had given up to marry her. She *had* to believe she could eventually win his love.

Marisa couldn't forget how it felt to be with him, joined body to body. It was this recollection, coupled with his coolness afterwards, that haunted her. Her glance would stray to him, mentally asking why, because her lips would not form the question. If he read the silent message in her eyes, he ignored it, pretending that nothing had changed between them.

And it had.

Things had also changed, it seemed, for her cousin and Jamie Covington. It pleased Marisa that there was a new light in Brianna's golden-brown eyes, a glow of warmth that dispelled some of the melancholy whenever Brianna was with Jamie. Brianna laughed more. Color began to creep into her cousin's wardrobe, though she still maintained her dark mourning. Just this day she had even agreed to go for a ride, alone, with Jamie.

Marisa approved of Jamie Covington. He was intelligent, with a steady manner and quiet dignity.

At this moment, Marisa felt anything but steady. She was restless, too restless to sit still and focus on the work she was doing. A walk around the grounds would be better, she decided, than remaining locked away.

Moments later, Marisa was enjoying the warm sunshine as she made her way toward the apple orchard, restored from its unkempt state. Suddenly, she felt a prickle along the back of her neck. Stopping, she raised her glance to the mullioned windows of the upper floor of her new house.

She saw a face peering at her. Recognizing the dark-gold hair and the familiar black eyepatch, she felt her heart quicken its beat. "Cameron." The whispered name floated on the air around her.

Cam watched Marisa walk slowly down the wide brick steps that led to the orchards and garden. *His* orchards and garden. Every inch and acre, every seed and sapling, every sheep and cow. All his, by her gift. Here at FitzHall, he was truly master, not simply a consort. Under English law and the king's command, he was the Earl of Derran, with all its attendant privileges. But this house was solely his, no matter what. Because of her.

He cast his glance around the large room. His tartan lay across the wide expanse of the heavy walnut bed. When he had traveled with the king in exile, he had perforce to leave behind in Scotland things which he cherished. The two-handed claymore that had been his father's gift on the occasion of his sixteenth birthday; the walnut letter casket with his initials from his elder brother Kenneth; the amber and gold pin from Duncan; and the brooch he'd had made years before, a copy of an ancient piece, done in gold with the Gaelic words inscribed inside that would be for his wife alone: *My own is mine.*

His wife.

His woman.

His love.

Cam unlocked the small drawer in his writing desk, removing the blue velvet hair ribbon hidden inside. He rubbed it between his thumb and forefinger. Marisa baffled him. He had withdrawn from her because he must, limiting his contact with her, though that had been nigh on to impossible on the journey from Dorset to FitzHall. Their days together were especially painful as he longed to touch her, to share with her his most personal thoughts. Instead, he kept a tight rein on his tongue, hoarding his conversation as if he were a miser.

Cam returned to the window, watching as she faded from sight. Marisa was beautiful—so alive, so perfect of body, yet shackled to a man who was so much less than she deserved. But he couldn't leave her, even if this slow torture was killing him day by day. His pride was as strong as his will.

His love was stronger still.

Brianna was happy that she had agreed to Jamie's suggestion that they take a leiurely ride across the property. They had passed the ruins of the old castle, about a mile from the new house, which had been bombarded during the civil war till nothing was left except for piles of stone, haphazardly strewn about. One of her cousins, Marisa's brother, had died there, defending his heritage. On the way to FitzHall, they had seen the ruins of another Royalist fortress, Goodrich Castle, the former home of the Talbots, the Earls of Shrewsbury. It, too, had been reduced to rubble at the hands of the Commonwealth. Like the old FitzHall, it was a monument to the Royalist cause, a once reliable bastion against the Welsh raiders.

Their meandering pace took them across the broad plains and rolling hills. Cattle and sheep grazed peacefully where once troops had waged war and destruction. This land was in her cousin's blood, Brianna knew. It was within easy riding distance of Wales, where once their common ancestor had brazenly crossed the border and wooed his English love.

They rode in comfortable silence, spotting an occasional farmer and children working the land. Jamie pointed toward a path which eventually led them to a secluded stream, a tributary of the Wye River. It was there that they stopped to water their horses.

Jamie dismounted first, stepping over to help Brianna. It was the first time that they had been alone since the night of the ball. As he lifted her slender body from the saddle, Jamie met Lady Brianna's eyes with his own.

She blinked first, moving away from him toward the water. Removing her gloves, she bent to sample the water. Cupping her hands, she drank from the cold stream.

Jamie watched her from where he stood, just a few feet away. She was like a deer, he thought, poised for flight in the woodland glade.

"My lady," he began, moving closer to her.

Brianna stood up quickly, her eyes widening in apprehension. "I'm thinking that we should be getting back," she said, refusing to meet his gaze.

Jamie took hold of her wrist. "No," he said firmly. "Not just yet."

"Please," Brianna said, "release me."

"I cannot do that," Jamie said, refusing to let her go.

"You must," she pleaded.

"If I do, will you promise to listen to me?"

Brianna considered his request for a moment. She could not outrun him, she knew, and fear of his male anger should she refuse him forced her decision. "You have my word," she agreed.

"Then let us sit down," he insisted, leading her toward a large oak.

Brianna settled on the thick grass, spreading her skirts about her. She folded her hands in her lap, her eyes downcast.

Jamie sensed that she was sore afraid of him, though he could find no reason that she should be. He only wanted to explain to her how he felt.

Their eyes met and he lost the words.

Brianna's fear vanished as she glimpsed the hesitation and lack of confidence in his hazel eyes. She relaxed, knowing that he would not hurt her. "What is it that you wish to say?"

Jamie knelt on the ground beside her, taking one of her hands in his. He took a deep breath and forged ahead lest his courage fail him. "I want you for my wife."

Brianna exclaimed, "Wife?"

"Aye," Jamie stated. "I know 'tis exceedingly bold of me to even think a lady of your birth and breeding would consider a man like me, but"— he lifted her chin so that he could look her in the eyes when he confessed—"I love you."

Brianna was shocked. A declaration of love was the last thing she had expected. And *marriage*? She didn't know if she could ever take that risk again, no matter what her feelings, and she did have feelings for Jamie Covington. Whether or not 'twas love, she could not truthfully say, or willingly admit at that moment.

Jamie took her reluctance to speak as a sign that she was insulted by his words. "Forgive me for my inopportune words, my lady," he managed to say. "Please forget that I ever spoke."

Brianna saw the visible pain in Jamie's eyes. Her heart reached out to him, as did her hands.

When he went to stand, she clasped his hand in hers. "Wait," she said softly.

Jamie, his pride wounded by what he thought was his stupidity, asked, "For what?" Sweet Jesu, how could he have made such a colossal fool of himself?

" 'Tis not what you may think."

"And what is that but the truth, my lady?"

Brianna touched his cheek in a tender caress. It was the first time she had willingly initiated contact with a man. "Your birth has nothing to do with my reluctance."

Jamie believed that Brianna was merely being kind. "I appreciate the sweetness of your lie."

"I am not lying," she protested.

"Whatever you say," he insisted.

She clutched the cross she wore. "By my faith, I swear to you that your birth has nothing to do with my decision never to marry again."

Her golden-brown eyes shone with truth. "Then is it our religious differences?"

Brianna wished she could use that as an answer. She was born of the Old Faith, but she was no religious zealot, intolerant of others' beliefs. "No," she murmured.

Jamie touched the black wool of her skirt. "You love *him* still?"

"Donal?" Brianna asked. "You think that I loved him?" Pent-up feelings of rage and hurt tore through her. Tears formed in her eyes, threatening to spill over her cheeks. She was so tired of pretending that her marriage had been what it should. So tired of protecting the memory of a man who abused her. "As God is my judge," she said, sobbing, "I loathed Donal MacBride. Do you hear me? *I loathed him!*" She brought her hands to her face to hide the tears that streamed from her eyes.

Jamie was stunned both by the force of her words and the anger behind them. He gathered Brianna in his embrace, holding her while she cried. "Hush, love," he crooned, "'twill be all right." He stroked her back, trying his best to give comfort to her.

His sincere warmth and caring reached into the fog of hurt and despair that she was temporarily trapped in. Here was a man whose arms sheltered instead of punished; here were a man's words that comforted instead of berated.

It was at that moment that a rash decision was born.

"Make love to me," she whispered while her courage held fast.

Jamie froze. Had he heard her correctly? Perhaps in his imagination he had only heard what he wanted to hear.

Brianna tilted her head back, looking him in the eyes. "Please love me, Jamie," she beseeched him as she shyly offered him her lips.

Jamie's mouth met hers in sweet demand. As much as he wanted her, he was certain she would regret the action should they anticipate their vows. "We should not, my love," he protested. "I can wait till . . ."

Brianna heard his words as she pulled back from their kiss. She placed her index finger on his mouth, stopping him from continuing. "Ssh," she said, not wanting him to say the words. There could be no marriage for her. But perhaps she could erase the memory of her husband's abhorrent touch with Jamie's. Replace the wretched anguish with something kinder.

She knew that she was allowing herself to indulge in carnal knowledge with a man to whom she was not wed, thereby willingly comitting an act of sin. Brianna accepted that, thinking that it could not be worse than enduring the brutality of Donal's base use of her body. Whatever penance was required of her she would do.

It must, however, be now, before her courage erroded further.

Jamie, his heart beating faster, moved behind her, unlacing her dress. Her small back was smooth when he touched it with his lips. Brianna shivered as he pushed the material off her shoulders.

Within minutes Brianna was clothed only in her chemise and stockings; Jamie's clothes lay across one of the tree's low branches, along with her dress and several petticoats.

Brianna's cheeks grew hot with color when she turned her head and saw Jamie standing less than a foot from her. Donal's body had been big and thick, covered in dark hair; Jamie's body was slender, his chest smooth. She closed her eyes and prayed that she would not regret what she was about to do. Her trust was in Jamie's hands, his to do with as he would.

Jamie bent down, observing Brianna. Her hands were clenched into fists at her sides; her eyes were tightly closed as if she did not want to see, almost as if she were in fear. He laid his hand on her throat. Her body was stiff, as if she expected a blow. "Brianna," he whispered, "look at me."

Her eyes opened slowly.

"I shan't hurt you," he promised. Seconds later, he could feel her body relaxing next to his. This time he closed her eyes with his kisses, touching his mouth to her lids, her cheeks, the curve of her jaw. Jamie kissed her mouth, gently at first, then with greater passion. He showed her how a kiss was supposed to be—a deep, mutual sharing of textures and flavors. When he broke from her lips, Brianna was breathing as urgently as he. Pushing aside her chemise, he bared her small breasts. Cupping them, he kissed each in turn. He could feel the urgency of his own body, his flesh hardening in anticipation of meeting hers.

He reached out his left hand, linking his fingers with hers. "You are so beautiful, though you must know that every time you gaze into a looking glass," he said, his voice getting huskier with his growing need.

Donal had never told her that she was beautiful. What he'd often said was that she was a "cold bitch who could freeze the balls off the devil himself." Donal had never touched her with gentleness as Jamie had, nor with the worship of a man who treasured instead of pillaged.

A tiny flicker of an unknown warmth ignited in her belly. She gasped in surprise, her left hand reaching for him. Her fingers dug into his back, holding him closer. Lulled by Jamie's unhurried pace, Brianna relaxed. He seemed in no haste to shove himself into her flesh, and she was grateful. Sounds of birds chirping surrounded her. Opening her eyes, she spotted a small rabbit contentedly munching the grass a few feet from them. It raised its head and stared at her before hopping off.

Jamie followed her gaze with his own, laughing when he saw the scampering rabbit.

Brianna immediately focused her attention back on Jamie, puzzled that a man ready to take a woman could still find humor in the antics of a woodland creature. "Oh, Jamie," she said, offering her mouth to him.

He accepted the token, slipping his tongue between her parted lips. Easing the material of her chemise above her hips, he moved between her thighs.

Brianna could feel the hardness of his manhood pressing against her and she involuntarily tensed. Slowly, he entered her. When no pain or discomfort followed, she relaxed.

Jamie proceeded with caution, moving further and deeper until he was well and truly within the moist haven of her flesh. Turbulence and tranquility blended in his soul as he brought them both to the heights of love and beyond.

Brianna's breathing was labored as she lay next to the man who had unlocked the doors to the gates of pleasure for her. In that instant, there was no right or wrong, no rhyme or reason. Only a happiness such as she had never known, nor expected to again. These stolen hours were hers to cherish, for Jamie had given her a gift of rare value—a sense of pride in herself as a woman. Much as she wanted to linger, to savor this new collection of sensations, she knew that it was over.

Sanity returned, and with it her innate modesty. Brianna moved from his side, reaching for her clothing. Dressing quickly, she kept her back to Jamie. "We must be going back before they worry that we have become lost, or worse."

Jamie dressed as rapidly as possible, unable to repress the smile on his face. In his heart he already looked on her as his wife; here, in the peaceful haven of God's benevolence, they had made their vows with the love they had shared. He wanted to let her know that this was, for him, a sacred contract.

"Would you be helping me with my dress?" she asked, her back to him as he turned around at the sound of her lilting, Irish-accented voice.

He pulled the laces tight and tied the ribbon securely. Stepping around her, he fell to one knee, taking her hand in his, saluting it with a kiss. "I, Jamie Covington," he pledged, "do take thee, Lady Brianna O'Dalaigh, as my wedded wife, here in the sight of God Almighty. Forsaking all others, through whatever God decrees, as long as I shall live."

Tears flooded Brianna's eyes at Jamie's heartfelt announcement. This meant more to her than she could tell him. If only she could repeat his words, because in her heart and soul she did accept them. "Jamie . . ."

"Now 'tis my turn to say hush, love," he responded, standing up. "I would have you know just what this meant to me, that my love for you is true. This was no tumble for my vanity, so that I could boast to all of my conquest. It was a way to show you, as best I could, what I feel. A seal, if you will, of my love. I am a poor man with words, Brianna, unlike most of the men at court."

"Who wrap their lies in pretty words of no consequence," she insisted. "I value your honesty, Jamie." Would, she thought, that I could be as deeply honest with you. Brianna believed in his love, and as she did, she could not condemn him to a life with a barren wife. He was a good man who deserved a whole woman, a whole marriage.

"Come," she said, severing the conversation, "we must not tarry longer."

"We will finish this conversation anon," Jamie promised, joining her at the stream's edge and helping her into the saddle.

"Aye, later," Brianna replied, keeping to herself the knowledge that for them there would be no later.

* * *

Marisa was strolling back toward the Hall when she saw the large contingent of riders heading across the property. They were still too far away to identify, but she was instantly alert. From the direction they came, she guessed that it wasn't her Welsh cousin. She'd recently invited Ravensmoor and his family for a visit whenever he wished, for she assumed that they would be in residence here for some months.

The sun struck the colors that the man who rode in the lead was wearing. Even from this distance, Marisa recognized the plaid. It must be someone from Cameron's family.

Picking up her skirts, Marisa began to run for the house, little caring that her actions were more suited to a saucy country minx without a care than to a peeress of the realm, so eager was she to greet the party.

From his window, Cam could see his wife racing across the grass. Fearing that she was in danger, he grabbed his dirk and cane, making for the door. He almost collided with Kendall coming in from the other side.

"Forgive me, my lord," Kendall apologized. "I thought you should know that a party of riders is fast approaching."

So that explained why Marisa was anxious to return to the house. He relaxed somewhat, releasing his tight grip on the dirk. "Have you any idea who they are?"

"No, my lord," Kendall responded.

"How many?"

"Seven or eight, my lord." Kendall followed Cameron out the bedroom door and down the stairs. "And there appear to be at least two women with them, perhaps a child as well."

That news heartened him. No one intent on mayhem brought along women and children. Most likely 'twas a visit from a neighboring family. "Where is Mr. Covington?" Cam asked as he reached the last step.

"He rode out with the countess's cousin some time ago, my lord."

"I would see him when he returns," Cam stated. He paused before he got to the door, taking a deep breath of air into his lungs. Another hurdle to leap, he calculated. To ignore the arrival would be to shirk his duty.

"Is aught wrong, my lord?" Kendall asked when he saw Cameron hesitating before going outside.

"'Tis nothing, Kendall." Before Cam could take hold of the door, a male servant was there, performing the duty.

Cam stepped out into the sunshine; Marisa came bounding up the wide brick steps towards the house. Her cheeks were kissed by the sun, as was the rich glory of her chestnut curls. She looked healthy, like a young, unspoilt country maiden; he wanted to carry her off to the nearest bed and make long, slow love to every inch of her flesh, strip the gown from her magnificent body, feel the weight of her full breasts in his hands as he tasted them with his mouth.

That was what he wanted.

But what he would do was to stand silent, keeping his desires locked tightly inside, safe from scorn and ridicule.

"It would appear that we are to have company," Cam said without a trace of emotion in his voice.

Marisa halted, catching her breath. "So I see," she managed at last to say. "And they bear your colors, my lord."

He registered the last part of her sentence first:

they were once again on formal terms. Then he demanded, "My colors, you said?"

"Yes." The pounding of hooves was coming closer. "The man who rides lead wears them."

A cold dread crept over Cameron's skin beneath his clothes.

Marisa saw Cam's hand tighten on his walking stick. He looked as though he were not a man of flesh and blood, but a piece of well-sculpted marble fashioned to resemble a living man.

Dogs barked; fowl scattered; horses whickered.

Marisa switched her gaze from her husband to the contingent that came to a stop just a few feet from her. She heard a low, Celtic oath from her husband's direction. The invective sounded harsh and bitter. From the corner of her eye, she saw that several of her men had stationed themselves along the cobbled path, pistols at the ready; two others were armed with deadly longbows.

Cam moved, taking his place beside her. The cold inflection he gave his words belied the summer sun. "'Twould seem, my lady wife, that we are being graced with a visit from the Earl of Tairne, my father, and his beautiful wife, my mother."

Chapter Twenty-Two

Marisa sucked in her breath at the harshly cold inflection of her husband's words. Whatever was wrong with him? she wondered. Her eyes were drawn to the big, bearded man who dismounted from a large dappled-gray gelding.

"So this is my new daughter," he pronounced with a hearty voice, his Scots accent deeper and thicker than his son's. "What a bonny lass you hae wed, Cameron." With that, Angus Buchanan leaned down and swept his son's English bride up into his embrace, swinging the startled Marisa around. Putting her back down, Angus embraced his son, clapping him heartily on Cam's broad back.

While father and son hugged, Marisa looked up at the woman who sat perched still on her brown palfrey, loftily above her. She was incredibly beautiful, past her youth, to be sure, yet with a loveliness that time could never dull. The older woman's eyes were the same, deep loch-blue like Cameron's, her hair the same rich old-gold shade.

Recovering her manners, Marisa announced, "Welcome to FitzHall, my lady." She glanced back to the Earl of Tairne. "And to you to, my lord earl."

"Aye," Cam echoed, "welcome indeed."

Marisa's gaze was once more drawn to the other woman after Cam spoke his perfunctory words. She saw a look of immeasurable sadness in the woman's face at the less-than-enthusiastic greeting by her son. The blue eyes pleaded for some sign of warmth, some hint of true hospitality beneath Cam's rigid stance.

Angus recognized the desperate yearning in his wife's eyes for Cameron's affection. His youngest son still had not forgotten, nor forgiven, his mother's unthinking cruelty. He left Cameron's side and walked the few steps back to where his wife waited. Holding his arms up, he helped her down from her gentle mare. He whispered, "Be patient, my love," for Alanna's ears alone.

Alanna Buchanan moved with consummate grace, crossing the cobblestoned path to where her son and his wife stood. She smiled as she bent, placing a kiss on each of Marisa's cheeks. "Angus is right, you are a bonny lass. My son has done quite well for himself."

"'Tis no thanks to you," Cam said in a quiet voice.

The bitter tone sent shivers down Marisa's spine. She heard the quickly indrawn breath of the Scottish countess at her son's barbs.

"Cameron," Angus growled a warning.

"Nae," Alanna responded, laying her arm on her husband's sleeve. Pain filtered through her words. "Cameron spoke the truth."

"Truth or no," Marisa said, "I think it best that we go inside." Cameron, Marisa noted, still had made no contact with the woman whose beauty he had inherited. "You must be tired after your long journey."

Angus interrupted. "A moment," he said. Leaving them, he moved to the back of his small caravan, raising his hands to a small woman who sat flanked between two men-at-arms. From beneath the folds of her mantle, Angus removed something. When he turned around, he held in his arms a small child, one thumb stuck in her mouth. He carried the girl back to where his wife, son, and daughter-in-law waited.

Alanna managed a heartfelt smile.

Marisa stared at the child and there was no doubt in her mind that the little girl was Cameron's. Her Fitzgerald pride kept her standing through the shock of confronting her husband's past.

Shock also coursed swiftly through Cam's body. It was like looking into a mirror, a mirror that reflected what he had once been. No physical sign of the woman who bore the child existed; she was Cam's alone, as if sprung from him like Athena from Zeus. "Elsbeth," he said, guarding his emotions lest the daughter he loved reject him outright.

"Papa?" Elsbeth asked in her small voice, her chubby arms outstretched.

"Aye, I am he," Cam responded, not quite sure what to do.

"Then be acting like it," Angus insisted, handing the child to Cam, and taking the cane from his son's grasp.

Cam accepted his daughter, his left arm cradling the girl. Elsbeth wrapped her tiny arms about his neck and held tight, as if afraid to let go lest he disappear in a puff of mist.

Joy flooded Cam's body. His daughter had willingly accepted him, no matter that he was less than an ideal man, his face and form forever cursed.

Angus and Alanna read the delight in their son's face, as did Marisa. The stoic mask had noticeably cracked. Marisa experienced a flood of hope as she watched the softening of her husband's demeanor. He was capable of receiving love; perhaps she could push aside his barriers further still and force him to see what she had to offer.

Elsbeth yawned, and laying her head on her father's broad shoulder, her blue eyes closed in sleep.

"I think 'twould be best to put the child to bed, husband," Marisa suggested, reaching out her hand and laying it upon the long blond curls that fell over Elsbeth's small shoulders. This was Cam's flesh, blood of his blood, and therefore, precious to her, no matter who had birthed the child. Nevertheless, curiosity about the mother pricked at Marisa. Was she the woman Cam had given up when he married her? Was this unknown woman the love he could not forget?

"Meg," Alanna called, summoning the nursemaid.

Meg hasted to do the countess's bidding, gently removing the sleeping girl from her father's arms.

"Cameron," Marisa said softly, holding out her arm, "let us show your parents the welcome family deserves."

Cam, his walking stick returned to him, took his wife's arm on his as they lead the way into the house.

*   *   *

"He hates me still," Alanna moaned, dabbing at her tear-stained eyes with a square of Irish linen.

"Give the lad some wee amount of time, my love," Angus insisted, gathering her naked body into his arms. He wished he could ease the pain his wife suffered, for now she knew how it felt to be rebuffed by the one person whose love should have been unconditional.

"Do you think his English wife loves him?" she sniffed, snuggling closer to the warmth of Angus's large body, taking comfort in his abiding love.

"I canna ken for certain," he answered, "though I believe she isna indifferent to him."

"And what of Cameron?" she asked, sliding her arm over his muscular chest.

"He is nae so easy to read," Angus admitted.

Alanna acknowledged that fact. Her youngest son had never been as open as her two eldest lads. Kenneth and Duncan wore their faces plain for all the world to see. Cam could hide behind whatever mask he allowed his face to wear.

Angus shifted in the wide bed, where the sun fell warm on their bodies. He kissed the top of his wife's head, holding her closer. "He does love his wee lassie, though," Angus pointed out, "'tis nae a doubt about that."

"Aye," Alanna agreed, "'tis true. But will his wife?"

Some time later, Marisa slipped into the room she had instructed be given to the child. It was part of a suite of rooms set aside as a nursery for the children she hoped to bear. Her hand touched the flatness of her belly beneath the material of her dress. There would be no child of her flesh and Cam's as yet. Her monthly course had come just two days after she and Cam had been together in the cottage.

She quietly approached the bed in which the little girl slept, her steps muffled by the expensive carpet underfoot. The child looked like an angel, all innocence and light.

"She reminds me so of Cameron when he was a bairn."

Marisa spun around at the sound of the female voice behind her.

Alanna moved closer to her new daughter. She searched the English girl's green eyes for any hint of malice toward her sleeping granddaughter, then breathed a sigh of relief. There was nothing to fear in the clear green eyes as far as she could tell.

"She does have the look of her father about her," Marisa agreed. "And what of her mother?" she queried bluntly, hoping that Cameron's mother would tell her the truth.

Alanna responded with a question of her own. "Then Cam has not spoken of her?"

Marisa reluctantly disclosed, "No."

"Perhaps we should let Elsbeth sleep in peace whilst we have our talk," Alanna suggested.

Marisa concurred. "I think that would be wise."

"Is there someplace where we can be alone?"

"My sewing room," Marisa said. "Follow me."

Alanna did just that, taking careful note of the richness of the furnishings as she made her way through the house. The walls were paneled in rich mahogany; artwork to rival that in a king's palace hung on display. It was a comfortable, well-appointed place in which to live. Windows let in vast amounts of light, bathing the sturdy oak floors in a golden glow. Thick carpets from the East were scattered about. The scent of spices and roses filled the air. Alanna saw a silver bowl set upon a small table filled with crushed petals and herbs. She stopped to take a whiff.

"How unusual," she commented. "I noted such a bowl in the room you gave my husband and me."

Marisa turned around, a smile on her mouth. "I find that they fill the house with such a bouquet that it banishes any and all dreariness."

Alanna liked the girl her son had wed. With each moment spent in her company, she found more to be thankful about. The lass was young and exceedingly comely; she looked healthy enough to bear Cameron strong sons. Aye, Alanna thought, this English marriage would benefit her beloved son well.

Marisa led her down the walnut staircase with its carved rail and into her sewing room.

She pulled a cord to summon a servant. Instructing that wine was to be brought for herself and her guest, Marisa chose to sit on a velvet-covered settle beneath a trio of mullioned windows.

Alanna took a seat in a small chair near her after admiring the handiwork of her daughter-in-law. "You are clever with a needle."

"Thank you, madam."

Alanna gave Marisa a smile. "I would be most happy if you would call me mother."

"It seems strange to call someone else mother whilst my own still lives."

Alanna nodded her head. "I can understand that, child. My given name is Alanna, if you feel more comfortable using that."

Marisa proposed, "If you have no objections, I would prefer to use the French term, *belle-mère*."

"*Mais non, chérie,*" Alanna responded.

"You speak French?"

"*Oui,*" Alanna replied. "I had a French nurse when I was a child."

"My mother taught me," Marisa explained. "Her own mother was French."

"Cameron speaks several languages fluently."

"So I have been told."

At that moment the servant entered carrying a tray. "Cook insisted on some of her fancy cake, my lady," the girl said as she placed the burden on a low table.

"That will be fine, Mary. Thank Cook for me," Marisa said as she handed her mother-in-law a glass of madeira and a plate of dark cake rich with fruit.

"I realize," Alanna began, "that 'twas a shock to you—and most especially to Cameron—when we descended upon you. If any blame is to be borne, it should be I who bear it. I insisted on this journey."

"You are my husband's kin, and as such are welcome to our home, whenever you choose to come," Marisa insisted.

"Would that my son felt as you do."

"Why does he not?"

"'Tis my fault, I can assure you."

"How so?" Marisa inquired.

Alanna sipped the madeira. She had decided to trust the English girl with her secrets. She had great need of an ally who could help her break down the wall she had erected between herself and her beloved son.

"Before I can answer that, I would ask a question of you."

Marisa ignored the plate of cake and the glass of wine. "What would you ask of me?"

"Is this a true marriage?"

Marisa raised her chin. "I was wed with the King of England as my chief witness. 'Twas most legal and fully binding on both partners."

Alanna shrugged her shoulders and sighed. "Have you shared a bed with my son?"

Her husband's mother was much like her own grandmother when it came to blunt questions, Marisa decided.

A flush of wild-rose color in Marisa's cheeks gave Alanna her answer. She rose from her seat and joined Marisa on the settle. "Do you care for my son?"

Marisa saw the earnestness in the loch-blue eyes. Alanna Buchanan desperately needed to know. *"Belle-mère,"* Marisa said, her voice strong and true, "I love him."

"Even as he is?"

Marisa took Alanna's beringed hand to reassure her. "I am not some shallow girl," she explained, "who must have a pretty toy to show to the world lest she be judged wanting. While I will admit to being shocked when first we met and I beheld his face, that was to be expected. I was unprepared.

"But have no fear, *belle-mère,* I can see beyond the scars."

"So, you did not run screaming when he was presented to you?"

"Of course not!" Marisa bristled at the thought.

Alanna opened her heart and matched Marisa's honesty with her own. "Then you are the woman for my son. Would that I had a measure of your courage when I faced him."

Marisa was perplexed. "What do you mean?"

Instead of responding, Alanna proposed another question of her own. "I will answer your question in due time," she promised, "but first I must know if you are aware of how Cam came by his scars?"

"No," Marisa confessed. "No one has yet spoken to me of the details. Both his Majesty and Cam's friend, Jamie Covington, know, though neither would enlighten me."

"Aye, the Stuart king has reason to love my son, for Cam proves his loyalty to Charles in the face he now wears. 'Twas a woman who dealt my son the disfiguring marks. A greedy bitch who sold information about Royalist agents for money."

"A woman?" Marisa asked, absorbing the information. "I had thought it to be Cromwell's men."

"Are you aware of what services Cameron performed for our king?"

Marisa nodded. "I know of his purposes. He told me but a little after Jamie revealed what his work entailed."

"He volunteered to return to London to find the traitor in the midst of the Royalist cause. Unfortunately, he was discovered first, by the woman he was bedding—she was part of a plot to kill the king. The knowledge my son carried within his head could be of great use to those who sought Charles Stuart.

"Cam refused to reveal the whereabouts of the king or any of Charles's plans. He would have died sooner than betray his king."

"I can well believe that," Marisa affirmed, "for I have seen the bond between his Majesty and Cameron. 'Tis very strong."

"Aye," Alanna said, her voice cracking slightly, "he is loyal to those he loves. Once given, it takes a lot to break Cameron's bond of faith."

Marisa heard the quaver in Alanna's voice.

Alanna paused, as if gathering her strength. "He was tortured for what he knew."

Marisa gasped.

Alanna Buchanan swallowed, her free hand coming to her lips as if to ease the trembling there.

"Are you all right?" Marisa asked. She could sense the other woman's turmoil.

Alanna saw the compassion in the younger woman's eyes. If only she had possessed that when her son had needed it. Cam's English bride was strong and capable of tenderness. Two very admirable qualities. A woman would have to demonstrate such traits to fully love her son.

"Aye," Alanna finally answered. "Cam is my third child. Kenneth and Duncan, his elder brothers, are much like Angus, my husband. Cameron was different. Elsbeth is his image."

"And therefore yours as well," Marisa observed.

The Countess of Tairne gave her daughter-in-law a bittersweet smile. "'Tis true. My son was born a most bonny child. One side of his face still retains that powerful beauty."

Marisa could well imagine what her husband must have looked like before—a man beyond compare, celebrated for the glory of his face and form.

"But I digress," Alanna continued. "The bitch chained him, hand and foot, naked and vulnerable, to her bed. She had a menial of hers break the bones in his right hand. Cam would not talk. She had her servant next smash his knee. Still, he did not talk."

Marisa could well imagine the excruciating pain Cameron had had to endure.

"When that did not force my son's tongue, the damnable bitch took a hot poker to him. She struck out his eye, blinding him, then seared his face and neck with her evil design. She would have killed him too, had not Jamie Covington come to his rescue."

Anger rose within Marisa that anyone could be capable of such blatant inhuman cruelty. Her free hand curled into a fist, fingernails digging into her palms from the force she exerted. She would have liked to submit the woman who had so casually inflicted pain on Cameron to a measure of Fitzgerald justice.

Then Marisa's heart was overwhelmed by the unsparing hurt her husband must have suffered. His life had been forever altered by a woman's destructive plans. A weaker man would have been destroyed, collapsing under the weight of society's scorn and his own self-pity. But not Cameron. He wore his scars both within and without. Anyone could see the physical marks; how many, she wondered, would ever look to see that which was not perceptible? The scars of the soul.

"You spoke of courage earlier?" Marisa questioned.

"I lacked it," Alanna sadly admitted. "When my son came back to us, after barely surviving the hell that the bitch had put him through, he suffered yet again at a woman's hands."

"Yours?" Marisa asked, puzzled.

"Aye." Alanna released Marisa's hand, folding both of hers into her lap, her eyes shielded by her lowered lids. "Like a fool I saw only the flaws, not the man. My own son, whom I loved beyond measure, I cut more deeply than she had."

"What happened?"

"We'd had word from Jamie that he'd been hurt, and that as soon as it was possible, he would send Cam to us. We waited many months for our son's return. Finally, he was once more within our castle. Safe within the fortified walls.

"He wore a heavy black hooded mantle, much like a priest's robe, so that his face was hidden from view. Then Cameron removed the garment. The face I saw revealed shocked me past all reason, past all maternal feeling. I screamed in horror at the sight of my own son. Instead of being grateful that he was still alive, I let my selfish vanity wound him further when I ran away in disgust."

Marisa could well see in her mind's eye the scene Alanna described. Cameron, barely recovered from the abominations forced upon his flesh, had come back to his home—the one place he should have expected to lovingly shelter him. How his mother's defection must have ripped to shreds any dignity he had left, isolating him even further when this foolish woman had fled from the sight of the man she'd once carried within her womb. The Countess of Tairne should have gathered Cameron to her bosom, showering him with all the love she professed to have for him.

Marisa fixed her green eyes on Alanna's upturned face. The shame of her former actions was plainly written there. Cam's cold tone and churlish manners now made sense to Marisa.

Even knowing what she did, Marisa could not find it within herself to condemn and despise Alanna Buchanan. It was clear to her that the woman had indeed suffered because of her imprudent actions. She had lost the regard of the son she loved, and if Marisa judged correctly, the son she had favored most.

"Too late I realized what I had done. Cameron refused every effort I made at reconciliation. He shunted aside my attempts at apology."

"So you have come here for a final reckoning?"

"Not so final, I pray," Alanna said.

"And what of the child?" Marisa hadn't misunderstood the love she saw in her husband's eye for his daughter. The child meant much to him.

"Elsbeth belongs with her father. She is a Buchanan; it is her birthright," Alanna declared.

"What about her mother?"

"She died giving birth to the child."

Would the spectre of this unknown woman haunt her marriage? Marisa risked the answer. "Did my husband love her?"

"My son has given his heart to no woman," the Scottish woman replied. "His body, aye, many times, for he was ever the virile stallion, particularly with Charles Stuart as a mentor. His seed he gave but once, for Elsbeth is the living proof." Alanna cocked her blond head to one side. "Does it bother you that Elsbeth is a bastard?"

"She is not responsible for the circumstances of her birth."

"And could you find it within you to love her? 'Tis a lot to ask that you take to your heart another woman's babe."

Marisa answered quickly. "She is my husband's child, and as such, a part of my bond with him. Besides, did you not gamble that I would accept her willingly?"

Alanna shrugged her shoulders.

"I thought as much," Marisa replied. "Have no fear, *belle-mère*, I will care for Elsbeth as if she had sprung from my womb."

"I pray to God," Alanna stated bluntly, "that your womb will in time carry brothers and sisters for my granddaughter."

"'Tis my wish also," Marisa replied.

*　　*　　*

Much later, as she soaked in a warm tub, Marisa thought back to the conversation she'd had with the Countess of Tairne. Cameron's mother had explained so much that was unclear.

With the information Alanna Buchanan had provided, Marisa could plan her next move. Like a general formulating a battle strategy, Marisa considered how she would win the prize that she desired most—the love of Cameron Buchanan.

What she had in mind was daring and involved risk.

She rose from the copper tub, a wicked smile on her lips.

His love was worth it.

Chapter Twenty-Three

"Ciamar a tha sibh?" Angus waited till he and Cameron were alone to ask his son just how Cam was faring.

Cam responded to his father's question in Gaelic that he was well, then switched to English. "I have not forgotten the ancient tongue, Father."

Angus gave a hearty laugh. "'Tis well that you don't, laddie, now that you be counted an English lord."

"I am still a Scotsman and will ever be so," Cam responded, proudly.

"Though you be a laird of some importance, now, in this realm." Angus regarded his son solemly. "Land and manors fit for a prince," he stated. "'Tis more than ever I could hae given you, laddie," Angus acknowledged.

"I dinna care," Cam said in earnest. "I had what I treasured most, Father—your good regard and your love." He reached out his hand and clasped his father's forearm, "I never resented Kenneth or Duncan."

"Nae, that I do ken, my son," Angus recognized. "No father, nor older brothers, ever had a more loyal arm at their side. I only wish that I had had more." Angus's voice was heavy with regret. "Then perhaps you would not have needed to leave Scotland to seek a fortune of your own. Then"—he stopped, taking hold of Cam's right hand—"you could hae been as you were born."

Cam recognized the underlying sorrow in his father's words and sought to alleviate it. "This face was no fault of yours. Do not ever think that," Cam stated forcefully. "I would have followed Charles Stuart no matter what," he affirmed, "for I believed in him and his cause."

"You are reconciled then?"

Can shrugged his broad shoulders beneath the fine linen shirt he wore. "I have long since learned to accept what is."

Angus, his normally deep, booming voice became softer, asked, "Then can you not forgive your mother?"

Cam walked away from his father, moving towards the stone hearth, wherein burned a small fire. He stared into the flames for a some time before Angus spoke again.

"She isna a perfect woman, Cam, just as I am nae a perfect man. I love Alanna; I have since first I laid eyes on her when she was but little more than a bairn." His voice grew wistful, "She was the most beautiful woman I had ever seen, or hoped to see. For her fair looks she was spoilt, first by her own father, then by me when we were wed."

Angus looked at his son, who had turned from the flame and met his father's gaze. "That she loved me was more than I could believe. But she did; she still does.

"And she loves you."

Cam have a harsh bark of laughter. "She loved me well when I was without flaw."

Angus agreed. "Aye, that she did, laddie. I shall nae deny that. *You* were her unblemished angel, her heart's true delight."

"Until I fell from grace, as it were," Cam said, his tone accusatory.

"She made a mistake. Have you nae done that?" Angus demanded.

Cam stood as straight as he could manage, his spine stiff. "I never claimed to walk the path of the angels, Father. Aye, I have made my fair share of mistakes." Faith Bellamy had been a major error in judgment; she had almost cost him his life and his sanity. The rough taking of Elsbeth's mother had been a mistake, but all that he could regret from that was the death of the woman, for he could never regret his daughter.

"Then, if you are nae without transgressions, give your mother another chance. Or did the merciless bitch who scarred you burn out all compassion from your soul?"

"Damn you, Father!" Cam shouted. "You go too far."

"I dinna think that, son." Angus walked the short distance that separated him from Cam and touched his son's shoulder lightly. "Think well on what I hae said." His voice was rough with emotion. "As God is my judge, Cameron, you and Alanna are what I hold most dear in this life, even before honor and personal safety, before king and country."

Angus turned and strode away, leaving his son to ponder his father's words in solitude.

*   *   *

"The Countess of Tairne," Charity said, "requests that she and the earl be excused from supper tonight as they are both exhausted from their trip and wish to rest.

"Your cousin, the Lady Brianna, begs you to excuse her also, as she has a headache and does not feel up to a formal meal."

Marisa absorbed the news. "Has Cook been informed?"

"Aye, my lady," Charity answered.

"Good," Marisa replied. "Ask Cook to send someone along later to the earl and the countess to see if they would like anything. What of my husband and Mr. Covington?"

"The earl and Mr. Covington are together in the library, my lady. A rider from London came with dispatches for Mr. Covington less than an hour ago."

Marisa gently shook off the sand from the note she had just finished writing. Placing the wick of her wax stick over the flame, she lit it. She let the melting wax drip onto the folded note, and blew the flame out. Taking her stamp, now bearing the seal of the swan, she pressed it into the melted wax. "Give this into my husband's hands."

Charity accepted the message.

"Wait till he reads it and bring me his answer. I shall be either in the nursery or with my cousin."

Charity answered, "Yes, my lady."

Marisa walked down the long hallway toward the rooms her cousin occupied. She hadn't seen Brianna since she'd ridden out with Jamie that morn.

She rapped softly on the thick oak door before entering. What Marisa saw therein stopped her.

Brianna's maid was packing her mistress's belongings into a large trunk. Arms akimbo, Marisa asked, "What is the meaning of this?"

"Edyth, leave us," Brianna instructed.

With a hasty "Yes, my lady," the maid fled from the scene.

"I have decided to return to Ireland," Brianna stated flatly, folding a garment and placing it into the velvet-lined trunk.

"Why?" Marisa was sorely puzzled, for her cousin had shown no signs of wishing to leave.

"Because I must," was Brianna's answer.

Marisa noted that Brianna's eyes avoided hers. She suspected that her cousin was hiding something. She walked the few paces to where Brianna stood, her hands busy with another garment. Marisa stilled her cousin's hands, asking gently, "What is wrong?"

"Nothing," Brianna responded.

"Nonsense," Marisa insisted. "You said nothing about leaving here before now."

"I have been thinking about this for some time."

Marisa raised a brow, "You have?" For some reason, she rather doubted that fact.

Brianna turned her back on Marisa. How hard her cousin was making this, she thought. If only Marisa had accepted her story about the headache, she could have been on her way before anyone was the wiser.

"What about Jamie?" Marisa asked, moving around her cousin to face her. She saw the tell-tale color in Brianna's cheeks.

"What do you mean?" Golden eyes met green.

Marisa sighed. "You must have taken notice of Jamie's attentions toward you?" She smiled. "He is very fond of you, cousin."

"It will be best for all concerned if I go," Brianna reiterated.

"I don't understand," Marisa protested. She wondered what had caused the desperation she saw in Brianna's eyes, like that of a caged animal trapped by a hunter. Was her cousin afraid to risk love again? "Brianna," she began, taking hold of her cousin's hand, "do you fear that you dishonor the memory of Donal should you choose to love again? Is it that you cannot think of anyone replacing him in your heart?"

At her cousin's gentle probing, Brianna's golden-brown eyes filled with tears. She knew then that she couldn't continue to keep up the pretense that her marriage had been with love. "My marriage to Donal was not what you think."

"How do you mean?" Marisa asked. "In what way?"

"Come," Brianna said, "there are things I should be telling you." Brianna began haltingly, revealing bit by bit the truth behind the facade of her wedded life to Donal. In Marisa's eyes, she witnessed the dawning realization of what a hell marriage with the wrong man could be. "So you see," Brianna concluded, "I felt more sorrow for the death of my servant than for Donal. She could stand my treatment at his hands no more, and damned her own soul to free me." Tears ran unchecked down Brianna's pale cheeks.

Marisa responded to her cousin's obvious pain. She drew Brianna into her arms, giving what comfort she could. At this gesture, Brianna collapsed against Marisa, pent-up tears flowing freely.

"Then you deserve to be happy, sweet coz,"

Marisa declared. "Jamie is far different from that spawn of Satan that you were wed to. He will understand, if you will only tell him."

Brianna hiccoughed as she tried to get her emotions under control. "I have told him, Marisa."

"And what had he to say?" Marisa had faith in her judgment of Jamie.

"He was naturally shocked and quite angry at the state of my marriage."

"As well he should be," Marisa stated.

"'Tis not as simple as that," Brianna insisted.

"I am certain that Jamie is a man you can depend on, coz," Marisa assured her. "He is not the sort to mistreat a woman."

"No," Brianna agreed, "he is a man of unquestionable good heart."

Marisa soothed back a few stray black curls that haphazardly fell around Brianna's face. It was then that Marisa noticed the small blade of grass entwined in one curl. "Are you afraid that he will prove a man unable to bed you with care and kindness?"

Brianna turned her face so that she met her cousin's green eyes. "After today, I do not harbor that fear."

Marisa suspected that she understood what it was that Brianna was telling her, but she wanted to be completely sure. "Are you and Jamie lovers?"

"Aye." Brianna managed a tentative smile. "It happened today, whilst we were out riding. He asked me to marry him, and 'twas then that I explained about Donal and me. I felt trapped by the bad memories, and I thought that Jamie could help me forget. With his loving, perhaps I could discover that elusive pleasure I've heard talked about."

That accounted for the grass, Marisa decided. "And did you?"

"He opened my eyes to what two people could share when they care for one another."

"Is that the reason you want to leave for Ireland? To inform Killroone that you are to wed again?" Marisa asked hopefully. "Should he have any questions, Cameron and I will vouch for Jamie, as will, I know, Charles Stuart himself if he must."

Brianna moved away from her cousin's embrace. "There will be no wedding."

Marisa was baffled. "No marriage?"

"I cannot wed Jamie. 'Tis why I am returning to my brother's castle, for I cannot face him to tell him. I am too much the coward."

Marisa's voice cut through the silence in the room with the force of her conviction. "You are no coward, Brianna O'Dalaigh. You have survived a hell that many others would not have."

"Two others did not," she said sadly.

"You are not responsible," she said. "Do you hear me?"

"I thank you, Marisa." Brianna's voice was scarcely above a broken whisper. "Your loyalty was ever a comfort to me."

"Brianna." Marisa was determined to make her cousin see reason. "Do you love Jamie?"

"I asked myself that earlier today," she admitted. "I wasn't certain then of my answer; but afterwards, I knew that I was, and knowing that, I could not trap him."

"Trap him? What are you talking about?" Marisa was again puzzled by Brianna's words.

"I am barren." Brianna uttered the distressing words with her hands flat on her stomach. "My womb will never quicken with a child. Could I be denying the man I profess to love the heir he deserves? 'Twould not be fair." Her eyes were filled with sadness. "'Tis better to let him think that I did not love him enough to wed with him."

"You will throw away a chance for happiness?"

"Aye, for I will not shackle him to me."

"You are a fool, Brianna," Marisa declared, "for you cannot speak for him. Mayhap Jamie will not care."

"Suppose he does?" Brianna's voice betrayed her concern.

Marisa responded with cool logic. "You will never know for certain if you say nothing."

"Should I force him to choose me over the heir he should have?"

Marisa vented her rising frustration. "May God spare me from people who would make decisions for others. Give Jamie a chance," she pleaded.

Brianna shook her head, "No."

Marisa tried anew. "Brianna, you must fight for your love."

"Would you?" Brianna leveled her gaze at Marisa.

"Yes," Marisa readily admitted. "I would, and I will."

"Then you do love the Buchanan?"

"More with each passing day," she replied honestly. "And," Marisa said with quiet determination, "I will have him as mine alone." A small smile crossed her mouth. "I know of his past, and it matters not, for I am his future, as you could be Jamie's if you would trust him with the truth. If he loves you, he will accept you as you are."

"Have you accepted the man you wed?"

"I have indeed," Marisa said. "His scars are there; I cannot change them." She walked to the wide bed, running her hands along the pulled-back drapes that could enfold the bed in darkness. "But I have seen the man behind the mask he wears. It is he that I love. A man of courage and loyalty, who has a quick mind and ready wit. An iron-willed man of strength who needs my love, even if he does not wish to acknowledge it as yet." She added with a small smile, "Just as I must have his."

"You set yourself a daunting task, cousin."

"Cameron is worth it."

"How will you accomplish your task?"

Marisa faced Brianna, a secretive smile upon her lips. "'Twould do no good to simply tell Cameron that I love him. Words have little meaning for him. I must *show* him, for 'tis with actions that he will understand, and I pray God, believe."

Marisa returned to the subject at hand. "You owe Jamie Covington the truth, Brianna. Will you think upon what I have said before you make a decision that could ruin your life?"

Brianna, weary, her mind drifting with all that had happened that day, finally agreed. "I yield, coz, and will do as you ask."

Marisa kissed Brianna's cheek. "'Tis for the best."

"I suppose," Brianna replied.

"It will be," Marisa assured her, and as she closed the door to Brianna's room, she met Charity.

"Have you an answer?"

"Aye, my lady," Charity said. "His lordship said I was to tell you that his answer is yes."

"Good." Marisa was pleased. She had cast out the bait and he had bitten. "Now," she said, lowering her voice, "come with me, for I have one more note that you must deliver."

* * *

"Another note?" Cam said, amusement shading his tone.

Charity smiled at the earl and handed Jamie the folded sheet of paper. "'Tis for you, sir," she said, withdrawing from the room.

Cam recognized the seal. Charity had recently delivered a similar note to him less than an hour ago. "From my wife?"

Jamie regarded the seal. "'Twould appear so."

"Then pray, open it," Cam instructed.

Jamie broke the seal and read the short missive.

Jamie,

If you want my cousin's heart, go without delay to Brianna's room, now. If you hesitate, all could be lost.

A bold M was scrawled across the bottom.

Jamie pushed back his seat. He stood, folding the note and placing it into an inner pocket sewn into his doublet jacket.

"There is something that I must take care of," he said to Cam. "If you will excuse me, we can finish this on the morrow." He gathered the documents and slid them into the leather pouch. "Will you see to these for me?"

"Best secure them now," Cam stated, "for I too have an appointment." His curiosity raised, Cam asked, "What is amiss?"

"Your good lady wife has informed me that something of value will be lost to me if I do not act at once."

Cam shot his friend a concerned look. "Can I help?"

Jamie took the papers Cam had been reading and put them with the others, turning the key and locking them securely in the pouch. "'Tis a matter I have to see to personally."

Cam posed the question, "Does it have to do with the Lady Brianna?" He realized that his friend was deeply in love with the beautiful and melancholy Irish noblewoman.

"Yes," Jamie responded. "'Twould seem that I made a miscalculation with the lady."

Cam found his concern for a member of his family roused. "How so?"

Jamie recognized the slight coolness that entered his friend's voice. Cam, he understood, was protective of those within his care and would defend those entrusted to him from harm. Marriage had broadened the boundaries of Cam's loyalties; had it also, Jamie wondered, broadened the boundaries of his heart?

"I asked her to marry me," Jamie stated.

"What did the Lady Brianna say?"

"She never fully answered me. Perhaps I did not press as hard as I should have."

"Be careful," Cam warned. "She has much delicacy about her."

"For good reason," Jamie responded.

"Which is?" Cam asked, one blond brow raised in question.

"'Tis not for me to say," Jamie replied. "I must respect the words she uttered to me in confidence."

"In confidence?" Cam inquired.

"Aye, in strictest confidence," Jamie responded. He picked up the leather pouch and walked to the door.

"I would see no harm come to her," Cam said, his tone dark.

"Nor would I," Jamie vowed. "The Lady Brianna

is dearer to me than anything in this life, Cameron. I want what is best for her, and I think *I* can be that for her. She fills a void within me with her gentle presence." His hazel eyes warmed with an inward zeal. "I would, if allowed, fill her life with as much happiness as I can."

"Then God speed your way," Cam declared.

When the door closed and he was left alone, Cam's thoughts dwelled on his own emptiness. Solitude had become his castle, and he had locked himself behind its secluded walls. Empty had been his life before Marisa entered. Empty was his bed without her beside him. Empty were the arms that longed to hold her to him. Empty had been the days since they last shared a thought or a direct, unguarded glance.

His father's words weighed heavily on him, as did the physical presence of his daughter and his mother. The child hadn't rejected him for the face he bore; Elsbeth had instead wrapped her tiny arms around him and kissed him.

And in that action was born the hope that perhaps he had been wrong. If his child could love him as he was, flaws evident, perhaps another could as well.

He had but to chance it.

Could he take the risk?

Brianna stared at the open trunk. Marisa's words floated in her brain, nagging like a gadfly around prime livestock.

Was she in the wrong to leave without talking to Jamie?

Soft and sweet memories of sharing her body with him replaced the words. With Jamie, she had felt more properly wedded in one afternoon than through all her married life with Donal.

Her arms wrapped around herself as she paced the floor. How could she endure parting from him when they had just begun? She had tasted the freshness of his love, and after the staleness of her wedded union with Donal, it was a blessing that she would find hard to live without.

Yet, because she loved Jamie, she owed him . . . What?

The truth.

A soft knock sounded on her chamber door. Brianna wondered who could it be, as she had sent her maid to bed. She doubted that Marisa would be paying her another visit.

It sounded again, barely louder this time. A voice followed it. "Brianna," it called.

Jamie.

Clad only in her bedclothes, she responded quickly. Opening the door a mere crack, she held it in front of her.

"May I come in?" he asked.

"'Tis very late."

"Obviously much later than I thought," he murmured, moving into the room. Jamie spied the trunk on the floor, saw the clothes half-filling it. "You are going somewhere?" He turned around, his mouth softening as he saw her standing there, her long black hair tumbled about her shoulders, her brown eyes wide. She wore a nightdress that resembled a man's shirt, with wide lace at the elbows and a ribbon at the throat that held it together. Her slim feet were bare.

Brianna moved and fetched a robe to cover herself. She should laugh at her modesty, especially after lying with this man and welcoming his body into hers.

"I was planing on returning to Ireland."

"Without telling me?"

"That had been my intent."

"Had been?" Jamie demanded. "Did you think that I would have been satisfied with that?"

"Marisa changed my mind."

"Thank God for that," he said with a deep sigh.

"It was she who made me see things in a new light."

Jamie closed the distance between them, lifting her chin to meet his descending mouth. His kiss deepened as he slid his arms round Brianna and drew her closer. When he raised his head, he whispered to her, "I love you, Brianna."

She finally spoke the words he longed to hear. "And I shall be forever loving you, Jamie. As long as there be a single O'Dalaigh in Eire, and even beyond."

"Then why would you leave?"

"Fear," she managed to say.

"Of what?"

"That what we had would not be lasting."

"Why would you think that?" Jamie inquired. "I am not an inconstant man. Nor, my sweet lady, do I make rash and false promises." He hesitated for a moment, doubt crowding his mind. "Or is that you think your family will object, since I am but an Englishman who shares neither your religion nor your place in society?"

"My family would be happy for me if I found a man whom I loved. No, Jamie," she said, the words bubbling to the surface. "'Tis for your sake that I would be leaving."

"My sake?"

"Aye, my love."

"You must explain to me how breaking my heart is in my best interests," he demanded, releasing his hold on her.

Brianna held out her hand, taking Jamie's and

leading him to a small couch. He sat facing her, his eyes clear and calm. She kept holding his hand, drawing strength from its warmth. Her voice was low, the words wrenched painfully from her throat. "I can give you no children. I am of barren stock."

Jamie sat silent for a moment. He considered how much it had cost the woman he loved to admit what was obviously so distressing to her. She had been willing to deny love so that *he* could have an heir.

Brianna was frightened by his silence. Had Marisa been wrong?

Jamie drew her hand to his lips. He kissed the knuckles before turning her hand over and kissing her palm. "Oh my love," he said, "I want *you*. I love *you*. If 'tis a choice of an heir without love, or a love without an heir, have no question which I shall choose."

Brianna's golden-brown eyes filled with tears of joy. "You still wish to marry me?" she asked, incredulous.

"If you would so honor me, yes."

"Oh, my dearest Jamie," Brianna sighed, burrowing into his arms, her hand on his heart, "'tis I who would be most honored to become your wife."

Jamie tightened one arm around her, as the other hand stroked her hair lightly. "I cannot give you the life you were born to, my dearest heart; I can but promise you I shall never give you cause to regret your decision."

"Then," Brianna said, her body relaxing around his, "'tis enough of an assurance for me." In her mind she uttered first a soundless prayer of gratitude to Marisa, followed by a wish that her cousin's love would prove powerful enough to reach through the darkness to the Buchanan's embittered soul.

For love, as she had found, her wisdom coming almost too late, was a powerful force to be reckoned with.

Chapter Twenty-Four

Marisa's daring gamble needed only her husband.

All was ready and waiting for him. The cold supper she'd requested lay on a small table brought to her room earlier. A breeze from the open windows stirred loose tendrils of curls around her face. Her hair hung down her back in thick chestnut waves, picking up the rich color in the golden glow of the myriad candles which lit the room. She had anointed herself with the rose perfume, even sprinkling some of the scent across the soft linen sheets.

The large clothes trunk at the foot of the bed was open. Marisa bent down, checking to make sure the long silk scarves she'd purchased were tucked inside. She picked one up, running the material through her hands, testing the strength. Satisfied, Marisa replaced the scarf and shut the velvet-lined lid just as the door to her bedroom closed with a decided snap.

Startled, she whirled around.

"It was open," Cam said, standing there. His gaze focused on the costume Marisa wore. It was unlike anything he had ever seen before—loose, of fine cotton in a deep shade of green, it matched the emerald ring ring on her finger; the long, full sleeves and ankle-grazing hem were richly embroidered in gold thread. It was cut into a deep V, exposing a glimpse of the flesh of her bosom to Cam's gaze. That the garment was her sole covering was evident as Cam could see the shadowy movenment of her lithe body beneath the cloth. He especially noticed the way the material clung to the shape of her breasts, outlining them in detail. She wore a golden girdle that hung loosely about her waist, the thick links fastened with an emerald clasp.

His own flesh stirred in response, raising the temperature in the room.

"Do you like this?" Marisa asked, her voice huskier in tone. Her slipper-clad feet made little sound on the wood floor as she moved across it.

"I've nae seen the like of it," Cam admitted. "'Tis certainly different." And, he added silently to himself, enticing, making a man crave a touch. If he did not know better, he would think the wench was eager to seduce him.

"'Tis from the East, called a caftan," she explained.

"How did you come by it?"

Marisa gave him a quizzing look. "The Fitzgerald family owns trading ships, remember? This was from a voyage many years past. Whilst we were in Dorset, my grandmother found it packed away in a trunk. She thought that I might like it.

And I do," Marisa said, turning slowly so that the garment floated around her like a green cloud. "I can think of some favorite concubine wearing this when she was summoned for her master's pleasure," Marisa finished.

Had it been he, Cam thought, the blood pounding in his veins, he would have ripped the gown from her body, eager to unveil the rich treasure which lay beneath the cloth. His mind and skin could readily recall the feel of her warm flesh against his hand, against his mouth. His ears remembered her soft moans and delicious cries as they rode the private storm of their shared triumph.

"You, too, it would seem, my lord, are wearing something different," Marisa observed, handing Cam a finely crafted silver goblet containing wine. Marisa had seen a costume such as this when she was a child visiting Scotland, though it was never worn in England. Her husband had on a simple white linen shirt, freshly laundered judging by the smell of the sun still clinging to it. But there was nothing strange about that. What was novel was what he wore instead of petticoat breeches and hose. A skirt of some sort was belted about his waist, ending above his knees. She recognized the pattern of the wool as that which Cam had explained was his family's tartan. His muscular calves were clothed in wool socks of charcoal gray banded in black. His feet were shod in plain black shoes, shorter of heel than court wear.

As he took the Celtic-designed goblet from her hand, their fingers touched briefly. Cam felt the tingling; from her hastily averted eyes, he could tell Marisa had too. Wine sipped from her lips would be all the sweeter, he mused; wine lapped from between her breasts and thighs would be all the more intoxicating.

Heat coursed through her with the intensity of his look. The loch-blue eye seared through the fabric of her gown until she could feel her nipples hardening against the material, felt the moist heat in her loins rising.

Marisa turned her back on him for the moment, needing to sort out her feelings and keep them under control. She had to remain calm for her the succcess of her scheme.

"'Tis of Scottish origin, am I correct?" she asked as she took a seat at the table. "Please," she said, doing her best to be the proper hostess, "sit down." His clothes somewhat changed her perception of the meal, and her husband. He appeared more at ease, and conversely more of the stranger.

"Aye, 'tis a gift from my father." Cameron walked the short distance and settled himself in the low chair. He looked around the room. "Where is Lionheart?" He was used to seeing the kitten about whenever Marisa was near.

"I took Lionheart upstairs to the nursery. I thought that perhaps Elsbeth would like to play with the kitten. It may lessen her fear of being in a new home. An animal is a reminder that though some things change, some things are the same no matter where one lives."

Cam was touched by Marisa's thoughtfulness regarding his daughter's feelings. "I was going to tell you about the lassie," he began.

"'Tis of no consequence," Marisa assured him.

"Aye, but it is," he stressed. "I love my little girl."

"As she apparently loves you," Marisa observed. "She showed me a silver locket. A miniature portrait of you was inside. She pointed to it proudly, saying, 'This is my father.'"

"She did?"

Marisa heard the wistfulness in his tone, the need to believe that he was loved, even as he disbelieved it was possible. "Indeed. Elsbeth was most happy that she would now be with you." Marisa sipped at her wine, wondering when Cameron was going to do the same. She counted on him drinking his fair share of the potent brew. Her plan depended upon it. "She even asked me if she was going to stay here with you, or would she have to go back with your family."

"And what did you tell her?" Cam asked calmly, taking a long drink of the wine, trying to appear unconcerned with her answer.

"That she was most welcome to make her home with us. Was that to your liking?"

Cam looked down the length of the table. "'Twas most generous of you," he acknowledged.

"Nonsense," Marisa dismissed the notion. "She is your daughter, Cameron. I was told by your mother that Elsbeth's mother died giving birth. Could I make her doubly an orphan by denying her her father?"

"She is a bastard," he admitted. "I wasna wed with her mother."

"That makes no difference to me."

"Thank you," Cam said simply.

"I have always wanted children, my lord," she said, lifting a linen napkin that was thrown over a platter piled high with a variety of roasted cold meats—chicken, goose, venison, and ham. Smoked salmon filled a smaller dish, as did figs, dates, and apples. A thick wedge of cheese topped another. "Take what you will," she murmured, her voice a gentle invitation. With a sharp-bladed knife, she cut a slice of cheese.

In a tone she managed to keep even, Marisa related another incident. "Elsbeth, as I was taking leave of the room, asked me if she should call me mother."

"What did you say?" Cam kept control over his own tone, fearing to reveal just how much her answer meant to him.

"I told Elsbeth that I would be honored to have her call me mother, as I would be honored to call her daughter." Marisa's green eyes fixed on his face. "Have I your approval?"

Cam's sensual mouth curved into a deep smile. "It would please me greatly."

"Then 'tis done."

He watched her, bathed in candlelight. These past few weeks, they had become uneasy strangers to one another; then tonight, she had sent him an invitation to take a private supper with her. Why? he wondered. And why was she dressed to tempt any man, him especially, beyond reason?

Marisa watched as Cam's hand came up to cover a yawn. It would seem that the herbs in the sleeping potion were beginning to work. They would have no ill effects on Cameron; he would soon drift off, perhaps for an hour or so. It would be enough time to do what she would. And, Marisa thought, how very easy her husband had made it for her with his choice of clothes this evening.

Cam yawned again. "Pray, forgive me," he said, not understanding why he was so tired all of a sudden.

"How long will your mother and father tarry with us?" Marisa asked, hiding her excitement that her plan was beginning to work.

"I dinna know for sure," he murmured, his head drifting slightly toward his chin before he jerked it upright. Lord, he thought, what ailed him? He had not been tired before he entered the room, and the sight of his lovely wife, clad in a gown that emphasized her small waist, her high breasts, her rounded hips, had triggered his own body's stirring.

"You are not eating, my lord. Is it not to your liking? Should I send for something else? Tell me what you want and it shall be granted."

Cam heard Marisa's voice growing distant. What he wanted was her, in his arms, her generous and loving heart accepting him. But he had grown weary of the futility of that hope. She would be as all others. Beauty would not willingly embrace the truth of his ugliness.

Yet, a voice inside his head mocked, *your child accepted.*

'Tis different, he mentally argued, *she is flesh of my flesh.*

Again the calm voice mocked him, *So was your mother. That proves nothing.*

Cam focused on the woman who sat at the other end of the table. Marisa was the promise of life, and of hope. For in loving her, he had been drawn to Marisa for more than her unquestionable beauty of body; 'twas her beauty of soul, her strength of purpose, her loyalty to her kith and kin, and her king that drew him. She was all he never knew he wanted, and all he doubted he could hold.

Feeling acutely woolly-headed, Cam decided that it was best he leave, much as he wanted to linger. This moment was too precious to squander. He rose to his feet, and the room momentarily darkened.

"Cameron!" Marisa cried, rushing to his side. Her arms went around him as he lurched forward. "Let me help you," she insisted, leading him to her bed.

"No," he protested, "I can walk." He hated feeling this sense of helplessness around her, as if he were an invalid. He blinked. His arm came around her to steady himself, his left hand closing around her breast for an instant. What was wrong? This was more than being merely tired. The wine? Impossible. He'd always had a good head for drink. Besides, he'd drunk only one goblet, as had Marisa.

Cam felt the thickness of the mattress beneath his legs. "My room," he managed to say, his speech thickening with each moment.

"Hush, my lord," Marisa's voice came to him as if from the depths of a thick mist. "You must rest." Her hands pushed gently against his chest, impeling him backward onto the lush density of plump pillows. The aroma of roses wafted around his head as he lost his battle to stay awake.

Marisa waited for a few minutes, watching her husband draw deep, even breaths. She leaned over, touching his shoulder. "Cameron," she said. When he failed to answer her, she knew the sleeping potion had finally worked. The right side of his face was turned into the pillows. How like an angel he looked, she thought, bending to remove the shoes from his feet. The thick, golden-dusted lashes of his left eye lay against his cheek.

While shifting his body, Marisa saw what her eyes had failed to notice before. On his right knee were ridges of scars. The bones had healed, though not as they had been. Her fingertips lightly grazed the spot. Her eyes went back to his face, peaceful in repose. *Oh, my love,* she thought, *would that I could ease your pain.*

Marisa rose, walking to the clothes chest. She took out the scarves and carried them back to the bed.

When she had completed her task, she returned to the table to finish her meal. She smiled as she lifted a thick slice of tender white chicken meat from the platter. The silver saltcellar in her hand, she tossed some salt onto the chicken. It would probably be several hours before Cameron awoke, and she would need all her energy for the battle yet to come.

Cam stirred, opening his good eye. He was still in his wife's bedroom. 'Twould appear he had slept some time in her bed.

As he went to move, he felt restricted. Panic rose within him. Sweet Jesus! He was tied to the bed. Silken scarves bound his hands and feet. He tried to loosen them, but they were tied tight, and he was still somewhat tired. How had Marisa managed this? And for what purpose?

It was the wine!

He'd been drugged. Something had been put into the wine he'd drunk.

How dared she?

"Marisa!" he shouted. "Unbind me."

"Please calm yourself. I am here, dear husband," she whispered sweetly.

"What is the meaning of this?" He pulled at his bonds once again.

"How does it feel?" Marisa asked as she joined him on the bed, sitting down.

"How do you think that I feel?" he demanded angrily, "like a prisoner."

"Then you can sympathize with how I felt, my

lord," she reminded him, "when you bound me to the bed in the cottage."

"'Twas different," he stated.

Marisa raised a chestnut brow. "It was? How so? Because you are a man and I am but a woman?"

"No," Cam muttered. "I had to do it."

"Why?" she questioned, laying her hand on his wide chest. With a pull, she unlaced the ribbon of his shirt. She slipped a finger between the linen folds, stroking the soft hair below.

He closed his eye; his hands balled into fists. Her touch was driving him mad for her. "I had my reasons," he said, refusing to elaborate.

Marisa gave him a small smile. "Not good enough, my lord."

"It will have to be."

"Think again," she challenged. Marisa leaned over to check the bonds, giving her husband another glimpse of her breasts.

Cameron could feel the immediate response of his manhood. Damnation! He was trussed like a prisoner, and the sight of her flesh quickened his.

It was then that he realized that he wasn't afraid. Annoyed, aye, damnably so. But afraid? Cam stared into his wife's green eyes. The last time a woman had held him like this he'd been in chains, and malice had poured out of Faith Bellamy's hellish eyes like slithering serpents spitting venom. Marisa's eyes held nothing like that. Her eyes were kind and clear. He had seen traces of anger in the emerald depths, but not hatred, not vengence, and not betrayal.

Could he tell her the truth?

Marisa waited for him to reply. The tick of the clock could be heard in the silence. The cry of a night bird echoed from a distance through the open window. The excited bark of a dog followed it.

"Was it because you thought that I would recoil from the evidence of the woman who abused you?" Marisa reached out her hand, and as she went to touch his scarred cheek, Cam abruptly turned his head.

"Cameron, please," she beseeched him, "listen to me. I know how you came to look as you do. I know about your mother and what she did to you on your return to Scotland."

"She told you?" Cam found it hard to believe that his mother would have confessed her actions to his wife.

"Yes. What she did was reprehensible, but"— Marisa stressed the words—"I am not her."

Cam gave a caustic laugh. "Aye, so you say now. I know what this face can do to those unprepared. Forget this," he commanded.

"No, I shall not." Marisa let her glance slide over his face, down his broad chest, across the wide belt that held the fabric in place. She tugged at his shirt, pulling the linen from beneath the belt and the fabric.

Marisa left the bed, coming back with a pair of silver needlework scissors in her hand.

"What are you going to do with those?"

"Get rid of unwanted material," she replied and placed the scissors against the linen and cut it till the shirt was ruined, cut straight up the middle, exposing his broad chest covered in dark-gold hair.

She dropped the scissors to the floor, rending the material even further with her fingers as Cam moved restlessly beneath her hands.

"Damn you, no!" he demanded.

It was then that Marisa saw the ragged section of flesh that covered the right side of his chest. Her breath caught in her throat as her hand flew to her mouth.

"Have you seen enough?" he inquired, his voice frigid.

Marisa answered him by leaning down and tracing the mark with her hand. "'Tis a badge of honor, my lord, for it was gotten in the service of the king."

"'Tis a mark of stupidity for bedding the wrong woman," he declared; "and underestimating her."

"We all make mistakes, Cameron," Marisa said. "Trust me," she urged.

"I know what 'tis best. . . ."

"Stop it!" Marisa insisted.

"No," he said, "you must stop." Cam tried to reason with Marisa before it was too late and she went past the point of no return, "else you will be sorry. Listen to me."

"How dare you treat me as if I were a child who does not know her own mind?" she demanded. "I know what I want and whom I love—you!"

"Love?" he asked. Cam was shocked by his wife's fervent declaration. Sweet Lord, he thought, 'twould make it all the more difficult when she rejected all that he was.

"Yes, love," she said with sweetness in her tone. Her angry outburst was over. All that concerned her was showing him the truth in her words. Marisa's hands were busy unfastening the wide leather belt with the plain silver buckle.

"Curse you!" Cam shouted.

Marisa ignored him, continuing to unfold the cloth as if she were unwrapping a precious jewel.

Cam closed his eye. He did not want to see

the look on her face when she beheld further evidence of his disfigurement.

Cam wore nothing beneath the tartan.

Scars crisscrossed his right leg; more wound across his flat belly and trailed downward to the gold hair that surrounded his manhood, which rose proudly defiant. The woman had burned a path of horror and pain on his flesh.

Cam felt the wet drops of her tears on his skin. Pity. He was a creature of pity to her now. Less than a man.

His eye flew open when the brush of her lips touched him, light as a feather, as her hair cascaded around his belly and between his legs.

Marisa could think of no other way to show Cameron that for him the darkness was over. That he now had someone to share the light with him. It required no courage on her part to kiss him where she would never have thought to place her mouth before she had read the book; all she needed was the belief that her love could heal him.

Her delicate kisses were like a gentle breeze on a midsummer's day, a balm of soothing ointment that somehow, as if by magic, repaired the damage done to his torn flesh. Her long hair brushed his skin like the silk scarves that bound him.

Marisa felt the deep shudder go through him as she made her way across the ridges of flesh. Emboldened, she continued her journey upward, across his taut stomach, along the arrow of hair that lead to his wide chest. Her fingers fanned along the golden forest until she came to one masculine nipple. Her tongue reached out and laved it as he had hers.

He drew in a ragged breath and she smiled in acknowledgment.

"Does that please you?" she asked, certain of his answer yet needing to hear it confirmed.

"Aye, lass, it pleases me," Cam responded, his voice husky with contentment. He couldn't believe what she was doing to him. Delight coursed through his body at an alarming rate, like a fire gone wild.

Marisa continued with her gentle assault, moving further upward. Her lips traced the bone in his shoulder, nipping it ever so slightly. His neck beckoned, and she followed the path there, skimming her mouth across the scar along his throat and across his cheek.

Marisa nestled for a quiet moment against his chest, loving the feel of his heated skin, his masculine scent, his response to her actions.

Now there was but one more scar to dispel.

His dark-gold hair was thick and soft. Her hand skimmed through the waves until she reached the tie that held the patch in place. Before he could object, she pulled it from his head, baring his eye.

Cam held still, his one blue orb unblinking, focused on her green eyes. He could raise no defense with his hands tied. She had now exposed his last secret by ripping away what he hid behind.

"Have you seen all that you wanted to see?"

Marisa stared at the results of the destructive wrath one woman had wrought. That bitch had deliberately blinded Cam, searing his flesh so only scars remained where once he had had an eye as blue as the one that watched her, waiting for her response.

"I see only a man," Marisa answered, her words flowing from her heart, "who has endured great pain, a man who possess more courage than an army of king's men.

"I love you, Cameron Buchanan," she stated simply. "You have the word of a Fitzgerald on that." With that pronouncement, Marisa bent and kissed first his blind eye, and then his sensual mouth.

At the touch of his wife's lips, Cam's mouth responded, meeting hers with all the passion that had been trapped inside him for so long. 'Twas as if a spell had been broken, freeing him from the that which kept him prisoner—loneliness.

His English wife had taught him much, especially the lesson of what power love really possessed. She had gone to great lengths to show him what he wouldn't have believed possible if she had simply told him.

"Release me," he demanded between kisses.

An enigmatic smile curved Marisa's mouth. "Not quite yet," she said.

"I want to love you," he said, his deep voice a caress along her skin.

"Later," she whispered. "This is for you, Cameron." Marisa worshipped her husband's body with her mouth and hands, skimming her tongue across every inch of his flesh, her hands busy learning the secret spots that could provoke pleasure. Her remembered reading of her grandmother's book, coupled with her own loving instincts, took over, tapping into the hidden richness of her passion, releasing it. She was at once shy and bold, experimental and certain, eager to try.

Cam's hoarse breathing, along with the sounds that rumbled from his chest, gave her added incentive. The hot, wild blood of the Fitzgeralds had been given free rein.

When her soft, teasing hands grasped him gently, gliding along the rigid staff of flesh, Cam thought he would explode from the sheer joy. Marisa slid her hand up and down, around and under, pushing him to the limits of his patience.

"I would ride, my lord," she said, her own breathing coming faster.

"Aye, lass," Cam entreated her, "do it. Do it now!"

Hiking up the hem of her caftan, Marisa moved with catlike grace as she melted over him. Adjusting herself carefully, she moved down upon the swollen staff, taking him completely into her body. He filled her with his hot, steely length. His husky whispered words of encouragement drove her on as he bucked beneath her thighs, pushing himself further and further into the tight warmth of her body. Each stroke, each movement brought them closer to the final ecstasy.

Marisa moaned low in her throat, almost losing what little control she had remaining.

With a potent thrust, Cam spilled his hot seed, and both soared into the heavens, breaking free of all barriers. Their shattered cries echoed around them. Marisa collapsed onto Cam's sweat-drenched chest, her damp gown their only covering, his body still connected to hers.

When coherent thought returned, Cam realized that in truth he had been a man who'd been only half alive until Marisa had resurrected him. She'd willingly come through the flames of hell for him, bringing him back to the wonder of life.

"I love you," he whispered.

Marisa lifted her head, her breathing returning to normal. Had she heard him correctly? She looked into his beloved face, asking the question to which she feared the answer. "What of the woman you told me that you loved and could not have?"

Cam whispered in his deep, seductive tones, "'Twas you, Marisa."

"Me?" she asked, blinking.

"Aye," Cam willingly confessed, "I have loved you these past months."

"Why did you not tell me?"

"'Tis very plain," he answered. "Fear."

She breathed a sigh. "That I would have none of you if ever I saw your face, or your body?"

"Aye," he admitted. "I have had good reason to think that you too would leave me if ever you saw what I chose to keep hidden."

"What about our wedding night?"

"Ah, that," Cam said, recalling how Marisa had dropped her robe and offered her lovely body to him. "I thought you were arrogant."

She slapped him playfully on his chest. "Arrogant? Me? 'Twas *you* who were arrogant, my lord. I was ready to . . ." Marisa halted.

"To what?"

"Do my duty," she finished honestly. "I had given my word before God and the king. I would have kept it."

"No matter if your wedded husband repelled you?" Cam demanded.

"You did not," Marisa insisted.

"Answer my question, if you dare. Would you have bedded me even if I repulsed you?"

Marisa responded solemnly, "I would have kept my vows. A Fitzgerald's word is law."

Cameron responded, "As is the Buchanan's, my love."

"Then what would you have, Cameron?" she asked, her voice a throaty purr of suggestion.

"Loose me," he commanded softly.

This time Marisa was happy to comply.

Cam rubbed his wrists where the silk had been tied. He watched as Marisa gathered the scarves and folded them carefully into her clothes chest. He then shrugged out of what was left of his shirt, throwing it across the floor. He peeled off his socks, sending them after the shirt.

"Come here," he said, holding out his hand to her, the long, lean fingers compelling her.

Marisa hastened to do his bidding.

With his loch-blue gaze taking in her body from crown to toes, he instructed her, "Remove the garment."

Her smile could have rivaled any courtesan's, except, he thought, that it was all the sweeter because it was reserved for him alone. The love he saw in her green eyes, the rapture he had witnessed on her face when they reached the pinnacle of love, would make the hell he had endured these past years easier to bear. That Marisa loved him as deeply and as passionately as he loved her was a miracle.

He'd lost faith on the journey of his life; she had brought it back.

Marisa eagerly removed the caftan, dropping it to the carpet beneath her feet. It had served its purpose. She moved slowly, with all the grace of an imperial cat. Her hand met his, fingers linking.

Cam pulled her back onto the bed, covering her body with his. Their lips met as each plundered and tasted the other. Their hands roamed, then lingered. They touched, savored, enjoyed, and discovered.

Their loving was slow and languid. When Cam eventually slipped into her body, it was if he were coming home. He'd found the haven his wounded soul had needed.

In Cam's strong arms, Marisa felt protected, cherished, and most important, loved. She snuggled closer as he drew the sheet over their still-damp bodies.

Tonight their loving had surpassed any fantasy, any dream she'd ever imagined. It had been strong as steel, soft as down.

It was real, and worth any price.

Chapter Twenty-Five

Cam awoke with the strange feeling of warm breath upon his flesh. His wife lay in his arms, her head resting on the broad frame of his chest, her hair trailing over his torso. His bonny Sassenach bride.

How sweet the night had been. In those hours past, he had discovered the true richness of love. Marisa had given him back a part of himself he'd thought lost long ago. Like a knight errant on a quest, she had successfully breached the walls of his pride to find the man within, breaking the spell of loneliness which had surrounded him these past years. Her tender regard had shattered his prison of pain, forcing him to confront the demons which had haunted him. Cam realized that he had been wandering aimlessly; she had shown him the light.

Cam tightened his arm around Marisa, rejoic-

ing in the feel of her soft, naked skin next to
his. With her beside him, all things were possible. Any boon she wished, he would see carried
out, whatever the cost. For love of her, he would
walk barefoot through the gates of Hell if need
be, endure any punishment or offense, so long as
he could be with her.

In loving Marisa, he had embraced life again,
reveling in its beauty, accepting its ugliness. Like
a novice come to an awakening, Cameron had
finally found his soul. It was Marisa.

It would always be Marisa.

Marisa heard the steady beat of her husband's
heart beneath her ear. A lazy, comforting contentment kept her where she was, curled against his
leanly muscled body.

She savored the taste of victory, for it was not
only hers, but Cameron's as well. She'd called
upon his heart to believe in her love, to grant
her access to the private chambers in his soul,
and he had.

Darkness and fear had vanished with the passing of the night. Marisa felt a link to her ancestors
who had risked much for love, who had been cou-
rageous enough to fight for what they wanted.
Their passionate blood ran in her veins, strong
and deep.

The power of her love for this man thrilled her.
Once she would have dismissed the idea that in
surrender lay victory. A lazy smile curved her
mouth. Now she knew differently. Their mutual
capitulation had proven her wrong.

Marisa moved her head, her lips seeking his
flesh. She kissed her way across the expanse of
his chest, her mouth mapping a pathway along
his body. She undulated her body so that she was
chest to chest, face to face, with her husband, his

body cradling hers. Marisa stared down at his face. The black eyepatch was once more in place, tied securely around his head. She had rescued it some hours ago, returning it to him. Before doing so, however, Marisa had taken the patch in her hand, her fingertips touching the smooth kidskin interior that rested against his flesh, and brought it to her lips.

Marisa understood that her symbolic healing kiss was not lost on her husband when she saw his loch-blue eye moisten with a single tear.

She leaned over his mouth, as if to kiss him, then changed her mind. Her hands reached out to bury themselves in his thick hair when, like her kitten licking the cream from a bowl, Marisa opened her mouth and stroked her tongue from his chin to the top of his lips.

Cameron's own tongue flicked out, wetting his lips, savoring the trail she had blazed.

She quickly accepted the unspoken invitation, melding her mouth to his as they kissed deeply, intimately, their breaths mingling.

With a deft movement, Cam shifted and drew Marisa underneath his body. Her legs parted for his entrance, wrapping around his hips as he plunged deeper, her body joining his in this primal exaltation.

When she recovered enough to move, Marisa sat up, her breathing still ragged as her heart slowed its rapid pace. How shallow and empty her life would have been had she never experienced this "little death." She tried to imagine sharing her body and her heart so completely with any other man but Cameron. The picture her mind conjured was bleak and empty, an emotional wasteland.

Vous, et nul autre, my darling, echoed through

Marisa's mind. You, and no other. She knew that for her, there would never be a love to equal what she had found with Cameron.

Cam's left arm encircled her shoulder as he rose behind her. Marisa's hands clasped the strength in his bare arm, her chin resting on his large splayed hand. "I was going to get something for us to drink, my lord. Do you wish aught else?"

Cam kissed her neck, his voice a dark seductive caress to her heightened senses. "Ay, lass," he murmured, *"you."*

"'Tis greedy you are," Marisa countered.

"I've years of depravation to make up for," he replied.

"Then shall we spend the day here?" she asked, loathe herself to relinquish the security the bedroom represented. Here, in his arms, she was safe and secure, loved and cherished.

He sighed. "Much as I would like to, I dinna think 'twould be wise."

Marisa shrugged her shoulders. "I suppose not," she agreed.

"Do you think that I truly want to leave this bed?" he demanded. "Or let you go from my arms?" His mouth trailed a path of fire along her neck. Marisa shivered with pleasure, closing her eyes in sensual appreciation. "If we were alone, I would keep you here in this room for at least a month."

"Only a month?" she questioned.

"Longer would be vulgar," he responded in mock solemnity.

"And it wouldn't do for an earl to be considered vulgar, now would it?" she asked.

"Nay, my love, it wouldn't," he replied. "So we must do our duty and keep company with our guests."

"Duty be damned," she sighed.

Cam lifted one blond blow. "Can I have heard you correctly, lass? My wife, shirking her duty?"

Marisa smiled, turning her head about so that she faced Cameron. "Quite right, my love," she stated as their lips met in a fiery blaze of passion, threatening to engulf them once again in love's flames.

When they broke the kiss, Cam whispered to Marisa in his deep Scottish accent, *"Gràdh mo chridhe."* He repeated the words to her in English. "Love of my heart."

The drink Marisa had been going to fetch was forgotten as they lost themselves in another kiss. So caught up in the rapture of their love were they that when Charity knocked on the door, they didn't even hear her.

Entering, Charity was unprepared for the sight which awaited her. Her mistress, the Countess of Derran, obviously naked, was in the arms of her husband, the earl, who also appeared to have little or nothing on, in her bed, kissing wildly. Charity inadvertently dropped the tray in her shock, which startled the couple.

"Oh, begging your pardon, my lady," she said, bending to the floor to pick up the pieces of the broken crockery. Charity's face was red with embarrassment at having intruded on the earl and countess's privacy. "I had no idea that you were bedding . . ." She broke off, her face getting even redder. "I mean that the earl was . . ." Her words trailed off as she raised her head, then quickly lowered her eyes. Whisking off her white apron, she dabbed at the spilled coffee. "Shall I get you some more?" she said, keeping her eyes averted from the couple on the bed.

Marisa, her mouth quirked into a grin, said,

"Yes, that would be fine. And I shall require water for my bath."

Charity scooped up the silver tray, keeping her eyes downcast as she backed out of the room. "As you wish, my lady."

Marisa errupted into a fit of giggles when Charity had closed the door. "Oh, Cameron, I am well and truly afraid that we have shocked her."

"Then," Cam said, adjusting Marisa onto his lap, "she will have to get used to being shocked. For we shall be sharing a bed from now on," he promised.

His long, clever fingers were working magic on her body, sending tremors shooting through her. Marisa forgot about Charity and everything else as she gave herself up to the wonder of his touch.

Brianna was happier than she could ever have thought possible. Sleeping beside her was the man who had shown her the wonders of love. She listened to Jamie's even breathing, watching him as if she expected that he would vanish at any moment.

Leaving her bed, Brianna drew on a robe. She opened one of the windows, enjoying the smell of the fresh air, the scent of the flowers in bloom. She was like a child in her wonderment. Everything was different, seen through new eyes, so long as she had Jamie in her life.

Life was once again meant to be lived. And love was meant to be shared.

She cast a glance over her shoulder and saw that the man who occupied her thoughts was stirring. "Jamie," she called. "Come here, my love."

Jamie woke to the sound of his lover's lilting Irish voice, beckoning him. He tossed back the blanket, pulling on his breeches and his shirt. He ran a hand through his hair, pushing it away from his face. His hazel eyes focused on the woman he adored, standing in front of an open window. In his wildest imaginings, he could not have not foreseen the incredible delight to be found in sharing love.

"Is today not the brightest morn you have ere beheld?" Brianna asked, holding out her hand for his, her golden-brown eyes shining like amber.

"It could be raining to overflow the Thames," he said, nuzzling her neck, "and I would think it perfect, so long as I had you."

"Ah," Brianna asked, "are you sure that there is not a drop of Irish blood to be found in your veins? With words like that, there must be some."

"No, 'tis but the truth," Jamie replied.

"'Tis of no matter, for it is indeed a day to praise God. He has given me many blessings."

"As he has me," Jamie agreed. "Now, are you not pleased that I kept you from returning to Ireland?"

Brianna's head bowed; her voice was soft. "I thought that complete happiness was to be forever beyond my grasp. That for me the shadows of life were all I could expect, or deserved."

"Nonsense," Jamie reassured her, "you deserve all of God's bounty."

Brianna continued her confession, "I had thought to go back to my home, perhaps to enter a convent. There, with time to reflect on my actions, I could find peace." She brought his hand to her lips. "'Twas God's will that you came to me."

"God, and your cousin," Jamie said with a smile.

"My cousin? What has Marisa to do with this?"

"She told me that if I did not want to lose that which I valued above all else, I should make haste to your room."

"She did?"

"Aye, her missive was most persuasive."

"Then I have her to thank?"

Jamie stroked her head, loving the feel of her hair under his hand. "Are you—thankful, that is?"

Brianna welcomed the feel of Jamie's arm sliding about her waist. "More than you know," she said.

"Then will you marry me?"

"Nothing would give me greater joy than to become your wife," she admitted truthfully.

"Then 'tis settled?" Jamie asked hopefully.

Brianna added, "I would marry in my faith."

"So long as I can wed with you," Jamie professed, "I will do it however, whenever, and wherever you choose. In England or Ireland, with a priest presiding if 'tis your wish."

"I would not delay, Jamie. I want to be your wife as soon as I can." Brianna knew that she was breaking the traditional year of mourning. When weighed against being without Jamie for months, Brianna couldn't continue to play the hypocrite. Donal was dead. God had sent Jamie to her, and she could not squander his love for the sake of false propriety.

"Then let me talk to the countess and see what can be done to expedite matters." Jamie tenderly kissed her mouth and took his leave.

Marisa was sitting in her garden, enjoying the warm breeze that swept over her. Nearby, playing with Lionheart, was Cameron's daughter, Elsbeth. The sun shone on the little girl's beautiful blond curls. Such a striking child, Marisa thought.

Marisa touched her belly with the palm of her hand. Could another child of Cameron's be growing inside of her now? A brother for Elsbeth? Or perhaps a sister, with the same coloring? She had said a special prayer this morn that last night's lovemaking had reaped an added reward. A child conceived from such passion would surely be doubly blessed.

"May I speak to you, my lady?"

Marisa turned her head and saw Jamie Covington standing at the entrance to the garden. He appeared to be wearing a most concerned expression on his normally phlegmatic face. She wondered if he had been in time to stop her cousin from making what Marisa was sure was a grave error.

"Of course, Jamie," she said with a smile. "Come, sit beside me."

Jamie sauntered over to join her on the wooden bench under a rose bower. He sat down, regarding the child. "Elsbeth, is it not?"

"Yes, 'tis Cameron's daughter," Marisa responded, then added proudly, "and now mine."

"I rejoice for my friend that you can embrace his bastard easily. Not many women would be so accepting."

"Elsbeth is not responsible for her birth. She is my husband's flesh, and so very dear to me."

"You love him, do you not?"

Marisa smiled, her eyes shining with the depth of her feelings. "Very much."

"Cameron deserves that, and more," Jamie stated. "You have courage and heart, countess. Two qualities that are important when loving a man like my friend Cameron."

Marisa blushed with the compliment from Jamie's lips. "I thank you for your good words,"

she said, "though something tells me that there
is another reason for your seeking me out this
day."

"Quite right, my lady," Jamie informed her. "I
wish to wed your cousin, the Lady Brianna." He
paused, allowing the import of his words to sink
in. "I would assume from your much appreciated
warning note of yesterday that you approve this
union?"

"With all my heart, so long as my cousin is
happy."

"Then we would summon a priest to marry us
without delay."

"You wish to be wed here, at FitzHall?"

"Yes, if you have no objections."

"My husband and I would be most happy to
give you a wedding to rival any at court."

"I think we would prefer something on a much
smaller scale."

Marisa nodded. "Mayhap 'twould be best," she
agreed. "I will dispatch a servant to Ross-on-Wye
to find a priest."

Jamie rose, taking one of Marisa's hands and
bringing it to his mouth. "I thank you, my lady,
on behalf of my betrothed and myself."

"I am Marisa," she reminded him. "Since we
are soon to be family, you must call me by my
Christian name. Again, I insist."

"And when she does that," a deep voice behind
them spoke, "I find that one should heed her
words."

"Cameron," Marisa said, the name falling from
her tongue like a benediction.

Cameron joined them, taking the seat recently vacated by Jamie. He kissed Marisa's cheek,
inhaling the scent of her perfume. He recalled
the fragrance on her skin, on the sheets as they

made love. His loins ached from wanting her. Like a perpetually thirsty man, he would never be satisfied. One lifetime could never be enough to show her how much he cared.

The same thoughts floated through Marisa's brain. A lifetime and beyond was what she wanted to share with Cameron. She had been prepared to sacrifice her own happiness to see her inheritance secured, her family's loyalty to the Stuart monarch unbroken. Now, she knew, she would abandon it should she ever be forced to chose between it and her husband. The love she felt for this man cut deeper and ran truer than any attachments she had felt before.

She watched silently as Jamie took his leave, and Elsbeth, her tiny arms full of the kitten, came ambling over to join her father and step-mother. The little girl begged to be lifted into her father's arms, kitten included. Cameron complied. Marisa saw the slight hesitation before her husband picked up his child and set her on his lap. Trusting would be difficult for Cameron, she realized, for some time to come. For far too long he had had to weigh any decision against the pain it could cost should betrayal occur.

Marisa vowed that her love would be the healing balm Cameron needed. She would make up for all the hurt he had suffered by letting him know that he was no longer alone. She stood beside him, now and forever. She loved him, and together they could withstand whatever they had to so long as they kept faith in their love.

Angus stood next to his son as Cameron instructed a groom to bring out several of the horses for inspection.

"My wife plans to breed the stallions to the mares she brought back from Ireland," Cam explained to his father as the two white stallions were led from the stables. He gave each of the large animals a treat from his hand, an apple apiece. "They are perfection," he stated proudly, taking the bridle from one groom. Grabbing hold of the stallion's long mane, Cam hoisted himself onto the horse's back. With a pull of the reins, he brought the horse to its hind legs. Man and beast understood each other, working as a team.

Cam dismounted, sliding off Romulus's back. He patted the horse's flank, relinquishing the reins.

"Your English wife has a keen eye for horse-flesh," Angus concluded as he inspected three of the Irish mares.

"Aye, that she does," Cam concurred.

"Your countess is a rare beauty, my son," Angus cheerfully admitted. "When the King summoned you, I hae thought that you'd be wed to some skinny milk-and-water Sassenach wench who'd be colder than a witch's teat." Angus stroked his thick beard. "I dinna mind telling you," he said with a laughing measure to his tone, "that I am glad to be wrong."

Cam joined in with his father's laughter, then sobered. "Charles Stuart gave me one of England's most precious treasures, Father. I canna imagine a life without her." Cam watched as two milk-maids walked by, wooden pails filled to the brim in each hand as they headed toward the kitchen. A wanton smile kicked up the corners of his mouth. His fertile imagination conjured up the image of Marisa in a copper tub, fresh milk covering her naked skin.

The bath, of course, would be big enough for two.

So intent was he on his fanciful notion that he failed to see the piercing glance thrown in his direction by one of the milkmaids, nor the malevolent smile that crossed her lips.

Chapter Twenty-Six

Disguised as a dairy maid, Faith Bellamy had secured a temporary position on the FitzHall estate. Careful applications of a dye made from walnut bark had darkened her hair, which was piled beneath a white cap. Coarse homespun cloth covered her body in a frock resembling Puritan garb, a size larger than she would usually have worn. Rough woolen hose and flat black shoes completed her disguise.

She hated being forced to wear these drab garments, but it was essential to her plan. She had to remove the threat that Cameron Buchanan posed for her, which meant he would have to be killed before she could feel completely free to enjoy the money she had waiting for her in London.

Faith had been working at the estate for almost a week, watching and waiting for an opportunity to kill Cameron. Nothing presented itself, and she was getting nervous. He never seemed to be alone. The surprise arrival of his family brought still more people to surround him. She'd considered poisoning him, but disgarded that notion as too chancy. If only he had ridden out on one of those great brutes that he was showing off to his father. She could have stolen a horse and gone after him. A bullet was more effective than poison, yet it was too risky to attempt to shoot him here on the immediate grounds.

Faith had almost given up hope of meeting her goal until she'd overheard some gossip about the earl's bastard child. It seemed his lordship had a fondness for his other-side-of-the-blanket daughter. Having heard that, Faith watched and observed today as she went about her tasks. She decided that she would have to take the child. If she could abduct her, the father was sure to follow. His life for his child's.

A wild light gleamed in her eyes. She could turn a large profit on the little Scottish bastard by taking her to London. Faith knew of a particular establishment that would pay handsomely for an unspoiled female child with blond hair and blue eyes. Within a few weeks, she could send Cameron a letter telling him of the whereabouts of the girl. He would hie to London to rescue the brat and there meet with an accident. Robbed of his purse by villains unknown.

Aye, she liked that idea. And Faith would, she reckoned, be doing the countess an enormous favor, making her a widow and removing the earl's bastard in the bargain.

Milk sloshed on her shoe as she entered the kitchen carrying her burden.

The sharp-eyed cook registered her displeasure, one hand waving a skinning knife as she stripped the fur from a freshly killed rabbit. "Hey, you there, be careful of that pail else you'll be spillin' it over my floor. Do that, my girl, and you'll be cleanin' it yourself."

Faith longed to shove the older woman's head into the pail, or failing that, douse the bitch with both buckets. She held her tongue and did nothing, keeping her eyes lowered lest the woman read her angry contempt. She took note of the back stairs, leading, she was sure, up to the family rooms. Faith tipped the liquid into a churn that another servant was using to make fresh butter, her gaze taking in the collection of knives that the cook had for her use.

Sweat ran down her shoulders and between her breasts. Faith smelled like a barn animal, ripe and somewhat stale. She wanted a perfumed bath to wash the stench of the dairy from her body, but she would have to be content to wait till she had accomplished what she needed to do. She listened as the cook directed several of the kitchen wenches to prepare vegetables, fetch ingredients, and gather more fresh herbs. Tonight's meal was to be special, the cook stated, as the countess expected all her family and guests to attend.

When Faith heard that, she allowed herself a little smile. Later this evening would be the best chance to steal away the child, perhaps whilst the rest of the household was at supper and the kitchen was busy, or possibly when the household slept.

Above all, she couldn't fail.

Marisa stepped into the dress that Charity held out for her, taking a deep breath as her maid laced the back of the gown. It was an elegant court dress of rose and cream silk, with slippers to match. Even though they would eat in the smaller family dining room instead of the larger, more opulent formal dining room, she wanted everything to be as beautiful as she could make it.

Marisa's eyes drifted to the wide bed that now seemed to dominate the room. Color crept into her cheeks as she recalled the delight she had found there.

A wickedly amusing thought struck her. Marisa wondered if she should lend the book to her cousin Brianna for future reference. She had certainly found it illuminating, to say the least.

"Marisa."

She spun toward the door. Seeing her husband standing there, one hand on a silver-tipped cane, Marisa ran to him.

Cam's arms opened and enfolded her within their protective grasp. He dipped his head; their lips met with a hungry demand that neither could resist. It was Cam who finally broke the contact, his breathing uneven. Damn, he wanted her. Looking into Marisa's luminous green eyes, he saw mirrored there the same depth of passion, the same excited fervor. She was dream and reality, goddess and woman, siren and saint combined. *His* woman.

His former rakish, cynical self would have once scoffed at that notion. Love had once been a word ill-used for convenience's sake, easily mouthed and just as easily forgotten. Now, having discovered the depth of love, he recognized the sexual life that once he'd led for what it was, dross.

How he wished that he could postpone this meal for at least another hour. He would rather the time was spent in Marisa's arms, learning

more about her, discovering all the parts of her
sensual nature.

Marisa laid a tender hand on Cameron's cheek,
trailing her fingers leisurely over his lips. Cam
nipped at her index finger, drawing it into the
warmth of his mouth before she slowly pulled
it free. Neither she nor Cam was concerned that
Charity stood watching the tableau.

"Supper awaits us, husband."

Cam lowered his voice to a husky whisper. "As
does our bed, wife."

"Then let us not waste time," Marisa replied,
linking her arm through his, "for the completion
of the first leads happily to the second."

As Cam and Marisa strolled down the long,
paneled hallway toward the broad staircase,
they met Angus and Alanna Buchanan coming from the other wing. The couples smiled,
exchanging polite comments about their choices
of dress for the evening, substituting trivial words
for what was really simmering just below the
surface.

Cam and his mother traded questioning glances.
Alanna's face was plain for all to see—she was
openly pleading for some sort of recognition from
her son.

Cam considered the other woman in his life. He
had changed his perception of his mother. Alanna
Buchanan had gone from his childhood notion
of perfection, the ultimate paragon, to the more
mature and sophisticated view he now held—a
woman as human and capable of making mistakes as was he. He still didn't know whether or
not he could ever forgive her for what she had
done—certainly he could never forget her turning
from him when he needed her comfort.

But Marisa's love had altered him. With the

mantle of her concern fresh in his mind, he had shed some of his bitterness at fate and of some people. Marisa's acceptance of his flaws had freed him from the stagnant bondage of anger and despair. Alanna's rejection *had* hurt him, devastated the young man he had been; but he could now put it aside, banished to the past where it belonged.

Marisa had given him the gifts of today and tomorrow.

Cam bestowed a loving smile on Marisa, then asked, "Mother, may I escort you to supper?"

Alanna's blue eyes filled with tears as she relinquished her hold on her husband's arm. "I would like that, Cameron."

Cam held out his right arm. "Then shall we?"

Alanna laid her hand on his forearm, sliding her fingers over the velvet of his jacket until she came into contact with the broken knuckles of his right hand. The difficult years had passed, she was sure. Love had irrevocably changed her son, for love was what she saw in the glance shared between Cam and Marisa, bringing with it a measure of tolerance. Alanna had much to thank her daughter-in-law for, the most important being the undeniable happiness she could read in Cam's loch-blue gaze, and his willingness to once more include her in his life. Her devout prayers had been answered.

As mother and son made their way down the stairs, Angus and Marisa waited behind.

Contentment showed on Angus's bearded features. A wide grin crossed his mouth. "You hae wrought quite a change in my boy," he pronounced.

Marisa demurred, and Angus pressed on. "You have, lass. I see in him this day a glimpse of the boy I raised." Angus took her by surprise when he put his big, callous-rough hands on her shoulders and gave her a smacking kiss on each cheek. "I love my son and would see him happy."

Marisa responded, "As would I."

"I had my doubts when he told me that he was to wed a woman at the king's request. I will admit I was nae too pleased to hear it was to be an Englishwoman that the King had chosen.

"But you're nae a puling weakling like I feared you would be. You seem a match for my youngest son. 'Tis what Cameron needs. He's truly a Buchanan in that respect. We hae always loved a challenge." Angus's dark eyes glowed with mirth. "Especially in our women."

"'Tis well then," Marisa countered, "for we Fitzgeralds are also well known for our love of a challenge, especially," she added slyly, "in our men."

Angus gave a hearty laugh, his big frame shaking from the effort. "I understand well now the king's choïce of a bride. Aye, lass, you are indeed the woman for my son.

"The *only* woman," she assured him. Marisa could never accept the shallow definition of love she had seen at Court. There was only one man for her, and she had no intention of ever sharing him with another.

"Shall we join the rest below?" she inquired sweetly, her heart suddenly light.

"You dinna need to ask me twice," Angus responded. "Countess, your servant."

Jamie and Brianna awaited the rest of their companions, eager to share their news. Seated at the gleaming table beside each other, they held hands and talked quietly, their faces aglow with mutual joy.

"I talked to the countess today. She approves of our wedding plans."

Brianna squeezed Jamie's hand. "I knew she would."

"She wants to host the nuptials here at FitzHall. Have you any objections?"

Brianna responded, "None. I've written a letter to my brother, the Earl of Killroone, informing him of my decision. I also was after asking him to send me what belongs to me." She bestowed a loving smile on Jamie, her brown eyes limpid. "I'm thinking that your house in London will never be the same when my trunks arrive."

Jamie stroked his fingers along her wrist. "I can handle a few more dresses, sweetheart."

Brianna lowered her eyelids as she said, "'Tis more than a few changes of wardrobe, my love."

"Faith," he questioned, "how much more?"

"A dowry fit for Killroone's sister."

Jamie laughed, dismissing the idea. "I want only you, Brianna; all else is unnecessary."

"Not to an O'Dalaigh."

He recognized the deeply ingrained pride in his affianced Irish bride. Much as he wanted to tell her brother that he could well provide for the Lady Brianna, though perhaps not luxuriously, Jamie hesitated in offending Brianna's family for the sake of something that mattered little to him one way or the other. "Very well, my love, I shall accept your dowry with appreciation."

"A wise choice," Marisa said as she and the Earl of Tairne, followed by his countess and the Earl of Derran, entered the room. "You would do well to keep faith with my cousin Killroone. He will be most generous to his sister, for he loves the Lady Brianna dearly."

"Is there to be a wedding?" Alanna asked.

In a few quick sentences, she, Angus, and Cameron were informed as to the whys and wherefores of the upcoming wedding.

"We would be honored, my lord," Brianna insisted, "if you would consider being guests at our wedding."

"I hae not been to a Sassenach wedding before," Angus declared.

Brianna laughed. "Half-Sassenach, if you please," she said, reminding Cameron's family that she was Irish and that Marisa, too, carried Celtic blood in her veins.

"You dinna mind if we lengthen our stay, lass?" Angus asked, aware of the terms of his son's marriage, that Cameron and Marisa shared the responsibilities of the earldom of Derran. Not wanting to offend his English daughter-in-law, Angus thought it best if he sought her permission. He had become very fond of Marisa in a short time, but as the English were a strange breed to his way of thinking, he decided on discretion.

Marisa's mouth curved into a delightful smile as she took her seat at the table. "'Tis not for me to say, as the estate belongs wholly by law, *English* law," Marisa emphasized, "to Cameron. So it will be for him to say."

"This is all yours?" Cameron's mother inquired, her head swiveling toward the place her son occupied at the other end of the table, taken aback by the Countess of Derran's words.

"Aye, Mother," Cam answered, helping himself to the meat from the platter that one of the serving wenches held in her hands. "The house and all its contents, the grounds, the livestock, the rents of the tenant farmers, the profits from what the land yields. 'Tis all mine, exclusively.

"So," he concluded, "I say that you and my father are welcome to enjoy the hospitality of FitzHall as long as you like." Cameron meant what he said, for after uttering the words, he felt as if a weight had shifted from his shoulders.

He lifted his wineglass. "I propose a toast—to the future."

"To the future," was the response as all within the room raised their goblets and joined in.

Creeping slowly up the back stairs, Faith Bellamy didn't try to hide the delight on her face. She was within minutes of achieving part of her revenge on Cameron Buchanan. Not only had she struck a blow years ago against his damnable pride, now she could wound him further before delivering the final stroke. He was all that stood between her and the comfortable life she wanted, and deserved. He stood between her and true happiness, she rationalized.

If only . . .

If only he hadn't been a damned Royalist.

If only he hadn't been so stubborn when she first questioned him.

If only he had been the resolute rake he had once seemed.

If only he hadn't forced her hand.

Faith hated him.

She had to, or else she would have to face the fact that beneath her contempt for his policies, for his heritage, for his politics, she, in her own way, loved him. No man before or since sexually excited her as he had. Once, and only once, had she questioned herself. When the men she had hired that night burst into her bedroom at the inn, binding Cameron's magnificent naked body

to the bed, she wondered if she could go through
with what was required of her. When Faith had
looked her fill at his straining muscles, at the
instrument of pleasure that hung limp between
his taut thighs, at the thick blond hair, at that
beautiful face, most especially at the face that
an archangel would have been jealous of, she
hesitated.

That he had caused the slightest doubt to form
in her brain worried her. There was no room
in her life for sentimental nonsense. She would
destroy him before he could destroy her.

Selling his perfect child to a London brothel would be a just punishment, she'd decided,
for the ruined nights of sleep, for the aching,
unfulfilled hours of torment she'd been forced
to bear.

If only . . .

In the pocket of her drab apron was a flat
smooth stone which fit in the palm of her
hand and which she could use as a cudgel
against the maid who stayed with the child.
She had questioned one of the household staff
regarding the beautiful child she had seen playing in the garden. The unsuspecting girl had
relayed the information that the child was that
of the new earl, and that the child had her
own nurse, a Scottish woman, to care for her.
The girl had concluded that everything here
was topsy-turvy with all the comings and new
folk.

Faith considered that, with her actions, 'twould
be even more so.

She slunk along the hallway of the uppermost
floor, holding to the shadows lest anyone see her.
A light spilled from an open doorway onto the
bare floorboards that the expensive carpet did not

cover. Faith approached cautiously, her heartbeat increasing as she neared the room.

Inside, the little girl lay asleep. Like a little princess, she was surrounded with luxury. A soft bed cradled her tiny body; sweet-smelling herbs scented the room; even a pet, a kitten, contentedly played with a large spool of dyed yarn in its basket. Such a contrast to her own ragamuffin childhood, fighting for shelter and food.

"What do ye be wanting?" asked the young maid, Una, rising from her pallet bed.

"I was sent to fetch you below," Faith stated. *Ignorant Scottish heathen,* she thought.

"And why would they be sending a dairy maid to deliver the message?" Una demanded.

Faith hadn't reckoned that the nurse would be so observant as to notice the difference in dress amongst the servants.

"I was called into the kitchen to help with the supper tonight, not that 'tis any of your business," she added sulkily. "Should I be telling them that you will not come?"

Una wasn't sure. Something bothered her, though for her life she could not say just what it was. "I must look to the bairn before I go," she said, turning her back on Faith.

That was all Faith needed. The stone was out of her apron. She struck the maid on the back of her head. Una crashed to the floor, blood oozing from the wound.

Faith stepped over the nurse's prone body, walking purposefully towards the sleeping child.

Marisa decided to pay a visit to her stepchild before retiring for the night. A slight smile creased her mouth. With Cameron in her bed, retiring was the furthest thing from her mind. They had left

the table after the delicious meal her cook had
set before them was devoured. She and Cam had
forgone the sweet course, and judging by the
mood of Cam's parents and her cousin and Jamie,
each couple would happily be following their lead
within a short time.

Cam told her that a surprise awaited her in his
bedroom, but Kendall had informed him that it
was not quite ready. It was then that she thought
to go and see Elsbeth. Tomorrow she would take
the child along with her as she and Cam rode over
the estate. Perhaps they could even find Elsbeth
a pony of her own.

As she moved along the hall, Marisa's thoughts
turned to her husband. She was as eager for
him as he appeared to be for her. She blushed
to think of her wayward thoughts at supper.
While she ate and conversed, all she could really
focus on was Cam, sitting just feet from her, his
strong hand gesturing as he talked. She longed
to feel those long, slim fingers on her flesh, sen-
sitively exploring, bringing her to paradise and
beyond.

It seemed as though all in this house tonight
had hope of love's beneficence.

Marisa entered Elsbeth's room. A scream tore
from her throat when she saw the inert body of
the nurse, blood staining the woman's clothes.
Fear choked off further sound when she saw a
woman bent over the bed where Elsbeth lay. A
blade glittered in the candlelight as the woman
snatched the sleeping child from her repose.

Kendall had seen to the arrangement of the
huge copper tub. Milk filled the inside.

At the wicked gleam in his manservant's eyes,
Cam dismissed Kendall with a laugh. "I dinna

think I shall be needing you the rest of this night," he said, removing the black velvet doublet that he wore, "nor at all tomorrow morning. At least not till I summon you. Understood?"

"I do believe that I understand, your lordship," Kendall responded with a grin.

It was just as Kendall opened the door to take his leave that they both heard the scream.

"Marisa!" Cam cried out, rushing past a stunned Kendall. A cramping pain tore through his leg as he bounded down the hallway and up the stairs towards the nursery. He ignored it as he forced himself to hurry.

"You shouldn't have done that, my lady," Faith sneered.

"Let her go," Marisa insisted.

Faith barked out a laugh.

The sound chilled Marisa's blood.

"No," Faith responded, "for the child goes with me."

"I cannot allow that," Marisa said as she stood between the woman and the exit.

Faith snarled her words. "Do you think I care what you will or will not allow?" She held her hand around the child's waist, the knife poised to strike if need be. Elsbeth whimpered in fear.

"Hush, my sweet," Marisa murmured in soothing tones, trying to stem the rising fear within herself as well as the child. "All will be well." Marisa had nothing with which to defend herself or Elsbeth, nothing save her own courage. "What do you want? If 'tis money, you shall have it," she assured the woman.

"Why do you care about the brat? You would be better off if she were gone. One less reminder of the beast you are wed to."

Marisa had to keep the woman talking till someone answered her call. As long as she kept the woman confined within the room, there was a chance to rescue Elsbeth. "Have you some grievance against me or my husband?"

"You could well say that," Faith answered.

"Will you tell me what it 'tis so that we may seek an understanding?"

"'Tis too late for that."

Marisa took a small step forward. As soon as she did, Faith raised the hand that held the blade. Marisa froze. "'Tis never too late."

"You are wrong. I am doing you a favor, can you not see that?" Faith demanded.

"By taking my daughter?"

"She's not yours. Even I know that. She's a bastard." Barely audible, Faith added, "Like me."

"I tell you that she is mine, and I will never let you harm her."

"Step aside and let me pass."

"Not so long as you have Elsbeth."

"I will kill her if you do not."

"Why would you wish to hurt an innocent child?"

Faith gave a bitter laugh. "Innocent? She has the devil for her sire."

"You are wrong," Marisa asserted.

"'Tis you who are wrong, countess. Cameron Buchanan is her father."

God help me, Marisa thought, for the woman is surely mad. Marisa took another step, her eyes never leaving the woman before her.

Faith warned her again. "Come no further, countess."

"What have you against my husband?"

"Better you ask him what he has against me, you fool," Faith muttered.

"You speak in riddles."

Faith gave a nervous laugh. "He had the face of an angel, once upon a time. Did you know that?"

Perhaps, Marisa thought, she could forestall the woman by going along with whatever she said. "You knew Cameron before the damage was done to his face?"

"You could say that," Faith admitted, loosening her grip on Elsbeth slightly. "'Tis my handiwork he bears," she claimed.

The blood chilled in Marisa's body. *"You?"*

"The same," Faith said with pride.

Had the woman not been holding Elsbeth, Marisa would have rushed blindly towards her, intent on vengeance. This was the bitch who had been responsible for Cameron's misery. Cold fury forced Marisa to remain where she was.

Cameron heard the bragging words as he burst into the room. There, standing but a few feet from him, his beloved child in her arms, was the malicious slut who had betrayed him years ago. Even with her color of her hair changed, he could never forget her features. Hot rage ran steaming through his lean body. "Mistress Bellamy."

Marisa risked a quick backward glance. Then 'twas really true.

"There is no escape," Cam warned.

"Much as I once thought you had none from my grasp," Faith countered.

"None but death for you," he stated grimly.

"You could never kill a woman."

"Do not test me." Cam clamped his lips together, trying to stem the pain in his right leg. "Release my daughter." Cam's voice was cold and commanding.

From the dim fog of her rational mind, Faith realized that her plans were in ruins. Even if she killed the child, there was no escape for her. Could she trust the honorable fools? And for what? Only death waited to claim her at every turn, like a long-lost lover patiently biding his time. Better she deliver a final thrust to Cameron Buchanan's heart.

Moments stretched painfully by as if on a torturer's rack.

Faith moved, raising her hand, but she misjudged her step and stumbled on the kitten's basket. The kitten screeched in pain. Faith dropped Elsbeth, and as she rose from her knees, Marisa, closer to her than Cameron was, lunged forward, catching Faith off guard. With a mighty push, Marisa sent the other woman flying backward, through the window. The glass shattered upon the impact of the woman's body.

Marisa, panting from the exertion, clasped Elsbeth to her bosom, hugging the child fiercely. Elsbeth cried and Marisa held her tighter, reassuring the child that it was all over.

Cam limped to the broken window and looked down to the courtyard below. Torches flared in the night as servants and stablehands came running at the noise. There on the cobblestones, glass surrounded the broken body of a woman, her hands and legs splayed at odd angles.

It was finally over.

He turned from the sight. His blue gaze beheld a purer vision. His wife and child, clinging to one another.

Cam moved the few steps toward them, extending his hand. Marisa took it willingly as he pulled her gently to her feet, Elsbeth still in Marisa's arms. He drew Marisa to his body, wrapping his arm about her and his child. Together they stood there, oblivious to the faces that crowded the doorway, ignoring the questions being asked.

They were a family—invincible, bonded by love, the greatest measure of the human heart.

Epilogue:
So Clear the Night
London 1663

The Beast was mightily content.

Cameron held his five-month-old daughter, the Lady Catriona Anne Fitzgerald Buchanan, in his arms while his eldest child, Elsbeth, chatted happily to her younger brother, Charles James Ross, Viscount Grayton, who lay in his cradle. The Lady Cat, blinking her green eyes sleepily, yawned.

"You simply must have a family portrait painted, my dear," the dowager countess declared, pleased that she had lived long enough to see her bloodline continue into her great-grandchildren.

"The king has already thought of that, *grand-mère*," Marisa responded. "His Majesty, as well as standing godfather to the twins, has commissioned his own court painter to do the work as a gift."

"Most excellent," Barbara stated. She could tell

from the radiant look on her granddaughter's face that Marisa was indeed very happy with her life, and very much in love with the man she had wed seventeen months ago. It was also plain to her old eyes that the scarred Scotsman was deeply in love with his wife. A crafty smile edged her mouth. That the blood ran hot between these two was easily apparent. Barbara believed in the power and passion of love; its memory had sustained her. With Marisa and Cameron, it had made two strong wills even stronger, forging an unbreakable bond.

"Tell me a story," Elsbeth begged of Barbara, having forsaken her brother's now sleeping figure.

"I would be glad to," Barbara said, rising from her chair. "Come." She held out her hand, and Elsbeth trustingly placed her smaller hand in the old woman's. Barbara whispered to the little girl in a conspiratorial tone, "Let us see if we can persuade the cook to send us a pot of chocolate, shall we?"

"Oh, yes, *grand-mère*," Elsbeth cried, employing the term she had heard her stepmother use.

"*Grand-mère*, if you must fill Elsbeth's head with tales, I would have you censure yourself. No personal recollections, please," Marisa chided.

Delight gleamed in the old woman's eyes. "Of course not," she said, "I wouldn't think of it." In her mind, Barbara mentally added, "At least I will have the sense to alter the names when I do."

Marisa watched the odd couple leave her bedroom. It had been a day for sharing. Brianna and Jamie had also stood as godparents for the twins. It was later that Brianna revealed a secret—she and Jamie were to have a babe of their own. Word had come from her brother Killroone that a young village girl had given birth recently to an illegitimate child that she could not support as she was barely older than a child herself, so she was willing to give the baby up. Brianna and Jamie were to set sail for Ireland in two days to claim the child, a boy. When they returned to England, they would be bringing their new son with them.

Marisa was thrilled that her cousin, who loved Elsbeth, Cat, and Ross as if they were her own, would now have a child. Brianna and Jamie had room in their hearts and home, where love abounded.

Marisa's eyes strayed to the crossed swords over the mantel. One day they would belong to her son, as would this London house. The words of the Irish woman from so long ago came ringing back to her through the mists. Daughter, wife, and mother to one name: Derran. Her destiny.

Marisa got up from her chair and crossed the room to where Cameron stood, irresistibly drawn to him. It would always be so, she acknowledged. She would follow him to the ends of the earth if she had to, surmount any obstacle in her path to be with Cameron Buchanan. He was her darkest dream, her deepest love.

Cam had placed his sleeping daughter in her own cradle. He stood there, marveling at his babies. Both so perfect, with a crown of blond curls and wide green eyes. Conceived that special night when Marisa had demonstrated to him the full capacity of beauty she possessed, the bewitching charm of her total love.

He watched her move toward him, ever graceful, her slim figure well displayed in the gown she wore of deep forest-green silk. His blue eye focused on the swell of her breasts above the lace-edged bodice. Just an hour ago Marisa had provided each of her twins with the nourishment that they needed. He and Elsbeth had shared in the very private moment. Cam cherished being part of his family, of every aspect of his children's lives. He treasured the memories he would carry inside his heart of Marisa, a baby at her breast.

The sun had set; the night sky was streaked with muted cool colors of pink, blue, and purple. Stars winked as they grew brighter. With a quick breath, Cam blew out the branch of candles nearby, holding out his hand to her.

Their skin touched.

Their gazes met.

Each was flame to the other, the fierce yearning of their desire bubbling rapidly to the surface.

Marisa slipped one arm around his lean waist as the other clutched his back, her fingers tightening in the soft white linen of his shirt. "Come, my beast," she whispered seductively, her green eyes warm and inviting, "have you no kiss for your beauty?"

Cam did, and would, for all the days of their lives.

I love to hear from my readers. Please write
to me at:

P.O. Box 717
Concordville, PA 19331

(SASE please).

FLEETING SPLENDOR

JULIE MOFFETT

For Alana MacKenzie, life in the majestic Scottish Highlands was filled with simple pleasures. But her tranquil life was forever changed the day broodingly handsome Nathaniel Beauchamp came into her life and vowed to make her his own. She soon found herself trapped in a marriage of convenience with the arrogant Nathaniel, struggling to adjust to her new life and shocked to realize love can sometimes blossom in the most unexpected places.

_3434-4 $4.50 US/$5.50 CAN

CREOLE NIGHTS

Deborah Martin

"A Must Read...I Loved It!" —Rexanne Becnel

Elina Vannier's life can't get much worse. Her father is missing, her brother dead, and the most attractive man she's ever met thinks she is a lying cheat. And soon she discovers her whole past might be a lie.

Convinced that Elina wants to destroy his family's reputation, Rene Bonnange lures the young girl to his lush plantation. But as the languid days pass, Rene finds himself longing for the deceitful beauty. No matter what the cost, he vows to uncover the truth about Elina—and to share with her a tempestuous ecstasy that will forever change their lives.

_3368-2 $4.50 US/$5.50 CAN

SHIRL HENKE

WHITE APACHE'S WOMAN

By the bestselling author of *Terms of Surrender*

Running from his past, Red Eagle has no desire to become entangled with the haughty beauty who hires him to guide her across the treacherous Camino Real to Santa Fe. Although Elise Louvois's cool violet eyes betray nothing, her warm, willing body comes alive beneath his masterful touch. She will risk imprisonment and death, but not her vulnerable heart. Mystified, Red Eagle is certain of but one thing—the spirits have destined Elise to be his woman.

_3498-0 $4.99 US/$5.99 CAN

SONG OF THE WILLOW

Charlotte McPherren

Ladies don't wear men's pants or herd cattle, nor do they curse or sneak whiskey, but Willie Vaughn does. Growing up in a household of five men, Willie can steal a base, rope a cow and hold her own in a brawl. But she never thinks she'll have to learn to seduce a man—until she meets the handsome and dangerous Rider Sinclair. After one look in the virile lieutenant's eyes, Willie is suddenly determined to hang up her britches and Colt .45 and teach the mysterious lawman a thing or two about real ladies.

_3483-2 $4.50 US/$5.50 CAN

The Queen of Indian Romance

Winner of the *Romantic Times*
Reviewers' Choice Award for Best Indian Series!

"Madeline Baker's Indian Romances should not be missed!"

—Romantic Times

The Spirit Path. Beautiful and infinitely desirable, the Spirit Woman beckons Shadow Hawk away from his tribe, drawing him to an unknown place, a distant time where passion and peril await. Against all odds, Hawk and the Spirit Woman will conquer time itself and share a destiny that will unite them body and soul.

_3402-6 $4.99 US/5.99 CAN

Midnight Fire. A half-breed who has no use for a frightened girl fleeing an unwanted wedding, Morgan thinks he wants only the money Carolyn Chandler offers him to guide her across the plains. But in the vast wilderness, Morgan makes her his woman and swears to do anything to keep Carolyn's love.

_3323-2 $4.99 US/$5.99 CAN

Comanche Flame. From the moment Dancer saves her life, Jessica is drawn to him by a fevered yearning. And when the passionate loner returns to his tribe, Jessica vows she and her once-in-a-lifetime love will be reunited in an untamed paradise of rapture and bliss.

_3242-2 $4.99 US/$5.99 CAN